For TOLCDIN, forever

the infinity chronicles

R.R.S PRESENTS

Piercing

Midnight

∞ PART ONE OF THE INFINITY CHRONICLES ∞

All rights reserved. Published in the United States by Faery Ring Press,
a private publishing platform in Baltimore, Maryland , USA. Printed by CreateSpace, a DBA
of On-Demand Publishing LLC, part of the Amazon group of companies. CreateSpace
headquarters located at:

21 North Pennell Road, Lima, PA 19037
Phone: (610) 566-7828

ISBN-13: 978-0692393215 (Custom)

ISBN-10: 0692393218

BISAC: Fiction / Dystopian

Summary: Fifteen-year old Raine Ylevol's life is in grave danger the minute she rescues an
enemy spy from an avalanche and begins keeping secrets from her government and those
closest to her.

1. Fiction, 2. Young Adult, 3.Science Fiction/Dystopian, 4.Romance, 5.Coming-of-Age,
6.Sexuality, 7. Action/Adventure

Printed in the U.S.A

The text type was set in Garamond. Additional fonts include A Quiet Sleep, Mrs. Saint
Delafield, Ruthie, Rock Salt, Nothing You Could Do, Arsenale White, good vibes-regular,
Times New Roman, Courier New, Hill Country, Algerian, and Metamorphous.
Cover artwork by Ronen Yakubov
Other featured artwork by Sanja Ice, Irene Javier, and Rachel Szpara
Book design by Rachel Szpara

Part One:

PIERCING MIDNIGHT

Wanderers this morning came by, where did they go?

Graceful in the morning light, to banner fair,
to follow you softly in the cold mountain air?

Through the forest, down to your grave,
where the birds wait, and the tall grasses wave,
they do not know you anymore.

Dear shadow, alive and well, how can the body die?
You tell me everything, anything true.

Into town, one morning I went
staggering through premonitions of my death—
I don't see anybody that dear to me.

Dear shadow, alive and well, how can the body die?
You tell me everything, anything true.

-Fleet Foxes, "Tiger Mountain Peasant Song"

chapter one

I was lighting the stove when it happened.

A hot, sizzling sort of sensation shot through my veins—
starting in between my eyes and rippling up to my temples,
making me gasp and drop the dishcloth straight into the fire.
And before I could make sense of what was happening, I was
blinded by a bright, white light.

Happy Birthday!

The words reverberated ominously through my head,
flashing in front of my eyes while blue and white fireworks went
off. For a moment, I could feel my surroundings again, and I
crashed into a chair, breathing quickly. Then the message
invaded again.

*Raine Xifeng Ylevol of Underbrush: you have aged another year.
You have now reached your 15th year, and the Majesty Council is so
thrilled to welcome you into the fast-working machine that is Thgindim's*

vast system of services and Careers!

"Raine! Are you trying to burn the house down?"

My mother's words reached my ears slowly under the voice still blaring from within my skull. Then, just as it had happened with Carmen last week, the announcement burst forth from the little chips embedded in each of my temples.

Please make your way to Peak Tower to receive your Career, immediately!

A sharp intake of breath. "It's...it's happening?" My mother's slight figure came gradually into my vision as the announcement subsided, and blearily I watched as she put out the fire with another damp rag, patting it down in haste.

"But I-I didn't do anything. I d-don't think I did, at least..." My tongue felt swollen in my mouth, and speaking was surprisingly difficult.

"Maybe there was something you *didn't* do?" my mother asked, sitting across from me at the table. I didn't answer, but I don't think she really expected me to. I scratched around the three small, black metal bars embedded in each of my temples. They still pulsed from the announcement the Majesty Council had sent through them. Shoulders shaking, my mother cut short my time to process what was happening. "You'll have to get ready then. Go change your clothes. I'll pack you food for the road."

It hardly fit me. The dress had been my mother's. She'd received it from my father as a wedding present. My shoulders were narrower than hers, and the worn blue silk sagged down my figure like a frown. I tried to pull out the stray threads, but only ended up unraveling some of the floral designs stitched in by the high-neck collar.

"Are you ready?"

"Just another second," I said, looking myself over one last time. The loose-fitting, outdated dress, the exposed white skin of my arms, the wild tangles of blue hair undone from my usual bun, all made me nauseous and dizzy. My black boots were the only thing keeping me grounded to who I was. *Breathe*, I thought, wrapping my cloak around myself and tying my hair back up.

Mom still scrutinized me intensely, pressing her folded hands to her lips as worry creased her lined face. Silently, she came over and pulled the red ribbon out of my hair, making the bun fall out and my hair tumble down to my waist.

"Mom…" I sighed. She circled me, eagerly searching for more to be fixed.

"Will you just let me put some lip colour on you? You look so good in red, Raine."

"No, Mom. I'm already going to be late."

She threw up her hands, shaking her head and returning to the kitchen while her long black braid swung back and forth. "I get it, I get it. You hate having to be such a lady for once."

I shifted back and forth in my boots, glad that she hadn't noticed them.

"Take this for lunch. Is it enough?"

My mother dropped a bit of toasted bread and cheese into my hand with a smile. After smoothing out my dress, I stuck the food into my cloak pocket and nodded. "Mmhmm. I'll be back by nightfall."

Her boney arms wound around me. "Don't worry. Just keep your mouth shut as much as you can, and don't forget your manners." She squeezed me once, then let go.

I left my little house and squinted in the morning light. The sunrise had splattered the sky with gorgeous scarlet and golds, and for a moment my hand itched for my coloured pencils or paints to capture the moment. The sketchbook in my skirt pocket seemed to pulse against my leg in waiting, but there was just no time for that now. I could recapture it all later.

"Hey!" a voice called from behind me. I spun around, my cloak stirring up a cloud of dust as I saw my neighbour Carmen, and friends Chantastic and Velle come walking up the road. *Crap! We had stuff to do this morning, didn't we?*

"Whatcha doin'?" Velle asked me, tilting her head to the side skeptically.

Her twin looked me up and down, a small smile playing on her lips. "You look so pretty, Raine," Chantastic said.

"Kind of...*too* pretty." Carmen's eyes narrowed. "We're still thieving today, right?"

"Not me." I tapped my temple with a finger, scowling. "It went off just a minute ago."

They gasped. Velle put a hand to her heart in exasperation. "Goodness, Raine, what did you *do?*"

"Nothing!" I protested, crossing my arms across my chest indignantly. Then a thought flickered through my mind. *Oh...*

"I...I think maybe I paid the weekly tax on time for once?" I suggested feebly.

Carmen rolled her eyes. "Well, that'll do it. How'd you even manage that?"

"Carmen, it doesn't matter," Velle cut in, striding up to me and lacing her arm with mine, "we need to get her up there, *now.*"

"We?" I asked, looking from Velle and Chan to Carmen who still looked pissed that I'd put a kink in our plans. "Just go without me this time. I can get up there— "

"You're late enough as it is," Carmen sighed, walking ahead of me and waving her hand for us all to follow. Chantastic shuffled over to my side and slipped her fingers through mine, smiling warmly at me. Carmen looked back at me, winking. "Just say thank you, dummy."

I knocked her shoulder, smirking. "Thank you, dummy."

We walked along the familiar path, past the shambles of huts and deserted alleys overgrown with winter-wisteria and thorns. From inside the houses, I could hear the clang of pots getting taken out for breakfast preparation, and doors creaking open and closed as people hurried off to their posts before the Justice Police would notice their absence.

"I think I'm gonna just skip this whole job thing. If I just hide at home sleeping all day I bet my chip won't go off," Chan murmured. "I'm not especially useful, anyway, so Thgindim wouldn't suffer much of a loss." She gazed upward at the Peak Tower, and I tilted my head all the way back just to get a clear view of it six miles up at the very top of the mountain. The frightening titanium structure gave our mountain a dangerously sharp point from this distance, but I'd always thought the scariest part was what was inside. Even my cloak couldn't chase away the chills Peak Tower gave me.

"You know that's not true, Channy. Just wait until you get to be one of the Majesty Council's Entertainers," Velle grinned, elbowing her sister in the ribs. "Remember, Granny said that sometimes they save the best jobs for last, and the assignment season is winding down, isn't it?"

Chan looked down, her black hair falling in a curtain to hide her blush. "My violin is too old. It was old and squeaky even when it was Mom's. There's no chance I'm as good as any Emergent or Canopian violinist, either."

Carmen groaned. "Don't degrade yourself, Chan. You know you're good."

"You're fantastic," I added, playfully flipping her hair over her shoulder. "You're *Chan*tastic."

Her eyes twinkled as she squeezed my hand. "I appreciate you saying that," she said. "But to the Council and everybody else I'm Chan Ai Song, Underbrusher. I don't think I should get my hopes up."

"Hmm...I don't know about that. You distinctly look like more of a Chantastic than Chan Ai."

"A Chantastic that can play exceptionally well," Velle added.

"*The* Chantastic that can play exceptionally well," Carmen finished, and we all skipped up a side road, laughing too loudly and earning a few glares from adults trying to get to work and the JPofficers reminding us to walk in single file. We drifted back into casual formation once we passed them. I linked my arm with Chantastic, who did the same with Carmen and then with Velle.

We made a silvery chain of fluttering cloaks moving through a wash of black smoke and faded green pines.

We picked our way up a steep hill in the roughly cut-out path, the mountain air making my head spin as we got higher.

The altitude started its usual throbbing of my eardrums, and since my friends weren't in formalwear, they'd moved ahead of me, waiting as I was forced to mind my stupid dress and struggle up the incline.

"What do you think I'll get?" I asked, knowing exactly what I wanted them to say.

"Let's see…" Carmen blew a chocolate brown curl out of her eyes, "you won't be a seamstress that's for sure, seeing as you couldn't even patch my mother's apron."

I laughed, thinking about Dolores Ajram and how I'd failed at sewing a few good stitches to fix the tiny hole. But then the worry sobered me up again. "I'm just not good at anything…useful," I decided as we crossed a trickle of a stream. "I'm scared of…I don't know. Getting something terrible." I said it casually so that they wouldn't be suspicious, "Like a Mother job. I've heard horrible things about that."

Once across the stream and about to climb a steep ladder up to another roadway, Velle grasped my shoulders and stared into my eyesas she assured me, "Don't worry. There is no way possible you'll be a Mother, and by the looks of it, no girl in our village will be this year. Maybe you'll get Scribe since you're literate. Then again…so am I…ooh, I'd quite like being Scribe now that I think about it…" Her eyes sparkled with sudden daydream and Velle instantly began tittering on about working in the Peak Tower literary archives and other dull things I couldn't latch on to.

If the Majesty Council would pick me for a Mother, I'd bear children as my Career. Mothers procreated with numerous men so that the population stayed steady in the upper levels of the mountain where conditions were most severe health-wise. The thin air near the top and lack of abundant food near the Base affected women's bodies to the point of where bearing children was either deadly or impossible. Most Underbrush and even some Starshade girls never menstruated because they lacked nutrition, and so those who did were kept under a watchful eye for being drafted into Motherhood. I was one of the only girls I knew in Underbrush who had started. Both Carmen and Velle had come back from their inspection declaring solemnly that they were barren. Chantastic had been too scared to find out and had feigned sickness at my house that day, which we all knew would catch up with her once her own chip went off. I'd lied and said I'd gotten the same results; the first and only lie I'd ever told my best friends, so far.

We had officially left Underbrush now, and had to show our Underbrush IDs to the JPs positioned at the gate to Starshade, the mountain's second level. They let us pass. A group of people came laughing up the other path from Underbrush that led to Starshade's entrance, and soon we found ourselves among our classmates: Aili Chow, Pula Wang, and Kris Yu. They were the popular kids at school and we didn't hang out with them really, but judging by the state of their dress, they were headed up to Peak as well.

"How's your morning been, Aili?" Carmen asked, the only somewhat social one of us. I smiled and waved at them, though, not wanting to seem too unfriendly.

Aili embraced each of us as if we were all her best friends. "Woke up to those birthday bells and whistles, so the morning's been nerve-wracking if anything. I knew it was coming but I still don't feel ready." She laughed nervously, her brown eyes wide with worry. Aili was a vision in pink and periwinkle blue silk, her hair shining like polished wood.

Pula eyed us three warily. "You *all* were summoned today? I thought I saw you in the goat pen, Carmen."

Carmen flushed angrily. She had had the worst of luck with her Career Day a month or so ago. Not only had she been put into the smelliest, muddiest job, but since the incident where a loose goat wandered off onto a cliff and Carmen had to coax it back by bahhing and crawling on all fours, she'd coined the nickname 'goat whisperer.' She was now quite the laughingstock of Underbrush.

She cleared her throat, "I'm just showing Raine the way."

"Ooh, you know the way?" Aili asked brightly, oblivious to Pula's jibe at Carmen. "Would it be all right if you showed us to the lift?"

Smiling politely, Velle chimed in, "Excuse me…but, 'the lift?' You don't mean…"

"The haunted lift?" Kris's eyes flashed giddily as we all jogged along. "Yup. Three miles up of pitch darkness, and only a creepy old JP stationed in the corner to keep an eye on us."

Aili lightly smacked Kris's shoulder. "Oh, don't be so dramatic, Kris. It's really not that bad, Velle."

"Ahh….I don't know, Aili. You can't even see your own hand in there," Kris said, holding out his hand and wiggling his fingers. "The JP waiting inside could chop your wrist and you wouldn't even see it coming. That's why Mr. Ping has to use that prosthetic thing now— he said it got chopped right off while he was on rounds to Canopia."

Kris was pretty silly and said some outrageous things sometimes, but he was right about the lift being haunted because I knew at first glance that something was wrong with it. The cables pulling it ran all the way to the Peak and disappeared in the clouds. They looked rusted and had been tied together in places after snapping a few times. A statue-still JP was standing in the corner of the lift as Kris had said, but he looked as average as any, not especially capable of chopping off limbs while cackling evilly as we shot up into the dark. I swear I'd even seen him picking his nose under his helmet as we approached.

The lift was a steel wire, cage-like box, with a lever inside that the JP operated to send us up. It could fit all of us with a little squeezing, but weight wasn't much of a problem seeing as we came from the malnourished level of Thgindim. My friends and I crowded into the back while Aili's group stood near the front where you could see out more easily as you rushed upward. As I clutched Chantastic's arm and felt her thin fingers stroke my hand reassuringly, the JP tugged down on the lever and we jolted off the landing.

Kris and Aili squealed and held onto each other while Pula hooted, peering out through the wire with lights reflecting off of her dark eyes. I craned my neck and saw green and brown and silver blurring by, unable to quite make out what anything was; but knowing that we were going really fast and about to enter the tunnel where all light would vanish.

The darkness was worse than I could have imagined. The lift shot up the cement tunnel, screeching against the sides and making sparks flurry on the metal edges. The black was thick and heavy and seemed to fill my lungs and snatch my breath; like I was being smothered by a great dark pillow and unable to come up for air. Chantastic kept me close to her, knowing how much of a wimp I was in darkness, whispering soothingly over Velle's shrieks and Pula's and Kris's conversation. "It's alright, it'll be over soon. It'll be okay," she said to me over and over, and I held my breath and waited for light to come back.

I really have no idea how long it actually took. But eventually, the lift slowed. That made the screeching of the cables even worse, and looking up I saw that a cord on the cable was splintering and slowly unraveling. The lift was really on its last legs. The stone-faced JP pulled back the wire netting so we could step out onto the smooth tiled ground, and we let our eyes adjust to the brightness of being so much closer to the sun. Our lungs fluttered weakly like moth wings, hardly able to fill with the horribly thin air. Aili had barely left the lift when the JP yanked back the netting and shot downward for another Canopia load of people venturing to Peak.

We prowled away from the lift docking station, up to the summit where Peak Tower stood clothed in glory of titanium shingles and thick diamond windows. The Tower jutted out from the center of the flattened courtyard like a thorn in the crown of Thgindim's head; silver and sharp among the mosaic spread of colourful stone. Smartly dressed adults climbed out of shuttles and fiddled with handheld devices and briefcases, Majesty Councilmen walked with pinched faces and their black robes billowing behind them— people from all over Thgindim flocked to and fro on their own paths that all eventually flowed through the big silver doors of the Tower.

Carmen, Velle, Chantastic, and I waved goodbye and good luck to our classmates and then we sat on a nearby bench to rest and eat. While I nibbled on the bread and cheese and took a swig from my water gourd, Carmen launched into instructing me on where to go. "Okay, since your name is N-Z you've got to go to the 32nd floor for Evaluation, a floor above where I went. They'll give you stuff to fill out until you actually go to the interview and then, *ta-da*! You now have an eternal position of servitude on Thgindim, the Everlasting Mountain." We all did an eye roll at the ridiculous title the Majesty Council gave our mountain.

Velle rubbed her temples, fingertips grazing over her own metal aging chips that had yet to go off."Wow…this really is it, isn't it?" she whispered. We all looked at her for explanation. "We're running out of time to be kids. For all we know, we could be courting tomorrow," she said dramatically, eyes wide as we all contributed to the woe of the situation through despairing comments.

"No more school."

"No more sleepovers."

"No more pranks or thieving."

"No more time to see each other."

I sucked at my lips to keep from whining, and tried in vain to control the spite burning in my thoughts. Because though the aging calendar in my chips would be disabled after today, I wondered about a thought surveillance feature I'd always felt had to be there too. It had never been outwardly stated to us by the Council that they could tell what we were thinking, but my teachers had always said the same thing to us: *Good little girls and boys think only good thoughts about their Majesty Council. Bad little girls and boys with bad little thoughts get punished.* After hearing stuff like this all my life, I never felt truly alone, truly at ease in my own mind. It was a heavy and anxious feeling, like I had my own personal police strapped to my back waiting for me to slip up.

As much as I didn't want to admit it, I depended on the Majesty Council just as much as they depended on my compliance. You listen, you pay the taxes, you adhere to the curfews, and you will live as long as you're able. To act selfishly for even a moment, and the Council would have no choice but to dispose of you. If we're all cogs in the Thgindim machine, one that stops moving or tries going the opposite way will clog up all progress and put things in a jam. I tiptoed the fine line of adherence with the occasional stealing, but in the scheme of the other ungodly things that were not to be messed with, pantsing a policemen or stealing sweets wasn't worthy of execution. And I'd gotten very good at being sneaky and keeping a blank head while the mischief occurred.

I looked at my hands. They had begun to shake uncontrollably. The bells chimed from the top of Peak Tower, signaling three minutes until it was time to go to Evaluation. I grabbed Chantastic's hand on instinct. She squeezed. *Breathe, Raine,* I thought, dizzily packing up what was left from my lunch as my friends waited for one last encouraging hug. *Don't worry, you won't be a Mother. Maybe you'll even get what you want…*

The bell chimed the second time. Two more minutes.

Suddenly the whole courtyard outside of the Tower was clearing out and flooding into the building, leaving me frozen. I felt like I was back in that haunting tunnel with no light for miles. My friends released me, I'd hardly felt their arms. Carmen nudged my shoulder to move. I couldn't. My breathing came out wispy and fast, images of someone else, someone better getting my dream job, clouded my mind. I had one more minute of being a kid, didn't I? Just one more minute until I was locked into the system and kept in it forever. I tucked a strand of hair behind my ear and smoothed out the tattered folds of my skirt, preparing myself.

"Good luck, Raine," Chantastic said quietly, her black eyes gentle, reassuring. She went on tiptoe and kissed me on the forehead, making some of the tremors roll away.

"Thank you," I whispered, holding her one moment longer,then forcing myself to move on.

The bell had chimed the final time. It was time for Evaluation.

chapter two

Covering the entire side of the tower were platinum sliding doors of elevators. Every time a door would open, a flood of people would pour out, and then twenty more would file in strategically. Thisoccurred steadily at every door, so my being early or on time for Evaluation seemed preposterous right now. I could barely move in the mass of Peak workers and new adults battling to get to their floor. Carmen had been carried away on an ocean of people running in the opposite direction, so I was left to find my destination on my own. And then, I spotted something so ancient, so unused, so simple, but useful and more familiar to my eyes that I smiled wickedly: STAIRS.

Elbowing my way through to the door, I glanced down at my directions and groaned; I'd have to climb thirty-two floors of stairs to reach my room. Well, it's a good thing I'd had a filling lunch. Taking a deep breath, I cracked open the door, and started racing up the steps.

I wonder what the punishment for being late to Evaluation would be...hmm. Honestly, these stairs are pretty lame for a monstrous structure such as Peak Tower, I thought, then unthinking the last comment, breathing faster and faster as I used the railing to pull myself up more quickly. The stairs were plain old cement, crusty and dirty and coated in a fine layer of dust that caused my feet to slip now and then. Obviously no one had used them in at least six years.

I'd raced up fifteen flights of stairs and was already huffing and puffing in desperation, ducking through the fifteenth level's door in the hopes of finding an elevator. The fluorescent lights tinted the scene a falsely bright white, blurring my vision. The doors lining the hallway were heavy iron with ten bolts and locks running up the edges to keep whatever was inside from escaping. Chills rippled like electric current down my spine as I quietly made my way over to the platinum elevator doors.

Howls sounded from one of the rooms, and fists hammered like thunder against the walls, "I'm telling the truth! It wasn't me, I'm innocent!"Fingernails scraped down the metal door.

I froze in front of the elevator, full to the brim with fear. My heartbeat seemed to throb right in my throat. As if in a trance, I turned back and walked to the door where the screaming was coming from. Not even thinking of breathing, I bravely peeked into the keyhole. All I could see was a man. He was dripping with bloody sweat, the tears pouring down his cheeks cleaning his grimy face. Once brown hair was matted and had great unnatural chunks missing as if someone had grabbed it at the roots and tore it from his very scalp. He panted and wheezed for breath, moans oozing from his bleeding mouth as he struggled against binds tying him to a chair. It was just him in there, so who was he screaming at?

Get out of here, idiot, you're not supposed to be here. My right mind hissed at me, warningly.

The prisoner's eyes flashed through the crack of a keyhole and dove into mine like missiles. He roared, the binds on his arms standing up and hissing. I realized they weren't ropes at all, but snakes.

Clamping a hand over my mouth and squeezing my eyes tightly shut, trying to force the memory of the obviously off-limits level of the Tower from my mind before I ended my future before it could begin, I bolted for the elevator and frantically stabbed at the up-button with a shaking finger. The door opened with a charming ding and I stumbled dazedly into the contraption, falling back onto the sofa inside. I couldn't stop trembling, thoughts struggling to form coherent words in my mind, *Accident, accident, accident! I didn't see anything. It was an accident, I swear.*

"Alright there, miss?"

The smooth voice came from the right side of the sofa. My words caught in my throat and I stared up into the face of an unfamiliar man. He had hard, brutal black eyes outlined with charcoal liner and a shiny bald head. His face was riddled with deep wrinkles, but he didn't have the appearance of a very old man; he was probably in his fifties. Clothed in silk midnight and crimson robes that fell loosely over his short and thin frame, he looked dressier than I did in my mom's best clothes. The mysterious smile he gave me and piercing eyes caused me to shiver further.

"I'm fine. Wrong floor, is all," I stammered with a slight edge to my voice.

His eyes widened slightly and his dark eyebrows rose in innocence, "Oh, now don't think I was accusing you of anything. You just don't look like you should be in such a…such a place." He finished crisply, making me nauseous with nerves, his eyes still intent on me. "What be your name?" he asked, cocking his head to the side. I looked him over again and decided that this stranger may as well be a Councilman. I tried to speak and get rid of the forbidden memories of the fifteenth level still biting through my brain.

"Raine Ylevol of Underbrush…your Majesty."

"Underbrush? Ah, yes, I see, I see. Very quaint little place, isn't it?"

I narrowed my eyes and smoothed my hair against my head uncomfortably. "Yes, very quaint," I muttered, quickly whispering, "Your Majesty." I loathed the manners I had to show to him. The way he spoke implied what couldn't be put into words. Some humor, then pity, and his nose was a bit wrinkled as if just saying the name left a bad smell in the air.

"I am Councilman Sebastian Lao if you care to know, but I doubt we will meet again in the future," He smiled sweetly, beginning a moment of awkward silence as he examined me, particularly my oddly colored hair. "Ylevol? That name...it sounds a bit familiar to me."

My exhausted eyes snapped open, "What?" I asked, curiosity peaking on the edge of my voice.

"Ylevol....Ylevol," he murmured thoughtfully with his teeth ground together. Just then, the cool feminine voice of the elevator spoke, *"Level 30, Department of Law Enforcement,"* and Sebastian smiled, pointing at the door. "Well, this is where I get off. I suppose I shall recall where I know that name once we are floors apart, as these things go."

I went rigid. This guy was head of Law Enforcement? He was the face spat on and set fire to in Underbrush. He was the man who chose whether or not to have you killed or banished, imprisoned or freed. Now that I thought about it, I realized he was the man who'd taken my father away. The person who'd made me grow up only with fuzzy memories of my dad's face just so that the overcrowded mountain could have more soldiers. I started shaking from putrid anger bubbling up inside of me.

When my father was drafted into the JP, I was only five and still a crybaby. We were in this small meadow looking for dandelion greens for Mom to cook when he took me upon his knee, stared at me with his grey blue eyes, and made me a promise in his gruff, whispery voice, "I'll be back before you know it, little raindrop, so don't you worry." We'd hugged and I still cried in spite of the honor it was for him to be chosen for such a job after all of his years as a tailor.His service contract would keep him at the base for fifteen years. All because of the man standing next to me.I couldn't even begin to contain the rampant thoughts I had for him.

"Until next time, Miss Ylevol." He smiled with false kindness, leaning into a slight bow and disappearing as the elevator doors slid closed.

I breathed a huge sigh of relief, slumping down into the sofa.*Phew, maybe Councilmen can't read minds after all...*

The cool female voice announced my level after another minute of waiting, and I stepped out onto a much quieter, much more comfortable floor and tried to regain my focus. The floor was coated in soft, thick, stubby, string of some kind— carpet! I'd heard of Peak having this sort of luxury, but to feel the springy stuff beneath the soles of my boot and know it was only for walking on and not for pressing to my face was unbearable! Even more exciting, a long, plush, sofa curled around the entire perimeter of the room like a white caterpillar, only stopping at a wide window where a secretary sat at her counter. I could see behind her many more workers bustling about by high-stacked cabinets and clutching holographic journals.

Mustering up my most sophisticated tone of voice and business-like manner, I walked up to the desk with my back straight as a door. A boy with shabby, but still formal looking clothes nervously trembled in front of me.

"Hello there, friend!" the woman chirped to the boy. She had spiky white hair that fell to her shoulders, a sharp, pinched nose, and blue eyes that twinkled behind pink boxy spectacles. Something about the prominent angles her cheekbones made when she smiled made me uneasy. "Name, please?" she asked brightly.

He answered in a slow, thick voice, "Er...uh...Bunky Gluts."

"Wonderful!" she piped as he smiled with huge cheeks puffing up. "And your level please, Mr. Gluts?"

"Canopia," he stated, shifting his weight.

"Bunky, your number is 233. Currently, we are on number 219. When you are called, follow the attendant to where you're Career Agent will be waiting, okay?" the secretary asked as Bunky nodded rather glumly.

As he shuffled away to the sofa, I gave the woman a mature, polite grin, very unlike my not very mature or polite self. "Good morning," I said as she looked up from some paperwork.

"Yes, it is, isn't it?" she sighed, looking me over and then averting her eyes. "Name?"

"Raine Ylevol, madam."

"Here you go. Fill it out, give it to your agent when you're called."

She shooed me away lazily with her hand and I raised an eyebrow, confused. *The number she handed me was 304, hadn't the last boy been 233?* I thought, turning slowly back towards her.

"Um...excuse me?" I began, trying to stay polite as my

mother had advised me. The secretary looked up from her desk planner, sighing.

"I think you gave me the wrong number. I'm Raine Ylevol? From Under—"

"I know quite well where you're from. Please take your seat before you get any more mud from those disgusting boots on the carpet," she hissed at me, eyes flashing. "Have a nice day, Miss Ylevol."

My face flamed as anger rose inside of me, but I stifled it, thinking of what my mother would say if she received a phone call about her daughter mouthing off to an official Peak employee. I turned on my heel and plopped down on the sofa as the secretary burst into sunshiny smiles at another Canopian arrival to Evaluation. Looking despairingly at the packet of forms I had to fill out, I glanced back at the bitchy secretary and pointedly put my feet up beside me on the couch, digging my muddy boots into the cushion. She flinched. I tried to hide my smile.

The forms were just repeats of the application I'd filled out in school, awaiting this day. It asked your top choices of Career and your skills, whether or not your body is able to reproduce, your parent or parents' jobs, and your height and weight. I thought about lying about my fertility, but Underbrush's doctor had already examined me and added me to a short list of other fertile girls being sent to aCareer agent in the Tower.

I drummed my fingers on my thigh, wishing I knew someone. I wondered if my friends were waiting in the Peak courtyard for me to come back with results. Bored, I doodled in the small sketchbook I'd brought along while Bunky Gluts twiddled his thumbs beside me. I caught him pick his nose a few times, and in spite of myself I awaited the moment when he might stick the booger into his mouth, but to no avail. He'd noticed me watching him and as I hastily glanced away, he whispered slowly, "I like your hair." His chipmunk cheeks were pink.

"Thank you. Good luck today," I replied, taken aback.

"Thanks, uh, you too."

Even though I usually didn't make much of an effort to chat with people other than my small group of friends, I tried to keep the conversation going. "So…what are you hoping to get today?"

His answer was immediate. "Anything but Locksmith."

"Why not Locksmith?"

He looked at me seriously. "Don't wanna get locked up."

A little creeped out, I subtly scooted away from him. Soon after, he went shuffling out of the waiting room for his interview. Another hour dragged by until the secretary told me to hurry down to room 27 and I tentatively made my way down the hallway that branched off the room. I knocked on the smooth obsidian door with a number 27 painted on it in silver ink, and waited. And waited.

"Come on in, kiddo."

I hesitated, sucked in my stomach. Then I turned the doorknob.

I know this is gonna sound silly, but the interviewer guy scared me to death when I first came in. I had seen upper-level Thgindimmers before, but this guy was the epitome of an Emergent, and therefore polar opposite of me.

His suit was a light, shimmery gold silk with embroidered birds stretching their wings across the lapels. His silver-white hair waterfalled in a long ponytail down his back, his harshly tanned skin etched deeply with wrinkles by the brows and lips. The only part of him not trying to blind me were his eyes; a dull, watered-down brown. He smiled at me, his trimmed mustache bristling, and motioned for me to sit in the chair across from his desk.

"Hello Miss…Ylevol[1]? Did I say that right?"

I slowly lowered myself into the seat, nodded. "Yes,

---

[1] pronounced yehh-VALL

actually.Most don't."

He laughed."Seems we are off to an okay start then."

"What's your name?" I asked.

He gave me a strange look. "*My* name?" His voice was clear and loud, too clear and loud for the tiny office. He laughed away my question. "Would you please pass me your file?"

I passed it.

"That's a good girl," he winked."Now, let's see about this resume of yours…" He licked his thumb and began flipping through from cover to cover. "You've been fourteen for…?"

"Nineteen months," I said quickly, trying to keep from playing too much with my hair. My hands shook and sweat in my lap.

"Ah, I see. Not bad, not bad…"

He paged through my file, re-licking his thumb every time his finger got caught. "You've been put down here as an early walker and talker, so you turned one-year-old after only seven months.Then,two-years-old and three-years-old at the average twelve month span; but what's this? Ooh… why did you take twenty-six months to go from nine-years-old to ten?"

I shifted anxiously in my seat. How was I supposed to know why the almighty Majesty Council had decided to wait to give me a birthday?I wasn't prepared to answer such a thing.Wasn't this supposed to be about my *future*, not my past?

But then,I remembered.

"Multiplication," I blurted out, blushing apologetically. "I couldn't seem to get that in school. It was the last and biggest unit and I remember getting scolded quite a bit since I couldn't grasp it."

He laughed a booming, amused laugh and I jumped, trying to join in, but beginning as soon as he stopped, wiping a nonexistent tear from his right eye. "Oh, boy, well I'll assure you there is no time for a multiplication test during this interview, so relax."

Easy for you to say.

The man stared at me a long couple of seconds, beaming with his mustache curled up above his lips. Then he looked away, clearing his throat and folding his hands in front of him on the desk. *Here it comes.*

"So. Here you are, fresh and ready at last. What do you want to do for your Council and mountain?"

I'd practiced this speech for so long now. I carefully took my sketchbook from my skirt pocket and set it in front of him, composing myself. "As long as I can remember I've wanted to be Thgindim's Sketcher." I paused, waiting for his reaction, but he remained unaffected by my statement. I tried to hold his gaze without letting my voice shake, "My father taught me some techniques before he went into the JP— I mean, Justice Police, and if you want to look in here, I have some sketches I've done of the mountain flowers, and my favourite is of Fluxaria. I did a landscape that focuses on its silhouette in the distance—"

"You painted Fluxaria? That's a bit of a dark subject matter," he said, chuckling under his breath and not even glancing down at the book placed before him. I took the liberty of opening it up myself and flipping to the page where I had done a watercolour of our twin mountain across the valley.

"Well... *literally*, it's dark, and I guess the concept too, but I didn't mean to say it's my favourite in that way. I just think the mystery of it is kind of...beautiful. There's just such a strong contrast from Thgindim's flowering meadows and greenery compared to how black and barren Fluxaria is," I explained, pointing out Fluxaria's shadow among Thgindim's colourful landscape. I'd taken so much care in painting the massive roof of clouds that perpetually stormed above it. I'd spent hours just getting the lopsided curve of Fluxaria's summit just right. The man now looked at the picture, squinting and holding it at different lengths to get it in focus just right.

"The drawing is very nice," he said, nodding with a half-smile, and I bit my tongue to keep from correcting him and calling it a painting. He pushed my sketchbook back towards me.

"Let's return to your forms, yes? I just need to skim over your…"

He rifled through to where my school grades and health information were listed, and he scanned them over carefully with his dull-coloured eyes.

I wish he could just look through my sketchbook more. Aside from language and art I don't think I got any superior marks…

"You are literate?" he asked, and I nodded. I noticed a clicking sound and glanced above his head to see a very confusing-looking clock. It had seven numbers and four hands. The numbers weren't sequential and some were upside down. This place was weird.

"I see everything here, and am not disappointed, Miss Ylevol. But there are many fair artists on this mountain, and what is it that sets you apart from the rest? That makes you deserving of one of Thgindim's most unique and ancientCareers?"

Go back to your speech, go back to your speech. I tried to speak, I tried to think, but soon the air in the room felt so thin that my lungs ached. I looked around, eyes watering, chest heaving, but no relief came as the desperation got worse. Finally, Mr. Whateverhisname gasped in realization of my sudden panic. But rather than a "what's wrong" or "are you all right," he exclaimed, "Oh my, I'm so embarrassed! Hold on just one minute, Miss Ylevol."

He pulled down on a gold lever that was attached to the wall and suddenly stale air exploded into the room from a little diamond-shaped vent in the ceiling. I inhaled and I could breathe again, but it felt fake and tasted like chemicals in my mouth.

"Being so high up, the thinness of the air can be very, very uncomfortable at times. We pump in some synthetic oxygen every few hours, but usually I just let it go unless I'm seeing a lower-level dweller like you who is not as used to thinner air. I assure you: the air's safe, it's made right here in the Tower." He winked again and I smiled even though I didn't find it very funny.

"Where were we?" he asked, more to himself, and then before I could remind him I was just about to make my case as being a viable Sketcher, he decided where the conversation was going. "Remind me...in your domestic home it is you, your mother, and your younger sister?"

I nodded.

"You mother is...what did you write here...a Spooner and Healer? Wow, that's a lot on her plate."

"She handles it well, though. I take care of my younger sister while she works. We all stay home and help out," I said.

He cocked up an eyebrow and spoke slowly, eyes scanning the page, "And your sister has a mental disruption? She's documented as an Inept Thgindim Citizen?"

My cheeks flushed, and I averted my eyes because I didn't want to see the smirk I could hear brimming on the edge of his voice. "Yes. Since birth."

"And you take care of her? I applaud your persistence."

"It's...she's my sister," I said stiffly, my throat dry and yearning for some real air. "She's really very amazing and kind. Everyone loves Gwen."

Everyone aside from the kids that used to tease her at school before she was taken out.Gwen could manage a few words, but aside from that, her language consisted of smiles, laughter, and blowing raspberries. She'd been progressing normally until she had been granted her third year, but after that, she just sort of stopped. She'd been three for 84 months; technically around ten-years-old using the 12 month to 1 year ratio. She'd always just be my precious baby sister. She'd never read, much less write, and it was my responsibility to watch over her and play with her while Mom worked. Hardly a responsibility.

"And you have here that your father is serving in our Justice Police?"

"Yes."

"Is his term almost over?"

"Not for five more years."

"Ah."

The ticking of the clock was bugging me again. I glanced

at it to try and tell how long I'd been at this interview, but all I could deduce was that each hand moved in a different direction and it was no use. "I like your clock," I said. It was a lie, but I needed him to like me. I needed Sketcher.

He looked puzzled for a moment, but then saw what I was looking at and beamed proudly. "Why, thank you. It's more useful than it looks." I smiled as if I understood and he said, "I have only a few more questions seeing as we're almost out of time now." He pushed my sketchbook even further from him and reluctantly I took it back into my hands. He gave a great cough to clear his throat and then folded his sausage-link fingers in front of him. I sat up straighter in my chair.

"If you had the chance to do anything, anything at all, and I don't mean even Career-wise, what would you do? What is a dream you have?" His voice was a softer tone now and I shut my eyes for a couple of seconds, dwelling on a good answer.

I had many dreams. Many of which I tried not to think about because of how tightly Thgindim had me tied to her, as well as my responsibility to my mother and sister. But I met the interviewer's eyes and said, despite my realistic judgment, "If I had the chance to do anything, sir, I would take my sketchbooks, go out into Mythland and draw and paint anything I found that doesn't exist on Thgindim. No one has seen those places and returned to show anything other than evidence of Fluxarian savagery, and so I would want to show the more natural side of the valley. I could just be off on my own to do it. I feel like there's so much more we can know and appreciate about a place if we take the risk to reconnect with it."

He didn't smile, but nodded politely and scribbled something on his little pad. My heart sank. At least I had been honest. He spoke while he wrote, "You are quite the independent young lady. But your sister is quite dependant on you, yes? Perhaps you'd do well in a Career that has you riding solo not far from home?"

I hesitantly said yes and he scribbled one more note before

flicking off the pad and looking back up with a grin. He extended his hand to me and I thought I was supposed to shake it, but in his hand he held a small scarlet envelope with a white ribbon wound around it.

Carefully, I slid it from his palm and stood, bowing deeply to show my reverenceas he returned my gesture with a slight nod.

"Best wishes, Miss Ylevol. It was charming to meet you."

I bowed my head, trying to keep from seeming too anxious to leave. "To you as well…thank you, very much," I said, waving and leaving the little office.

The envelope vibrating in my uncontrollably shaky hands, I took the stairs down again and this time got off on the correct floor. I'd have to find my friends. I dashed down the steps and nearly tripped as I tried to multitask and read the schedule that had printed out for my interview. I was not allowed to unveil my Career until I made it past the Peak Tower doors and said Thgindim's pledge.

I slowed down and fixed my hair before entering the tower lobby again. It was still as hectic as the morning. A few heads turned as I walked through to get out to find my friends. Heads always turned when people saw me. At this point, people had stopped asking me questions and they just gossiped. *What a strange colour. Like ink.Maybe it was a dye accident.* I heard those all the time.

The Peak courtyard was no longer the overcrowded center of attention. Surrounded by the electrical fence keeping them from the edge, a few Councilmen and workers flitted around from person to person. From here I could see across clearly, and my eyes instantly focused in on the black-haired girl standing on the bench waving her sweatered arms. That reminded me of how cold it actually was, and I slipped my cloak back on over my dress, ducking in between crowds to get to Chantastic. I could see her grinning, and she hopped down, running forward to meet me as well. Running made it even harder to breathe in the thin air and I found myself gasping again. Could they pump that fake oxygen stuff out here? Or would it just float away? I was never all that good at science so I wouldn't know.

"Chan!" I called hoarsely, feeling a sudden fear grab me at being somewhere so strange and unfamiliar. Chantastic was the black beacon at the end of my vision. As soon as we came close enough, I leapt, throwing myself into her arms, pressing the stiff envelope into her back. She held me tightly, stroking my hair and giggling.

"You're acting like it's been a hundred years," she whispered into my hair, pulling back and taking my hand. She touched the envelope, eyes widening and then coming closer to me. "The others had to go, the altitude was making Velle feel faint and Carmen forgot she had a weekend assignment at the goat pen. You have to open it! Let's see, let's see!"

And so I did. I went to reveal my job as if I had been shocked by lightning— fumbling over the white ribbon and shaking worse than ever. I tore the scarlet envelope and pulled out the little folded bit of paper. I read the beginning aloud. "'And so today, your life begins as a contributing person to this mountain. After years of learning and studying; now you will become a true gear in Thgindim's cycle of life and serve her Majesty Council justly.'"

Chan came to my side when I stopped reading. I just stood there, holding the letter in front of me. The mess of blocky capitalized letters swarmed before my eyes.

Raine Xifeng Ylevol:

THGINDIM LAUNDRESS

CONGRATULATIONS!

Forever serve Thgindim, the everlasting mountain

chapter three

I was blind. Rage and shock and disappointment and hysteria and something I couldn't even begin to describe overtook me, and the card with my Career was mangled and crushed in my fist.

It was too dark to see what shapes were trees and what shapes were merely bushes. I'd gone off from Chantastic hours ago, but now I was lost and not even sure of what level I was on. I think it was probably somewhere in between Canopia and Starshade. I was surrounded by trees and knew there couldn't be a village for at least a mile from here. In fact, I thought I might have been running in circles.

Laundress?LAUNDRESS? It had come out of nowhere, where did that jerk come up with Laundress? Did he make a mistake? Maybe he meant to write…I don't know…just….Laundress? The thoughts stung the inside of my skull like wasps and buzzed twice as loudly.

I slashed some branches out of my way and earned a nasty cut on my wrist for it. Cursing loudly, I stopped running and slid down a tree. I was too angry to cry or even form any words. I kept my mouth closed tight because if I opened it I might have actually started crying or screaming. I was such a whiner, or at least I probably was taking this too harshly because I'm an Underbrusher and should've known an Emergent or Canopian would get Sketcher this year.

I *had* known though. I'd just hoped really hard that I would be surprised and get it after all.

Who had gotten it then? How much had I sucked compared to them? It was probably some rich boy who had a drawing tutor that got to spend hours learning how to sketch orrectly and perfectly, while I just winged it and scribbled things and that probably looked laughable to the interviewer compared to what else he'd seen.

How stupid could I have been? I'd sounded so arrogant and ignorant, shoving my crap sketchbook in his face while he probably was handed oil paintings and flawless reproductions of the mountain roses and grasses.

I stood up and brushed some dirt off my skirt. Mom was going to be so disappointed in me. I'd ruined the dress she'd given me, my hair was full of leaves, and my skills had led me to receiving a crap job that I was stuck with for the rest of my life. Stomping over roots and ducking under the pine branches heavy with snow, I stumbled into a meadow clearing. It had dense woods on one side, and faced out onto a cliff that gave a breathtaking view of Mythland and Fluxaria in the distance. A little crystalline stream danced over smooth silvery and bronzed stones, reeds and river poppies bobbed and swayed on its muddy bank. I stepped carefully into the meadow, breath rattling louder than the breeze in the needles of the pines. I fell to my knees and began to drink from the river, scooping up the cold water in my hands. I splashed some on my face and picked a violet river poppy. The river poppy is unique to Thgindim, and it was my favourite flower to sketch.

They have five petals of a royal purple that are brushed

with periwinkle near the black center and fuchsia near the edges of each petal. When they die, red veins appear in the dried out blossoms and the entire flower turns crimson as blood. As I fingered the flower, a crackling of twigs sounded from the trees ahead of me.

Beside the stream was a pile of logs bound with twine and a bow and quiver of arrows leaned against it. At the sound, I was hit first with the desire to hide, terrified JPs were moving about and that I'd be in big trouble for being so far from my level. But the only hiding place close enough to leap into was a bramble bush, so instead I grabbed the bow and struggled with latching in an arrow. I wasn't very bright at archery either, but I'd figured I could just feign courage with the stranger's bow to scare off whoever was sneaking up on me

A boy came hesitantly out from the trees, his steps cautious in his black boots. I drew the arrow back and pointed it at him bravely, my lips mashed firmly together. He had messy blonde hair that fell into his eyes and wore a red knit beanie hat. His eyes were a clear silver and he had a shadow of stubble along his jaw. Shocked, a puff of breath came from his chapped lips, and he raised his arms as if to say, *I surrender*. But he was smiling, and I raised an eyebrow.

"What's so funny?" I snapped, eyes narrowed as he kept chuckling and leaned against a tree, arms folded across his chest. He was wearing a grey wool coat with copper buttons that ran from the high neck to the hem, a knit white sweater beneath, jeans that had seen better days, and a red scarf he had tied in a fancy knot around his throat. His grin spread up his face. Something about that smile hit me as being very familiar. Did I know him?

"Hey, maybe you should answer the person who is pointing a weapon at you?" I suggested, and he nodded, his wavy bangs falling into eyes.

When he spoke, his voice was gruff and amused, "You're holding the bow upside down. Oh…and look at that form…"

He came over and I was so shocked that my arrow flopped off of the bridge. He tapped my knee with the toe of his boot.

"Stop it!" I protested, getting off balance. But he then flicked my shoulder and blew air in my face and I toppled back onto a bed of pine needles.

"I think that's my weapon, thank you very much." He sighed, scooping up his bow and stowing the arrow back in his quiver. I followed him with my eyes as I continued to lie on the ground. Usually you could distinguish a person's mountain level based on their looks; tanner skin and lighter hair and eyes higher up, darker eyes and hair and lighter skin the lower you go. But even though he had the fair traits of an Emergent, his body gave away that he was definitely an Underbrusher. He had no fat on him. But instead of having the near-skeletal-Underbrusher body type that my friends and I shared, he was solid muscle. I could see how his coat bunched up on his arms as he lugged a pile of the wood over to another tree.

"What's a girl like you doing this far off from town?" he asked, not facing my direction, but pulling an axe from a leather case on his back and splitting some of the lumber. I jumped at the first slice.

"A 'girl like me'?" I asked, flushing.

He dropped the axe and turned back to me, pursing his lips. "I'd say...if it weren't for the awesome hair...sixteen year-old Canopian? Only child. You play piano and eat cake."

It was difficult, but I forced myself not to smile at the comment he'd made about my hair. "Wrong. Not even close," I said, and I half hoped that would shut him up but he just nodded and grinned more broadly.

He rolled his eyes. "I'm just joking, Raine."

My breath caught in my throat. "You know me?"

He crossed his arms again. "We did go to school together for six years, didn't we?"

And at that moment, the memories flooded back to me. A boy with badly cut blonde hair and grey eyes. Tall and quiet and didn't have any friends. Had I noticed him back then? Not especially, not many people did, and if he was noticed it was by boys like Kris or Jian who would make fun of him. He'd disappeared after sixth grade and my classmates had assumed he'd fallen off the mountain one day or thrown himself off because nobody liked him. Our teacher had just said he was having family and money issues at home and could no longer attend class.

But I remember in my first year of school, when my father left, my mom had still made me go to school that day, and I was crying all during class. My teacher beat and spanked me in front of everyone to show how shameful it is to show someone your tears and especially over such an honor in your family. She called me selfish and made me sit outside the cave we had class in until

I was ready to come back without crying. But I couldn't stop. I kept sobbing and sobbing and sat outside class for the rest of the time. My face was pressed into my hands when I heard my teacher scream at another student to leave class. This boy stumbled outside, tripping over a rock and gasping. His cheek was red where my teacher must have struck him. He sat beside me and dangled his legs over the edge of the cliff as I stared at him.

"I'm sorry about your dad," he had said, this being the first and last time we'd ever talked in school. "My brother's in it and I miss him a lot. He's gonna come back and your dad is too, though."

I had nodded and we sat in silence watching the trees sway in the Mythland valley. I couldn't figure out if he had gotten himself kicked out of class to talk to me or if it was just coincidence. His brother was killed only a week later from an avalanche, and I couldn't bring myself to talk to him again. People stopped making fun of him, but he still walked home alone every day until the day he didn't come back.

"Destan, right? Destan…?"

"Abrasha. Wow, I can't believe you even remember that much," he said softly. "So why are you out here? If you're lost, I know a lift that will take you into Underbrush."

I got up from the bed of pine needles and brushed off my dress. "Where am I, exactly? What level?"

"You are actually right on Underbrush, just a good distance away from being near any village," he said.

"Oh. Well…today was my Career Day. Were you at Peak too, today?" I asked.

He shook his head, reaching at his belt for a water gourd. He bent down near the stream and filled it. "I'm already employed. I have been for years." Then he offered it to me and added, "Happy birthday."

I muttered thanks and took a long draw of water, looking over him skeptically. "But how? You *are* my age right?"

"Yeah, yeah. Money just got too tight early on, and I

applied for the woodcarver's apprenticeship when I was eleven to start bringing back money for my family," he answered, surveying my face. "What? Are you one of the people who thought I fell off the mountain?"

My face went pink. "I didn't know what to think. I mean…I don't really know you." I set down the gourd on the grass and hugged my knees to my chest. How late was it now? The clouds were bleeding red and gold. It had to be sunset. When I had been running in the thick of the trees it had felt so much later due to the forest's dense darkness.

"So, what job did they give you?" Destan suddenly asked, sitting beside me. I ripped at some grass clustered around my boots, my throat closing up again in frustration at being reminded of my failure.

"I got Laundress," I whispered, and it hurt to say out loud. I looked over to see his expression. It was unreadable, his grey eyes looking off into the distance. My stomach fluttered and I looked away, confused at my reaction to just looking at the near stranger.

"I thought you were into art or something," he replied, and my lips parted in astonishment. Had he paid that much attention to me so long ago?

"I am. But I wasn't good enough. I'm not good enough," I stuttered, running my fingers through my hair and letting out a long breath. Destan got to his feet and whipped out a little flute. I watched in curiosity as he began to play. It made a deep whistling sound that mimicked a sleepy hoot of a bird.

A great animal came stalking out of the darkness. It was a slender grey wolf, with green eyes and black streaks in its fur. My voice froze in my throat and Destan held up a hand as if he knew I was going to scream. He went towards the wolf calmly and I saw that the wolf had a basket on her back. Destan lifted the wood he'd bundled up and placed it in the basket. He turned back to me. "It's not your art. It's them. Underbrushers come with a label that have only so many options listed for us that the

Majesty Council's written themselves." He gave me a small smile, quickly looking away and stroking the wolf's side.

"Thank you," I whispered, rubbing my arm as a shiver traveled through me.

"If you're looking for a way to get home, I can give you a ride," he said.

I bit my lip uncertainly. "Um…you don't have to," I began, then stopped as I envisioned myself tripping through the woods once it got even darker, falling into JP animal traps or falling right off the mountain. I looked back up at him. "Well, if it isn't any trouble for you…"

"It isn't," he said, shrugging. "I was just about to head out anyway."

He helped me up onto the wolf's back and I straddled it, situating myself comfortably on the saddle. He eyed my dress amusedly, how I'd so easily plopped on with no problem, and climbed on himself, hooking his feet into two little holders sewn to the saddle. Destan looked at me out of the corner of his eye. "You ever ride on one of these before?"

"No," I confessed, heart hammering like a woodpecker had nested inside my chest. I couldn't imagine the look on my mother's face when she'd see me arrive home like this.

"Then I'd advise you to hold on. Siri goes faster than fast," he said, a smile in his voice.

I awkwardly wrapped my arms around his waist and closed my eyes and swallowed my fear all at once. "Let's go," I breathed, and he smacked his foot against Siri's side.

She took off instantly, moving in great bounds, muscles coiling and springing beneath me and I held onto Destan for dear life. Siri dodged trees as only an animal could, going so fast I found that she was outrunning the sun, the sky brightening as she ran. In a matter of seconds we had left the woods and now were on a narrow, unfenced mountain path that if she were to trip, we'd plunge off the very edge of Thgindim. But was the view worth it. Leaning my head into Destan's back with my toward the sky, I saw every valley and colour of Mythland and Fluxaria beyond us. The sky was more beautiful than I had ever seen it, and I screamed, "Destan, this is amazing!"

He howled and Siri joined in and then so did I, and we kept running until we reached Underbrush's gates. He leapt over it and I laughed as the JP men stationed there cursed after us to stop and give our IDs, but we kept going and I pointed at my house. He slowed Siri to a trot, and I missed the kiss of wind on my face.

"Could we stop a little bit away from my house? I don't want my mother to have a fit," I gasped, winded from the ride.

"Yeah, of course," he said, and he rode Siri a little away from Carmen's house that sat beside mine. My once neat and wavy hair was blown around like a crazy person's, but I didn't care, and grinned at Destan who stayed on Siri's back.

"Thanks for the lift," I said, sincerely, bowing my head a little, but Destan waved his hand to brush the gratitude away.

"No problem," he said. "It gets lonely up there. It was nice to reconnect with an old classmate."

I stood there for a moment, meeting his eyes and looking away nervously, murmuring, "Still…thank you."

He nodded and took off. "Till next time, Bluehead!" he called, bounding back into the trees.

chapter four

When I went inside, my mom was busy stirring a stew that looked like it was all greens and nuts. It had been a bad week. Usually we could score at least some chicken. I snuck by to her bedroom and tried to do something with my hair before approaching her. After knifing through the worst bits with her antique jade comb (a gift from my father), I gathered myself and stepped quietly into the kitchen.

"Hi, Mom," I said and her dark eyes squinted at me from behind the cabinet where she kept her spices.

A smile splintered her gaunt face. "Raine! Get Gwen and then you can share your news over some supper, alright?"

I nodded and went into the room my sister and I shared. Our sides were separated by an old shower curtain that had been hung up when she was born. Gwen had long, curly black hair and the same dark eyes as my mother. I stuck out in the family like a frozen thumb: blue and pale, with my father's light eyes.

I pushed aside the plastic curtain and saw Gwen playing on the dirt floor. She looked up at me and smiled, her eyebrows shooting up her forehead. She had gotten dressed with her sweater tunic on backwards and her leggings inside out, and was chewing her nails down to the soggy cuticle. My first day away from home, and Mom couldn't even dress her properly?

As I bent down, she stumbled to her feet and toddled over into my arms. "Rayyy!" she giggled, my name being the clearest thing she could pronounce due to her mental disruption. She could hum an 'm' sound for Mom, wave, nod, and shake her head, but that was it for direct communication.

"Gwennie! How was your day?" I asked in a small voice that made her giggle.

She squealed, squeezing me with her thin little arms into a tighter hug. Then she did a clumsy twirl and plopped back in front of her stuffed wolf and fox that I'd knit for her last birthday. She looked up at me and hummed, reaching out with the wolf in her small fist. I took it and knelt beside her, stroking  the yarn hair I'd sewn on for a tail. Gwen touched the fox's nose to my wolf's and made a kissing sound. She was darling, so precious. I couldn't imagine not spending my days with her anymore while I was busy washing and collecting stinky clothes from all over the mountain. If I'd gotten Sketcher, I could have taken her along with me. Drawn the flowers she'd collected for me in every meadow imaginable. Lie under clouds and laugh because it was her most favourite thing to do (second to dancing).

"Um, *girls?* Your bowls are getting cold!"

I gasped, pressing a hand to my mouth. Gwen copied me, placing her broad palm flat on her face and then sliding it up and down the flat bridge of her nose while she laughed. I wrestled her into a tickle hold for being so silly and sighed, "C'mon! Let's go to Mommy."

Holding hands, we walked into the kitchen where we had a little fold-up table and a few bowls and cups. We'd set up the table whenever it was time to eat and keep it folded up in our cabinet for most of the day so that Mom could move around the kitchen and brew more easily.

Gwen and I sat down, and I watched my mom work. Her job made sense. She had already had a passion for cooking and told me she had aspired for so long to be a Healer. The Majesty Council had favoured her talents and given her what was perfect for her. Thinking of this made me doubt Destan's reassuring words, and then I just blamed myself again. I wasn't good enough, that was all it came down to.

My mom ladled some soup into her own bowl and tossed us a fork and spoon. I let Gwen take the spoon tonight and smiled as she dipped it into the thin broth and tipped her head back to taste the first spoonful. Mom sighed and wiped away a stray drop of soup that trickled down Gwen's chin. Then she erased all trace of her stress with a single breath and grinned encouragingly at me, rubbing her hands together in anticipation. "So? What did they give you?"

I blinked at her, mouth open to say it and I couldn't spit anything out. Her bushy eyebrows travelled up her forehead expectantly and Gwen rocked back and forth in her chair. I took the crumpled up envelope and ribbon from my skirt pocket. When she saw how much damage I'd done to it, she let out a short breath.

"I'm guessing whatever it is, you aren't very happy."

"I'm a Laundress."

"Oh, well that suits you."

I choked on my forkful of soup. "How? Do I really look that much like a Laundress?" My mom shrugged and my veins flowed with fire.

"I'm just saying, that's better than what Mrs. Ajram told me Carmen got. She got 'goat whisperer' or something ridiculous.

Well, you can't blame the Council for giving that messy family the short end of the stick." She lit a cigarette she had stowed down her dress and Gwen gave a little cough at the smoke, her orb-like eyes focused on me.

I stared dubiously at my mother and shook my head. "Unbelievable. Mom, I'm a Laundress forever, and Carmen's a 'goat whisperer' and I don't know why you still insist on holding a pointless grudge against the Ajrams in the first place." Carmen's family had originally been from Canopia, but when her father ran into trouble with some sort of black market, the Majesty Council imprisoned him and forced them out of their life of near luxury.

"I'm not holding a grudge, Raine. I'm just saying it makes sense that she wouldn't be in the Majesty Council's favour. Anyway, don't blame this on me if you weren't good enough for Sketcher or whatever it was that you were setting yourself up for."

I swallowed my annoyance with another forkful of soup. There was silence as we all ate, Gwen pouting and making a whining sound for some more soup that didn't exist. And then my mom sighed, "But you are right. We're talking about your future and since you're starting your adult life as of tomorrow, you and I need to discuss what my parents discussed with me on my Career Day."

I drained my bowl and met her eyes. Gwen slid out of her seat and began slowly shuffling toward our bedroom door, her eyes inquiring.

"You can go ahead," Mom said sweetly, nodding so that Gwen felt that it was okay to escape back into her room and play with her stuffed animals. As she shuffled off, Mom dug the tip of her cigarette into her empty bowl and asked gently, "Could you make me a cup of tea, Raine? My back aches from all that brewing today and I need to relax, honey," Mom asked me, and I got up to fix some. While the leaves soaked in the barely warm water, Mom whispered, "Raine...I think it's about time you start courting."

Courting. The word sounded gritty in my brain and it took me awhile to understand it. "Courting as in…" then it clicked and my voice became feeble, "Marriage? Me? Me get ready to get married?"

"I know it sounds like it should be so far off, but I started courting your father once I received my Career. It's really a fun and relaxing process, Raine. It isn't as bad as it sounds."

"What if I don't want to get married?"

"You're going to get married Raine, that's something you don't have a choice about."

I started pacing and then threw my hands up in the air, "Well what do I have a choice in? Right now it seems like nothing!"

"Don't be so melodramatic, dear," she scoffed, and for a moment I almost hated her.

"I don't get to choose anything! Not my Career, not anything, not even something as personal as who to commit to! Mom, can we please talk about this when I'm not about to jump off the mountain?"

"We're going to talk about it now. And I'd have you know that courting is an act of meeting with several men your age or a little older. *Several.* You can choose out of them which one suits you best. There, you have a choice, don't you? Stop acting like such a child." She wasn't joking anymore, but neither was I. I clutched my head where an ache throbbed between my eyes.

"When will I have to meet with them?" I collapsed into a seat again and poured her another cup of tea.

"As soon as you can. One of my most loyal customers in upper Starshade has a son about your age that she speaks very highly of. I'd like for you to meet him if you've swallowed this fantasy of yours of remaining single. I mean, really Raine, people gossip about my odd, thieving, blue-haired daughter enough. I'm doing this for you. For your reputation. For your happiness." She reached for my hand across the table, but I left the kitchen without saying another word. I was too exhausted for anything else and didn't want to keep fighting an unwinnable battle.

Kicking off my boots and releasing myself from the stupid dress, I fell onto my cot and tried to drown myself in the quilts. Gwen peeked at me from the edge of the curtain and I rolled onto my side, turning away from her innocent face. If she saw me cry, she would freak out and scream for Mom to come and make me feel better. As if that would do any good at all. Just that morning I had been full of hope. Now I was full of dread and hoping I'd go somewhere nice in my dreams.

chapter five

I left early in the morning to make it to the Laundress pavilion in the middle of Underbrush's square where all of the Career centers were set up. I knew where it was because this was where Underbrushers dropped off their weekly laundry and picked it back up days later. Apparently, every level above ours (even Starshade) had a Laundress pick their clothes up at their own homes. We really were the poor ones.

I was dressed normally now. Everyday I wore a variation of the same thing. Thgindim was cold and rugged and dangerous and only got worse as you went up the mountain, so we all had to dress warmly. However, we couldn't be too bundled up or else we wouldn't be able to climb over fallen rocks or trek up through the forests. To cope with this climate, I tied my hair up into a messy bun with a red ribbon. My bangs stayed floppy in my face so that I could avoid eye contact by hiding under them. I pulled on thick knit leggings and socks, denim shorts, a worn and stretched brassiere that I've had since I was thirteen, long sleeve shirt, thick scarlet sweater, and fingerless gloves so that my hands didn't get frostbitten and could move freely. I also had a tool belt I kept on me always along with my water gourd, dagger, a leather money pouch, and a little scrap of fabric I could tie up my lunch in. I also brought my bow and quiver of arrows just in case I had wanted to try and scare anyone off with the idea of me shooting them. Maybe it could work with someone not as clever as Destan.

Glancing around, I saw three other girls from my year had been given Laundress too. They nodded at me stiffly, and hurried ahead as we all made our way to the pavilion. In all of Thgindim, there were about 25 Laundresses and they all came from Underbrush. The current Laundresses were on the move to their assigned level and elbowing through us newbies. I approached the counter where the Head Laundress was writing up orders on a typewriter. She had on a jade pendant and looked surprisingly well fed for an Underbrusher. Working for so long in even a shabby Career like Laundress must have it perks, I guessed.

The Head Laundress glanced down at us and smiled. "Good morning, ladies! I just got word of you new runners this morning, so just let me finish up with your name tags and I'll give you all the info ya need to know.

It hardly took another ten seconds, she typed up nametags so quickly her fingers were a blur. She then slid them into little pins and said, "Pin these on so people know you work fer me."

I slid the pin through a stitch in my sweater and looked back up at her. She reached behind her and pulled out handfuls of folders and various papers from the line of baskets.

"Here's how it goes. This is your map. You won't be needing this fer long because you'll be goin' all over, but until then, I advise you to hold this map to yer precious little hearts." As my eyes combed over it, I felt a flurry of almost excitement rise inside of me. I'd get to see much more of Thgindim than I ever had before, so much more that it was even overwhelming to imagine.

"Get here before dawn, be back before dark. You'll only be responsible for one level at a time so work at yer own pace. We alternate duties in shifts. Don't talk to each other, don't hardly talk at all. You have to act like ghosts or little faerie godmothers that take or leave the clothes without a word. If they say thank you, curtsy and don't look in their eyes, got it?"

We all nodded in awed silence, shifting from foot to foot. The Head Laundress looked us over in amusement, unable to contain a sudden burst of laughter. "You're all so adorable! Now gon' get yer wolf from that little spot over there, and here is your schedule. Keep it on you and make a copy for home to check if you'll be gathrin' or delivrin'. Even if you are bringing clean clothes back, once yer done you have to come to me and wash some of the clothes that have been dropped off here. Pick a spot to do yer washing. We got basins in the back of thispavilion and I'll even turn on the radio for you girls if yer workin' at a good pace. Am I clear with all that nonsense?" She squinted down at us still with a smile and we all answered in unison.

"Yes, ma'am."

"Don't you *ma'am* me. Just call me Auntie Jun," she laughed again, waving her hand and passing out our schedules. She dropped some battered pieces of money for the wolves into each of our palms, and I thought of Destan; how riding on Siri's back had made me feel so free and light, like the wind.

The Travelshack, as we Undebrushers called it, had public, borrowable transportation devices. There were wolves and horses in little stalls filled with hay and dry grass and bones, scooters and small gas-powered carts lined up for paid rental, and then a wall with some metal rickshaws. So many animals and contraptions had already been rented out or stolen that by the time I made it to the stalls, the only sign of wolves was in the lumps of dung left in the wolf-pen. I had visited here with my dad when I was little. I'd pet a wolf's muzzle and Dad said that because he didn't growl or move that he was depressed from living in such a tiny place. He said that if I held out my hand a little farther, the wolf could snap its jaws, get a few of my fingers, and be made instantly happier. I squealed as he pretended to throw me in the stall and I decided then that I didn't like my dad's sense of humour one bit.

Just me and another one of the new girls were without an animal. The horses were too expensive and knowing my mother, she'd throw a fit if she saw me riding something so flashy. The girl didn't talk to me, but moved like my shadow behind me as I went up to the counter where the animal keeper read a tattered book. He looked up, chewing on a toothpick.

"Excuse me," I said, having to cough to get his attention, "how can we request wolves? We're new Laundresses and this is how we were told to get around."

The guy glanced up for a second, and then shrugged, "What you see is what you get. We won't be getting any more until at least end of the month."

I swallowed my disappointment. *So I don't get to fly like Destan,* I thought, nodding at the man and then asking, "What should we take, then?"

The man licked his thumb and flipped a leathery page of his book. "Most Laundresses use a rickshaw. Don't know why Jun suddenly thinks I have beasties ready for all of her girls."

The other Laundress and I begrudgingly went to the row of rickshaws lined up outside the front of the Travelshack. Each of the contraptions consisted of a simple  bicycle, the seat padded with worn wool, and a large bucket of some sort that seemed to serve as either a basket for the clothes gathered, or an extra spot for people to ride along.

After thanking him, the other Laundress and I took a rickshaw, paid the man with the money Jun had given us, and we wheeled our vehicles out into the square. Thgindim was waking up now, more pots clanging from inside of houses, smoke rising from chimneys and JP trucks barreling down the road.

The schedule given to me said I had to pick up from Canopia, the third level. I couldn't help but contain the bitterness in my thoughts. *Great, give the new girl the biggest level on the mountain for her first day.* The other girl had disappeared so now I was on my own. I retied the ribbon in my hair, stubbornly climbing up onto the bike and trying to gather my balance. *I can make it to Canopia without getting lost*, I thought. *I was able to make it to Peak yesterday, hadn't I?*

What I instantly realized as I started pedaling was that I'd need more leg muscle. Underbrushers already had about 0% fat on their bodies due to lack of food, but pedaling along the increasingly steep main road that wound around the mountain made me realize we must not have that much muscle either. I thought of Destan on his wolf and became so jealous that the frustration actually helped me surge forward out of Underbrush and on my way through Starshade. I wondered if I was too slow, if I could get fired for being too slow, if I could get fired at all. But the Majesty Council couldn't expect everyone to be masters at their position if they hadn't even considered their talents.

I'm. Supposed. To. Be. A. Goddamn. Sketcher, I thought over and over, shivers zigzagging across my spine as the rusted gears of the bike-chain squeaked with every pulse my foot put on the pedal.

I chugged up to the JP at the gate into Starshade, taking a breather and putting my foot down to balance myself to get my ID. His eyes scanned over me in no more than a blink. "I see your badge. Proceed." The gate opened and I kicked off, trying to suppress a groan as I had to force my exhausted legs to keep pumping.

Once the gears were used to the amount of movement I was demanding, the squeaking and screeching of badly-oiled parts ceased and all that was left was a soft, soothing clicking. Starshade had smoother roads than I was used to on Underbrush and I slipped through the shops and homes breezily. I took notice of what made Starshade different from my level. The buildings were less of the ramshackle cabins and huts I was used to, each having at least two rooms and topped off by elegant, arching roofs tiled with shiny obsidian. When I passed by the school building, I almost had to make a complete stop to take it all in.

The Starshade school was tall and narrow, with bamboo balconies and the Majesty Council flag flapping in the smoke the chimney coughed out. Kids trudged up together in little monochrome clusters into the school building. I wondered how many classes they got. I'd had six: arithmetic, language, history, science, crafting skills, and morality. Morality had been my least favourite. It was all just talk of rules and how to live and why the Majesty Council was the only source of protection and wisdom we had against the Fluxarian savages across the valley. I pedaled away, my brain stuck on my memories of Underbrush's big cave, packed with hundreds of kids in chairs, writing on their laps with stubby pencils while one teacher screamed and pointed at a board set up by the front.

After getting through more thorough JP clearance at the Canopia gate, I swerved off the main road to avoid the steady flow of uniformed workers trooping down to the different factories and mills. The air reeked of sulphur and gasoline, and the dirty, heavy fragrance of burning coal lay like a blanket over the entire level. I pulled my turtleneck over my mouth and nose, squinting in the haze of fumes I saw pumping out from each crooked chimney. Every building on either side of the road looked industrial, made of stone and metal, hardly comparable to the mansions and cozy cottages I'd once expected to be found here. *Where do I pick up the laundry if there doesn't seem to be any houses?* I thought, face burning as my clunky rickshaw took up the entire width of the narrow sidewalk.

"Oi! Watch where you're going, Underbrush scum!" A hand came out and shoved me against the side of the mill I'd been wheeling by, and I tipped off the bicycle seat, getting smashed in between the wall and bucket of the rickshaw as a great horde of men and women all clad in the same navy jumpsuits jogged past. When the pack of Canopians dwindled, I pushed the stupid thing off of me, dragging it off into an alleyway and taking a moment to calm my heart rate. I leaned over, bangs falling down in front of my eyes, shaking hands pressed to my knees. My fingers were red and even starting to blister from gripping the rough handlebars so tightly. *Get a grip, get a grip,* I thought, still breathing raggedly, but trying desperately to calm it. I wheeled the rickshaw into the shadows, unhooking the basket in the back from the wheels and bike and holding the huge bucket in my arms.

I left the alley, hardly able to see around the laundry basket in my arms, and before another person could block me, I took off running down the sidewalk. Seeing a gigantic laundry basket with legs caused a lot of gasping and expletives to be uttered as I plowed through, eyes quickly darting left to right in search of where I might find a place to pick up. I felt wicked and funny plowing through like this, I'd never dare to draw so much attention to myself back home.

Why hadn't Jun told me about Canopia and how weird it was laid out? My throat hurt from breathing so hard and sucking in the polluted air. Just as I narrowly avoided a pack of teenage nurses that had been obliviously giggling and skipping toward my rampage, I suddenly remembered something the head Laundress had said. What she'd said just moments before me and the others had bolted.

The map! I realized, slowing my sprinting to an uneven, fast-walk as I dug around in my pocket for the rolled up pages she'd passed out. I backed into an alley again so that people could pass without fear of running into a giant rickshaw bucket and blue-haired girl. I scanned over the map, flipping through pages until I saw the layout most similar to what I was experiencing. Scrawled in messy red handwriting at the bottom was a note; a note I'd guessed was from Jun:

CANOPIANS' APARTMENTS ABOVE BIG FACTORIES— TOP FLOOR. STINKY, STINKY, STINKY!!

I raised an eyebrow. Looked back up and blew some hair out of my eyes. *Welcome to the rest of your life, Raine,* I thought, stowing the map in my boot, picking up the laundry basket, and making my way to the apartments to get the stinky, stinky laundry.

chapter six

I let the slope of the road carry me down, the weight in the basket behind me helping me gain some speed as I cruised farther and farther from that awful third level of the mountain. The stench of the factories followed me still; reeking from the soiled uniforms and sweat-drenched garments in the bucket. Now my priority was just going somewhere to get them clean. Jun had said that basins were in the back of the Laundresspavilion, and for a moment I considered this because I'd rather do my busy work in the presence of strangers than my crazy mother busily brewing, and Gwen yanking on my sleeve to play with her the entire time. But after the hours I'd already spent in swarms of not so friendly higher-level Thgindimmers, I felt so drained and desperate for some solitude and rest that I found myself heading toward an opening in the woods. Before I knew it, I was finding my way back to that meadow, trying to retrace my steps and quell the sudden longing twisting in my chest.

Riding the rickshaw over roots and rocks was nearly impossible. I had to stop repeatedly to go back for a sock or blouse that had fallen out while the cart jumped over the bumps. It was only a number of minutes until my ears perked at the sound of the stream lying ahead.

I hopped off the bike, padding along on the frosty moss, my boots loving how soft the ground was in comparison to the pedals. I rolled the rickshaw into the meadow clearing. Unlike yesterday, the sky was no longer aflame with sunset. Wisps of feathery clouds laced the edge of the blue horizon. The pines sparkled with snow, their needles drooping with glassy drops of sap. There wasn't a bow leaning against a rock this time or a stack of logs or any sign of wolf prints, and the stream babbled almost more giddily than it had yesterday. *It would be perfect for washing my Canopia laundry! And so relaxing...*I thought serenely, scooping up a pile of the smelly stuff and kneeling by the water. Cold dew seeped through my leggings at the knees, and I shivered.

The water was icy on my fingers, but all of the pedaling I'd done had made me feel sweaty and overheated. I stared at the clothes for a moment, and then fell onto my back and just closed my eyes. So much for being motivated, but I was starving. Still flat on my back, my hand patted my little fabric bundle of bread and water gourd.

A bird chirped somewhere, a low hoot that I recognized. A meadowlark? Seemed fitting for the setting. I craned my neck back, my hair digging into the grass, but as the world looked upside down from my angle, I saw a shadow perched in the pine tree. It grew an arm and waved. I jumped and sat up as Destan Abrasha hopped down, a slightly bewildered smile on his face and flute in his hand. It hadn't been a bird at all; it had been him playing again.

"Didn't expect you to come back," he said.

I nibbled on my bottom lip, brushing back my bangs as I replied, "I need a place to do my washing."

"Isn't there an entire Laundress pavilion for that?"

"Isn't there a woodshop for your work?"

He narrowed his eyes, appearing a little amused. "Fine, fine, I see how it's going to be. Stay if you want then. Just don't chop down my trees or anything."

"If you like trees so much, why do you cut them down?" I asked, unwrapping my lunch and taking a swig from my gourd. The wellwater tasted like mud and I emptied it to fill it in the stream.

"I don't really chop entire trees down. I just take down branches and get logs from the fallen ones for carving," he said, and then he gave me a sideways look. "Why are you talking to me, Raine?"

I flushed, unsure if the question annoyed or embarrassed me. "I can stop if you want," I shrugged.

"No, I don't mind. Just…"

"Just what?"

"I just don't get visitors often," he shrugged, then I saw a small smile spread on his lips. "Actually, I don't really get visitors ever. Not used to this whole communication thing." He stood back up and sauntered over to his axe, beginning to roll out a few logs to set on his splitting-stump. But before he could make the first chop, he paused, hands on hips, "And you know, since you've invaded my most secret and beloved place, I think you owe me a bite of that bread."

His silver eyes gleamed mischievously as he returned to the stream. Begrudgingly, but knowing it was fair, I tore the soft part off the crust and set it down in his open palm. He had gloves too. Ratty, dark and fingerless, with little holes and splinters tucked in the stitches. His fingers were calloused and rough and covered in faded white scars.

In a smooth movement, he whipped a small amber jar of molasses from his pocket and painted some of the sweet stuff on the bread. How had he gotten that? Had he found a maple and drilled into it? But when I thought he was going to stuff it in his face, he passed the hunk back to me with a smile."A peace offering. Now I'll let you get back to work." He went into the trees, whistling. *What an odd boy. What goes on in that head of his?* I stared after him for a moment while I ate the now sweet bread, and then got to washing.

I felt washing the clothes this way was even better than if I had done it all in a basin back in the village. The water rushed at the soapy fabric and helped me attack the stains. I could rub the rocks on them to scrub the harder marks out and move on to the next article of clothing. The only problem was how numb and pruney my fingers became from working with the cold water. I bet the basins back at the pavilion were warm.

Destan came back into the clearing off and on; sometimes hauling some lumber and other times it looked like he was just wandering over to check if I was still there. It was sort of charming, and so I mostly pretended not to notice and let him do his stalking. I finished the entire load by what I think could have been a little over an hour. The sun was still yellow and shining and I had until dark to go home. Going downhill would be much faster too so I was ahead of schedule already!

After folding the clothes and stowing them in the bucket of my rickshaw, I stood back and looked at the meadow. He would be back soon; I could just feel it because he hadn't checked on me for a while. Leaning against a tree, I started sketching the stream, and soon enough, Destan appeared, hands in his pockets.

"All finished?" he asked

"Yeah. I just finished a moment ago. You?"

He pursed his lips. "Actually, I finished two days ago. I get a weekly load and spread it out on my own time." Destan walked a little closer to me, looking a little bit nervous which at this point struck me as strange behaviour for such a usually cocky person. I closed my sketchbook as he motioned towards my archery set, "Would you mind if…could I try it out?" he asked.

I felt like asking him where his bow was or saying

something to make him go away so I could draw in peace, but for some reason all I could say was, "Sure, go ahead."

Destan treated it so tenderly, like it would break even though it was made of thick, supple ebony and strong leather cord. "It's made beautifully. Looks better than I could have ever carved." He strode away from me and loaded in an arrow, pulling his elbow back to his ear.

I could never pull it back all the way, his extension was perfect and I couldn't help but admit, "I can't use it. My dad left before he could show me how to do it correctly—"

"Come here," Destan said suddenly, lowering the arrow and beckoning me. I cautiously set down my sketchbook, but then he waved his hand dismissively, saying, "Wait! Tear out a piece of paper if you can."

My journal was already nearly full, but reluctantly I listened and carefully pulled out a leaf and handed it to him. He marched up to a tree and fastened it to a branch. "Do you want me to show you?" Destan asked. "Show you how to shoot?" His eyes were sparkling and eager, fingers drumming on the neck of my bow.

I stared at the target he'd made and licked my lips. "I…I really am not good. Remember how you embarrassed me yesterday?"

"C'mon, I wouldn't call that embarrassment. We were alone and I wasn't laughing AT you. I was laughing because you amuse me."

"*Amuse* you?"

"Yes, Raine Ylevol, you are a very funny person."

"Okay, fine, but I don't have a single hope when it comes to archery," I insisted, crossing my arms self-consciously. "You can use it all you want, I really don't mind if you do. But I really don't want anything to do with a bow and arrow."

"Then how come you brought it along with you?" he asked, raising one eyebrow accusingly. I opened my mouth to speak, then closed it, looking guiltily at the ground. Destan came closer. "I've got a bow for myself, and while yours is quite the charming piece of weaponry, I don't know how I feel about a little blue-head like you going through the woods without something to protect herself. I mean. If you intend to keep showing up here to wash."

He waited for my response a couple beats, and then I gave him one, stating simply, "I do intend to wash here."

"Then you better also intend to learn how to use that thing in case a JP decides to jump you one day," he said.

I sighed. "You make a good point," I looked up into his eyes, pushing my bangs out of my face, "so where do I start, oh, archery-master-Destan?"

A mischievous smile gleamed on his mouth, dimples pinching his cheeks. He shoved the bow into my hands, whispering, "Let's start with that wobbly stance of yours."

chapter seven

And from that day on, Destan Abrasha gave me archery lessons and I answered any questions he wanted an answer to in return. I would blur through my pickups and deliveries in anticipation of seeing him again, and when I'd check back in with Jun at the pavilion she'd see how sweaty I was and think I'd been scrubbing really hard and not firing arrows at paper targets and rotten wood.

"Raine, you're *so* much stronger than you think. Only use two fingers! Three at the *most*," he pleaded, moving to fix my grip again. My fingers shrank away from the string before he could touch them and the arrow flopped out, making him sigh. "*Really*, Bluehead?"

I exhaled, glaring at him. "I *told* you I was bad. And would you stop calling me that?"

"Whatever you say, Bluehead," he answered, shrugging

and stepping back as I tried not to stamp my foot in protest. "Again."

I held my tongue, plucking up the arrow, hooking it back in, and trying to keep it on the bridge of the bow; what he called the arrow rest. My arms quivered with the potential energy rippling through the drawn-back cord.

I heard him sigh. "Release your stance," he said, coming over to demonstrate again. "You're not nocking in your arrow correctly."

Nock: that was a new term he'd taught me. There were a series of things about archery that I had never bothered to understand before, and now Destan made it his mission to engrain the art of the bow-and-arrow into my heart, mind, and soul. When going into your stance, you had to stand with your left side facing the target and face turned towards the target; if your weight isn't equally distributed onto both feet, your aim will be off; the arrow must be 'nocked' (a.k.a hooked in) perpendicular to the bow string; the cock feather must be the one away from the bow because if you have it turned in, it will hit the bow on the way out and the arrow will fly crooked. And he promised there was so much more.

I steadied myself and pulled the arrow back. My pointer and index finger trembled from the pressure. "Good! Keep going, more, more!" Destan called. "The string should touch your chin and tip of your nose. That's how you know it's being drawn back far enough."

In a quick motion, I released my right fingers and the arrow shot off, stabbing the plank of rotten log Destan had found to use as a target. It worked much better than ruining my sketching paper and Destan said that shooting directly at a living tree will cause the arrow tips to either fall off or dull. I wiped at my forehead, prepared for the onslaught of criticism he'd send at me. "I know, I know. I should've just let the string roll off my fingers or whatever you told me, but I'm getting tired."

"On the contrary," he said, "I think that was quite

astonishing. Especially so because this is only your fourth or fifth lesson." He beamed at me encouragingly and tossed me an apple. I sat by him on the shore of the river, watching as fierce wind ripped at the trees around us. Thgindim's weather these days was so unpredictable. Some theories floating around were that some scientists at the Peak were tampering even more with our atmosphere to thicken the air on every level and control rainfall, but I couldn't see how such a thing could even be possible. Destan looked at me and I knew he was going to start asking me unusual questions again.

"Do you know if anyone ever in your family had such great hair as you?" he asked, and he lifted a finger as if he wanted to touch it, but I tucked the strand behind my ear self-consciously.

"Nope. Only me. My Mom tried to dye it once," I said.

"Her hair or yours?"

"My hair, dummy," I smirked, nudging his arm, unsure of why I was smiling about something that had been so mortifying. "It was against school rules, against the rules of the heavens, against nature, everybody said, and so since I wasn't normal and had to be fixed, my mom just one day, when I was eight, cut off all my hair and painted it black with ink from her calligraphy ink pots. I looked like a boy with black hair for one day, and then a sad little Bluehead the next after getting a bath."

"I think I remember that..." he trailed off, nodding. I knew he couldn't possibly remember since it had been so long ago and we hadn't ever really been acquainted with each other, but it was nice of him to say. He came up with a completely different question in the next instant. "Do you still see your friends often? The friends from town?"

I shook my head slowly. "I see Carmen at night when she's coming in from work. She's at the stables and has to take care of the pigs and goats. She doesn't deserve such an awful job." Carmen's pretty hands were always muddy now and her naturally floral aroma had become tainted with the smell of feces and rot. I suddenly realized how much I was sharing, how weird it was that I was so openly telling him these things. But I couldn't seem to stop. And the calm way he just sat by me put me so at ease. "Velle's always up at Peak since she got a position as one of their maids, so I never see her. And her twin, you know, Chan Ai? She works down here as a Florist so I try to see her, but overall we've sort of been blown apart." My voice trembled off, and I tore up some weeds sprouting up by the heels of my boots.

He opened his mouth, probably about to tell me something like our jobs were crappy excuses, that we must not really care that much for each other if we don't put in the effort. But then he closed his lips again, staring off thoughtfully before murmuring, "I don't think you're necessarily 'blown apart.' You just have to work through the shit handed to you. Make time for each other, yeah?"

I tossed a stone into the river, watching it get carried away. "Yeah. Well, I'm off Sundays except now I have to do this 'courting' business my mom thought up. Have you courted anyone, Destan?" I wondered, picturing him with some pretty Canopia girl who thought he was from her level because of his lighter hair and eyes.

Destan barked a single laugh and waved his ratty gloved hands in front of my face. "Do I look like I've been holding some girl's hand with these things? I don't have the time or the ability."

"You have time to teach me archery," I pointed out, and his silver eyes went to slits.

"I see how it is. Let's get back to work now then—"

He got cut off as a low rumble started vibrating through the air. Our eyes met and for a moment this connection sent a shiver down my spine, but the rumble was getting nearer and nearer.

"Do you think we're having a rockslide or another mini avalanche or something?" I whispered, setting down my apple core and gathering up my things. My heart was pounding so hard and so suddenly that my chest hurt. What if it was headed for the meadow? Even if we made it out in time before the boulders started crashing in, what if it ruined our perfect spot for practice and laundry and everything?

I moved toward my rickshaw, but before I could hop on, Destan seized my wrist in his big hand. "No! Raine, it will slow you down and we need to get out of here as fast as possible."

It was only a light and easy Underbrush load, but the bike and bucket itself was still so clunky. I hated the idea of Underbrushers being the ones who lose their clothes due to a rockalanche, but I nodded, "You're right, you should call Siri."

He took my hand and started running into the trees so fast that when we jumped in unison over the fallen branches and little pits of leaves we stayed airborne for a full three seconds. While I ran obediently with my hand in his, trusting where he was taking me, he groped in his pocket for his flute and then he started hooting it with as much of a melody as he could. Siri came bounding into view within seconds.

"You're smaller, so get in front of me. This way you won't fly off," Destan said, lifting me up by the waist without warning and placing me on his wolf's back. I straddled her and pressed my calves to her balmy stomach while he slid on behind me. He scooted forward and his arms folded around me so that he could grasp the reins he had fastened to her saddle. When he touched me I felt uncontrollable colour rise in my cheeks and my already frantic heart start to dance faster. Destan tugged on the reins and Siri took off like a bolt of lightning.

I lost hope in the idea that Destan knew where we were going. The forest was getting thicker and blacker and the noise of cracking and crashing rock resounded thunderously no matter what direction we seemed to go toward. Still, we ran and ran, the wind biting our faces, Siri's movements lithe and powerful. We raced out of the thick of trees and when all we saw ahead of us was sky, Destan kicked Siri's side hard to stop and yanked on the reins. She howled and backtracked, whimpering at how hard he'd kicked her.

While he stroked her side and murmured apologies, I leapt off the wolf and looked down at where we had almost fallen. We had reached some sort of valley where the road had cut off and caved in, no longer making a perfect circle around the mountain. All of the rubble looked like rock though, no sign of houses or village. Just rock. It almost seemed as if Destan and I had found another mountain because we hadn't thought the Majesty Council would let anything on Thgindim go uncharted.

He came up next to me, panting and his cheek marked with a new cut under his eye, and he stared down with me. Rocks waterfalled down the mountain face into the pile of rubble and squinting, I could make out something or someone, squirming as if stuck on the opposite side of the broken road. "Destan, I think someone's over there," I gasped, grabbing his arm for support to keep from falling into the deadly pit of boulders and crag.

"It's….a girl." Destan's eyes widened, he went on his knees and peered into the valley that the rockslide had created. The face of whoever it was turned to look at us. We couldn't see much with her being so far away, but the terror shone bright and noticeable in her faraway eyes.

"Should…should we get her help? Find someone?" I suggested. He returned the proposition with a look of absolute incredulity.

"We're nowhere near anyone, Raine! If we don't get her, she's going to get smashed. I'm going in and will need your help to pull her out," said Destan, brushing himself off and getting prepared to dive down there and get her. Thinking about it, I decided that good results would be more likely if our roles were switched.

"Destan, I have a serious case of lacking upper body muscle, and you seem to deal with hauling heavy things everyday, so let's switch. I can climb. I'll go down and get her, and then you can lift us both out, okay?"

He seemed a bit put off by me having the harder part of

the rescue mission, but I attempted to be confident and make my gaze as firm as I could. Then he nodded, wrapping his wood-bundling rope securely around my waist and repeatedly tying complex knots. "This way, if you fall I can catch you. Okay?"

I nodded, and began to ease myself down the first side. There were so many rocks already stacked up from the avalanche that I could step from rock to rock pretty easily without ever having to go perfectly vertical on the cliff-face. This all felt unreal, like a dream. How could my day go from picking up Underbrushers' laundry to risking my life for a stranger stuck in a valley? She was only a few feet away now.

"Hey? Are you doing alright?" I called out to her. Her hair was dark and in a thick ponytail, "My friend and I can get you out of here. Can you edge any closer down to where the rocks are all stacked and away from the other side of the broken street?" She clung to the wall and tried lowering her foot down onto a rock ledge, but the ledge crumbled away and I heard her squeak.

"Edge down slowly!" I shouted, picking my way across the rocks to her, "I'm down here, if you fall I'll catch you."

"No! No, I'll just...don't hurt me! I'm sorry!" she said wildly, for some reason scrambling in the opposite direction of me.

Hurt her? Why's she scared of me? "I'm not going to hurt you, come down and we'll get you some help."

"I don't believe you!" she laughed hysterically.

"Well I didn't come all the way down here to help you and now just leave you, so get the fuck over here!" I roared, insides boiling in annoyance with this idiot. I was *not* ready to get crushed by a rock because some girl was too chicken to let a stranger save her. She made a squealing sound, slid down the broken side of the road, and fell onto the pile of rubble with a thud. Her front was soaked in blood, same with her right hand and leg. Her breathing came out ragged and frantic. I moved toward her, but felt the rope pull taut. I glanced back at Destan and saw he couldn't let me move any farther forward to get her.

"Try to crawl over to me," I said, entire arm quivering as I reached out to her.

"I...I can't," she wheezed, rolling onto her stomach and pushing herself up with her hands. A great slab of rock hurtled between us, spraying rubble at our faces. I stumbled backwards, cheeks stinging. Boulders showered down the mountain face, picking up speed, and before another could come between us, I leapt across to the landing where she lay, took her hand and dragged the girl to where Destan could pull us up. The girl was small, but compact; with heavy muscle that my toothpick arms could hardly support.

"Do you have a good hold on her?" Destan yelled down to me.

The girl managed to get to her knees, and then flung her arms around my middle. I linked my fingers tightly together around her, hoping that would hold when Destan yanked us up. And surely enough, his lumberjack muscles paid off as he carefully lifted both me and the stranger by the rope tied around our waists. The pressure hurt like hell against my stomach, but I gnashed my teeth and tried to focus on how many breaths the girl was sucking in.

He pulled us up and my knees scraped against the rough rock face as the girl scrambled off of me. *Oh, so now she could go fast?* But as soon as she reached the landing, her obviously broken leg turned in and she keeled over with a howl, clutching her ribs and gasping for air. She was bleeding badly, and she had a deep gash going from her black eyebrow to her temple that looked oozing and infected.

"Oh, shit, Raine." Destan's eyes went wide as he looked from her to me. "We have to get her help."

"No doctors! No doctors, I just need some...some," she yelped, eyes streaming, "Oh fucking *fuck,* FUCK that hurts..."

I stared at her, at her blood-wet black shirt and crooked leg that I could nearly see bone protruding from. "Are you crazy? We're taking you to a Healer now!" I exclaimed, thinking of my mother and quickly filling with dread at how pissed she' be to have such a serious case sprung on her like this.

Destan bent down near the girl's twitching body and tugged out something that was hidden under her turtleneck. IT was a pendant, or medal; a golden sun. Destan inhaled deeply, piercing me with his eyes as if I understood. I raised my eyebrows as if to say, *"What?"* But all colour had drained out of his face.

"We're not taking her to a Healer or anywhere near the village, Raine," he whispered.

The girl started breathing like her lungs were failing to work, but as the sun touched her hair, my eyes widened. In the sun, her dark black hair almost glinted blue. Like the blue of my hair except mine was that colour all of the time.

"She's a Fluxarian," he said.

chapter eight

If I had thought Destan had me Siri could run fast before, a girl from our enemy on the wolf's back made Siri speed ahead so fast that even as I clung to Destan as tightly as I could, I felt myself floating off the wolf's back. We were in big trouble. Helping a Fluxarian? Even with it being pure accident, the Majesty Council would have our heads, I knew it. I already felt like I was riding to my execution. Should we turn her in, give that a chance? But still, she was nearly incapacitated at the moment and didn't try and hurt us, right?

Not yet, I thought, heartbeat racing frantically. *Raine, Raine, she's still a Fluxarian, and Fluxarians are savages.* That's what the Majesty Council had told us. In the distance beyond Mythland, Fluxaria throbbed in the valley like a bruise. Black smoke, perpetual storms, lightning and thunder. The legend everyone went by was that Fluxarians and Thgindimmers were originally one tribe, on one mountain. But the tribe started feuding within itself and split into two, each picking a side of the mountain. Even separated, we kept fighting and so many people died that the spirits came with a great bolt of lightning, gust of wind, and whip of fire that split our mountain in two and put impossibly terrible lands in between us to keep us from destroying each other. Now I'm not sure I or anybody on Thgindim still *really* believed in spirits sending magic to divide us and our twin mountain across the valley, but we did for sure hate each other, and from what we'd learned of Fluxaria, we had good reason.

The thought that this girl had made it through Mythland was the most unnerving of all. No one dared cross Mythland, enter its unpredictable forests with trees tall as towers and winds that whipped tornados up to Thgindim's Base in the dry seasons. People were banished to Mythland, that sentence equal to nearly immediate death or endless torture. And yet here was a girl no older than me, her hair almost like mine, unconscious and injured, her head leaning on my shoulder and blood seeping through my sweater.

We rode back up to the meadow, and no rocks had hit my rickshaw or even touched our little practice space. Destan laid the girl on the grass and turned to me. "You said your mom's a Healer right? Could you sneak some medicine? I know that's asking a lot and it's not fair but—"

"Yeah, of course, I'll be right back," I said quickly, wanting to leave, grabbing my quiver of arrows and bow and running from the meadow. *Her hair is like mine. Her hair is almost like mine and she's a Fluxarian and no one else in Thgindim has hair like mine.* The thoughts cycled in sickly whispers in my head, and I had to cover my ears as I bolted down the mountain path. *Her hair is black, it only looked blue in the light because of some weird reflection. I am not a Fluxarian.*

Sneaking past my mother was easier than I'd thought. She was busy sealing lids on some soups she was sending out and so I could go into the kitchen and be alone to snatch some topical ointments and grab a roll of fleecy bandages. I also grabbed a vial

71

of sleep medicine just in case. Now I was breaking more rules. I hadn't only unknowingly helped a Fluxarian; I was stealing from a Thgindim employee and using those materials on the Fluxarian very knowingly. I couldn't get caught now. Gwen was napping, her mouth slack, stuffed animals tucked in the crook of her elbow. I quickly kissed her forehead and fled, hysteria creeping up on me.

Since I didn't have my rickshaw or Siri to ride back up to the meadow, it took some time to make my way up, but the sun was still out and I was already done my laundry for the day so time wasn't an issue. The girl's health was though. I sped up, but when I was about to duck into tree cover, I ran straight into a man walking and reading from some shiny metal tablet. It fell to the gravel and I bent down to pick it up for him, stammering, "I-I'm sorry, I'm s-so sorry, I was in a hurry…"

My voice faltered as I saw him. It was a JP. But not just any JP. He was wearing thicker, shinier silver armour and had cruel blue eyes with dilated pupils through the slits in his mask. I looked back at him for a moment, backtracking and hyperventilating in panic that he'd been looking for me, he'd be arresting me now, but when he didn't do or say anything, I took off again, more terrified than ever.

"Perfect. Here, I'll lift up her shoulder while you wrap it," Destan said as soon as he saw the materials in my hand. I dropped to my knees by the girl who was awake now, her eyes screwed shut in pain.

"What's your name?" I asked, unwinding the fluffy white bandage and applying the ointment to the gash.

"Irene," she rasped, "But don't spread that around, you hear? I'm Fluxaria's most notorious…most feared," she squealed at my cold hands, "spy of all the land! You won't get away with my murder!"

"Isn't it a little obvious by now that we're not planning on killing you?" Destan sighed.

"Well, it would be bizarre if you didn't," she replied

gruffly, wincing again.

"If you're a spy…is Fluxaria going into serious war with Thgindim now?" I asked, ripping off the end of the bandage and taping it down. Red was already creeping through the thick padding I had just given her.

"Are you kidding? You're the ones who want war! I'm just scoping this place out to see what kind of bombs you have ready to fire at us," she whispered, breathless and trembling as I poured some disinfectant over the deep gash in her arm. Then she closed her eyes and her face twisted with pain, "Water…please, some water?"

Destan hastily passed her his gourd. I couldn't quell the curiosity rising inside of me, and kept the questions coming. "That's impossible…we haven't heard anything of war, I thought we were just trying to keep to ourselves."

She laughed then, and I jumped back in surprise as she rolled her eyes and covered her mouth with the broken fingers I'd taped together. Her laughter sent ice shooting through my veins.

I watched her, feeling nauseous. "And how did you get all the way through Mythland? I thought it was impossible."

"I swear, you two think everything is impossible." Irene sucked down all of the water from Destan's gourd. "I'm not saying it was a short or awesome journey, but if you know where to stop within Mythland, it is very possible. Not a whole lot of fun though. I do not recommend it." As she had begun to sit up straighter, she suddenly gasped, clutching her back and falling face first into the grass. Her short tan fingers yanked up grass as she whimpered in pain.

Destan shot me a look and said slowly, "Irene…Raine and I have to discuss something alone for a moment, we'll be right back."

She didn't flinch, and her whimpering had quieted. She lay facedown in the grass as more red blood budded like poppies on her bandages. Struck with fear that she'd finally kicked the

73

bucket, Destan immediately dashed over to her.

He held his fingers under her nose. "She's breathing, but unevenly," he whispered.

I nodded, pacing frantically back and forth, everything seeming to blur at the edges of my vision. "What are we going to do?" I asked, my voice coming out two octaves higher than I'd expected. "Do we tell someone? Do we turn her in or something?"

"We can't do that now. We've already stolen your Mom's bandages and patched her up which already earns you and me a decade in prison."

"But they're *going* to find her anyway, people are going to find out what we did and…" I stopped pacing and leaned my forehead against a tree. "They'll kill her, Destan. I don't think I can deal with that no matter who she is."

His voice came softly into my ear, "I couldn't either." He sighed, and I felt a hand cautiously rest on my wrist. He'd never just touched me before. I felt my face fill with heat, slowly turning around to face him, now a foot or two apart. His hand left my skin and its absence caused me to shiver. It was starting to get cold and night would fall very soon and quickly, we needed to make a decision now. I tried to meet his eyes but found myself only able to talk to him by staring at his forehead.

"So…what do we do now?" I whispered.

Destan took off his hat, the dark blond curls flat and sort of funny looking where the beanie had squished them down. He wrung it in his hands, looking distressed. "I'll…I'll let her stay at my place."

"No, that's too dangerous. Like you said earlier, JPs are everywhere around here. We can't bring her in the village at all," I said.

"I wasn't going to take her to…shit, never mind," he cursed, running his fingers through his hair, then gathering himself. "We'll think of something. There has to be something."

I tapped a finger on my lips, thinking. Then I murmured,

74

"She could stay here. We'll be back tomorrow for work. She's too injured to run away, and wouldn't even know her way around."

He nodded. "Maybe. Yeah, I think that'll work." Then Destan snapped his fingers, adding, "And we'll have to take that knapsack she was carrying just in case she tries to make a run for it. Who knows what sort of weapons or spy junk she's got hiding."

"Ohh, you're right…"

I put my hands on my hips, wondering if Irene would try to kill us and flee once she had healed. I glanced back at her sleeping body, curled up like a cat by the stream. She looked so…normal. She couldn't be any older than us. She may have been in those black spy clothes and in apparent servitude to a corrupt mountain across the valley, but the longer I looked at her and the way her hair shone like jewel and I remembered how her owlish eyes were so dark and fearful when I'd first reached her, the more I felt that she wasn't as dangerous as we were making her out to be.

"I really want to talk to her," I mused, lost in thought. I met Destan's eyes again. "Don't you want to hear a little about Fluxaria? It might be…interesting." That wasn't the right word, but it was the best I could do.

"Yeah, actually." He smiled a very tiny smile, but then returned to the tense state we'd been in before. "Raine, you have to promise me not to tell *anyone* about her, or this, or what we've done, okay? Not even your mom," Destan said, in a quiet rush of words, gripping my shoulders and bringing his face closer so that he had me locked firmly in his gaze. His misty grey eyes were so serious.

"I promise," I said, my voice catching a little bit.

His chapped lips turned up slightly at the corners. "Bluehead. We're criminals. It's a bit exciting, isn't it?"

I rolled my eyes and lifted his hands off my shoulders. "At least I now know what kind of influence you're having on me."

His explosive laughter couldn't help but make me grin despite how dead I'd be if anyone else knew what was going on.

Still shaken from finding the spy and tired from the day of running around, I trooped back to Underbrush longing for something to calm my nerves. I dropped off my load at the Laundress pavilion, and as I made my way home, started rubbing my arms. It was really cold. I could feel the icy mountain air filtering through each stitch in my sweater and my leggings and I exhaled smoke like a dragon. As my boots crunched on the gravelly mountain road, I glanced wearily at the Songs' cabin, the overlapping pine logs and tin roof like my own house. Theirs was two floors though; their father had to add an addition to the house when they were born because he was already living with their mother and both sets of grandparents. But after a sweep of disease knocked out an awful 189 residents of Underbrush just eight years ago, including their parents and all but one of the Song twins' grandparents, the second level now remained unused and empty.

I stopped my walking, staring at their cabin and then glancing back at the sunset. I hadn't seen Chantastic or Velle in so long. Not even Carmen, and she was my neighbour. Deciding to push my mother into the back of my mind, I took a deep breath and approached their front door. I knocked softly, timidly, having a bizarre hope that maybe no one would come to the door so I wouldn't have to face them. It was an odd fear, to see them. Maybe I was just scared they'd see me and instantly know the crime I'd committed today. Maybe work had beaten them so hard that they'd be unrecognizable to me.

After a few tense moments of weight-shifting and back-and-forth pacing on their porch, there was a creak of the door and a dark, slanted eye peered at me from inside. I couldn't tell if the eye was Chantastic's or Velle's, but as soon as the door was pulled open a little bit wider, I saw the closed-lipped smile, the pink rising in her cheeks, and I knew which twin was in front of me.

"Chan!" I gasped, nearly breathless as Chantastic came smiling out, leaving the door ajar. She was wearing a huge, hole-ridden sweater that Velle had crocheted for her and thick, thigh high knit socks. She slipped on her way out the door, blushing as she pushed some black hair from her eyes.

"Raine! Hi…" she sang, embracing me tightly and rubbing my back with her warm hands. "I wasn't expecting anyone to come over, the place sort of looks like crap."

We shuffled inside, and she drew the chains across the door since it was getting dark and this was when the nastier Underbrushers tended to come out. I glanced about the room; the wooden staircase in the corner, the sofa and table where the family could both eat and lounge. The sofa faced a large, antique radio that had belonged to Chantastic's father before he passed away.

"It looks fine. Comfy as always," I commented, sitting on the couch and realizing instantly how tired I was after the crazy day. Chan stood awkwardly in the doorway, holding her elbows and looking nervous. I decided to try and keep the conversation going, "Will Velle be coming around?"

"In an hour or two."

"Oh. Cool."

She nodded, and the silence was getting more and more unbearable. I looked at her and tried to focus on my best friend, but kept thinking of how Destan was in a meadow with Irene, and how he could be attacked if she wasn't as injured as she let on, or he got caught…

"Why are you here, Raine?" she asked quietly. I averted my eyes to the floor.

"I miss you. I was wondering if maybe…I could sleep over?" Inviting myself felt rude and weird, but I never used to have to even ask. Her face softened and I could feel myself start to break on the inside, thinking of the Fluxarian again and what I'd done.

"Are you okay?" she asked gently, coming towards me,

eyebrows drawn together in worry. I nodded, lying to the both of us. And then I ran to her, giving in, wrapping my arms around her thin body and trying so hard not to burst into tears the moment my nose buried into her warm shoulder.

She squeezed me tightly.

"My job's just really wearing me out," I said. "I just sort of need you right now, if that's okay."

"Of course," she whispered, stroking my hair with her pretty fingers. We pulled away and she said, "Let's go upstairs. I still have all the blankets laid out from when you used to come over before."

We climbed up the squeaky set of steps to the second level and Chantastic lit a lantern at the landing so that the empty, dusty room shimmered with cobwebs that hadn't been swept away in weeks. Ratty quilts and pillows were thrown all around the hard pine-planks of the floor, and cream coloured candles dangled from chains hanging from the ceiling. She went on tiptoe and lit each one, as well as a stick of lavender incense she had stuck inside an empty milk bottle I had painted for her ages ago as a birthday present.

"I've been saving some roses for you," she said, blushing a little bit as she pulled out a wicker basket from below a side table. She pushed the basket towards me and I saw a collection of dried rose buds and blossoms in every colour imaginable. Florist really was the perfect job for her. "I remember we used to go out and pick them by school sometimes, so when I have to go out and gather for my master, I always save some for you."

I brushed the paper-like petals with my fingertips and looked up at her, smiling. "Thank you…I wish I could say I've brought you something from my job, but I don't think you'd appreciate dirty laundry very much." Chantastic laughed and bumped me with her shoulder affectionately.

We laid back on the pile of blankets and I took her hand in mine, swirling my thumb over her fingers. She held mine more tightly and tilted her head so that it rested on my shoulder. I kissed her forehead lightly and whispered, "Chan?"

"Mmm?" she hummed drowsily.

"Let's always be friends, okay?"

"Okay…"

"Good…because…" I could feel the words swelling inside me, anxious to come out. I had to tell her about Destan and about Irene and everything, I couldn't just keep holding it in, especially not from her. "I've done something…bad."

"Bad?" she asked, lifting up her head and leaning her cheek on her fist. "How bad?"

"Worse than stealing mountainberry cider and pantsing JP 21996."

"Oh my. Do you wanna talk about it?"

I rolled around to face her and pressed my forehead to hers. My stomach hurt from the guilt and my head hurt from the anxiety, but I couldn't form the words I needed. Her hand caressed my cheek and she murmured, "You can tell me anything. I'll even keep it from Velle if you need me to."

"I just…if I did something bad that I believe to be good, but have the choice to decide if I should keep on doing the bad thing, should I keep on doing it?"

"That is *beyond* vague," she began, and I groaned, but she continued. "So…if it's hard for you to be honest with me now…what are you afraid of? Me judging you? Thinking it's bad?"

"It's perceived really bad. But for some reason I think I'd feel worse if I hadn't done it."

"Then stop worrying," she said earnestly, poking my cheek and nuzzling me with her nose, "From what you're saying, I think you just need to think about how it's affecting you. If you're really guilty, then stop doing whatever it is. But if you think it is right despite what other people believe, that's never stopped you before, so why now?"

"Why are you so much wiser than I am?" I smiled, feeling relief wash over me even though I'd never even said the exact thing that was tying my stomach into knots.

"I wouldn't say that," she mused modestly, and I pulled her small body closer to me. Her hand rested on my chest and she breathed softly. I could feel her stomach expanding and contracting on mine. Gently, I tugged the blankets over us and rested my mouth in her shiny black hair.

"I love you, Raine."

"I love you, too."

The candlelight faded to yellow blurs behind my eyelids, and I drifted to sleep comforted by the warmth of her body and scent of the fragrant incense smoke swirling in curls of light grey throughout the room. The grey was so close to the colour of Destan's eyes, and that thought calmed me further somehow and shocked me all in one. I closed my own eyes and tightened my hold around Chantastic, feeling sleep slip over me in a wash of comfort.

chapter nine

My mother decided that I would start courting a boy named Skye Zanying the very day after Destan and I found Irene. Skye and Raine. Hahaha.

In order to go on the date, I had to go knocking on the Ajram's next-door and ask for Carmen to babysit Gwen while my mom and I were gone. Carmen was on her way to court a boy of her own, so her mother Dolores came over and began to try and tame Gwen's wild black curls with a wire hairbrush. Gwen shot me a desperate look as she released a few mumbling moans, but Mom soon pulled me into our tub room to scrub me down. She even went as far as to pluck the crap out of my bushy brows with cheap tweezers and trim the ratty split ends of my waist length hair since she was forcing me to wear it down. Once I was clean and my lips painted with that blood-coloured stuff my Mom adored on me, I slid into one of my nicer sweaters; a forest green knit pullover with fancy designs crocheted into it (a gift from Velle). I borrowed one of my mother's skirts; a soft brown rawhide material. Then I kept my leggings on and laced up my boots. I didn't look too much like myself, but not too much unlike myself that I felt uncomfortable.

I woke up early in the morning to check on the spy, and found Destan sleeping by a tree with a lantern that had long gone out. Irene was still curled up by the stream, but her knapsack was no longer with her since I'd advised Destan it might not be safe. I was glad that Irene had been on close watch, but then guilt settled like a stone in my stomach that he'd had to stay overnight. Tiptoeing over to his tree, I laid a note and some clean bandages by his axe and hoped the letter wouldn't make him too mad:

Sorry for the short notice, but I have to go out with my Mom today to start a stupid courting thing. Sorry! If I'm not back by night, can you change her wrappings? Thank you so much, and I'm sorry again. I'll see you two tomorrow, if something happens just come by my hut.

—Raine

Skye and his mother wanted to have lunch at some generic Starshade eatery called *Majestic Dining #4*, and so I rode my mother up to the second level. She sat in the bucket of my rickshaw. It was funny to take my Mom on the route I used for work, and she pointed out all sorts of things like, "Oh, Raine, do you pick up from that house? I bet they have nice things," or, "The air's a bit thinner up here, but it's nice not smelling shit every waking minute, you know?" It was obvious that my mother hadn't left Underbrush probably since she was a girl and heading up to Peak for her own Career assignment. I got to go up and down and see everything everyday. I'd never really appreciated how lucky I was compared to the people whose jobs kept them stuck in one place.

But then as we passed by the school, her voice sank from wonder into grouchiness, and the volume of her speaking became nearly inaudible. "That Majesty Council. If they can afford to give Starshade enough money for a proper school building, why do we get the cave?" Out of the corner of my eye I watched the two-story building disappear into the noontime mist, and then I focused ahead and pedaled harder than ever.

Once we reached the cafe, I parked the rickshaw on the little lot on the side of the eatery, and helped my mom out of the bucket seat. She was wearing her silver and lilac dress to complement her raven hair, and she'd actually put on proper stockings rather than the thick wool socks she went around home in. A woman I vaguely recognized poked her head out of the restaurant and waved with a big smile, "Pearle! Oh, it's so lovely you and your daughter could make it!"

She came out and embraced my mother and then hugged me too. She was softer, not as boney as an Underbrusher, but not as soft as I assumed a Canopian or Emergent would be. She had a kind face, and led us inside. There were about eight tables, most with people already sitting and eating. *How expensive is it here?* I glanced at some plates and felt my mouth fill with saliva and my stomach seem to do a cartwheel of longing. Tender looking meat and gently cooked vegetables. No soup. *No soup!* I thought giddily, swearing to myself to bring Gwen back something other than the dull brews my mother would make for us every single night.

As we walked into the eating area, a boy at one of the tables stood up. *Skye,* my mind whispered to me. I had blurry memories of him as well. My mother and his had been close ever since my father left, and my Mom began working even harder with new soup recipes to bring in more money. That's how she'd met Mrs.Glade Zanying. She'd gotten a letter in the mail praising her hazelnut and celery broth, as well as an invitation to come and show Mrs. Zanying's cooking class how to prepare the soup correctly. Naturally, they were fast friends, and after learning they both had kids around the same age, they tried to set me and Skye up on play dates over the years, but I was one of those, "LET'S PLAY OUTSIDE!!" people, and he was horribly allergic to grass and sun, so you can see how well we'd hit it off.

I almost did a double take now, though. He was actually fairly good-looking. His eyes and hair were the same shade of chestnut brown, and his skin was smooth and freckled across his nose and under where his eyelashes brushed. He was tall and thin and a little weak in the arms and legs, but he was dressed exceptionally nice for someone only one level up. His suit was jade corduroy and his tie swirled like a silver snake to where his vest met the curve of the fabric. A pocket watch peeked out from his diamond patterned pocket. Almost too formal for just a simple lunch. He pulled out a seat and said, "Miss Ylevol? Would you care to sit with me?" His voice was as smooth as his manners.

I curtsied, feeling silly and not like me again, replying in a soft voice, "Yes, I would. Thank you." As I sat, my eyes met his and remained connected until he sat down across from me with his mother. I wasn't sure if queasiness was a sign of liking him or if it was just my nerves.

"What a nice young man." My mom beamed, and Skye blushed bashfully and looked at the table.

He's shy? I thought curiously.

My mom jumped in again, "So Skye, tell us about yourself. How's work?" I found it funny that my mom addressed him as his work defining him. I found it even funnier that I had this thought as if Destan had planted it there for me. I picked at a loose strand of yarn unscrewed from my sleeve and tried to shove the woodcutter and fugitive from my mind.

Skye smiled, nodding. "Work is fine. I'm studying about the judicial court with a Majesty Councilman. Just the past cases, but I'm still learning so much." He sipped whatever it was that was in his cup. I saw I had a drink in front of me as well. Glancing up innocently, I hesitantly took a draw. It fizzed like bad fruit on my tongue and I didn't like it, so I politely set it back down as Skye focused his attention on me. "What about you, Raine? How do you spend your days?" He was looking at me, and my mouth was already open to answer when my mom butted in.

"Raine's a Laundress. A bit disappointing, but she's great at working around the house," my Mom said, a big gross grin on her face.

Skye must think I'm so boring. I wrung my hands together under the table. "And I like art," I piped up. My mom gave me a stern look, but if I was actually going to try to find a husband that could like me, then I should show him myself, right? "And archery," I said without thinking, witnessing my Mom's utter confusion because last time she'd checked, I couldn't shoot anything a foot in front of me. Bringing up archery also hit me with nausea as I was once again reminded of who I'd left Destan with. Would Irene hurt him? Could she, or was she too hurt still? The worms in my stomach turned into writhing snakes.

"Wow, archery? I bet you're really good," Skye said. "I've never been very sports-oriented, myself. But I'm very interested in literature. Do you read?" His brown eyes were so eager that I couldn't help but embellish the truth a little.

"Read? Oh, yes! Yes," I said, laughing nervously and having to use a lot of restraint to not just hide back under my hair.

"Who do you read?" Skye asked cheerily, punching a hole right through my facade.

I blanched. "Well...actually..."

I was able to buy another moment to think as a server came over and set down some plates, making my stomach growl quite audibly. I was given chicken in some sort of spicy smelling sauce with stir-fried vegetables and a rice ball sprinkled with sesame seeds. "I mostly just like reading the legends, if those count." The truth was that my dad used to put me to bed with the spirit legends, and aside from the 'the end' on the last page, the storybook was purely told through pictures.

"Sure, the legends count," he said warmly, scratching his head. "Are you familiar with the texts of Zhongli Quan or Li Tieguai? If you like the legends, you'll surely like them, they're very interesting and…"

I wasn't able to follow whatever it was Skye was going on about. He was sweet, his voice was kind and his eyes kinder and I smiled and nodded to act like I knew what he was saying. I even laughed where I thought it was appropriate and hit the mark every time. The real problem was how distracted he made me. I didn't care about what he was passionate about and he didn't understand what I was passionate about. I'd try to talk about sketching or riding on the back of wolves and he would look shy again and say something polite or just say, "Wow!" or "That's…neat!" Our mothers, on the other hand, were just reveling in everything, oblivious to the awkward silences and increasingly strained conversation. They were looking, but not seeing. When the lunch was over and we all were saying our goodbyes, Skye touched my shoulder. I turned to face him and I saw red rise in his cheeks. Did I really make him nervous?

"I would like to bring you to a cotillion a few weeks from now. It's for my 19th birthday. I really admire you, Raine, and would love if you would see me again." His voice broke off near the end almost like a question.

My heart heaved a great sigh of wishing he wasn't so nice and that it would be easier to tell him I didn't feel like we could go anywhere. "That's really sweet of you, Skye," I said, glancing at my mother beside me, whose eyes were so bright and hopeful. I gave a Skye a pained smile, "but I'm actually afraid that—"

"That she doesn't have anything to wear yet," my mother

interrupted. Her hand tightened on my arm, the nails digging through my sweater and into my flesh. "But we will make our shopping rounds, won't we dear?"

My face was burning and my arm hurt within her stony grip, "Oh. Um…y-yeah sure. I would…love to come. Yeah. Thanks, Skye." Dammit, Raine.

The grin on his face was so big that it was heartbreaking, "Wow, no, thank *you*! That's great! I'll see you soon, then." He turned back for a moment, but then faced me again, gingerly taking my hand and pressing a kiss onto my knuckles. "Until we meet again…Raine," he breathed, pulling back and jogging to his mother to relay that I had said yes.

As we were walking back to my rickshaw to start home, my mom held out her arm to stop me. "Raine."

I gently pushed her arm down and took another few steps toward my bike, eyes stuck on the gravel beneath my boots. "Mother."

"Were you going to refuse him?" she asked quietly.

My fingers drummed slowly on the scratched up handlebars of my bicycle. The rubber had been picked away by the nails of Laundresses before me. I began a new crevice in the rough material as I whispered, "Yes."

"Can you tell me *why*?"

"It's…it's just—"

"Did his upper-level Career intimidate you? Is it that he's from Starshade?"

"No, but—"

"Did he say something…*rude* while I was in the restroom?"

I covered my eyes with my hands. "Mom, no, he was the perfect gentleman, he was kind and seemed to like me, maybe—"

"Then don't you dare ruin this, Raine," she scoffed, coming around to look at me with her eyes like burning coals. "This is your best chance to move up on this mountain!"

"Mom, you said it yourself. I could see multiple suitors, why do you insist so much on him?"

"Because as of yet, no other young men have come knocking and we're...we're running out of time, Raine," she said, her expression switching from anger to a painful sort of sad. She hopped into my rickshaw bucket, and I settled myself on the bike's seat, trying to rotate my shredded rubber tires on the ground without tipping us over.

After letting the last of the JP shuttles shoot across the road, and checking both ways, I kicked off and stood up on my pedals to get some extra power to pump at the gears and get us moving. At least riding downhill wouldn't be as hard on my lungs and scrawny legs.

As we coasted along the edge of Starshade's road, I drowned my eyes in the emerald green tree cover. "Running out of time for what, Mom?" I asked suddenly.

Her voice hovered between wind and sound. "The department called again, just two days ago."

I squeezed my handlebars, fear stirring my stomach. The department, meaning the hordes of JPs dressed in white carrying syringes instead of rods. The department with a big padded room where all of the kids like Gwen were hidden— or *protected* as they'd told us. Protected from the *normal* people.

"They got wind we missed last month's tithing period. Just what they needed to believe Gwen was stressing us financially," she whispered, barely loud enough for me to hear her above the frantic hum of my own thoughts.

"B-but..." I stammered, hardly able to keep my rickshaw upright as the road made a dip just as the tremors began, "she isn't stressing us financially. Not just her or because of her, if anything, it's all those taxes stressing us—"

"That's just not how they look at it, dear," she sighed. "And it would be great if we had the luxury of taking our time to find you the perfect husband, but we just don't. We don't. Unless you'd rather have your sister taken away?"

Her voice was rough as rust, and I abruptly pushed my pedals in the opposite direction so that we came to a complete stop, now only a block away from the Underbrush gate. Even from here I could see that the Underbrush main road ahead was swarming with JPs in comparison to here at the end of Starshade. It was like the sky had rained down rats on our level for the entire flock of vultures to come for.

"I understand," I said.

"Good," she said.

We both coughed as a dump truck rolled past spewing exhaust into the air. The electrified fence buzzed like a buggy meadow.

"I know it isn't fair, Raine." She reached around the side of the bucket and touched my trembling shoulder. "You just have to start making sacrifices. It can't be so easy for you anymore."

Easy? I scrunched my eyes tightly closed, so tightly that I almost thought I could see the imprints of my eyeballs. All of my thoughts had died now. My whole head felt cold and full of air. I pedaled and pedaled, trying to keep us out of the Underbrush traffic, trying to keep myself from floating straight into space where no one got married and no one took away little sisters and everyone washed their own clothes and enemy spies didn't happen into perfectly peaceful meadows and I would be able to rest for just a moment.

chapter ten

"Oh, you're here now," Destan said, his usually melodic voice threaded with a cold edge. "Irene read me your note. How did the courting go?"

He was making some sort of stake or pole, his carving knife sliding up and down a severed branch so that it was sharpening the stick to a point. I figured that this was just how he kept calm while having to watch the spy I'd left him saddled with. He averted his eyes from mine, jaw set and breath coming out like smoke in the chilled air. Irene remain slumped against a tree, dozing with her hands bound together.

My throat tightened. "Look, I'm sorry, but I had to meet the guy with my mom and—"

"Raine, I know why you weren't here. I asked how did it go?" He raised his eyebrows and then went back to dragging the blade along the soft wood of his pointy stick.

Tying back my hair into a bun, I picked up my bow and

went to where we did target practice. "Fine, I guess. He's nice and my mom's obsessed with him. He's trying to work his way up to Peak as a lawyer or something."

"Well, isn't that fancy," he said sarcastically in a low growl of a voice. I raised my bow and saw Irene watching me with an intrigued look. I tried to focus on the target and not her. "That's not the anchor you used yesterday. It has to stay constant," Destan groaned, barely even glancing at me. Anchoring is the hold of the bow.

My neck prickled with annoyance and I brought the string to touch the tip of my nose, "Better?" I asked.

Suddenly, he was behind me, arms folding around my body to hold the bow with me. His rough fingertips poked out from the snipped-off tips of his gloves, and they laid delicately atop mine, drawing back the bowstring even further. His index finger tapped my thumb. "C'mon, Bluehead, you can't use your thumb! We've been over this so many times..." he sighed, the smile evident in the way the words reached my ears so lightly.

A hot blush crept up into my cheeks, and I knew he was trying to steady me, but suddenly I felt like I could vibrate with the quick way my heart was beating inside my chest. Alarmed by the sensation, I hesitantly removed my thumb, felt the taut string grind down into my knuckle, and pushed the feelings aside.

"Quit calling me Bluehead, Beaniehead," I hissed, touching my toe to his ankle to signal I could hold it on my own now.

His chuckle tickled my chin and then he backed away. "Release."

The string rolled off my fingers smoothly and within one second the arrow pierced close to the center of the rotten piece of wood. My tense body relaxed, and I even felt myself smile.

"Thank you," I said, nervously meeting eyes with Destan, now standing a couple yards behind me. He grinned, taking a deep bow, and we both laughed. Within the sound of our giggling, suddenly I heard a whistle.

Destan and I both looked at Irene, who had evidently woken up. Wrists still bound together, she managed to sit upright now, fiddling with her bindings as her bandaged fingers slipped clumsily over the fabric. She looked like a doe spotted grazing, her dark eyes wide and frightened, her lips still rounded from her whistle, her shoulders rising.

She grunted, avoiding eye contact. Her voice came out quietly. "That was a good shot. That's all."

Destan and I exchanged glances, filled again with the awkwardness and confusion we'd had when we'd first found her. What were we supposed to say? What was her friendliness supposed to mean? I knew she was tied up and injured, but even talking to her seemed like it would end badly for me. Every tree's shadow now took on the silhouette of a JP officer, the thin branches like lightning rods poised for the stab. Did the Underbrush JPs know about the meadow? Could they find her? Find us?

"Yeah, she's getting good," Destan broke the silence, snapping me out of my temporary panic.

Irene looked over at me. "How long you've been shooting?"

Taken aback, I replied, "Oh. Um. N-not too long. A couple weeks."

She made that whistle again. "Damn," she said, shortly.

Hesitantly, I looked to Destan. And after he nodded, I took a deep breath and strode over with him to meet Irene. She misunderstood and held up her hands to be unbound. Destan stared at them warily, his lips parting in apology, and then closing again. He cleared his throat. "Irene...we want you to know how we're going to handle this situation."

Her eyebrows arched. "My situation?"

"Mmhmm," I mumbled, my fingers yanking up grass anxiously.

Destan remained cool and collected. "Raine and I are going to tend to you just as we've been doing, okay? We'll hide you and bring you food and medicine until you're better," he explained. The spy's face remained unreadable. "But I'm not sure if we can fix you up 100% because hiding you for an extended amount of time is risky for all of us." His voice hitched up into a question at the end, his eyes imploring her.

"Okay," she said.

Now it was my turn. I tried my best to mimic how measured Destan had been in explaining what we'd decided on. "Also…" I began, voice quivering ever so slightly as my fingers ran out of grass to pull, "once you are all healed, you have to promise us you'll leave and go back to Fluxaria right away."

Irene slouched back, crossing her muscular arms across her chest. "Sorry. Can't do that."

I gulped. "Can't?" My voice sounded squeaky, I felt like scurrying away, and this girl was a cat ready to come bolting after me, a mouse.

"Fine," she said, eyes flashing, "I *could* go back after getting patched up. But I won't."

"Then don't expect any more help," Destan scoffed, brow furrowing in frustration. "We're not healing you so you can continue on your merry way to destroy our mountain. I'd say it's only fair that due to keeping you alive, we deserve a favor from you."

"And that favor is me returning home empty-handed?"

"Well…yeah," he said. This was the first time I could see that in that rapidly working mind of his, there were no more words stocked up and ready. The realization made my stomach lurch. If he couldn't reason with her, and I was too timid, how were we going to make it through this?

Irene licked her lips and stared him straight in the eye. "Fine. Then don't help me anymore. I can take care of myself here just fine, do what I need to do, and get out. Sound good?"

"No!" I sighed, exasperated. "It doesn't 'sound good.' Look, I know sending you back without accomplishing whatever it was your government wanted you to accomplish will take a toll on your job or whatever, but that's not more important to me than keeping my home safe—"

"Thgindim's safety? What enemy does your mountain have to fight off? What diseases are being spread here, what people are being slaughtered and taken captive, what bombs are being dropped?" Fueled by anger, Irene was able to break free of the wrapping we'd had around her wrists with a single jerk. She reached forward with her good hand and jabbed me hard in the chest with her pointer finger. "Because how I see it is you guys live in candyland while MY mountain is the one in danger!"

Destan reached across and pushed her hand down, crawling to kneel in front of me and keep Irene from getting any closer. "Hey! Don't you think of touching her like that or—"

"Or what?" she laughed coldly, struggling to her feet and wincing as she tried unwrapping her broken fingers. "How about we just end it here? Thanks a whole bunch for getting me out of that rockalanche, but now I think I'll just go it alone."

"We won't let you," Destan said.

"I'm not waiting for your permission, blondie," she hissed. As she and Destan stood face to face, her forehead only level with his broad chest, I slipped back to where I'd set down my bow and quiver, wondering if I could actually shoot her if it came down to that, if I could ever bear to actually shoot anyone. *Maybe I could toss the bow to Destan,* I thought. *He's brave enough to protect us from her if it comes to that.*

"I made it through Mythland, the whole hundred and fifty miles of trees and beasties that are twice, *triple* your size," Irene sneered. "I can take on the two of you, easy."

"Not in the shape you're in," Destan said, narrowing his eyes. "And we've got your weapons."

I had my bow now, and nocked in an arrow with shaky fingers, taking a step forward, crunching on some leaves so that Irene heard and looked up, realizing I had it pointed straight at her. "And more importantly, we've got *our* weapons," I said, locking my knees and standing firm.

We had her trapped now. With Destan towering a good foot and a half over her, and me trying to put on the act that I'd actually shoot her, Irene shook her head, shoving past Destan and plopping on a rock by the stream. She laid her head in her hands, and from there I could hear mumbles trailing out from between her fingers. "Are you two really the same soulless robots as your Council? Do you honestly not even care that an entire culture is set to be blown to bits?"

She lifted her face out of her hands and stared down into the stream. She had her back to us, but I could see her reflection rushing by over the rocks. The water flowed so quickly I couldn't tell if the big black eyes it was mirroring were running with tears or simply staring. The meadow went silent.

My aching fingers relaxed, and I slowly drew my arrow back in, unhitching the notch from the bowstring and smoothing out the silky feathers on the end. As I dropped the bow to my side, I felt Destan's shoulder rub mine, and I looked over at him, now standing to my left. His face looked as guilty as my heart felt. This was just as school had warned us so many years ago. The teachers had said, *"You won't think it now, but just know that the Fluxarian race is skilled in manipulation and you will find yourself easily falling under their spell. If you ever encounter the enemy, just keep your head and duty to your Council in mind, and let that protect you from experiencing empathy for such a barbaric breed of human."*

I swallowed my fear, and with my hands balled into sweaty fists, I came closer to the rock where she sat, keeping my voice just above a whisper. "Of c-course we don't want that. We don't want anyone to die. That's also why we can't just let you stay here, though. We can't let our home be destroyed, either."

The wind blew at the fine, black, flyaway strands of her hair, and the crickets in the reeds began singing more loudly. She turned around, narrowing her eyes and laughing wryly, "What alternate universe do you two live in? Fluxaria hasn't done a damned thing to this place, and only will if your stupid Council won't calm down about crap that happened hundreds of years ago."

Destan's jaw clenched and unclenched, his face furrowed with confusion. "That…that can't be it, though," he looked at me to back up his statement, and I nodded. But suddenly I was just as uncertain about what we'd been told as much as I knew he was. "There's no way Fluxaria is innocent like that if it's true we are planning to attack you—"

"Tell me *one* thing we've done to you," Irene yelled, leaning on her good arm to stay seated on her rock. I could see the pain burning through her body in the way her limbs shook in supporting her, and yet she kept her face free of emotion, only her eyebrows dug hard over her eyes and her teeth ground together as she spoke, "Because I could damn well tell you a *thousand* things your mountain has done to us. I'm dying to hear at least *one* thing you think mine has done to fuck up yours."

My mouth opened then closed. I looked at Destan kneeling beside me and he was scraping dried clay from the toe of his worn black boots, also submerged in thought. What *hadn't* Fluxaria done to us was the better question. It was mandatory that our radio be on all the time, but in the mornings my mom would turn it up loud to hear the Peak news and reports of Fluxarian invaders attacking the JP military base, Thgindim hostages taken, and even just two weeks ago, blaring through the kitchen while Gwen and I ate breakfast were the cases of Mythland-sent Thgindim soldiers mauled by Fluxarian savages, skinned alive, and partially eaten. I saw my first photos of the aftermath of a Fluxarian attack when I was just seven. My class had squatted in the cave as the visiting Peak representative flipped through the gruesome black and white images on her fancy projector screen and held up a baggy of long, red stained teeth that she said were taken from a Fluxarian man's body. I know Destan remembered too, because as Irene finally let herself slide from the rock and lie on the riverbank, I caught him checking out her mouth as she breathed; looking for signs of teeth sharp and long as eagle talons.

Neither of us answered, just sat there as the reeds bobbed in the chilly evening wind and the meadowlarks flew to their nests in the tall green grasses. *I could damn well tell you a thousand things your mountain has done to us,* her words reverberated in my head until I found myself asking, "What have we done to you?"

But she couldn't answer.

Sirens shrill as screeching ravens shot through the air, attacking our eardrums. All three of us were bent over or curled in on ourselves, clutching our ears and closing our eyes as the alarms blared to a steeper frequency and made my knees buckle.

Destan caught me before I fell, grasped my arm. "It's a drill; you have to get back to town before the blackout."

"Blackout?" Irene cried, breathing loudly and quickly as

she dug her nails into the soft ground by the stream. "What blackout?"

Just as I was collecting myself, the dreaded rumbling came rippling through the wail of warning sirens. I grabbed Destan's wrist, heart pounding, fresh fear flowing through me. "No, it's a raid. Destan, it's a real raid."

His eyes widened and looked to the sky. I followed suit, anxious that any moment an airship would come and cover the sun. But knowing how low on the mountain we were, I jogged over to the edge of the meadow, pushing aside pine branches and staring out from the cliff overlooking the Mythland valley.

"RAID FROM WHO?!" Irene hollered behind me.

I squinted into the distance, my gaze skimming over Mythland's green roof of leaves, up to the black dot at the end that was Fluxaria. Emerging from the thickest of clouds was one even smaller black dot, the size of a sesame seed. As the seed came closer though, the rumbling got louder, and soon the seed sprouted wings and propellers and I gasped, backtracking to where Destan was hooting on his flute so vigorously that Siri came bounding back within seconds from wherever she was prowling.

Anger pulsed through me as I spun on Irene, who had her knees pulled to her chest. "You lied!" I shouted, pointing at the now marble-sized shapes of the Fluxarian airship in the distance. "You aren't innocent at all, that's your ship, coming for us!"

"We don't send airships out!" she demanded, but as she limped over to me, Destan quickly cut through us and bound her wrists together with his lumber rope. Using the longer end of cord hanging off the end, he wrapped it around a tree and did a hasty double knot.

"Well, there's a first time for everything," Destan said, hopping onto Siri and pulling me up in front of him. I started, not used to riding with him behind me.

"Destan, you should be—"

"We're going to have to ride faster than ever, Bluehead,"

he said in a rush, his arms folding around me as he yanked on Siri's reins. I felt the hair on my arms rise in reaction to feeling his body surround mine so protectively, and as we lurched forward, he brought me even closer, keeping me from sliding off as we left Irene and the meadow and surged into the wood.

Usually, the forest skirting Underbrush was much darker than the town, but the moment Destan and I propelled out of the tree cover, we were met with lantern-less streets, pitch black houses. Doors were shut, and as we bounded along the main road, we passed through the musical clicking of locks being switched into gear. The only other people in the street were rows of JPs, their rods raised and helmets on. Destan pulled back on Siri's reins, gently, and slowed her sprinting to the town speed limit. But no sooner did we slow down when a horde of JPs leapt in front of us and added their whistle blowing to the sirens blasting all the way from Peak Tower. Siri dug her claws into the gravel, jolting us to a stop, her long pink tongue hanging out of her mouth as she panted.

"Halt!" a JP yelled, his voice barely rising above the alarms, "All Thgindim citizens are to be in *lockdown*!"

I unconsciously leaned back into Destan fearfully. But as soon as I'd noticed it, and in embarrassment meant to resume sitting with a comfortable space between our bodies, his right arm found its way safely around my waist, the other busy keeping Siri in control. His hand was warm on my side, comforting, and I gulped, realizing how much I liked it resting there.

"We were working in the fringes of the town when we heard the alarms," Destan explained, his voice booming by my ear, but in truth barely even reaching the JPs in front of us.

The row of JPs parted in front of us. "To your houses, now!" He didn't have to tell us twice, Destan sent Siri loping faster than ever, the dark houses in combination with the rumbling of airships turning Underbrush into a thundercloud as we ran.

"Which one is it, again?" he asked.

"Fifth one down," I said, not daring to lift my hand from Siri's soft muzzle to point at my hut. I heard Destan count off the houses in my ear.

As we came to a halt, Destan's first matter of business was placing both of his hands on my waist to lift me off and set me down. As my feet touched the ground, I heard a horrible scraping noise, and saw the tall points of the pines smashing against the black underbelly of the airship, now arrived. Just minutes ago it was still over Mythland, how had it made it directly over here so quickly?

"Come on!" I yelled, grabbing Destan's arm and using all of my might to try and pull him toward my cabin. I could hear my mother fiddling with the door, my name being shouted from inside. Destan looked at me, reluctance and protest flashing across his features. I didn't want him in my house with my mother any more than he did, but there was no time to worry about introductions when we may or may not be bombed by the same enemy we accidentally saved in a rockalanche.

I seized Siri's reins in my hands and sprinted to my door, driving Siri and Destan straight through the entryway and into the hallway. Siri's massive grey body strained against the narrow hallway, and I squeezed through to pick up the door she'd ripped off its hinges. As I struggled to lean the door against the frame to give us at least a little separation from outside, I heard the synchronized panting of wolf, boy, and women echoing through the cabin.

My mother and Gwen had themselves flattened against the back wall. Gwen was smiling, like she thought this was all one big game. My mother on the other hand, was the most distressed I'd seen her in my entire life; her braid undone, her eyes wet and bright, her chest heaving so hugely that it made it seem she gained weight with every breath only to lose it when she exhaled.

Destan was sandwiched between Siri's back and my house's tin ceiling, groaning as he slipped out and tumbled onto the dirt floor, making Gwen burst into laughter. Mom hushed her, gently stroking Gwen's curls and then flashing me a furious look. Meanwhile, Destan struggled to his feet, his 6ft stature too tall for the 5'10" house, conking his head against the ceiling, making the whole roof shiver. He rubbed the crown of his head with his dirty palm, face scrunched in pain. Seeing my mother's expression, he ducked his head, giving a slight bow and forcing a small grin, "Oh. Um…I'm Destan. Raine's archery instructor."

chapter eleven

The kitchen table was no longer big enough to hide all members of the Ylevol household under it in case of a drill or raid. My mother, Gwen, and I crouched directly below it, while Destan knelt awkwardly on the outside, only his Beaniehead and dirty face under cover. Siri had no choice but to remain smushed in the entrance hallway, her head resting patiently on the paws she had stretched in front of her. Every time she lifted her fluffy tail, the roof lifted on and then off the cabin' structure, making us jump and Gwen giggle. At least she was enjoying this.

My mom slid from her toes to her backside, crossing her legs comfortably and then scratching her head. Her dark eyes flickered to Destan. "So…Destan, you said?" He nodded. She cleared her throat, "Got a last name to go with that?"

Strangely enough, he hesitated. I noticed his mouth lifting from a grimace into a smile. "Just Destan, actually."

Her eye twitched. "How do you know Raine, Just Destan?"

Oh jeez. This is all too weird, I thought, *Oh you know, we met in the woods and have a pact to keep an enemy spy a secret. Oh, yeah and we shoot arrows!* I couldn't suppress a little hysterical chuckle, making both my Mom's and Destan's heads turn. I flushed, sucking on my bottom lip and staring at the floor.

"We work in the same area. I'm the woodcarver's apprentice."

"Ahh, okay. I didn't think the woodcarver's station was by the Laundress pavilion."

Destan forced a grin. I could still see the anxiety quivering in the lines between his brows. "I get around."

"How old are you—?"

"Mom!" I hissed, blushing apologetically as she looked at me with that intimidating spark in her dark eyes. "Please, don't quiz him. He's just a friend."

Destan cleared his throat, a smirk playing on the edge of his mouth. "Teacher."

Face flaming, I turned and stared at the door so that I couldn't feel his playful gaze. "Teacher," I corrected feebly. My heartbeat was thrumming rapidly again, like dragonfly wings beating in a blur. *Raine, stop it, stop it! Why are you feeling like this?*

"Well, it's about time you kept that bow from gathering dust." My mom's sudden appreciative tone sent a wave of relief flooding through me. "Especially with you going about the mountain so frequently. That dagger isn't enough to defend yourself."

I nodded, sneaking up a glance at Destan as my Mom yawned. His eyes found mine the same moment and he smiled, close-lipped, eyes squinting. I smiled right back, trying to suppress a laugh as he suddenly crossed his eyes and stuck out his tongue. Both his tongue and eyes returned to their original spots quickly as my Mom looked back at us and away from Gwen.

We were saved from more uncomfortable conversation as the rumbling abruptly ceased and alarms cut off, leaving

Underbrush in a cold hush. The all-clear bell chimed twelve times, and JPs went down the street re-lighting the paper lanterns swinging from our porches. My mom padded over to the radio and screwed the dial this way and that to try and hear the news, but there was still interference from the flux of JP radio transmissions being made, and she ended up turning it down once more.

Thgindim was still under house lockdown until dawn, so my mother really had no choice but to let Destan stay. Luckily, I was able convince the stationed JP to let Siri lounge outside rather than stay cramped in the hallway. Other than that quick exchange, I was shut back in the house, hardly able to sleep, listening to my strange friend breathing on the other side of the curtain.

Squished next to Gwen on my cot, I lay on my side, vision bleary and out of focus from concentrating so hard on the fabric of the curtain dividing the room. I had the quilt pulled up as far as it could go and my toes poked out. I slid more of it onto Gwen and pulled my knees to my chest, testing the quiet.

"Destan?"

"Yeah, Bluehead?"

My stomach did that uncomfortable fluttering thing when I realized he was still awake, and I steadied my voice, whispering, "Why didn't you tell my mom your last name?"

There was a rustle on the other side of the curtain, and as I combed my fingers gently through Gwen's curls, I heard Destan yawn. "Do you remember my last name?"

"Of course. Abrasha. But only since you told me."

"Hmm," he sighed. I could just imagine him laying on Gwen's bed, feet hanging two feet off the length of the cot, arms behind his head as he stared at the ceiling. I wondered if he was sleeping in those ratty gloves and red hat. "My family just doesn't like getting a lot of attention," he finished, slowly, choosing his words with care.

"Do you have any brothers or sisters?" I asked, and then

hastily correcting myself, "I mean, other than your older brother that…y'know…um, died in the police?"

"Mmhmm. Three half-sisters, all younger."

Gwen rolled over into the wall, her cherubic cheeks squished together as she let out a sleepy breath. I brushed the dark hair off of her face. "I'm…I'm sorry you couldn't be with them during the blackout. I'd be so scared not knowing how Gwen might be."

I snuggled closer to my sister. Her body was so sharp and small after all of these horrible years of thin soup and bites of bread. I softened the edges around her hipbones and back with the quilt and stuffed fox, and buried my face into her hair, wishing I could see her dreams and make sure they were better than her life awake.

"It's all right. Now that it's all over, I can breathe easy, y'know?" he said, words blurring into a yawn.

I gulped, "Is it?"

"Is it all right?"

"Is it…over?"

I heard the springs of his cot screech as he must've gotten up or changed positions, then the soft sound of his socked feet moving on the dirt floor. Then he spoke, so quietly that I had to sit up and lean forward to catch them. "I had a thought, Bluehead."

I blinked sleepiness out of my eyes. "What is it?"

His fingers crept over the side of the curtain, then one of his bright eyes appeared in the little gap between the fabric and the wall. He looked left and right, from the door to me, then whispered, "Just in case your mom is still up, could you come to the curtain for a minute? I don't want to talk too loudly and wake her."

"Yeah," I said, slipping off the lumpy mattress and hugging myself to keep warm. Coming over, I went on tiptoe and brought my eye to the crack where he peered through. "Okay. Talk."

He nodded. "About Irene."

"Uh huh."

"You don't think she has anything to do with the airships today, do you?"

My stomach dropped. "I hadn't really thought about it. I was just so scared."

"I'm just wondering how much she means to that mountain of hers," he murmured. "Would they send ships as a threat for just *one* spy? Was it just coincidence that you and me are sort-of-hiding-sort-of-holding-her-hostage when they came?"

He pulled the curtain back so that now we were completely face to face. "Because the key here is that, yes, we've had monthly air-raid drills before, but never an actual attack as long as you and me have been alive. They decided to come *now*. And even weirder, it seems they didn't actually drop any bombs."

"Well, we still haven't heard about the other levels. Peak would be the most likely target," I pointed out, scratching my head and yawning.

Destan held my gaze steadily, bit his lip. "True."

The way he was looking at me so straight-on sent my gut plummeting again, and I glanced down, rubbing my arms self-consciously. All of my bangs fell in front of my eyes, giving me my own personal curtain to hide behind. But then his hand suddenly appeared behind it and he lifted up the thick shield of blue hair, leaning down to look at me, a curious smile on his lips, "Why do you do that? Hide?"

As he lowered his hand, his fingertips brushed ever so slightly against my cheek, leaving behind a tingle where they'd touched. We were standing so closely, the night was so abuzz with crickets and whipped with wind coming through the pines, and I was hit with the desire to have him touching me again. I felt dizzy with confusion at these new kinds of feelings, and scared of how vulnerable I was, here and now, with him, a boy I think I trusted, both of us awake during the sacred in-between hours of night and morning.

I sucked in a breath, backing away and letting my hair come falling down again, turning away from him as my chest was assaulted inside with such a rapid beating that I wondered if this was what a heart attack felt like. "I…goodnight, Destan," I stammered, walking quickly back to the cot where Gwen continued snoring softly, curled up like a kitten.

I heard the curtain separating the room pulled back into its proper place, and as I hid under the quilt, still shaking with nerves, Destan answered faintly, "Goodnight, Raine."

chapter twelve

It had been confirmed that the attempted attack by three Fluxarian airships was a result of the Fluxarian government demanding ransom for hostage JPs and not receiving it on time. Or so the radio said. I wasn't completely sure if that sounded quite right. Of course, I knew that the act of sending over airships was a threat, but when the way to go about the situation involved raising taxes on Underbrush another 30%, it just seemed wrong.

Still, life went on. The day after the blackout, the Ylevol family woke up to an empty cot where Destan had slept and a pile of dirty coins on the kitchen table serving as a thank you. And now, with the weekend beginning, and no excuse to see Destan in the meadow during my Laundress work, I took it into my own hands to check up on the spy. I left the house in the early afternoon when Gwen was napping, and my mother was gone for a yearly Peak evaluation.

I was forbidden from my rickshaw when not working, so I lessened my quiver a few arrows and added another layer of sweaters for my trek up to Irene. As I walked, I noticed different looking officers milling about town. These were all women, unlike the completely male Justice Police force, and they wore smart wool coats the colour of ink and hats that looked sort of like these paper ships Chantastic and I used to fold and send down the river when we were little. Each of the women stood tall with their arms flat at their sides and hair cut short and slicked smooth at the napes of their necks. Like the JP men, lightning rods swung lethally at their hips, but in their arms were bundles of long scrolls.

I paused in my walking, blowing hair out of my face and ever so slightly hiding behind a stack of crates as one of the women came marching to the nearest house. It turned out to be my boss's hut, and she opened the door slowly, eyeing the woman officer suspiciously. Jun hadn't done her hair up yet, and without her rouge and eye makeup she suddenly looked much older and a bit unkempt before this woman standing smooth and stiff as a statue.

"May I help you?" Jun asked, leaning a hand on her hip.

Briskly, the woman pulled a scroll from the stack she had pressed safely under her arm, and held it out. "As decreed by the head of Law Enforcement and Foreign Affairs, it is mandatory that all private residences of Thgindim citizens wave the mountain's new national flag from their roofs or have it hung on their door," she reported, not even blinking as Jun took it and shook it out of its tight roll.

The flag billowed down, the dark blue fabric glistening in the clear morning light. I was pretty sure my mom already had one of these flags somewhere, but then as I looked more closely and Jun held it out, I noticed the insignia was different. Rather than the emblem of seven silver stars around the figure eight design, two big letters dominated the center of the flag, *MC*. Circling them were small silver stars lined up like soldiers.

Jun looked the flag up and down. "Mandatory, eh?" She glanced at the woman, who nodded. Then Jun cackled a laugh, jovially placing a hand on the woman's prim shoulder pad. "So I'm assuming there is *mandatory* payment for a shiny new banner as well, yes?"

The woman officer's mouth slid into a forced smile, and she awkwardly shifted out from Jun's grasp. "The only payment is compliancy. This symbol of nationalism comes with no other price then the loyalty, pride, and support of Thgindim's citizens."

I could just tell my boss was fighting against an eye-roll. She bunched up the fabric into her fist and backed into her hut. "Why then, thank you very much. Bye bye, now, goodbye." She shut the door quietly, and the woman curtly stiffened her posture and made her way to the next house.

I skirted the main road to keep out of the eyes of the female officers moving about, and within the hour I had made it back up to the discreet patch of trees leading to the meadow. The forest was eerily quiet today. Frozen dewdrops hung on the ends of pine needles like pearl earrings. A lacy coating of snow crackled under my boots, and blackbirds darted to and fro, swifter than shadows. For a moment I thought of my Dad, and how I'd cling to him every time he took me walking through the woods to gather herbs or simply get away from Underbrush's swirling world.

Before Gwen had been born, we could afford to just take walks. My dad had worked for Peak Tower in his early adult years as a JP officer trainee, but when I was born he postponed employment and paid an absurd extra tax so that he could watch me while Mom worked. Mom said I'd spent my earliest years more in the forest than in the house, that I could recite the names of rocks and minerals and flowers before I could say the Thgindim pledge with the rest of my kindergarten class, that my father and I were even scheming up treehouse plans and hadn't yet chosen a spot when he was stolen back into the force. He'd raised me for the first third of my life, and yet it was such an early piece of my existence that I couldn't even begin to remember anything more than blurred images and the sound of a knife cutting through river poppies as I watched water ripple down the mountainside in glass ribbons.

Hesitantly, I drew back a fern and peered into the clearing. Irene wasn't tethered to the tree anymore. My stomach lurched, and gasping, I stumbled into the clearing, dropping the satchel of food I'd packed for her. I looked left, right, up, down, then felt my entire body relax as the spy came yawning out from the other edge of the clearing. She raised an eyebrow.

"What?" she said. "You think you could keep me on a leash for two whole days? No way, Jose. Even with these crappy injuries I could bust out of that little harness your boyfriend put me in."

My face heated up. "He's not my…never mind." I crossed over to her, reclaiming the food sack and then passing it over to her. I held it out at arm's length, still fearful of getting too close to the stranger. "Breakfast. And probably lunch. I'm sorry I couldn't come by yesterday."

She eyed me curiously, taking the food. "It's no big deal." Then she fell back onto a squishy cushion of moss and started digging into the amla berry stew, poking her chopsticks in and out to gather new bunches of the bitter chunks of berry. Irene added new sound to the woods, providing it with deep breaths in between swallows, loud gulps as she drank deeply from the stream.

It seemed that Destan was not going to show up today, so I decided to give myself a break and take some time *not* doing shooting practice. I knelt by the stream and took out my small tray of watercolour paints; hard, cracked, and so old that even dry brush techniques made the colours seem watered down and cloudy. Then I flipped to a new leaf in my sketchbook and began sketching the outline of a certain river poppy I especially liked. Unlike the others, it stood straight up, not wilting under the weight of morning dew and cold winds. The flower's black center faced the sky and the two leaves bobbed up and down as if in prayer to the sun. But it was only after a few moments of preliminary sketching that I noticed the eating sounds had stopped. I paused, setting down my pencil, and glanced behind me. Irene was stretching, testing out the movement in her fingers. I could have sworn I saw her eyes dart away from me. Now on edge, I tugged my paintbrush from behind my ear and dipped the frayed end into the stream, getting it nice and wet. As I smoothed the bristles over the last bit of red on my paint tray, however, I could feel warm air touching ever so slightly on the back of my neck.

"Are those sunset poppies?"

I jumped, brush falling into the stream and instantly getting carried away from me. Irene had appeared behind me, leaning over and snooping on my drawing. I quickly shut the sketchbook with a *snap* and then hastened to close up the paint tray. "N-no…river poppies," I stuttered, almost speaking entirely through my teeth as I fought the urge to move a good three feet away from the girl.

She leaned her chin on her fist. "No. Sunset poppies. I'd know them anywhere."

I drummed my fingers patiently on my thigh, my words coming out clipped and clear, "*River* poppies. And they're native to Thgindim, so I doubt it."

"Nice try, but wrong," she smirked, pulling up a flower and using her good fingers to flatten out the petals. Her black eyes crossed in concentration as she slit down the stem with her pinky nail and then pushed two of the leaves through the new hole. "See, if you go about trimming and fastening the poppy this way…"

She held the oddly prepared flower between her middle finger and thumb, and with her tongue sticking in between her lips, pushed the river poppy through the air, releasing it like a paper airplane. It soared up and did a few loop-the-loops before landing blossom first on the grass, the fancy leaf folding coming undone. My jaw dropped in surprise, and I blinked slowly. "Where did you learn that?"

"Figured it out with some friends back home," she answered, reaching for another. "There's this holiday celebrating the sun spirit and somehow it became some mushy couples holiday, and so when all the people are sending these flowers back and forth using lovebirds, my buddies and I would catch the birds, set them free, and then dive bomb the flowers like this to the lucky receiver." She grinned, shooting the next flower-plane straight up into the air and then watching as it came twirling down like a dancer.

I laughed, catching the poppy in my outstretched palm. I looked at her. "So, you're into mischief?"

Irene relaxed back into the grass. "I would say so. Nothing mean, just good fun."

I smiled down at the river, watching my reflection sparkle over the river stones. For a moment, I envisioned the time not so long ago that my friends and I had done the easiest and most fun thieving we'd ever tried. We were trying to steal some milk from the animal pen for Carmen's baby brother Luca, and before JP 21996 and his bozo cronies could snatch us by the collar and lock us up for a night in Underbrush's misdemeanor center, Chantastic and I had exchanged conspiratorial glances and picked up the big gross bowl of milk fat and dumped it into the JPs' helmets. We wouldn't actually waste good milk, but this was the stuff sifted out of it that had been sitting out for two days too many and smelled so sour it hurt your nose. Long story short, the thick white gunk stuck like glue on the inside of their visors, and as the officers stumbled around into each other, accidentally stinging one another with their unsheathed lightning rods, my friends were able to make a quick getaway with two gallons of good milk and plenty of laughter filling the somber Underbrush streets. "I'd say I'm into some mischief too," I said, dipping my fingertips in the cool water and swirling them around.

Irene sat up quickly, flinching as she must've strained an

injury, but her face showed no sign of pain, only pleasant surprise. "Oh, really? Honestly you've come off as pretty goody-goody to me."

"Goody-goody?" I said, turning on her. "What gives you that idea?"

She pursed her lips, tilting her head to the side as she looked me over. Then she said, slowly, "Well, okay I get that you're breaking your law or something, but you're so tense and timid all the time. Like the only reason I'm still alive is because you just don't have the guts to get rid of me."

I blushed. "Well...that's sort of a reason, I guess, but it also just doesn't seem right."

"Even though you think my mountain wants to destroy yours, you still think it isn't right to kill me?"

"I don't know! Okay, I don't have the guts. Happy?" I fumed, crossing my arms.

The spy smiled impishly. "Yep. I'm real happy you can't get past your moral dilemma. Being alive is awesome."

The situation was weighing heavy on my chest again, the fleeting friendliness settling into stone between us. "I might have a moral dilemma, but after the airships Fluxaria sent over, I don't know how long Destan's will stand," I said, glancing back at her.

Irene groaned dramatically, covering her face with her hands. "There you go again with your annoying ignorance about everything! You know I really thought we were hitting it off for a second, but as I told you, and I'll tell you again— it wasn't Fluxaria."

"Irene—"

"Just *listen* for a second, gimme just a second!" she demanded, laughing bitterly. "You think you know more than me about a place you've never visited, much less lived. I get that. So to give you a nice and pretty picture, Fluxaria has trees, and flowers, and some nice humans and some stupid humans just like anywhere else, and we've got good food, and some weird food, and too many statues that need to put some clothes on, a lot of sickness, and *so* much fear! But we most definitely do *not* have airships, we most definitely do *not* eat Thgindimmers or even make it our mission to go after and torture them. And believe it or not, I'm the first spy to actually make it here in the last decade, so get out of fairyland and take a good look at the real world we live in—"

"Stop!" I suddenly shouted at her, wanting to plug my ears, my heart racing faster and faster as it tried to keep up with the hurricane of words leaving her mouth. "Just stop this; you know you can't prove any of this to me—"

"Then let's change up the deal, how about that?" she cut in again. "If I can prove to you and your friend within the…let's say…*week*, that your mountain is up to no good and that mine is up to real good, then you'll let me carry on my mission and get out of this dumb place. If you two draw a blank and there's no crazy shit just like you thought, I'll go straight home, spy's honor. Because then you're right and I'm wrong and deserve to pack up and skedaddle. But I'm not leaving empty-handed without getting the chance to turn over some rocks and show you what nasty critters might be under them."

I clutched my sketchbook to my chest, staring straight into Irene's big, dark eyes. In the short while we'd been tending to her, already she seemed to be getting better. She'd slept off some of the vertigo that came from her assumed concussion, and her bruises were going through the green stage of healing. I was just thankful her broken fingers, cracked ribs, torn shoulder muscle, and leg injury hadn't been totally fixed yet or else there was no way Destan and I could depend on her not to hurt us and flee.

Getting to my feet, I retrieved the archery gear I had neglected to practice with, and strode to the entrance of the meadow. It was all getting to be too much. I felt like the girl had shoved marbles into my head and now they kept rolling and bouncing around to keep me from focusing. "I'm willing to give it a shot," I sighed, wanting the arguing to stop before my head actually did decide to fall off of my body. "I'll talk to Destan about it next time I see him. Probably Monday when the weekend is over."

Irene coughed, hand shooting to her ribs as each jerk yanked at the fractures. She let herself release a solitary gasp, but then gritted her teeth and raised a shaky thumbs-up. "S-sounds good. I'll…I'll just be here."

I nodded, averting my eyes and slinging my quiver on. I left the meadow, then; submerging myself in the soothing green of the pines and the cool smell drifting off of their needles. It helped to clear my head. Now all I had to do was get back to Gwen and take her out shopping for groceries since my Mom was gone for the day.

I watched my boots as I walked, the way the frosty grass crackled under my toes and then sprang back up with such inspiring energy. I tried avoiding the scattered clumps of mushrooms so that I wasn't trampling some rabbit's lunch. And as I made it nearly to where the woods met the town, a hand came out from the shadows and grabbed my wrist, its grip cold and hard as ice.

chapter thirteen

"Hey beautiful, what're you doing so far away from your girlfriends?" he chuckled, voice rough and breath reeking of some disgusting kind of moonshine. The JP was only half in uniform, no helmet and only his chest shield, his legs in a ratty pair of jeans. I struggled in his grip as he tried to back me up against the nearest tree, a dying conifer with sharp, yellowed needles. I tried to read what number was on his badge but then gave up, knowing his voice anywhere. One of 21996's rats.

Another hand appeared then, stroking my hair like someone would pat an old dog, and I whipped my head around, seeing to my left a pair of bright blue eyes and crooked teeth. "Oh, baby, give me a smile," he giggled, a JP no older than I was.

The third and final hand, wiggling fingers coming closer and closer to my neck, finally taking hold of my scarf and unwinding it, all of them laughing as I tried ducking out, only to be forced more roughly against the tree.

"I have money," I panted, voice quivering so much that I wondered if they could understand me. I only had the few pieces of copper Destan had left the night after the blackout, and panicked thinking of what else they'd like to take. I'd lost count of the JP horror stories of what would happen to girls a little too far away from town.

"How about a kiss, gorgeous?" the second one begged, standing only an inch in front of me now, coming forward with his hand. He flicked down the strap of my brassiere with his pinky and grinned. "Whoops."

Repulsed, I spat straight at his face, getting him square in the eye. As he went tottering back, the other two exploded into booming guffaws, the first JP grabbing my face and scrunching my cheeks together, his other hand trying to crawl up my shirt as I frantically forced his hand down again and again. The other JP in the meantime fiddled with his belt and pants zipper.

"Just takes a couple minutes, beautiful," the man grinned. The JP I'd spat at stuck his hand in my pocket and withdrew my money pouch, shaking out the contents and grinding them into the dirt with the toe of his boot.

"Only three fucking coppers…" he hissed, disappointed.

The one holding me prisoner brought his lips an inch away from my mouth, his fingers grazing over my thighs, "Just give me a kiss—"

His jaw was knocked hard by a flat-fisted punch, his gross big hands leaving my skin as he reeled around in fury. "Who the fuck—?!"

A kick straight to the groin, sending him yowling like a fox, and Destan came charging at the next two, smashing their heads together and shoving them down onto the ground. His eyes were steely and scary, and swinging his fists, he clocked in the eye and gut the one who had been touching me. The JP with the terrible teeth staggered back to his feet and threw a punch that Destan caught even without glancing behind him, twisting around the boy's arm and kicking back with the heel of his heavy-duty boots into the boy's shins.

Now all of them were distracted and wailing in pain, and as quickly as he'd come to my rescue, Destan grabbed my hand and ran us out of the woods, taking us down along the rows of huts and trees. I clung to his arm, biting back tears and trying to keep up with the rapid pace his feet moved on the gravel. We went so fast that for a moment we were flying.

We peeled around the abandoned corner-store, stopping abruptly in the alley, both of us needing a good minute to catch our breath. I put my hands on my knees, bending down as I made as much air as possible move in and out of my lungs. My ribbon had come loose, my long, heavy hair hanging around me in a navy curtain. I resurfaced, hand over my heart, feeling it slowly return to normal speed as Destan readjusted his hat, which had gone askew.

He placed both of his trembling hands on my shoulders, eyes intensely diving into mine. "Are you okay?" he rasped. "Did they hurt you?"

I shook my head vigorously. "N-no, no, I'm f-fine."

"They didn't try to...so they didn't...?"

"No, no, not yet," I said, forcing a shaky smile, unable to sustain it as tears filled my eyes and a few came skidding out. I quickly caught them and wiped them gone with my knuckles, breathing out a cloud of air and using all of my willpower to not start crying in front of him. My whole body was trembling uncontrollably.

Destan dropped his hands from my shoulders, still staring at me. And then all of a sudden, he threw his arms around me and hugged me. I gasped, face buried in his chest, too short to be able to look over his shoulder. I felt so small and protected, and he squeezed me, rocking us back and forth silently. My shivering slowly came to a

120

stand-still as I relaxed in his arms.

We broke apart and he first unwound his own scarlet scarf, putting it snugly around my neck seeing that mine had been ripped off by the JPs. Then he took my satchel and bow, stuffing it into his own knapsack and moving to leave the alley. Checking to make sure the JPs were nowhere in sight, we crossed the road and began walking south. I wasn't sure where he was leading us, but I followed obediently behind him.

"I don't think it's a good idea for you to be alone right now," he began, glancing back at me and then pausing, rummaging in his jeans pocket to pull out his flute. He piped a few notes, then spoke again, "Who knows if those assholes will be lurking around, still looking for you."

I nodded, rubbing my arms to chase away the chills caused by the oncoming evening cold. "Good point. Where are we going?" I asked, tripping over my untied boot laces and hopping on one foot while I attempted to tie it again.

Destan waved ahead of us. "Isn't your house this way?" He tilted his head to the side in question.

Smiling, I shook my head and jerked my thumb behind us. "North, actually."

"Oh, shit. You'd think I'd know this by now."

"It's fine. We just need to hurry and get to Gwen. I left her alone all day," I said, just as Siri appeared, looking oddly haggard and bleary-eyed. We had just woken her from a nap, and Destan took her reins, guiding her alongside us to give her time to wake up as we started jogging back north.

Destan looked at me sideways, panting, "How come you were hanging around the meadow for so long?"

I tossed my bangs out of my eyes. "I was nervous about leaving Irene unsupervised, y'know? Speaking of which, she had an idea, which I agreed to, that she wants me to tell you about."

"Cool. What is it?"

I opened my mouth to speak, but then shut it again, silenced by the Underbrushers I saw now among us, sweeping their porches or selling something on the road. Rather, I cleared my throat and ran closer beside him, whispering, "I'll tell you later. Too many ears."

He nodded. "Gotcha."

We made it to my house in no time, but as soon as we'd gone inside and found Gwen most happily playing with a few pairs of my socks, I remembered that I had had to go shopping so that Gwen and I could eat dinner. I sighed, eyeing the pantry shelves and wondering if I could somehow fashion a meal out of parsley flakes, three walnuts, and an unopened can of fish sauce.

"What's up?" Destan said, from behind me.

Hunger gnawed at my stomach just looking at the sparse choices. I scratched my head. "I was supposed to go out and get some food for dinner," I turned toward him, leaning against the kitchen counter, "but the JPs took my money and I really don't want to take Gwen out there in the open with those jerks still around."

Destan frowned, then surprisingly burst into a sunshiny grin I'd never seen him wear before. "Aha!" he cried, smacking his hand down on the table. "I know! Okay, you're going to have to trust me, but may I take you and Gwen out for a surprise?"

I pursed my lips, arms across my chest. "And this surprise involves food and no chance of getting hounded by perverted police officers?"

"Hell, yes."

I slipped past him and peeked into Gwen's and my room. She looked up from her twisted knot of socks and blew me a raspberry. I blew one right back and called, "Gwennie! We're going out. Get your coat."

Destan waited outside while I got Gwen's coat and hat on. I tried putting a scarf on her, but she kept whining every time it made one loop around her short neck, so I gave up and guided her outside. Siri stood majestically in the silver, evening light, her rider poised at her flank. Destan bowed, offering his hand to

Gwen.

"Your Highness?" he asked smoothly. Of course Gwen didn't know what he was saying, but she looked to me excitedly and then put her small hand in his. He helped her climb onto Siri's back, using an overturned milk crate as a stepping stool. Then he turned to me, extending his hand once more for the taking. Even with the ratty gloves and muddy boots he looked like a prince.

"My Bluehead queen," he whispered, looking at me from under his long, gold lashes.

I attempted a curtsy but nearly toppled over, catching myself and hiding my face under my bangs nervously, but still smiling. "Thank you, King Beaniehead."

He hopped on in front, Gwen sandwiched between us, and sighed, "There you go calling me *Beaniehead* again..."

With a gentle but officiating kick to Siri's flank, Destan had us take off south, Gwen screaming with joy the entire way. My sister's curls flew out in every direction, hitting me in the face as she tipped her face to the sky and burst with laughter. I couldn't remember the last she had been so happy, so much like a real ten year old girl. Her eyes were shut in ecstasy, arms extending out as if she were soaring— she probably thought she'd turned into a bird.

We rode so far south that I was sure we were going to delve into Justice Police Base territory. But then Destan swerved off the main road onto a dirt trail, and we trotted through a tunnel of conifer trees as brilliant as emeralds, paper lanterns bobbing from the overhanging branches. We followed the path all the way down, and at the end of the trail appeared a medium-sized log cabin with smoke billowing from the chimney. Stacked up against the right wall were bundles of wood, bound by the same rope Destan always carried with him. In front of the lumber pile was a splitting block, an axe wedged deep into the sturdy tree stump.

"What is this place?" I asked, my curiosity rising. "Do you

live here?"

"No way, you kidding?" Destan laughed, slowing Siri even more and leading her off the trail to a patch of moss on the side of the cabin. "Didn't your dad or mom ever bring you here?" I shook my head. He opened his arms wide above him, "This is the woodshop! My home-base where the boss is, where we sell the lumber we cut, and knick knacks that we carve."

He helped Gwen off Siri's back and I hopped down myself, and as we approached the wrap around veranda of the woodshop, Siri relaxed onto her patch of moss, gnawing on some sort of big bone. The planks of the veranda creaked as we climbed the steps and waited, and then Destan entered first, holding open the door for Gwen and I to come quietly in.

The shop's interior took my breath away. The walls looked smooth as marble, and yet as I ran my fingertips over the paneling I realized it was birch polished and sanded to a shimmering white. Shelves upon shelves of statues, hand carved name plates, forks and spoons and plates and bowls, pinewood window shades, toy figurines and nicer ones made of mahogany and petrified oak, anything you could imagine being fashioned from wood was probably somewhere in this cozy little shop. I had never realized just how many shades of brown there could be, how different a set of maplewood plates could look from the willow-wood plates, how much detailing and craft could bring a hunk of dead tree into a life-size model of a swan with its neck extended and elegant.

I had to keep Gwen's arm tightly linked with mine to make sure she didn't go over and touch everything she laid her shiny eyes on. Even with her insistent whining and yanking on my sweater sleeve, "Ray…Ray, *Ray*?"

"Not those, Gwen," I hushed, guiding her away from the table of painted jewelry boxes.

Destan walked backwards to smile at me. "So?"

"It's amazing, you…you made all of this?" I asked, just noticing the overhanging fixture of branches weaving this way and that to look like a chandelier, candle nubs stuck on each end, jade beads hanging down in a canopy around us.

"Naw, Ling makes probably three-fourths of it. I do the bulk of the lumber-jacking." He flexed his muscles, and we all giggled.

"What's all that hootin' and hollerin', boy? You bring a circus in here or what?" a voice I assumed to be Ling's shouted from behind the door labeled *Checkout* with its own fancy nameplate.

"Not a circus, Ling," Destan called back, rolling his eyes and grinning as he ushered us through, "Underbrush royalty."

Inside were two workbenches and stools, an old record player spinning under the back window, and a checkout counter where an old man sat chewing on his thumbnail.

"Ling, may I introduce you to the lovely ladies of the Ylevol clan," Destan announced, and the old guy at the counter squinted and then smiled with at least three front teeth missing.

"Well, I'll be darned if you aren't Solomon Ylevol's daughters," Ling snickered, getting to his feet and planting both of his hands on his hips. He leaned forward and smiled crookedly again at me. "Now I don't know about this here hair, but them eyes I'd recognize anywhere. You even got those long girly lashes I used to poke fun at him for."

I tried to hide my excitement at the mention of my father, and just simply nodded, pushing my hair out of my eyes. "Yes, yes…do you know him? Or knew him?"

"*Know* him?" Ling croaked, frowning. "You're telling me you don't remember 'crazy old Ling the wood guy?' I helped your old man build that house you're livin' in, I gave you that red shiny rocking horse? You're Raine. Little blue Raine, and that there is Gwen Lin."

Now the rocking horse I vaguely remembered, but it was still ten years ago. I feigned my recollection of the memory. "Oh! Yes, I think so!" I chuckled, still feeling a bit out of place, Gwen humming and shifting back and forth at my side.

"Ling, I would like to share our supper with these girls tonight," Destan said, appearing at my side. Our arms were touching, our hands nearly hitting into each other. My fingers wanted to curl around his and take his hand, but that panicky part of me kept them hanging there, waiting for Destan to be the braver one again, waiting to be held.

Ling rubbed the short quills of his stubble, grimacing, "Well, I hope you haven't told them this is some high class joint, because you know there usually isn't even enough for the two of us, boy."

"I already ate," Destan said quickly. "They can have my portion, no problem."

Ling shrugged, face splitting into a grin again. "Then go ahead and serve them like a real gentleman!" He came hobbling over and took our hands, leading us out the back door onto a patio overlooking the dense, dark woods. Out on the patio were a series of pine needle stuffed cushions, and a low table for us to sit. Gwen and I sat, and when Ling went back inside we heard the music crank up even louder. It was some trio singing in harmony, a cheerful folk song. Gwen swayed back and forth, humming happily.

In a few minutes, Destan came out with two wooden mugs in each hand and plates balanced skillfully on each forearm. He set down a plate in front of me, "Here is one for the queen..." and then he did a clumsy, silly spin, making Gwen collapse into laughter and clapping as he slid her plate across the table, "and for you, beautiful princess."

My little sister peered down at the plate and then into her mug, a look of awe glowing from her face. I reached across and tucked a napkin into her collar to keep her from getting anything on her dress, and then settled back on my cushion. My face physically hurt from smiling so much, and yet I couldn't seem to stop. Not so long ago I thought I was going to be assaulted by the police, and now I was listening to scratchy music, trying to eat the roasted rabbit slowly to hide that I was starving. All the while, Destan watched me, head down on the table, eyes sparkling like moonlight on water, his mischief-laced mouth hidden behind his arm.

"It's good?" he asked, voice lilting like music.

I nodded enthusiastically, trying to ration out smaller bites to make the single rabbit leg go farther. I decided to eat the string beans and rice to save the meat for last, and before sending another forkful into my mouth, I looked down at him, blushing. "Thank you so much. I promise I'll pay you back."

He frowned. "No. No paying. I still owe you and your family for letting me stay during the blackout."

"But you paid us remember? And you saved me from those guys back there. I think I'm in your debt, now."

Destan shook his head, sitting cross-legged. "Definitely not. There's enough debt going around this stupid level. Let's just call it..." He tapped his lips with his fingers thoughtfully, staring up into space, then smiled, not as goofily this time, more sweetly. "An act of friendship."

I leaned my cheek on my hand. "So, we're friends now? Not just partners in crime?"

Nodding, he murmured, "Yeah. I think we are friends, Bluehead. It's been a while since I could call someone that, so know that I really mean it."

There was that inkling of confusion again, just as it had been there when he had been isolated at school from the very first day he stepped inside the cave. Just as it had been when he'd hid his last name from my mother, and said his family didn't want attention. All I knew of him other than what he showed me was that his brother died in the Justice Police and that he had three half-sisters. But what about parents? Why didn't they want attention? I stared at him quizzically, trying to figure him out, scared to bring up any questions of this sort again and risk him putting up another joking defense or distraction. Instead, I sighed and twirled the rabbit leg-bone in my fingers, bowing my head appreciatively."Well then, I'm honoured, Destan Abrasha.

I'll try to live up to being a good friend."

He exhaled sharply, jerking his thumb back, saying, "You can *try*, but it's going to be hard to beat Siri. It's not every day you meet a girl who comes when you call and carries you on her naked back."

We burst into laughter, Gwen looking away from her licked-clean plate and joining in on the giggling. Destan turned to her and sprang to his feet, holding out his hands. "Let's dance, your majesty! Oh, we must!"

Gwen didn't even wait to hear his request, she clumsily got up off the cushion and grabbed Destan's rough hands, jumping up and down, swinging his arms back and forth. They galloped in a circle in rhythm to the music blasting from inside the shop. Then they would stop with a gasp, go in the opposite direction, and Destan picked her up and spun her around. Gwen glowed with happiness and laughed the purest laughter I'd ever heard. I clapped my hands to the beat, watching them dance like a bunch of wackos and sing along loudly and off-key, Destan replacing the lyrics with things like 'yummy yummy food tastes so good,' and 'let the Majesty Council eat our poop.'

It wasn't long until he dragged me into the dance with them, lifting up his arms and trapping me in a circle as he and Gwen came round and around me like a carousel. I was so dizzy, protesting that I was going to throw up all the food I just ate, but also laughing so hard that eventually I gave in and spun myself inside of their moving ring, singing along to the nonsense words, so happy to not have to carry any laundry or take care of anyone, so happy to be a kid again with my hair flying like a storm and arms reaching to the stars.

chapter fourteen

"Have you ever thought about a boy?"

She looked at me, smiling curiously. "You mean…*thought* about a boy?"

I rolled my eyes, standing on my pedals to give the rickshaw more power to move forward. Chantastic walked beside me, her arms full of fresh-cut flowers, all white roses. She was taking them to Starshade to set up a small selling table, and I had an Emergent load to do for the first time, so for now we walked together. I already missed her like crazy, and secretly hoped that I'd get the worst level again and again so that I could see her every day.

My bike wheel rolled over a twig, breaking it in half with a squeaky snap. "Like…have you ever had a crush on someone?"

Her cheeks pinked, and she sucked on her lip, musing, "Mmhmm. But I'm not…I didn't pursue anything romantic with this person. Why do you ask?"

"I was just curious, I guess." I sighed, clenching my stomach tightly as I tried to make it up the steep incline of the road, my legs aching. Chan panted beside me, having just as much trouble with the hill as her mary-janes had the soles hanging off like black tongues licking up every bit of gravel.

"Do you have a crush on someone?" she asked suddenly, looking at me with those pretty dark eyes.

"I don't know, that's the problem." I frowned. "I don't really want to, y'know? It's so alien to me and I feel like there's enough to worry about with Mom and Gwen and especially Irene and stuff…"

I hadn't been able to catch myself.

Chan's brow crinkled. "Who's Irene?"

My face flooded with heat, brain too panicked to conjure up a single valid excuse. I missed the pedal with my boot the moment Irene's name left Chan's lips, and my rickshaw tilted to the side, making me fall over.

Chantastic gasped, coming down to help me off the road. "Raine, are you okay? What happened?"

"Missed the pedal, that's all." I didn't even try to brush the powdery dirt stains from my sweater tights, just shakily climbed back onto the bike. Chantastic's face was still riddled with concern, but she followed silently behind me, fingers gently stroking the silky rose buds as we continued up the main road.

When we passed through Starshade and hit the point where we'd have to split off, I got down from my rickshaw to give her a hug. She embraced me extra tightly, whispering into my ear, "Are you sure everything is okay?"

I shut my eyes. "Mmhmm."

"You'd tell me if something was going on, right?" she asked softly.

"Of course," I lied, the fib stinging on my tongue and leaving a nauseating taste. *I can't lie to her, I can't lie to her, I can't, I can't. She's my best friend. I can't keep this all from her.* My thoughts whirled and whirled until I was sick with them.

She pulled away, beaming. "Good. I'll see you soon, then. I love you."

I tried to look as normal and not totally freaked as possible, "Love you, too."

We parted ways, me planning to just blur through the house calls and pick up and drop off the clothes as quickly as I could without messing up the folding I'd done back at the pavilion. It is an understatement to say that going up there was a shock. Before I became a Laundress, the distinction between levels had seemed very subtle; with Starshade only appearing as a cleaned up and polished Underbrush. Then came Canopia, all smoke and filth and metallic clinking but still structured so that at least I could believe such a place existed only a couple miles away from home. But Emergent was unlike anywhere else on the mountain. I'd completely underestimated the wealth flowing into this high level of Thgindim. Emergent was an alternate, distant universe, miles and miles away from what I thought Thgindim and the Majesty Council were even capable of.

One family alone had enough to fill my entire bucket, sometimes more if they were the rich Emergents. I had to take trips from the Laundress pavilion to Emergent, to the meadow to wash the clothes, and then repeat the cycle five times until I had done all that Jun had assigned. Jun sent groups of ten Laundresses to tackle Emergent. Not to mention, it was mortifying to ride my crappy rickshaw around such a lavish place.

I passed groups of gorgeously dressed and made-up ladies that didn't bother to hide their laughter when they saw me on my ridiculous bike with my threadbare sweater and gloves, torn leggings, and muddy boots. I was a shadow as Jun had told me to be. But I could have been singing loud and off key like I had done with Destan and Gwen in the woodshop, and *still* no one would tell me to shut up because I was nothing to them.

Houses were few, buildings were many. The mountain terraces extended out at least forty feet farther than Canopia and supported entire towers made of metal and glass. None were nearly as tall as Peak, but they rose up to ten stories like clear cliffs. The road I pedaled on was so smooth that my wheels left scuff marks on the white reflective stone, and the traffic was unbelievably minor compared to the busy, clockwork movement of Canopia. I rode in a mostly vacant lane of my own for the sub-level delivery vehicles as bullet trains and chrome scooters of every colour whizzed through the center of the level, honking tinny horns and blasting music from their vehicles' radios.

I rode by a long shopping center made completely of blue glass and silver piping that stretched on for a quarter of a mile, and inside I could see girls flitting from one rack of silky clothes to the next, couples holding hands and fawning over different sofas and tables to choose from, and most unnerving of all, there were so many people just smiling. I'm not against smiling, it's my mission to make sure Gwen gets a smile in every day, but it made me so furious as I rode by the same smiles again and again. The "*I love my job*" smile, the "*Payday! Let's go treat ourselves*" smile, the "*I love life so much*" smile, and everywhere I looked, those new Majesty Council banners were flying in the wind, flapping like big navy wings, and glistening like gossamer in each tall house or apartment building's window. This was a carefree fairyland, the kind of place Irene thought me and Destan lived in as well.

I pedaled faster than ever to get out, thinking over and over, *How is this real, how is this real, how is this real?* I only saw a couple JPs every minute or so, rather than the entire leagues of them that stomped up and down Underbrush's road from dawn to dusk. I had proof now that the Majesty Council trusted Underbrush the least, gave its greatest attention and wealth to this thin-aired slice of mountain. And the more I thought of the Majesty Council, the more I thought of what else they might be keeping from us, what Irene might be right about.

No, I didn't trust my government. But did I trust an enemy spy? Of course not. In my mind, both of them were spinning their own lies that just got tangled together. Fluxaria did seem like it would be in danger now from us because they've always been the perpetrators of violence against us— or so the Majesty Council claimed. But even with my doubts about the Council, there's no way Irene could talk around the Fluxarian warships coming for us. I'd *seen* them coming. If there was a war, it would be because both countries were crazy and ready to shoot each other out of existence.

"Raine! Look where you're going!" one of the Laundress girls riding behind scolded suddenly.

Dazed, I shoved my pedals back and jammed up the gears so that my rickshaw screeched to a stop and a bunch of warmly dressed Emergents could cross the street without a blue-haired idiot crashing into them. They whispered behind their hands as they walked, eyes scanning me up and down fearfully, as if just now they'd realized an actual person still did their clothes for them. A group of teenage boys didn't even attempt to hide their laughter at me, their eyes flashing in amusement at the rusty old bike, the mud on my boots, and the greasy hair around my face.

The moment the last pedestrian's foot touched the sidewalk on the other side, I took off immediately, going as fast as I could to the high and shining gate that separated Emergent from Canopia, speeding through and not looking back.

I made it to the meadow for the final time just after lunch, stumbling through the leafy entrance, rolling my rickshaw beside me, and panting for breath. Destan had done quite a lot of lumberjacking, or whatever you call it, and had a big pile of cut pine branches stacked in the center of the meadow. He was systematically moving them from the middle over to where our target tree was, building a sort of log-cabin style structure. It was only up to his waist when he saw me come in, and he beamed. "Bluehead! Is that an empty basket I see?"

I fell onto the ground, arms and legs spread in exhaustion. "It sure is."

I felt something tickle my nose, and I wrinkled my face,

opening my eyes to see Destan twiddling a cluster of pine needles over me, smiling. He pulled them away, chuckling, "Well, I'm glad you're all done, because Irene just had the *best* idea ever and needs your full attention."

"NO, I did NOT!" she hollered. Irene sat grumpily against a tree, turned away from us.

Raising an eyebrow, I looked at Destan for explanation. He made his way over to one of the twistier trees and climbed lithely up a few levels of the winding branches. A big black satchel fell down with a thud onto the ground, and Irene spun around immediately, trying with all of her might to drag herself over to it before Destan could hop down. Just as her tan fingers reached out to touch one of the frayed straps, Destan swung back down and snatched it up.

"Ah, ah, ah," he chided her, waggling a finger and loping over to the odd stack of wood he was making.

Irene rolled onto her back, fuming, her palms tight against her eyes as she growled, "Blondie, this was NOT part of our deal!"

"It doesn't exactly go against it, though," he pointed out, setting her satchel atop the tower of wood. Destan took his own bow from across his body and reached back for an arrow, backtracking to where we shoot from, cocking his head at me for me to come over.

"What are we doing?" I asked, hesitantly taking out my own bow as Irene's cries of frustration got even louder and she banged the ground with her fists like Gwen in one of her tantrums.

Destan raised his bow into that perfect stance I tried so hard to imitate, and as he closed one eye, tongue coming in between his teeth, he murmured, "Trying to give her some incentive..."

My brow furrowed. "Incentive? What do you—?"

He let his arrow fly, and it pinned one of the satchels straps to the tree, making Irene curse loudly and try hastily again

134

and again to get to her feet, only to come falling down face first every time. Her face was beet red, with more and more grass getting stuck to her cheeks and sweaty forehead.

"For her to tell us the real truth of what Fluxaria is going to do to us," he explained quickly, taking an arrow from my quiver and placing it in my hands. "Here, Bluehead, for practice today your assignment is to hit that bag—"

"Stop! Just stop for a second would you?" Irene screamed, leaning against a tree with her knees trembling, trying to stand as long as she could. "You're already keeping my stuff from me, you don't have to ruin it too!"

I was on her side with this, remembering the deal we'd made just the night before. "Destan," I urged, tentatively placing a hand on his arm and pushing it down. "I know it's urgent, but this is what I needed to tell you about. Irene had an idea and I said we'd treat her fairly for a week if she found proof Thgindim's also up to something."

His freckly cheeks surprisingly grew a little rosy, and he looked at my hand on his arm, lips pinching in an almost smile. I quickly removed my palm to pretend to cough into it and then I watched as he went to the target and tugged out the arrow, the strap falling limply back down the satchel. I thought he was going to be defensive, make a joke, but I was taken aback as he walked slowly over to Irene and shoved his gloved hands deep into his jeans pockets, curls falling over his face as he clarified, "You two really made a deal?"

Irene gaped at him, mouth hanging open in a big 'O', "No shit! It's not like I've been saying that for the last fifteen minutes or anything."

"Sorry! At least I didn't aim so well for the first—"

The zing of something rubber flying past, smashing a good two inches away from where he was standing. And then we heard the voices, the distorted, robotic speech the JP helmets made, rattling through the trees near the entrance, coming closer. The sizzle of lightning rods next, more zings, and a hundred of

135

those rubber bullets tore through the leaves and came straight at us.

I ran to Destan, who hoisted Irene over his shoulder and knocked down the pile of logs, trying to clear our tracks and avoid the onslaught of bullets that managed to bruise deep into my calf and ricochet off the rickshaw with sounds deep and clanging as gongs. He swung his axe at the brambles on the side of the meadow leading to deeper wood, Irene covering her head with her hands as they wriggled through the opening. I had a moment of pause, thinking about the lumber and the rickshaw and how even if we left, we'd be able to be traced. Acting on impulse, I shoved Destan's head down hard with all of my body weight, making him and Irene fall onto all fours in the brush, both of them looking at me in shock.

"Go, go, go, don't make a sound. I'll find you," I hissed, fearing my courage would run out if they had a chance to protest, and I threw a fern in front of them just as all twenty of the JPs doing the forest raid came bursting through with their rifles and lightning rods raised.

"You there!" The leader of them, in the darkest metal with 22278 gleaming on his tag. "Out from the shadows!"

My chest seized up, and I pointed shakily at myself in innocent question. *Sell it, Raine, don't let them think you're doing anything, but washing clothes.*

"He's talking to you, bitch! Listen to your superior officer!" The one on his right flank roared, shooting a rubber bullet at my ankle and making me come forward in haste, lips trembling in fear. I prayed and prayed Destan and Irene were well away now.

"On your knees," 22278 barked, grabbing me by the shoulders and forcing me down so that my eyes were level with his thighs, my face close to the belt where a long, electrified blade hung. I heard a familiar, gross and greasy laugh, and JP 21996 came out from behind an officer, waving at me mockingly with a smile of glee stretched against his yellow teeth.

I avoided eye contact with him, and gulped, trying to

speak, "Is...is there a problem, officer?"

"What was that?" he bellowed, roughly tipping my chin up. "Speak up, girl. These are men you are talking to."

My whole body shook, I had to swallow down my breaths to keep from tearing up in panic. "I'm sorry, sir," I said, more loudly, and the captain of the fleet stepped back. His horde of men stalked into a circle around me, trapping me like a rabbit surrounded by wolves.

"Are you aware that you are currently trespassing in territory our Majesty Council has prohibited *all* citizens from entering without a license of residence?" he asked me.

I shook my head vigorously. "No, sir. I'm not living here, I just come here to work..." my voice faded out as JPs tore across the meadow, chucking Destan's lumber into the stream to get it out of their way, some pawing at my quiver and rolling the arrows around in their fingers. My least favourite officer turned over a rock where Irene's spare gauze and ointment were hidden, and my eyes widened.

"Cap'n, have a look at this," JP 21996 called in a singsong voice, holding up the fistful of materials I'd snuck from my mother's medicine storage. He looked my way and gave me a sickly, satisfied grin.

The only way I can explain the relationship between me and this certain police officer is this— I ruined his chances with a girl a couple years ago. He was trying to flirt with this girl, the gorgeous Lili Jung (already way out of his league), but then I ran by and snatched the pistol from his hip, and in his attempt to lunge out and grab me, 21996 split his pants and Lili never spoke him again without bringing up his floral underpants. So obviously, I was tacked as #1 on his Underbrusher-Hit-list.

More than just the captain went trudging over, a number of JPs pulling apart the fluffy white bandages and squeezing out some disinfectant ointment to smell it. The captain pointed his rod at two officers and then at me, and they came from behind, hoisting me up by the armpits and dragging me over to him.

"Where did you acquire official medical materials of a Majesty Council-chosen Healer?" he demanded.

I winced, arms hurting under the pressure the men were applying as they held me up. "My mother, she's a Healer. Pearle Xue Lin Ylevol, northern end of Underbrush, Healer and Spooner," I spilled out, the torrent of words muddling into gasps as the JPs dropped me at the captain's feet. I remained kneeling, head down, knowing that even my mother didn't have the right to give, much less use, her Healer materials on me since they were paid for by the Council. When I had the flu a few years back, I was forced to stick it out in bed for three weeks with some natural remedies my Mom could scrape up on her own, while paying customers were given advanced, medicinal elixirs that took only hours to kick in and kill the viruses. I bore my eyes into the grass, adding, "I'm her daughter...Raine Xifeng Ylevol, northern end of Underbrush, Laundress."

"What use of medicine does a Laundress have in her field?" a JP scoffed, the others muttering in agreement, 21996 being the most vocal with his snorting.

Anxiously, I ducked my head lower. "My job...it has risks, it's dangerous sometimes...my job..."

"Louder, scum!"

"My vehicle— the rickshaw over there —has rust. It cuts me and needs regular disinfecting," I fibbed, feeling how the blood pulsed hard and fast in my temple. "And I get knocked around on the roads; I needed some first aid to keep with me—"

"So you're legal guardian betrayed the policy of fair trade and gave you these materials, free of charge?"

JP 21996 blew air between his lips, crossing his arms and then jerking his head at me. "She's a stinking *thief*, Cap'n. I know this gal. Raided the cafe just a month or so ago and made a real mess, has been in the klepto business for years now."

I gritted my teeth, biting back the lies of defense I'd had planned. All 21996 would have to do is pull up my record on one of those Majesty Council-issued metal tablets and scroll through the list of specific discrepancies. Or at least he'd threatened me with such things before, and it turned out to be partially true as the captain whipped out his own and asked for confirmation of how to spell my name.

"It's Y-L-E-V. With that sneaky little 'L' in the '*yev*,'" 21996 directed, making air quotes as he spoke. The captain brushed him aside, glancing from the tablet and back to me rhythmically. Then he nodded at four other officers to take hold of me.

"This is now her third proven and documented demerit in the past half year," he sighed. "Supplemented with the array of unconfirmed acts of theft and trespassing, she'll need some probation paint to put this crime to rest."

chapter fifteen

Destan's red scarf around my head and tucked along my face, I crept inside my hut, careful to skip the creaky step on my way up to the porch. I shook my feet out of my boots, quietly setting them by the broken door and slipping into my room. Relieved to be back home, but tense with nerves about Destan and Irene and where they could be hiding, I drew the curtain between Gwen's and my room, crashed onto my cot, and pulled the covers over myself completely. I needed a moment to think and figure out how to work my way around this new issue— my punishment.

"Gwennie? Are you up from nap already?" my mother called from her bedroom, obviously in the midst of her own afternoon nap from work. I let one ear peek out from the blanket to check if I could hear Gwen's gentle snores, and then once the familiar sound struck my ears, I went completely under again, just in time for my mom to come padding in.

I stared through the fibres of the quilt, trying to discern

what expression my mother was making as she came to Gwen's, then my side. The *scritch scritch* of her slippers on the floor stopped as a shadow passed over the blanket. "Raine? You're home from work already?"

These days I usually stayed out until nightfall keeping an eye on Irene and finishing the archery practices Destan gave me. This made my mother think I was just very dedicated to the clothes I was washing. I was home at least an hour early today due to the JPs I'd gotten mixed up with.

"Got off early," I whispered, picking at the stitches of the blanket with my dirt-caked fingernails. And then, the inevitable occurred, and she forced down the quilt. Her lips parted in surprise, hand flying to her cheek as she appraised me and my not-so-ordinary appearance.

"My goodness...Raine..." she gasped, and I begrudgingly rose from my bed, heading to the mirror to see just how bad it was. "What did you do?" And before I could turn my face away, she grabbed my arm and made me look at her, her eyes reading over the crimes the JPs had painted on my forehead. Her voice shot instantly from the appalled whisper to an angry shout, "Theft? Trespassing? *Three* demerits?"

"Shh, shh, Gwen's still asleep..." I pleaded, wrapping Destan's scarf more securely around my face to hide it, and going out to the kitchen.

"When were you going to tell me you've been stealing again?" she demanded, following behind with surprising speed. "I saw the cider bottle Gwen had stashed under her bed, but I thought that'd be the end of it since you are actually doing something with your life now!"

"I know, Mom. This time it wasn't even really stealing, and I didn't know I couldn't be there—"

"Where?" she snapped.

"The woods, this meadow close to Starshade," I grumbled, setting my head on the table.

"Oh. So this is about that boy and those lessons you say he is giving you with your dad's old bow," my mom scoffed, sitting beside me. "You can only take your chance with the woods around town if you don't make your comings and goings a pattern, Raine. Your dad and I taught you this time and time again, so why are you getting caught now?"

Remaining silent, I continued letting my forehead rest on the cool kitchen table. After a few moments of the stony silence, my mom gave up, returning to the kitchen and trying to light the gas stove so she could cook. It clicked and clicked until finally a flame burst out, and she set a pot down onto the burner.

"Skye called the house today," she said softly. I lifted my eyes so I could see her; how her mouth was set in a disapproving line and she plucked the seeds from a little jar with such care. And then she groaned, putting down the seeds and rubbing her forehead. "He called to ask if you were still coming to his party next week, and also that he was coming down to Underbrush after work today to see you."

Now I sat up completely straight. "Wait, what? As in *today* today?"

"And now you have that paint all over you that you very well know won't come off at least after a few sleeps and washes, so it is almost in my right mind to just call and cancel," she answered, drumming her fingers on the counter. I could almost see her decision volleying back and forth from her head to her heart, and then back and forth again.

I twiddled my thumbs, muttering, "That's probably a good idea. He won't get a very good impression from a girl wearing her crime all over her face." And then, a devious thought struck me. *Or maybe that's why he should see me. So he gives up and I won't have to go on with this courting business or go to that awful sounding cotillion.* But that single spark of hope was snuffed as I heard Gwen whimper in her sleep, and I was suddenly reminded of where she would be taken if we couldn't pay the coming tax. If I didn't marry Skye and didn't get the money to pay the tax, if I didn't fall in love with him or at least go so far as to liking him enough.

"You *will* be seeing him tomorrow, no matter if it takes us all night, and blood and tears to get it off." My mom rubbed her hands together, tugging out the jammed kitchen drawer and picking through for whatever herb she needed next. "I'm not having you shame yourself and your family in front of the man you need to marry. I've got a recipe for getting that crap off. It'll sting and the imprints will still all be there til' they decide to fade, but I'm not putting our future in jeopardy because you decided to do something stupid."

I picked at the chipped edge of the table, wondering if I had been stupid after all. I had no idea where Destan and Irene had gone. What if we'd all just gotten away and had hidden somewhere together? It would be a lot more suspicious and we would have had to change our meeting place, but at least my face wouldn't have been painted completely black with *thief* and *trespasser* inked in with a rust colour; a stronger dye that would soak in and remain after all of the black was scraped off.

The thing about probation paint— it is exactly what it is named, you are officially on probation from not just a snoopy JP like 21996, but the entire fleet of police for your level. Any misconduct no matter how minor, and you are locked up in one of those scary rooms I'd come across at Peak on my interview day. I don't know, maybe not exactly as bad as that bizarre snake torture chamber, but still I would be taken away and holed up where I couldn't see Gwen or my friends or anyone for at least ten years. I would be betraying Destan and leaving him to handle hiding a spy all on his own.

This was the first time I'd gotten it, surprisingly. Being so thin and small and quiet, I was usually able to hide well and skip punishment, getting away with taking food or setting booby traps where I knew JPs would stumble into them. I'd been ignoring the minor laws in Underbrush for at least half of my life now, so the probation paint I received today was well overdue in the grand scheme of things. I'd known some boys in school who'd gotten it for scuffling with each other too much, and not only did they look frightening with it on, but everyone in Underbrush was forced to ignore them while the paint lasted. Once it came off, they still complained that their faces stung with the irritating effects of the stuff.

My mom cleared her throat. "Go to your room for now. No supper tonight, maybe not tomorrow, depending on how much you can get off before your date with Skye. And if the date ends well." She wouldn't look at me, and this time her hands weren't even busy. Her brew was trying to boil on the stove, and from the creaking of the cot coming from my bedroom, Gwen was trying to sleep through all of the conversation.

I got up and she gave me the bowl of herbs and minerals she'd mixed with water. It smelled strongly of vinegar and rubbing alcohol, with a hint of marigold. I swirled it around a little. "Okay. I'm sorry, Mom."

She patted my shoulder, facing away from me. "Just get it off," she said.

I shivered, pressing the bundle of snow to my cheeks and feeling the relief from the burning fade slowly only to be replaced pain from the cold. I snuggled into Gwen, who had come over to my side and laid down when she heard me crying out from having to scrub and scrub at the probation paint. I still had patches of black around my eyes, where my skin had been just too tender to put the harsh mixture my mom had made, and I couldn't tell if I'd lightened any of the writing on my forehead.

Shaking, I tried to absorb some warmth from my sister, pressing myself against her and hugging her close. Gwen hummed, nuzzling me with her nose and letting herself be used as a space heater. As I held her and set down the snow pack, I tried to focus my mind on falling asleep, on not thinking of anything at all, so I could finally rest.

The brief instant of thoughtless calm ended the moment I heard the tap on my window. I ignored it at first, opening my eyes and staring into the bush of my sister's black curls, thinking I'd probably imagined the sound. But then it came again—*tap... tap...*faint as anything, but insistent as a woodpecker beating against a tree.

I swallowed, slowly sliding off the cot and moving to the back wall, stepping on the pile of sketchbooks I had placed under it so that I could see out. As my eyes rose above the metal sill, I found myself staring at two moons, big and silver and full of craters. With a yelp, I fell, the sketchbooks spilling out beneath me as I hit the floor. I rubbed my tailbone, wincing and immediately going back up on tiptoe to make sense of what I'd seen. This time when I looked out, I realized that they hadn't been two moons at all, but a pair of wide, silver eyes, now much smaller since the owner of these eyes had moved back from the window and was busy trying to keep his balance on the stack of crates outside.

With a gasp of both relief and surprise, I pushed at the glass, sliding the window frame to the side and gripping the sill, shocked at how cold it was outside. "Destan?" I hissed, poking my head out. "Destan, is Irene here? What happened? Are you all right?"

"Shh, shh, there's no time, Bluehead," he whispered, looking left and right, pushing down on his red beanie and then looking at me seriously. "You need to come out here, now. It's urgent."

"Is Irene okay? No one saw you two, right?" I asked, heart speeding up fearfully.

"No, we're good with that, just..." He bit his lip, increasingly nervous looking. "Yeah, she's in a bit of trouble again. There's just something you gotta see."

I gulped, going down from my toes and looking at Gwen. She was perfectly awake, eyes gazing at me accusingly. She knew that I was going to leave even before I did. I looked out only once more; just letting my eyes rise above the bottom of the window. "I'll be out in two minutes. Do I need to bring anything?" I asked.

He shrugged. "Just yourself and your bow. I'll wait near the front."

I pulled on another two sweaters and a pair of jeans over my leggings, searching my desk in the dark for my red ribbon. Once I found it, I tied up my hair, kissing Gwen on the forehead and sneaking back into the kitchen. The house was dark and sleeping, chilly now that the fire had been out for a few hours. I stuck my feet into my boots, tapping the toes on the floor ever so gently to get my feet in more snugly, and I took up my tool belt and archery stuff.

If I leave the house now, I thought, *Mom will kill me, no doubt about it.* I closed the door quietly, jumping down from the porch without even touching the steps. *But I can't stay, he needs me.*

Destan came out from the shadows, offering his hand to

me. "Come on," he said, his rough voice breaking the silence of midnight.

I didn't hesitate, taking his hand and running beside him, letting him guide us. We disappeared from the street after a couple of strides, melting into the alley, and then into the forest easy as if we were made of smoke. Everything looked so black ahead of us, I couldn't understand how Destan could possibly see to avoid the trees and roots sprawling from the ground. But I soon realized we were not running in the direction of the meadow or even the spread of woods, rather the ground beneath my feet grew increasingly steeper and rockier, making my feet stumble and thighs ache from having to suddenly run uphill.

We stopped after about ten minutes, catching our breath and wiping our brows. Destan motioned upwards with a lazy wave of his hand. "We gotta go up this tree. About halfway up there is a cliff landing to jump to."

"Is this where you two went when the JPs came?" I asked.

He nodded. "Yes. Irene is inside."

I craned my neck to look up. "Inside where?"

Destan pushed aside the long fluffy pine branches and found his footing on the tree, sighing, "I'll show you. Follow me."

I ducked under the pine needles, searching for a good finger-hold. I found a sturdy branch and pulled myself up, placing my feet on some lower bows. Destan was climbing slowly enough for me to follow his path, and I put my hands over where I'd last seen his boots. Then he paused, moving toward the trunk so that I could join his side. I held onto his arm for balance, and he pointed to the rock face a few feet away. "There's a ledge. You can't see it from here, but you have to trust me— I've climbed in and out of there twice now," he said.

My stomach turned anxiously, but I nodded. "A-alright. Are...are you going first?"

"Yeah," he said, edging to the other side of me, and jumping without another moment of hesitation. For a moment I was paralyzed with fear, scared I'd hear the thump of his body smashing into the ground, and that would be that. Rather, I heard a grunt, and from the cliff landing, he pushed aside the branch blocking my view.

"I'm here, grab my hand and jump."

I grabbed it, holding my breath and hoping I could leap far enough with my heavy toolbelt and archery bow and quiver hanging off of me. Airborne for only a split second, I felt strong arms encase me and lead me safely back to earth, or in this case, rock. I wobbled in my boots, Destan and I holding tight to each other as we gazed out above the trees and then glanced back at the door hewn into the mountainside.

Confused, I asked him, "But...how is there...?"

"You'll see. It's unbelievable, Raine, just completely unbelievable," he said in a rush, edging along the ledge and then leaning against the door. The stone groaned against his weight, and slid to the side grudgingly. I pushed against it as well, trying to have it slide aside faster. Once the chink between the wall and door was big enough for us to slip through, we went inside and were shocked by a sudden heat thick and burning in the air.

The dark was less black and more orange now, and everything smelled of smoke. Not the kind of filthy, chemical-tainted smoke I'd get engulfed in when I'd ride through Canopia, but a smoke so thick and earthy and dense that it swelled in my chest and nested there. I glanced around blindly, only making out the hard walls of rock and stalactites dripping with water above us. It was so hard to breathe in the hot air.

"Is something burning?" I asked.

"Not exactly." Destan's figure was hardly discernible; his shadow more formed than his body appeared to be. He took my hand safely in his, and together we began to walk down the tunnel, our boots crunching over the broken rock. It became brighter and brighter, everything rimmed in gold as we approached where the tunnel opened on the other end.

As soon as I stepped out, I was hit by a sudden wave of stale, bitter smoke, like the breath of a dragon. I backtracked, covering my eyes and trying to breathe through my scarf only. From where I stood, I could see that all of Thgindim, from the Peak to the Base beneath us, was entirely hollowed out. Towers and towers of dark metal, webs of truss bridges and chains, mazes of smoking steel vents, were branching out from the mountain walls and terraces here and there, crisscrossing above us and disappearing into the darkness above that seemed to continue on forever.

Conveyor belts moved mechanically, rhythmically, carrying uniform metal objects, some looking like guns, others like clocks, and other tank-like contraptions so big that they moved sluggishly from one end to the other. Even more massive vehicles dangled from thick cables, many of them only half-built; their carefully constructed insides of gears and wires and engines on full display. The only source of light came from the scarlet lava heaving and churning at the bottom of Thgindim, kept contained in a pool made of the blackest metal I'd ever seen.

"What is this place? Destan what is all this?" I clutched my hands to my chest, having to scream over the roar of the heat and mechanical movement of the factory so that Destan could hear me.

His eyes were fierce and bright in the firelight. "It's what Irene said we'd find," he yelled back. He unbuttoned his coat, stifled by the heat. "Or, at least, what she expected."

Dazed, I walked along the ledge, which gradually evolved from the crudely hewn rock we'd started on, into a steel crossing area with handrails and carefully crafted steps leading to different levels of construction. My brain wasn't working properly. I couldn't think, not even a quick thought, not even a single word of what this could mean or how it affected anything. I simply peeled off my extra layers as the hotness became too much, leaving me only in my sleeveless undershirt. I kept walking behind Destan with my eyes combing over every inch of the terrifying place.

"Where…where is Irene?" I asked.

"She's stuck," he said gravely. "As soon as we'd made it in here and had inklings of what this could maybe mean, she just took off limping! Probably completely undoing all the setting of her leg we've been working on, and even though I could keep up with her fine and restrain her, she made a jump for this lift sort of thing." Destan reached up at a lever drilled into the wall, and cranked it down, standing back as the chains on the floor next it started unwinding and being pulled taut by some invisible force.

"She was trying to get to some sort of office she claimed was floating right in the middle of the mountain. I don't know, Raine. She sounded like she'd damned lost her mind," he sighed, rubbing his face and taking off his beanie. He shook his sweaty curls out, the wild cream-coloured corkscrews pointing out in fifty different directions. I pretended not to notice the way his Adam's apple bobbed when he saw me only in the thin short-sleeved undershirt, and I crossed my arms across my chest, worried he might be able to see the outline of my brassiere through the cotton fabric. Appearing unfazed, he stuck the hat in his back pocket and helped me tie my long bangs back with the ribbon wrapped around my head. He sighed again. "All I know is that Irene went up, and then the lift came down without her."

I gasped. "Is anyone else in here?"

He puffed up his cheeks and blew out some air. "Definitely. I'm pretty certain we found an entrance that isn't really an entrance though. Like it was meant for trash disposal or something, so I haven't seen anybody around here yet."

"Thgindim is a few miles tall though..." I murmured, looking up and seeing the first glimpse of the bottom of the lift come towards us. It wasn't even the size of my pinky nail.

"Not to mention more than a few miles just going around one level," he added, extending his arm and moving it across where we assumed the perimeter of the big cavern must be. "This place is crazy huge. As big as Underbrush, if all the trees were cut down and we had miles up of sky."

We could now hear the lift screeching down to us. It was

150

different than the one I'd taken from Canopia for my Peak interview. Instead of wire netting and the lever inside the lift, this lift was completely open air, just a platform that rose and fell when commanded by the lever where we stood. It came shooting down with such velocity that it landed with a deafening crash, undamaged, but trembling from the force. I nervously touched Destan's shoulder. "Are you sure this is meant for people to ride?"

He glanced behind him at me, his previously worry-stricken face now brightened by a mischievous half-smile. "I am quite sure this is definitely meant for everything other than people." His theory was practically proven as I nervously looked about the mountain interior and saw similar lifts loaded up with bundles of steel beams and crates of JP armor scrap.

"Great..." I whispered, reluctant to set foot on the worn out thing at all. Destan was bent over, holding onto the side rail with one hand, his other gripping his longbow. I joined his side, taking off my fingerless gloves to make sure I got a firm enough hold on the bar, and then I felt his warm hand cover mine protectively.

"Ready to fly, Bluehead?" I was suddenly reminded of the first time he'd taken me riding on Siri when I'd first found him in the meadow. It felt like a century ago.

I shook my head, opening my eyes that had been scrunched closed in anticipation."Nope, but let's do it, Beaniehead."

Destan rolled his eyes. "*Beaniehead...*"

And then with his free arm, he reached out toward the lever with his longbow and whacked the long metal handle like a hammer. It took a couple hits to get it to activate the chains and begin to carry us upward. The moment he made the final hit, we shot up with a jolt, my stomach seeming to fly straight up my throat and then ricochet around my ribs as we increased speed and the unsteady lift shifted back and forth. My knees buckled beneath me without warning, my entire body suddenly forced down against the rail I'd been planning to hold onto, and then went from being smushed uncomfortably against the rail, to getting face-planted against the scratched up metal floor. His hand covering mine was now pressing down so tightly it hurt, and then it slid down and he too was forced onto the floor, both of us on our backs and unable to even open our lips to release the terrified screams bursting inside of us. I could feel the skin on my face being pulling back from the force, sticking tightly to my skull by what felt like the weight of the entire universe acting against us. I couldn't move my limbs from the spread-eagle position they were forced into, and the only conceivable thought running through my head was one intelligible word, *Destan, Destan, Destan, Destan.* I couldn't turn my face to look at him and see if he was alive, if he could still breathe because I felt like my lungs were using all of their might just to keep pumping under all this pressure and the faster we went, the faster I seemed to need to breathe and the slower I could catch my breath.

The most alarming thing was that we just kept going and going. Up, up, all black, the only distinguishable things around us were the landings we flew past, making it through the square cutout in the platform that came every ten seconds or so, but never once slowing. Where would we stop? *How* would we stop; if the lever that controlled it was on a wall now at least a mile below us or at a rest stop where no one was waiting for us? What if someone was waiting for us, a JP who would have our heads the minute we stepped off?

Now in a violent panic, I didn't even use my strength to breathe anymore. I clenched all of my muscles and dragged myself closer and closer to the edge of the lift platform, feeling every nerve of me get tugged in the opposite direction. Then I took a break, concentrating on moving my hand to Destan's. If I could just reach his fingers without having my fingers break under the pressure in the meantime. I waited and waited to feel my skin touch skin and not warm and rigid metal, and as soon as my power gave out, I felt him slide his own to mine. He even

152

managed to grasp my wrist tightly, turning our arms so that I could hold his just as securely.

I kicked out my legs in a sudden movement, my foot halfway hanging off now, almost enough to suck me over the edge. Head spinning from lack of good air, I put the rest of my will into jolting myself off in only a few kicks so that I wouldn't have bones broken one by one. Destan helped, pitting his weight against mine, sending me off the platform, my entire body feeling a thousand pounds heavier as suddenly it was just me against the will of gravity, and if it hadn't been for Destan rolling onto his stomach and clamping both of his hands around my wrists so that I hung off the lift, I would have been sucked down to a death in a bubbling pool of lava.

Agony ripped through me, my arms straining in their sockets as he kept hold of me, and then as we came close to a platform, I acted on instinct, letting go from his grip and slamming onto the metal landing as he and the lift continued up. Every bone quaking and feeling cracked in seven different ways, I struggled over to the wall, heaving myself onto the lever to force it down, hearing a great squeal as the handle slammed against the rock. The chains once moving in a rapid blur, carrying Destan up, pulled taut and still.

On my knees, gasping for air and coughing so hard I thought my lungs would come out of my throat, I gazed upward at the small silver square that was the unmoving lift, and then felt my eyes roll back, a thick tiredness tipping me into an uneasy unconsciousness.

chapter sixteen

I was walking through the trees at dawn, my bow so tiny that I could carry the little thing in my palm. The arrows were holding my bangs back like hairpins, but when I touched the back of my head I felt that hardly any hair was there at all, just a short prickly fuzz, and when I withdrew my fingers they were black and covered in ink.

"Raine...."

A tap on my shoulder, a girlish giggle and singsong whisper into my ear. But as I spun around, no one was there, not even a bird that I thought maybe could have perched on my shoulder to speak with me.

"Goodbye, Raine."

Two hands this time, gripping my shoulder with scalding hot palms, the voice deep and robotic. They forced me to my knees, and I looked up, frightened, as a JP in glistening black armor rose up from the ground, from a pool of ink growing like grass. He put a gun to his helmet with one hand, and a gun at me with the other. I screamed, seeing the bullet come out the size of a dinner plate, covered in flaming numbers and flying toward my eyes. The bullet he'd shot at himself drilled a hole through the thick, dark glass with a sickening screech, and blood came pouring out thickly, melting his armor, lava gobbling up the ground—

"RAINE!"

I awoke with a wheeze, forced back too quickly into the sweltering, deafening heat and noise of Thgindim's belly. Sitting up with limbs loose as jelly, I breathed heavily, unable to see anything through the smoky film settling over everything. A warm hand touched my cheek and I cried out in surprise, comforted abruptly as I saw that the hand belonged to no one other than my friend, Destan. He had his arm around my shoulders, keeping me from lying back down on the metal landing. I was suddenly made aware that I was draped across his lap, my head leaned against his chest, the soft sweater fibers pleasant against my chapped and stinging cheeks.

"D-Destan? Destan, what happened?" I asked weakly. He eased me up to sit on my own, his arm remaining behind my back for support.

"I just made it down a little while ago, did something hit you?" he asked, concern streaking his features. His fingers hovered lightly over my cheeks and forehead where I knew he could now see the harsh imprints of the leftover probation paint on my face.

I shook my head, nauseous and dizzy from the heat still clogging up the whole place. "No, no, it's from probation paint…I think it just got too hot and all of that speed just sort of knocked me out…" I pinched the bridge of my nose as a headache blazed through me, lingering and throbbing like the brain freeze I used to from eating too much snow when I was a kid.

Destan assisted me to my feet, gripping my arms securely to make sure I wouldn't topple over again. He frowned, "You got quadruple P'd so that our cover wouldn't be blown."

'Quadruple P'd' meaning 'Police-Probation-Paint-

155

Punishment.' I shrugged, looking at my boots and regretting the extra layer of socks I had put on for this late-night expedition. Destan knocked my shoulder with his in a friendly manner, whispering, "You really are brave, aren't you, Bluehead?"

Feeling awkward and self-conscious about getting that sort of recognition from the boy I fearfully realized I was growing quite attached to, I just shrugged again. I was about to swing my bangs in front of my face to hide, but before I could make a move, Destan anticipated it, sliding his hand under the thick blue curtain and pressing it back against my scalp with a grin. "I knew you were going to do that if I said that," he laughed, letting them fall back down after a few seconds, and then putting his hands on his hips. "But it needs to be said. You saved all of our necks from something way worse. Not to mention you became some sort of flying beast and managed to stop that suicide lift." He looked up at the platform hoisted a good fifty feet above us and whistled.

*He climbed down all the way from up there to reach me? Did he go down those chains? They're so rusty, his hands must be raw...*I thought. My eyes traveled over him, taking in the freshly scraped hands that had carried him to me. Destan looked at me, and this time I didn't immediately chicken out and avoid his ghostly grey eyes. I wanted so badly to know what I looked like to him, what was different or better or worse than what I thought I knew of myself. But the stare was getting too intimate, I felt drawn to come closer to him with every passing second, felt my heart-rate jump faster and faster in a frantic sort of beating, and so before I could give in to any of these increasingly affectionate and bewildering feelings, I cleared my throat, tucking sweaty strands of hair behind my ear and bending down to pick up my bow.

"So, now that we're both here, how are we going to get to Irene?" I asked, aiming to return to the rescue mission's urgent pace, and leave the slow thickness of conversation.

Destan turned on his heel, walking to the edge of this lift-landing station and taking hold of the guardrail, peering down into the black depths of the mountain. "We fortunately only missed the center room where she was aiming for by only four stations," he said, and I bristled at his use of *fortunately*.

"Four docking stations? There's at least a hundred feet between each one!" I said, coming to his side and feeling my stomach lurch at how far below that little place was. I hadn't been able to see it clearly before, but amidst the assembly lines and conveyor belts of products, a glass watch-room of sorts hovered directly in the center of the inside of the mountain. It was at the halfway mark of Thgindim itself, and suspended in the middle by braided cables extending out from each corner where the glass walls connected. The only way I could assess how an actual worker would make it in there was if they had something to fly on to get there, or that there was a staircase or bridge that was out of my frame of vision.

"I can't see if she's in there or not," Destan murmured, squinting his eyes and gritting his teeth in yearning to make out what lay behind the frosted glass.

"Me, neither," I sighed, tapping the guardrail thoughtfully. "Did she say why that place was so important? Why she needed to get there?"

"No idea. All she said before running off was that it'd give her proof," he replied, leaning his chin on his hand, both of us lost in contemplation of what to do next.

I tried to replay the story he'd told me. So, they entered this hot and extremely vast factory, which produces what appeared to be big weapons and specialized armor and vehicles of some sort; the stuff that the Canopia factories didn't have room for. And then even with herself literally crying out in pain and limping unstably to the lift, she shot up somehow without Destan activating the lever, so she must've thrown a heavy object at it or something to force it down. Then she went up, and the lift came down without her. The questions now were: how high did she actually go? Why did the lift come back down on its own? Did she get off all right?

I turned to Destan, trying to clarify. "You said she was stuck. Does that mean you somewhat know what situation she's in or were you just guessing?"

"I heard her calling out to me, very faintly, but at least that meant she wasn't too high up," he explained. "All she said was that she was stuck, and to get you, so I did just that. She couldn't hear me when I tried to answer; she obviously knows how to yell better than me…"

"Okay, well assuming she's still conscious, that must mean she landed *somewhere*. If she'd just flown off, there'd be no way she'd be okay enough to call for help," I said.

Destan opened his mouth to answer, but just then there was a whirring, increasing in volume until it became a roar. Big doors camouflaged with the mountain rock slid apart, about thirty JPs or men of similar looks marching out in rows, directed by a black-robed man in the rear, shouting commands. I couldn't distinguish what was being said since they were spilling out a good seven platforms below us. Destan and I ducked down by the railing, glad to have taken off our hats and scarves a while ago so that we wouldn't stick out like red sore thumbs among the dark shades of grey and black.

The JPs broke up into pairs, climbing into small carts that ran across a bridge and into a tunnel on the other side. Two other tracks diverted off the main one and continued down in patterns I couldn't discern because the rising heat hurt my eyes to stare down too long. The man in the black robe remained on the platform by himself, arms behind his back, apparently bald head shiny in the lava light. "Wait a minute…" I said, putting my head between the widely spaced bars of the guardrail and trying to see closer. And then as I leaned a little too forward, I knocked a hunk of rock off the edge of the platform and it fell down, down, until it conked right on the robed man's bald head. The man whipped around in surprise, a hand on his head, and then suddenly his piercing black eyes shot to where we were perched.

"Shit!" Destan gasped, grabbing me and yanking us away

from the railing and out of sight. I clung to his arm, not daring to breathe, beads of sweat trailing from my forehead and down the

tip of my nose. I moved only a few inches forward, yearning to see when the man might decide to walk away. He was still rubbing his head, but now was standing closer to a shuttle, knocking with one hand on the door. It opened, he slipped inside, and with him gone, I slumped back into Destan, exhaling loudly in relief.

I closed my eyes, and no longer had I tried for a moment of peace that a thought struck me. "This is the second time we're risking our lives for a Fluxarian," I whispered, dumbfounded at my own words.

He pursed his lips, rubbing the nearly untraceable shadow of hair that went around his mouth and along his jaw. Destan replied softly back to me, "Last time we didn't know, though. We just thought she was a girl."

We sat, slouched in silence, now waiting to see who would make the decision either to abandon the rescue mission altogether and escape the way we'd come, or figure out how to get to the glass room for the spy who still hadn't shown substantial proof against us, the spy who might not even be alive anymore. I gulped, feeling strangely cold in the once sweltering hall. *It would wipe my slate clean*, I thought, *There's no way this could be traced back to us. Destan and I could go back to archery and wolf rides and make the most of what time I have left before getting married off and sent to Starshade. It would be as if Irene hadn't even come.* The thoughts made my heart race in a neither positive nor negative state of excitement, simply just the rapid response to something so suddenly profound.

Destan looked at me, eyes big and imploring. "What do you want to do?"

I bit my lip, feeling the sting of the probation paint still caked on in places and the bruises I'd earned all along my right side from my rough landing. *You didn't get this beat up for nothing*, a more tender voice said in my head, beginning the steady flow of adrenaline to pump through me like caffeine. *This is important. You know it is.*

I put my hands on the warm metal floor and pushed myself up to my feet. Striding calmly over to the rail and looking out, I saw the coast was clear for us to go either way. I looked back at Destan over my shoulder, answering steadily, "We've got to get her. We promised her we'd give her a chance to find proof."

A small, sly grin lit up Destan's face. "I was hoping you'd think so."

chapter seventeen

"As your extremely experienced instructor, I trust your skills at something like this, at this point in your archery training," he said in a mockingly pompous voice, patting me encouragingly on the shoulder as he eased himself off of the landing and onto one of the thick, circular cables.

My brain was exploding with horrible images of him slipping off, and before his hand left the metal, I said, in a squeak of a voice, "Don't. Die. Destan. I mean it."

He held up my tool belt with a reassuring smile. I'd removed the water gourd and dagger, leaving just the inch-thick, three feet long strip of supple cattle leather I'd stolen from a warehouse a few years ago. Destan wrapped it under the cable, holding each end of the belt and sliding it down so that he was beginning to lay belly down on it. I tentatively leaned forward, securing his hands better to the belt with my red hair ribbon wound around them both and then tied. He tested the hold, and then nodded, making to move ahead.

The moment his feet left the platform, I could already sense the strain suddenly put on his body to keep from flipping to the cable's underside. He moved like an inchworm, knees scrunching in and out while his hands kept a rhythmic motion of going forward. I noticed that with every readjustment of his position, he was sliding more quickly, seeming less like he was getting the hang of it and more like he was losing control over the speed down the increasingly steep cable. Destan was past another platform, in the midst of sliding a full six feet down too quickly, when the toe of his boot slipped off the coil of the cable. Hearing him gasp from over a hundred feet below me, I stood jumped anxiously over to the guardrail, leaning so far over that were on tiptoe. He'd flipped over so that he was clinging to the underbelly of the cable, shooting down it like the first bead threaded on a necklace.

I opened my mouth in panic to call for him and ask if he was okay, but then grit my teeth together again when I remembered we were not the only people in here by far, and that even if he could hear me, he wouldn't be able to answer with so much to focus on at the moment. Stiff with impatience, I clutched the rail with white knuckles, waiting for him to emerge out of the smoke on the roof of the glass room. My throat hurt from breathing so hard, and without my ribbon my hair draped down my back, scratchy and thick, making me sweat.

"Please," I whispered, lip trembling as the room's roof remained shrouded in smoke and clear of the woodcarver's apprentice. I held my breath, making a pact with myself not to take another until I saw him off of the cable and alive. *Seven, eight, nine, ten,* the seconds were getting longer, my eyes stinging in the effort to stay open without blinking.

And then I heard a few bars of music from a flute, and as I blinked a few times and caught my breath, a hand waved from out of the smoke, then an arm. Sent into action, I found the arrow I'd tied to some spare chain I'd found, and sank into my anchor, straightening the level of my arrow against the bridge of my bow and pulling the string back, making sure to touch it to the tip of my nose.

Not sparing a thought, I released the arrow, watching it fly at that odd angle of the cable and toward the glass room; losing speed and the perfect height as it came close to the smoke. The chain was really weighing it down. I'd never shot an arrow with something connected to the end, and already I was seeing how it changed just about everything about the accuracy of my shot. I backed away so that the chain could unfurl smoothly, and I helped feed it over the side of the platform so that it might not slow the arrow down any more than it was already.

I saw Destan run out from the smoke, doing a quick jump in the air to catch the arrow in his fist. When I saw his pinky and ring finger manage to snatch the feather just in time, I yelped joyfully, clapping my hands together and trying to restrain my joy at seeing that the arrow had reached him after all.

Now comes the scarier part, I thought despairingly, bending down to pick up the end of the chain and tie some of it in a thick knot. The tar coating it slimed over my fingers as I tried to work the knot tighter, my thoughts humming and humming. *What time is it? How long until Mom and Gwen wake up and realize I'm gone?*

I gripped the chain tightly in my sweat-slick fist, waiting until Destan gave the thumbs up that he'd secured it. Then, seeing him hoist up his fist signaling me to go, I hopped onto the knot in the chain, my boots on either side, and with a gasp I swung from the platform and across the cavernous hall of smoke and metal.

The terror and excitement was split evenly inside me, I both was silenced by the thoughts that I'd fall or perish right in the hot air, and silenced by the exhilaration of soaring. I was weightless and small. Wind rushed past me and I swung perfectly in between the rows of conveyor belts and chains. I felt secure standing on the knot with my hands plastered around the chain and knees tucked stiffly around it, my cheek tucked close to the warm metal links, my eyes wide open to see everything rushing by.

It felt like I'd had a lifetime in the air, when suddenly time returned to its original speed and I plunged towards the glass room, bound on slamming against the wall if I didn't get off soon.

"Let go!" Destan yelled at me, running on the roof as I approached closer and closer.

I obeyed, unclamping my hands from the chain and jumping from the knot I'd tied for my feet to balance on. I flew for only a few seconds before hitting hard into Destan. He caught me safely in his arms and crashed down onto the roof. We rolled together, groaning, until he jut out his boot and stopped us on the edge of the building.

Painting and stumbling to our feet, we took each other's hands, dashing instantly toward the stairwell hatch on one end of the building. The rubber soles of our boots were so worn that they would no longer squeak on the metal steps, but each footstep made an audible *thud* that would surely alert anyone who happened to be in there.

The stairs from the roof led down into what appeared to be a lounge. Lockers lined the back wall and JP helmets and weapons hung from hooks on the wall adjacent. There were rows of soft vinyl chairs facing out at the two grand glass walls, and on a couple end tables there were still glasses of ambrosia wine sitting out, the drink gone lukewarm and still. A big white crate with cold steam blasting from the bottom was the final piece of this odd place. I tiptoed over to it, eyeing the handle curiously. *A cabinet of sorts? Maybe one of those fancy coolers I'd seen in the JP cafe back home?*

"Raine, I don't see her. Let's try one of the floors below," Destan urged me, making his way to the next set of stairs. But the white glass of this cabinet was moving, shaking ever so slightly, and it had some sort of brownish looking thing inside of it running along the glass, tracing lines in the condensation from the inside.

"Destan…" I whispered, torn between leaving whatever it was in there, and opening it to see what was inside. I took a cautious step back, bumping into Destan who now was peering at the cooler thing as well. He cocked his head to the side, eyes darting from line to line as the brown thing moved shakily across the glass.

"Are those…letters?" he murmured, and I squinted at the glass, suddenly making sense of the swirls and shapes and feeling a rush of horror overcome me.

I didn't let her finish tracing the words with her finger. I yanked at the handle, twisting a little knob with my other hand and forcing the door open. A blast of wintry air slapped into us and Destan and I came face to face with the spy herself, frost lacy all over her forehead and dotting her jet black hair. She stumbled forward, tear tracks frozen under her eyes, and some snot visible and just as frozen beneath her wide nostrils. She breathed out clouds of steam. "Y-you f-f-found m-m-me," she wheezed, hanging onto our arms as we helped her out of the cooler.

"Did someone put you in there?" Destan gasped, brushing the snow out of her hair and blowing at the frost on her face to help it melt.

Irene shivered, shaking her head and gasping for air. "N-no. H-h-i-d-ding."

I inhaled sharply, "Is someone in here? Police?"

She shook her head again, flakes of snow flurrying from her hair and gathering on the navy carpeted floor. Wiping away her defrosting mucus with the back of her hand, she said, "Not any-m-m-more. Saw them t-t-ake off some t-time ag-g-go."

I took the sweaters I'd shed due to it being so hot everywhere else outside and pulled one after the other over her head. "Soon you will be overheated," I said, pulling her arms through the sleeves, "but for now this'll help you defrost."

Her head poked through the turtle neck hole and she bowed deeply. "I am eternally g-gratef-f-ul. Doubly eternally grateful n-n-ow."

Destan put an arm around her shoulders, leading her carefully over to the next set of steps. Every movement made her inhale more sharply, wince more profoundly, and I was frightened to see that her abdomen was bleeding again. She must've jounced the fractured rib out of healing and now it had cut something. I gulped, swallowing my unease and joining Destan in helping Irene down the next stairwell.

This second floor was vastly different from the third. Rather than carpet, the ground was tiled with thick black metal diamonds, and rather than lockers, chairs, and freezers, we came face to face with a myriad of extravagant machines. Taking up the entire length of each of the four walls were big blinking screens of mountain surveillance; staticky images flickering from level to level. At one point it even displayed the main Underbrush square where Careers clumped together, and I saw Jun shuffling new delivery schedules at her front counter in great detail. The resolution the cameras provided was so intensely sensitive and accurate that as I came closer I could see how her curls waved at the side of her face, how the lines at her eyes crinkled in concentration as she tried to work an ancient stapler

166

on the thick piles of paper.

"This is…creepy," Destan whispered, touching a calloused finger to a screen where it showcased even incredibly deep parts of the outlying woods. My heart beat faster as I wondered if someone had been able to see the meadow with Irene and us for weeks now. But watching the screens go through their full cycles of areas, we could all breathe easy seeing that our meadow hadn't yet been hooked up to whatever security device this was.

Beneath each of the screens were control boards thorned with thousands of switches and knobs poking up in all different colours, labeled with numbers and some symbols I couldn't decipher even after staring at them for a good minute or so. Destan was busy circling the contraption in the center of the room: a wire cylindrical tower a few feet tall topped off by a huge glass dome. Cables and electrical wires ran in between the netting of the metal and disappeared into the floor below.

"Did you…have you seen this before, Irene?" I asked nervously, removing my arm from her shoulder so that she could sit on one of the stools surrounding a control desk.

"No, I haven't," she replied, her pink lips parted in an equal amount of shock as the rest of us. But then she cleared her throat, looked at me. "I didn't get down here before. But I can't say how long it might be until those creepers come back, so if you'll let me, may I try to scrape up some of that evidence you wanted? Or is this enough?"

I bit my lip. "We don't know what any of this stuff does—"

Destan sneezed, the room growled, and me and Irene's heads swiveled to see Destan by one of the control boards, his index finger just over one of the buttons. He looked at us in alarm, stepping back, hurriedly saying, "I…I didn't mean to…shit, shit, shit, shit…"

"Wait!" Irene gasped, pointing crookedly with her bandaged fingers at one of the screens. "Look!"

It had gone blank, the surveillance of various towns gone now, replaced by an ever increasing array of shots of the mountain wall, completely in colour. Brown rocks, darker brown rocks, rocks with moss over them, multiplying and multiplying into a brown-green-grey grid until Destan hesitantly jabbed at the button again, making the computer or whatever it was stop producing these images and focus in on a segment of the wooded mountain. By the looks of the smoothed stone, this was probably on Canopia or Emergent, a good while away from any of the towns. Two JPs had their masks off and seemed to be slowly trying to remove each other's armor, bringing their mouths together again and again hungrily.

"Okay, *what* is going on?" Irene said, raising an eyebrow, and Destan cautiously just touched that same button again, causing the tower and dome in the center of the room to come alive.

It produced a ghostly image of the JPs and the area around them, making them nothing but wavering black and white figures. Parts of the mountain rock were illuminated in red, labeled with numbers and those symbols on the control board. I came to Destan's side, attempting to make sense of this odd thing. Glancing from the image in the dome, and then back to the control board, I slowly tapped on a button labeled with a figure eight symbol.

Every screen in the room suddenly lit up with different angles of the same shot of the JPs attempting to have a romantic escapade and the trees and mountain wall. The image floating in the center of the dome brightened, the red marked spots with the figure eight turning green as those rocks and trees in the area began to tremble. Then the marked areas began to fall toward the men silently, and as they fell there was a crashing sound above us, and little bits of rock sprinkled down from miles up onto the roof.

I watched as the JPs scrambled with their helmets, dashing out of sight as the area became a rockalanche danger zone, and I backed away, horrified at what I just caused to happen. "That's…that's not possible. How can I…did I do that?"

"Raine."

Feeling light-headed with shock, I turned to Destan, who was at a control board across the room. Irene was busy limping over, and I seized her hand, helping her across as we both came to see what he was looking at so intently.

Now that I was closer, I could see that on the screen above him were what appeared to be models of vehicles of some kind, big and black, without wheels and only with great wings and weapons secured beneath like an extra set of claws. I gulped, "The Fluxarian aircraft?"

Irene's quite audible sigh was lost in the clearing of Destan's throat as he pointed at the ship's logo. A big, threatening, white, *MC*.

Irene stood up a little straighter. "I wasn't gonna say it, but, hell…I told you so."

chapter eighteen

"It's not…you don't think it could be a replica of the Fluxarian ship, do you?" I asked quickly, head spinning. "I mean, could it be in response to the one they sent here? Like to fight back?"

Irene groaned, throwing her hands in the air in frustration. "There is no 'fighting back!' Don't you see they've been fooling you all along?"

Gravely, Destan shook his head. Then he rubbed his eyes, sighing loudly, "Well clearly, Bluehead, there is a shit ton that's been kept from us."

"Not to mention, sent at us," I added, envisioning that avalanche I'd made happen. I glanced at the control board beneath the airship, not daring to even try out this one, and then shut my eyes despairingly, walking away and pacing about the room. Destan was coming towards me, about to state the next step of action from here, when a subtle roaring sound came. Darting to the window, I saw one of those big shuttles the JPs and that guy had gotten into pull up by the door to this very room.

"Get down!" I ordered, voice just above a whisper, taking Destan and Irene's hands and making for the set of stairs. "Go, go, go…"

I heard the door to the control room floor open and JPs filed in as we thundered down what turned out to be the last set of stairs. The lowest level of the building was completely filled with a mess of wires and energy generators and hot machines making the room one big broiler. Together, the three of us sank back into the tangle of electric cables feeding up into the ceiling, vaguely reminded of the sensation of melting through the forest and the overhanging vines and branches. I watched my feet, careful not to undo any of the plugs from the generators they were attached to, and then froze completely as a set of footsteps pounded down toward us.

We crouched down, none of us daring to breathe. And the JP came, knelt, fiddled with one of the many metal boxes lying about, and then stood up, calling, "Sir, everything's in tip-top shape."

"Good," a silky voice replied, softer footsteps resounding around the basement as the man in the black robe who'd almost seen us on the docking station spoke. "Must have been carelessness on an officer's part to forget to shut down those programs. As you were, 30087."

Recognition struck me. "Sebastian Lao," I whispered automatically, receiving a warning squeeze on the wrist from Destan. *So, the Councilman from the elevator really is as nasty as he seemed,* I thought absently as the JP saluted and made for the stairwell.

"Yessir!" he cried, waiting for his boss to begin walking up to the control room before following obediently behind.

The men above continued with their noisemaking and trooping about, and at this rate I think we'd all guessed that they would be sticking around for quite a while. So, Destan scooched over to face us and whispered, "Okay, so any ideas?"

You don't have one? I felt compelled to ask, usually so certain that he would have thought of one of his genius plans by now. But by the looks exchanged between us, even Fluxaria's most notorious spy and Thgindim's blue-haired mischief-maker were drawing a blank.

Irene let out a puff of breath, now fully dethawed and stripping off the sweaters I'd loaned her. "Okay, raise your hand if you think that stealing their wheels to take us back to the outside would be a good idea?"

Both Destan and my hands rose up and down, caught indecisively between wanting to go for it, and doubting that we could actually get away with it.

Irene made a face, sighing, "Okay…raise your hand if you know how to hijack a motor vehicle?" Irene stuck her own hand into the air, obviously taken aback at how neither of her companions could admit to it. She gaped, and then looked at me accusingly. "Hang on— didn't you tell me you were into mischief? And you've even got 'thief' written on your forehead?"

I flushed, shaking my leg back and forth nervously as I admitted, "Well, yeah, but it's not like I can drive anything other than a bike. I've only started one of the police trucks once a long time ago; I don't even know what sort of vehicle this is."

"I can guess how it works," Irene said, Destan looking up attentively. "If you can just get me in there and help me get the engine going before they can stop us, then I can get us out lickety split."

"You're sure?" Destan asked.

She nodded, black ponytail flapping against the white glass wall behind us. "Yep. This is what I was trained for, believe it or not."

He and I exchanged glances, him being the first to speak, "Okay. We can try it, but we'll need a diversion so that we can get up there."

I scratched around my eyes, getting some of the dried

black paint under my fingernails as I contemplated what to do now. The salve my mom had made for me had left my skin rougher and even blistered in areas around my neck. Then an idea hit me, and I looked up at them, a slow smile creeping up my face. They looked at me in question, and I whispered, "Would a stink bomb work?"

Irene stared at me, jaw hanging down and eyes narrowed as she obviously demonstrated her disapproval of my plan. Destan on the other hand, rubbed his jaw thoughtfully, brows furrowed, asking, "Where would we get the stink?"

I was already ahead of him, yanking my spare water gourd from my tool belt and uncapping it, saying, "This salve. To get the paint off, my mom made this horrid smelling salve that can even burn away skin if it's left on too long or exposed to too much heat."

Irene blew some air through her lips, whistling. "Huh. Good thing we're in a volcano…plenty of heat…"

Destan was grinning now too. "That…might just work, Bluehead." He waved his hand above the gourd's lip, wafting the vinegar-rubbing-alcohol-marigold-stink towards his nose. Destan gasped, passing the gourd back, coughing. "Yup, that will most definitely do some adequate stinking."

"The alcohol is highly flammable too," I added, capping the gourd and breathing through my mouth since my nose burned from the harsh stench.

Irene nodded. "Okey dokey then. So…what now? Do we just set that thing on fire and chuck it up?"

"I think you and Raine should make your way to the shuttle and start hijacking it first. Then when the bomb goes off, the JPs don't have the chance to flee to the shuttle and try to get away and run into you two. We need a quick escape," Destan said, beginning to move out from the tangle of wires and back into the middle of the basement. "I'll be right behind you and throw the bomb when the time is right."

"How are we going to go through without being seen?" I

interrupted, fingers nervously wringing each other. "The last thing that can happen is that they figure out who we are. This might just be too risky."

Destan grasped my shoulders, staring deeply into my eyes. "Bluehead. Your instinct was good, don't let your brain go and start to mess you up. The stink bomb will be great, and...I don't think hiding our identities will be a problem."

I swallowed. "How?"

Destan loped to the stairway, hollering up in a deeper tone of voice, "12345! 2468-ten! 10101! I need you knuckleheads down here for a moment!" Then he hastily unplugged one of the generator boxes and heaved it into his arms, motioning for Irene and me to remain hidden in the shadows of the cables.

"What the hell does he think he's doing?" Irene hissed into my ear, shaking her head. She looked at me, an eyebrow raised, "Is he always this crazy?"

I watched him, ready and excited at the foot of the steps, tongue between his teeth, bouncing on the balls of his feet as JP voices and the thunk of footsteps carried down towards us. Smiling, I shrugged. "He's like a big kid. A big, wise kid. Occasionally impulsive."

Then I went instantly dead quiet, freezing to the state of a statue as three JPs came cautiously into view, their visors flipped up on their helmets. One of them spoke, slightly crouched as he struggled to see in the dark, "Uhh...someone call 23145?"

Destan appeared from behind, crashing a heavy generator onto the top of the JP's head. Even with the helmet to take the impact, he toppled down unsteadily, groaning as the other two withdrew their rods and glanced back up the stairway.

"Captain—!" One of them began to shout, abruptly silenced by Destan's sweater sleeves as he tied the extra knit jumper around the man's mouth, yanking him down to the ground and knocking his head just hard enough against the wall so that he'd be in dreamland.

Destan's eyes flashed onto mine and he whispered

urgently, "Start putting on those uniforms, quick—"

The last conscious JP slugged Destan straight in the mouth, grabbing him by the throat and squeezing before Destan could fall to the ground. That's when I started, darting up from the ground and sinking into my stance, not even fumbling with my arrow, nocking it in with such instinctive speed and accuracy that I fired within the five seconds it took for the JP to glance over and realize what was happening.

I'd had no intended aim in the forefront of my mind, but was pleasantly surprised as it struck in the chink of armor between his forearm and elbow and he cried out, dropping Destan and clutching his arm.

"You little…" he seethed, lunging for me, and in response getting lassoed back by Destan's scarf he had looped around the JPs neck. He choked, falling to his knees as Destan loosened the hold and copied the motion of slamming down the JP he'd done before to make sure he'd be unconscious long enough for us to get away. Destan's teeth were red, a thick slug of blood oozing right down the corner of his mouth. Seeing my concerned stare, he looked away self-consciously and wiped it with his knuckles, sticking the helmet over his head and beginning to strap on the armor.

Irene was all finished, mine just missing the heavy, awkwardly huge steel-plated pants, and after Destan helped me hoist them at least to my hips, we heard the stairs creak.

"What's all the commotion, officers?" a harsh voice shouted down.

I pushed the sleeping bodies into the mess of wires as Destan poked his head into the light of the stairway and took a step up, saying gruffly, "Generator got busted, caused a bit of a noisy mess."

"Well, get it done. Sebastian wants those ships ready to fly by next Thursday and you haven't even designated the takeoff and transmission status yet," the JP I guessed was the captain barked at him.

Destan nodded, clearing his throat and leaning against the stair railing. "Oh. Yes. I will definitely do that right away."

Silence.

"Sir!" Destan corrected, "Right away, *sir.*"

No response, the captain walked away and Destan looked at us desperately, whispering, "Okay, you two go up and out, I'll get the bomb ready. Try not to talk, just get out of there and go to the shuttle."

We nodded and began up the steps, me sweating under the task of lugging Irene behind me since she couldn't walk without making a fairly feminine squeak. She helped as best she could; grabbing onto the railing and pulling us up. When we emerged into the control room, it had taken on a completely different atmosphere.

Every control board was surrounded and in action, screens blinking from place to place, weapon to weapon, strange rows of numbers and maps with lots of blue dots and red lines. I gulped, supporting Irene and limping toward the door the JPs had entered through. The captain, a man in armor closer to dark grey than black, spun on his heel eyeing us as we were about to make it out.

"Injured, that one?" he barked at us, hands stiffly behind his back.

I opened my mouth to speak and then bit down hard on my tongue, remembering what Destan had said about the risk of having too girlish a voice. I just nodded, grunting and pointing at the door and then at us. My hands were cold and shaking inside the thick black gloves.

The captain raised an eyebrow, clearly not amused with the silent treatment. "All right, I see you need to go, but how exactly did this injury come about?"

Irene cut in, lowering her voice so much that it almost sounded like she was speaking in slow motion, "The busted generator...uhh...blasted my leg open. Need to...get...a band-aid."

It took much of my willpower not to slap her upside the head for that, and I nervously laughed, copying the growlish voice she'd created, "Haha, he also got hit in the head when it burst. Rookies, you know?"

The captain scoffed, "You're one to talk, 36672."

*Crap...*I thought, realizing I should have noticed the shiny new badge the armor had on it. I grit my teeth, panic tickling at my spine. I sidestepped the captain, saluting with my free hand, and hurried through the door with Irene in tow, calling, "We'll be right back, sir!"

Soon as we got out and the automatic doors slid shut, I hastened to lean Irene against the big silver vehicle and started eyeing the handle. I'd picked locks before, easily. But there wasn't even a keyhole. Just a single hand grip on each side.

Irene groaned, pushing herself up taller and limping over to me. "I got this one. Stand back."

I obeyed, moving away as she unhooked the lightning rod on her JP armor and systematically jabbed the electrified end all along the edge of the shut door. The metal pod glowed from the inside, and I realized that it wasn't metal at all, but thick, hard, silver frosted glass. Then, with a click, it slid open smoothly, too slowly, and I couldn't help but ease it along the track faster so that we could squeeze inside.

"Neat trick," I muttered, sparing a half smile for the spy as she shrugged and plopped into the front row of padded benches inside.

"Thanks," she replied, staring at the blank dashboard of the shuttle and sighing. "Oh, great."

"What?" I asked, worried at her reaction. "You said you knew how to work it, right?"

"Mmm..."

"Mmm?"

There was a blast and some surprised yells from inside. Smoke hissed under the door of the glass building and then it was knocked open. Destan came sprinting out, helmet instantly yanked off, arm covering his mouth, eyes wet and streaming as he leapt inside.

"Drive, drive, drive!" he ordered, slamming the door closed and coughing as we got the first nasty whiff of the salve-turned-stink-bomb.

Irene bit down on her lip, drumming her fingers on the blank dashboard and then accidentally popping up the lid to where the controls were. "Aha!" she cried, typing in something rapidly and cranking around a wheel so that the door closed with a secure sounding screech and we shot forward.

Pressed against the bench, I took off the helmet and shook out my hair. Irene did the same and joined me and Destan in the back, trying to undo the hooks in the armor with her taped-together fingers. I aided her, working on the shoulder pads first. "Don't you have to steer it?" I asked.

"All done," she replied briskly. "Tapped in the exit location and hit go. It's not like there's a very wide range of where this little thing can go other than the track beneath it." Irene then relaxed back on the bench and closed her eyes, appearing to be in the process of taking a well-earned nap.

Destan draped his arm around my shoulders, pulling me close and whispering in my ear, "That was one hell of a stinkbomb, Bluehead."

I smiled, looking up at him and leaning my head on his shoulder, the scent of pine and cut wood and the odd after scent of vinegar-marigolds greeting my nose. When I hit the stinkbomb smell, I wrinkled my nose, taking my head off his shoulder and sighing exhaustedly. "Let's just get home. I think we need this weekend to forget about all this stuff."

He rubbed my shoulder gently, leaning his cheek on the top of my head. "Couldn't agree more."

Nervously, I touched my fingers to his, filled with comfort when he twined them with his own and his lips smiled into my hair.

chapter nineteen

I tripped, flying flat onto my face and making the blisters from the paint sear as they came in contact with the road's gravel. Pushing myself with my hands, I forced myself to keep running even though I felt so dead exhausted that I could sleep through the entire weekend ahead. I'd retrieved my ribbon and tied up my hair, but now my bun bounced against my neck loosely, all of it coming undone and tangling around my face again. *Come on, come on, make it there before she wakes up. Come on Raine…*I thought insistently, increasingly nervous as Underbrush began to wake up and set up their shops and sweep their front porches for when the JPs would come to collect the daily police fund donation.

"Morning, sweetheart!" I heard Jun holler as I sprinted past the Laundress pavilion, where I thankfully wouldn't have to go until Monday.

I hastily waved at her, not even able to spare a quick smile as I ducked through the first JP trucks rambling through the street. I hurried to where I could see my tin roof wobbling under the morning's harsh wind. *So close, so close, come on!* I bopped Carmen on the head when I went by her house. She stood bent over, pulling out weeds spiraling from under her porch, and yelped when I touched her so quickly.

"Good morning?" she called quizzically, and I could just imagine her eye roll as I moved aside my still unhinged front door and dashed inside.

The pot was already set on the stove, but not boiling. I gulped, leaning over the water basin on the counter and splashed water on my face, trying to get off the dirt that had gathered during the night's expedition and my clumsy trip back home. I shoved up my sleeves and saw that even my arms were covered in dusty mountain mud and filth, but before I could dunk them in the basin, my mother came peeling around the corner. I quickly forced my sweater sleeves back down, still out of breath and mussed up. I grinned, teeth bared, anxious that she hadn't seen me just run in. "Morning, Mom!" I saw out of the corner of my eye that I'd tracked in mud, and ever so subtly pushed the throw rug over the boot prints with my toe, pretending to stretch my legs.

She narrowed her eyes at me. "Good morning," she said, tone of voice unreadable, moving past me and switching off the stove. The just-boiling water lost its bubbles, cooling back to a still surface.

I let my smile sink back into my more neutral face, rocking back on my heels and casually leaning against the counter. "How l-long have you been up, Mom?"

"About half an hour," she answered, not taking her eyes off me or moving from where she stood, hunched slightly with her hands on her hips. Then she blinked. "I'm shocked. I didn't even hear you leave your room."

My breath caught, heat rushing into my cheeks as I began stammering, trying to collect the words that wouldn't have me infinitely grounded. "Mom I can explain, I just couldn't stay in bed, it was an emergency and I promise I will…I know I should have— "

"Calm yourself!" she scoffed, adding some rice to the water and re-lighting the fire. She brushed away my bangs from my forehead and touched my face. "I told you I wanted you to get it all off, and the fact that you spent a whole night in here doing that instead of wallowing in bed actually makes me *quite* impressed."

I gaped at her, heart rate still at a panicky pace, my brain feeling numb. "Oh. Well. You're…welcome?"

She coughed into her elbow, turning up the radio for the only report she cared about listening to (the one about the state of the herb farms including the one she so depended on up in Canopia), and sighed. Then she picked up a limp chunk of my hair and dropped it, scolding, "I do wish you hadn't been out here so late into the morning though, you look a wreck otherwise. I'd cut your hair here and now if Skye wasn't—"

Three polite knocks on the door. My forehead banging three times against the wall in frustration.

Mom's brows drew together, and she muttered, displeased, "— already here."

I took a deep breath, twisting up my waist-length blue hair fast and pausing before the door to tie it up more securely. "Just a second!" I called, struggling to make a good knot and wipe some of the mud off of my boots on the floor-mat all at once. Shaking my bangs to the side and out of my eyes, I carefully lifted the door enough so that I could move it, and stepped down to the porch where eighteen-year old Skye Zanying waited, flowers in tow.

His grin shined from ear to ear so happily that it made even me feel a little sunnier and less like the dark, sleeping side of the moon. He offered the flowers to me. "Good morning."

I accepted them, touching the white rose buds and feeling a yearning to be in Chantastic's attic with the flowers and candles and piles of pillows where we could take a nap together. I forced myself out of that daydream, coming down the steps with him, saying, "Thank you, Skye. How did you know white roses were my favourite?"

He laughed nervously, eyes on the ground as we began walking slowly down the Underbrush road. "Actually," he said, "when I went to the florist, I asked what she might give you if she were in my place, and this was her suggestion. Also, I just thought that they were sort of unique on such a cold place like Thgdindim." His brown eyes lifted and rested softly on me, looking up at my hair, his voice gentle, "Like you, Raine."

Oh jeez, oh jeez. I couldn't control the rush of red I knew had made its way into my cheeks, and I tried to give as appreciative a reply, utterly failing. "Thank you…uhh…you are pretty unique yourself." I ended the compliment with a clearly strained laugh.

Skye tilted his head to the side, beginning to dig in his pocket for his Starshade ID as we approached the gate to the next level. "You think so? I can't see how I'm any different from many other guys from my level— maybe it's different on Underbrush?"

Well, you're definitely not Destan.

I held my hands behind my back, willing my brain to shut up and my lips to start working. "Well, it isn't usual that someone would add an Underbrusher to the list of who they want to court if they're from somewhere higher."

Skye sucked in his lips, a curious look on his face as he admitted, "You're sort of the only girl on my list, right now."

I was too scared to say *'me too!'* Once again torn between wanting to make this work with him so that my family could get the help we so desperately needed, and between wanting to seem uninteresting and bland enough that I wouldn't have to keep spending my extra time courting when I could be tossing jokes and shooting arrows with Destan. Not to mention figuring out how to solve the issue of the illegal spy still in my care. So, rather than boosting his ego and mentioning how I also wasn't going to see anyone else, and rather than lowering it by saying it was just because my Mom was making me and we needed money to keep Gwen out of the crazy-house, I decided to keep the questions coming. "How come? Have you courted anyone else before me?"

He nodded. "I have. I've gone on dates with some girls from my old school, but it never really worked out the way I'd hoped, you know?"

I blushed again. "Actually...I don't. You're the first guy I've courted with, so I'm not so good at determining what means 'working out' and what doesn't."

"*Really?*" he sounded genuinely surprised at that, and then we went into a one floor shop with nice stone tile flooring and robin's egg blue wallpaper. Rather than the messy bins of produce Underbrush had strewn down the street to serve as markets, this place was put together so nicely, like a pretty illustration in a storybook. At the front was a long wooden counter where a woman in a clean apron was stacking meats, cheese, and what looked like slices of cabbage onto thick chunks of bread. There were only a few shelves around the place, selling jars of stuff like mustard and rosehip jam. At the side of the counter was a metal basin filled with ice and snow, bottles of cider and beer and juice nestled safely in the white tundra. Picnic tables were set up outside and inside the shop, with halved-log benches and teams of Starshade miners stuffing their faces with the generously portioned submarines.

Skye was walking slightly faster than me to the counter where the woman had looked up and expectantly pulled out a new cutting board from somewhere under it. When he noticed me standing open-mouthed still at the door of the deli, he smiled sweetly, beckoning me forward. "Come on up, Raine."

I didn't feel as self-conscious here as I had before in the more upscale cafe we'd had our first meeting. Even though my hair was nothing but a rat's nest strapped up to my head and there was a considerable amount of dirt painting my body under the sweater, knowing that I was eating among average, working

Starshaders like the miners relieved a great amount of anxiety. Scared I'd embarrassed him by just standing awed by what should be an average sandwich shop, I hurried up to him, mouth watering as I got a whiff of the different scents rising from the fresh bread and thinly sliced meats.

"What can I do you for today, Master Skye?" the woman at the counter asked, beaming at the both of us and brushing crumbs from her hands.

"Just the usual lean variety please, Mrs. Fan," he replied, shocking me with his specificity when there wasn't a menu in sight.

"Of course," she smiled, laying her striking blue eyes on me. Light eyes like that could only come from higher up the mountain. "And what would your lady be wishing to have to start off her day?"

I looked at Skye for help, hoping he'd conjure up some mystery meal or know what I liked as he'd done with the flowers earlier, but he just furrowed his brow, apparently both confused and amused at my hesitation. He motioned at the glass top of the counter which showed the bins of meats, cheeses, and more toppings under the counter. "Just tell her whatever you want."

"Anything?" I asked. "As much of it too?"

They both laughed at me, Skye saying, "Of course!"

"He's paying anyway, so get away with piling on what you can." The woman winked.

Going on tiptoe to peek at the toppings clearly, I pointed at everything I didn't recognize, as well as all of the meats, asking, "So…may I have one slice of each? Is that all right?" I paused, taking notice of the hard-boiled eggs kept to the side, "And one of those too?"

"Your wish is my command, dear," she replied, sliding open the drawer and beginning to build up both of our subs.

Skye told me to wait outside at a table while he waited to bring back our food. I slid onto the bench that faced out toward the distance, awed at how much more magnificent this view was in comparison to the one I could see from Underbrush. *Being up higher has its perks,* I mused inside my head, fingers suddenly restless and itchy for a pencil and paper. I glanced back at Skye, who was pondering over the cooler of drinks, and then I took one of the napkins from the pile on the table and began sketching on it with the pen I kept tucked in my waistband for impulsive-art-emergencies. I was nearly done filling in the pine's bottom branches with quick slashes of ink when I heard the bench creak and saw Skye set out our breakfasts before us.

"What's that?" he asked me, setting a bottle of milk in front of me and a glass of water in front of himself.

I glared at the milk, regretting not choosing the cider while I'd had the chance inside. But then I quickly folded up the napkin. "It's nothing, just a drawing I was doing."

"May I see it?" he said, voice gentle and polite, but still very persuasive.

Who knows? Maybe we'll find common ground, I thought hopefully, slowly unfolding the wilty napkin and spreading it out on the table.

Skye bent over it, smiling. "You're really good..." he murmured, uncapping my milk and taking a sip of his water. "I'd always been so bad at art. I like looking at it though."

"Really?" I asked, taking first notice of how enormous my sub was. It was a foot long and five inches thick, with peppers and sliced egg and so much meat of different colours and cuts that I might as well have eaten an entire farm. I picked it up, attempting to nibble off the first few inches of it and not just try to jam the entire colossal thing into my very, very hungry mouth.

"Oh, yes, it's my favourite thing about being able to go up to Peak when I have to," he explained, pinching his *'lean variety'* two inch thick sub of thin grainy bread, a couple pieces of lettuce, and some shiny looking bean sprouts. "In the Department of Archives, there is an entire floor of classical Thgindim art from as far back as a thousand years ago, just when we broke away from Fluxaria. There's even a gallery showcasing the work of the most talented Sketchers throughout the ages and libraries of their observation notebooks."

I was actually beginning to get very interested in this conversation, not to mention excited about the fact that the big tower had more than offices and jail cells. "No way! That sounds so incredible; I've only ever seen some Sketchers' stuff when I'd peeked over their shoulder, while they were doing their records when I was little!" I said.

Skye nodded. "It really is. Too bad the job is practically useless in this day and age, though."

Okay— what?

I stared at him. "I thought you just said you loved their work, that Peak has huge archives of all of their contributions."

Skye shrugged, finishing his dainty chewing and accidentally wiping his mouth with the napkin I'd drawn on. After he swallowed, he replied, "Well, they're just not exactly contributing anything to Thgindim's constantly advancing system. There's so much less work to be done by just hiring photographers, and not as many people to pay if the Sketchers are cut; boosting the economy."

"But it's about preserving a culture," I argued, not wanting to stir up anything so much that we actually started fighting and ruining my chances of hitting it off with him. Not being able to let my dream Career be deemed so useless, "not just the culture of the land they are documenting, but the culture of artistic expression and interpreting the world through different lenses. Photographs will just show viewers what we already see, the sketches can invoke feeling and show what approaches we would take toward the world at that time, what approach and feeling the Sketcher had towards his or her subject."

My plate was mess of fallen bits of egg and fatty segments of corned beef, while Skye's was immaculately clean. He pushed his away from himself, standing up and looking a little put-off. He glanced at my plate, then me. "Are you finished?"

My stomach was so full it could explode. "Mmhmm," I

said, tucking some hair behind my ear and meaning to take my plate back inside, but instead watching as he stacked it on top of his own and carried them both in. Guilt moved like a slug through my stomach. *Raine, that was not cool.* I thought, shaking my knees anxiously and staring off into the store as he opened up his wallet to drop a tip in the owner's jar on the counter, and then came striding back to me.

I smiled timidly at him, brain working fast to figure out how to return things to the cheerful atmosphere we had before. Skye offered his hand to me. "Shall we?"

Nodding, I took it and contemplated the sweatiness of my hands as we walked down the road. His hand was smaller and softer than Destan's, and rather than it feeling like his was embracing mine, Skye's fit against mine gently, swaying our arms back and forth as we continued onward. Wherever that might be.

"Thank you for the food," I said, kicking a pebble with my shoe.

"You really liked it?" he asked, a hopeful grin on his face.

I nodded. "Yeah, it is rare that I don't have soup for every meal so. It was really a treat."

"Because your mother's a Spooner, that's right…"

He seemed to be taking us to what looked like Starshade's equivalent of Underbrush's Travelshack; a tall building with bikes and animals and some fancier sort of motor vehicles and carriages that would never grace Underbrush's dirty street. Within a couple minutes, he had paid for a wolf-drawn sled to carry us around the border of Starshade's woods, which already had a couple wispy inches of snow covering up the grass.

As the sled bumped over the lumpy grass, giving us only a view of the woods on our left and the backs of buildings on our right, I tried to relax and just enjoy the ride. The man driving the horses was humming some song that Skye said he had an interesting fact about, and as I closed my eyes and interjected with the appropriate "Mmhmm"s and "Wow, really?"s, I felt myself rock into a near sleep.

But then, Skye nudged me. "Raine?"

"Mmhmm?" I hummed, forcing myself to sit up straighter and keep my eyelids from drooping back over my eyes.

Skye looked down. "I apologize sincerely if I may have offended you with my talk of Sketchers. I promise it was unintended."

I was taken aback by this, now much more attentive, replying, "Oh. Um. It's no big deal. You can have your own opinion."

"But I like hearing yours," he chuckled, looking up shyly at me. His eyes watched me fondly. "If there's anything else you might want to prove me wrong about, I would love to hear about it."

I pinched my lips, feeling them about to smile at that remark. "You would?"

"I would, indeed," he murmured, glancing away with a nervous laugh.

Sliding down slightly in my seat, I thought about it for a while. Then I whispered, "How do you feel about meat?"

He wrinkled his nose. "Why?"

"Your sandwich. It was all greens. Why no meat?"

He pushed some of his soft brown hair off of his forehead answering, a little embarrassed, "It just doesn't do wonders to my body. It makes me sick to my stomach." Skye chuckled, "But I've noticed you have quite the penchant for it."

I nodded. "Yes, I do."

He stared off ahead of us, where I could now see where we'd taken off. We'd almost come full circle. After that I was going to ask him to take me home. I didn't want to spend my day off leaving Gwen home alone while Mom cleaned and left her to make a mess of our room. Skye spoke again, quietly, nervously, "I would like to see you again. After my birthday, I'm thinking, since you seem to have quite the packed schedule."

You have no idea, I thought, trying to keep my palms from sweating as I thought about Irene and Destan and the nonexistent plan of action we'd have to make now that Irene had fulfilled her end of the deal and had shown us proof that she wouldn't have a home to go back to.

Skye continued, "But I want you to take the reins for the next date. What do you think?" he asked, as the sled slowed and the wolves pulling it panted, trotting us back into town to the Travelshack. "You could show me where you like to go, what you like to do." He smiled encouragingly, climbing out first so that he could help me off of the sled and onto the stool to the ground.

I batted my lashes, feeling snowflakes catch on them as a noisome squirrel ran across a snowy pine branch above us. I contemplated what Destan would think if *I* were the one taking time away from dealing with a seriously dangerous and treasonous situation to schedule and go on a date with Skye. It was one thing if my excuse was that my mother or Skye had arranged it, but if it was my own doing, what would he think? That I thought courting was a bigger priority than keeping an enemy spy under wraps? That I liked spending time with Skye more than him? Just the thought made me frustrated.

Skye's just the small side job Mom's assigned me to in order to make sure Gwen and us are safe and secure with enough money, I thought, glancing up at Skye and imagining a red hat, pair of grey eyes, and strong jaw in front of me. *Destan is…oh, I don't know what Destan is. He's just important.*

A cloud of air condensed out of my mouth as I spoke, "We shall see."

chapter twenty

"What now?" Destan asked, obviously still a little uncomfortable with the reality of Irene having the right to decide what to do next. We'd even given her back her satchel, and now while I washed clothes and Destan chopped wood, Irene had a good old time getting to know the knick knacks she'd had stashed in there the whole time.

Aside from the handgun, collection of bottled poisons, and foldable pouch with a dozen different types of knives, the spy had packed more or less normal things. She had a field notes book and plastic baggy full of wrapped up sweets and granola bars. Her grey knit blanket was soiled and grass stained, but otherwise still "smelled like home," she said. A well-worn stuffed panda was swaddled safely inside of it. Next to the mostly used-up first aid kit and stacks of folded black pants and tunics was a well worn comic book with the words *Mystery of the Missing Tomb:*

A Kaoren Byrd Adventure. Irene was poring over that now as Destan asked her again, "Irene? Can you tell us what you were planning to do next?"

She glanced up from the water-damaged drawing in the book, dog-earing the page and sitting up. Only one finger was bandaged now. "You mean the original plan? That Fluxaria gave me?"

I wrung out the pair of stockings I'd been washing and patted around the grass for my bar of soap, saying, "Whatever you think we should do next. As long as it isn't sitting around doing nothing for another couple of days. The JPs could decide to check back and see if there are trespassers here again."

"Yeah, sitting and wasting more time is real bad. Just..." Her big dark eyes stared intently at the ground, brows drawing together seriously as she took a moment to think. Then she tried stretching out her arms above her head, only to withdraw them immediately as her rib seemed to cause her a great, sudden amount of pain. She took deep breaths, shaking her head, "...there's just not even the teensiest thing I can do in shape like this. I'd love to do my business and get out, but even with all your nice bandages and creams I'm still...I'm still real broken in places." Irene withdrew her hand from her abdomen glumly, muttering, "At this rate, Fluxaria could be wiped off the face of the earth by the time I can even use all of my fingers again."

Destan and I exchanged sympathetic glances, trying to figure out what to do. He slid the blade of his axe into the leather holder on his belt and came over to the river with me, picking up some of the wet clothes from my Canopia load and draping them in the sunny spots of grass after I'd washed them and wrung them out. As he tried to keep the dirt from his fingers off of an absurdly white shawl, he asked her, "Well...what specifically is it you need to do? Whatever it is will keep us out of an open-fire war, right?"

She nodded, rolling up the comic book and looking through it at us like a spyglass. "Yep," she said. "My job is to bring back information about what kinds of weapons there are, when they'll be launched, where it's all hidden, y'know just all sorts of warning. Luckily we got that last one finished seeing as we now know where shifty stuff and weapon-making is happening."

Irene set down the comic again and practiced bending and unbending the fingers we'd taken out of the tape and gauze splints. "Not to mention your life actually sucks a shit-ton more than I'd thought, so with this stuff taken care of, your nasty Council will get what was coming to them and you can have some more fun around here."

Destan chuckled, shrugging. "Sounds like a win-win to me."

Irene snorted. "Yeah it would be; if the person on the job wasn't stuck laying by a river all day waiting for her boo-boos to get better." She bitterly placed both hands on the ground, attempting to hoist herself up onto her own two feet. As she showed signs of toppling, I leapt up and caught her arm, steadying her as she fought to bear some weight on the broken leg.

"You think we're really running out of time this fast?" I whispered, guiding her as she tried taking a solid step on her own.

"I've been here what, almost two months?" she began. "I was in Mythland for another good chunk of time, I'd say it's almost been half a year since I was home and even then, things were already heating up. Any moment it'll be the boiling point, honey." Her last word came out as a gasp, and I instantly pulled back on her, easing her back down to rest and not worsen things by moving too much. She stubbornly resisted, but then gave in, groaning as she lay on her back with her arms over her eyes.

"Well..." I bit my lip, reluctant, yet sure of what I wanted to suppose. "What if we were able to do some of these things for you? Just until you're well enough. If it's helping both of us, we could share the responsibility— you, Destan, and me." Destan paused in his laying out of wet blouses and skirts, staring at us both inquisitively. I flushed, adding, "Well...I mean, if he also thinks so."

"No, I think that sounds pretty reasonable," he said, making a face as he held a dripping pair of stained bloomers between his thumb and forefinger. I went over to him and put it back into the water, grinding soap into the dirty spot as he sighed in relief.

Irene hummed uncertainly, her eyes squinted and lips pursed as she considered it. Then she said, slowly, "Thing is…it's not like this is easy stuff, you guys. There's sort of a reason why Fluxaria hasn't been sending over spies for quite some time." Irene scratched her head, yawning hugely. She looked at us solemnly, "Your Council and all of their dirty little secrets aren't just under lock and key, as you probably noticed from the burning hell-pit where we found all of those tanks and stuff."

True, I thought, suddenly queasy.

"Were you supposed to bring back entire weapons? Or what exactly is it that you were supposed to retrieve, Irene?" Destan asked.

"Just the weapon blueprints. And I need to get my hands on as many military records and written out plans for any new offense Thgindim has planned."

"What have we sent at you before?" I whispered.

Her eyes suddenly looked as if a shadow had sucked the shine from them. Irene may have been putting on a brave show for us so far, but moments like this made the war really feel real. She had seen something horrible, it was lurking in the hidden wrinkles around her mouth, it was draining the liveliness from her eyes. She had witnessed true loss and death and it didn't even take her explanation to convince me she was telling the truth.

"Couple of years ago, about thirty Fluxarian hostages were returned by your Justice Police. It was a fake peace offering. Turned out the hostages had been infected with a deadly, fast-spreading disease and it killed off entire villages in just a month," she said, clenching her jaw.

I looked at Destan, a lump in my throat as I said softly,

"Remember that virus a few years back? The one that took out so many of the elderly down here and a lot of really little kids?" Both of the Song's parents had been in that mix and two of Carmen's little sisters.

He nodded gravely. We were both thinking it. Irene brought it to the surface. "Wouldn't surprise me if your Council unleashed it on you lot too, maybe even before Fluxaria. You know, as a trial run."

Kill off the poor ones, I thought, filled with a sickening feeling that I'd thought this before, that I'd known this was always what the JPs and Council had been doing to Underbrush. *There are too many of us. Let the police run wild and without punishment for whatever pain they inflict on us. Take our money and tax us into our graves since we aren't even given enough food to spend it on.*

"Where are these records?" Destan said, breaking into my nauseating stream of thoughts. He must've noticed how increasingly anxious I was getting because he took the bar of soap from me and took my hands in his, warming up my fingers that had gone nearly numb from the icy water. His touch made a tingle go up my arms.

"Most of 'em are virtual, my government thought," Irene said, leaning her chin on her fist. "So I'm guessing on the hard drives or personal tablets up in that shiny tower."

"Virtual?" Destan and I asked dubiously.

"Like a computer file or online message. Do you two seriously not know what a computer is?"

Our answer was given by the rushing of water on rocks and Irene cussed quietly in shock. "Well, you'll have to steal the tablet of Head of Law Enforcement and Foreign Affairs. They're the same person now due to a recent death or something that my queen told me about."

"So Fluxaria really does have a queen?" I asked, conjuring up a fuzzy image of the tall, dark-skinned woman with red eyes and a crown of knives. The pictures our teachers used to show us in history of the Fluxarian royal court used to be so terrifying, but now that I was recalling them, it seemed absurd. It suddenly was laughable that a short and sassy spy who brought along a comic book and stuffed animal could be under the supervision of a ruler crowned with pointy objects.

"She's the face of our country, but other than that, doesn't have much to do with making decisions. Just sort of serves as a blood descendant to the original leaders who helped establish Fluxaria as its own nation." Irene got another yawn out of her system, stretching and slipping off her soft, black boots. Her socks were purple.

"So, who runs everything? Makes the rules?" I asked, unable to keep my curiosity stifled as this spy rewrote the history I was taught with every word she spoke.

One of Irene's thick black brows arched. "Do you want to hear about how my mountain works, or do you want to discuss how to have it not get blown up?"

"Of course we need to get through the plan of action," Destan answered for me, crouching down by her. "But, Irene, you gotta understand that we know next to *nothing* about who you and your people actually are."

"Show us who you want us to save. We…we trust you now, but could you please give us an idea of the home you could lose? Just for the sake of understanding?" I added. My palms were sweaty, and Destan let go of my hand, draping an arm around my shoulders as Irene cleared her throat and settled into storytelling. Or, more accurately, she gave us a history lesson; arranging river stones in the grass to stand in as certain villages and Fluxarian citizens.

She mapped it all out like this: the social classes were the peasantry, the Wise, and the royal family. That's it. And Fluxaria wasn't even divided into distinct levels. Individual villages were arranged less geometrically than Thgindim's and there were hardly any terraces built into the mountain at all. Where the air got thinner, rather than pumping in fake oxygen, the upper half of the mountain was simply not civilized. The foliage and environment remained wild and untouched, save a huddle of towers that served as spiritual temples closest to the top. The queen lived a little while away from the peasants, but not as cut off as the Majesty Council was from their citizens.

The villages were completely run by the townspeople themselves, each one having different regulations put in place and Careers to aspire to. Irene kept both of our heads from bursting at the sheer ridiculousness of such liberty by affirming that there was still a guiding figure. A Wiseman or Wisewoman watched over the peasants. They didn't have direct or absolute control over the village, but if there was trouble, they'd step in. When there was a major decision to be made that involved the entire mountain, the Wise figure would listen to what their town had to say and cast a vote for the royals to see.

A person could only become a Wiseman or Wisewoman after going through many spiritual, social, mental, and psychological tests. All who passed these tests were then voted on by the mountain to decide who should be counted as one of the Wise. Then the Wiseman or Wisewoman could pick a town to sponsor. Just as Irene had said, the royals really didn't have hardly anything to do with the legal system at all.

When Fluxaria had just split, Irene admitted that they had been the group that had been more corrupt, more isolationist. They had wanted to keep an absolute monarchy and expand off from the mainland to see if there were other nations out there to take control over. When that ultimately failed, they reconsidered their ways and went to the spirits for guidance. Since then, the mountain was kept in motion and thriving through the efforts of each individual town working to sustain themselves and work together when conflict arose. The remaining descendants of the original royal family lived just as humbly as any working person or Wise figure, but they resided in the originally built palace and kept their titles just to carry on tradition. They also had to be put through intense diplomatic and humanitarian training since they were designated to deal with extra-mountain issues. Best example being Thgindim and the increasing number of threats and sneak attacks that had been worsening for almost a quarter of a century now.

By the end of Irene's description, I felt like I had gone back in time to when Underbrush still had a fairly up-and-running library, and I had just read another great story of how a nation came to be and how it drifted toward destruction. I was so lost in the moment that I nearly asked Irene, *What happened to Fluxaria, then? Did they make peace? How did they fight back?* But then I realized that the answers to those questions depended on two fifteen year olds sitting in a meadow; that the responsibility had been shifted from the broken hands of a young spy into the cautious arms of Destan and me who were just beginning to have our initial fears subside.

"So…" I breathed, my vision unfocusing as I stared long and hard at the grass, "we need to steal from Peak Tower. Give that stuff to you, and that's it."

Despite the certainty of my tone, it was meant to be a question, and Irene replied as such. "I am not asking you or him to do anything, Raine. I'm still eternally grateful you've kept me alive so I can do what I came for."

"But you are under a time crunch, yeah?" Destan asked quietly, gazing at her intently.

There was the sound of the gong, and Destan and I looked at each other sadly. Curfew had crept up on us so quickly. Irene understood, nodding and dragging herself back under the tree where she had her blanket spread out and her satchel propped up like a pillow.

"You two let me know what you decide," she said, wincing as she eased herself into a laying position. She smiled a little, and I noticed she had a little black mole above her lip. "I'll just be, y'know. Here. As usual."

Destan and I nodded, patting a sleeping Siri on the muzzle and gathering up our supplies and the clothes I'd laid out to dry. Once we were all packed up and had covered up the entrance to the meadow with some more fern branches, we started back toward town. He had Siri moving at a slow trot to remain in step with me on my rickshaw, and after we made it out of the woods and I could unload at Jun's pavilion, Destan called to me again, just as I had been about to start on home.

"Hey," he said, that sly smile on his mouth, "Bluehead, mind if we take the long way to your place?"

I blushed, hands on my hips. "Doesn't your mother want you home at an appropriate time?"

At the mention of his mother, Destan's grin flickered for a moment, briefly looking a little stressed, and then he rolled his eyes, laughing it off. "It will just be a few minutes more. Ten minutes, tops."

There it is again, I thought, even more interested in his reluctance to mention his family, much less a mother or father. I scuffed my feet in the gravel as I came up to Siri, and then was swept up onto her back.

It was dark and calm, and Siri skirted the outer road so closely that JPs didn't notice or hassle us about getting home as promptly as possible. We walked the edge of our only known universe, and all I could see around me were stars budding in the purple sunset, ready to bloom. I was sitting in front of Destan again, his arms around me so that he could hold Siri's reins. And his warm breath grazed my neck as he murmured, "Raine?"

I turned my head to look back at him. His eyes were the same colour as the moon now wide and high behind us, and twice as bright. "Yes?" I answered, my voice also soft. There was something about night time that made whispering seem ritual and necessary.

"For the past three years, I've entered in a shooting contest down at the Base, and never won. But I think maybe this year…I could enter you in instead? I feel like it would motivate you to learn all the stuff I'm teaching you if you have an exciting goal to reach," he said, brows raised ever so slightly in anticipation of my answer.

198

My eyes squinted uncertainly. "I...don't know...if you've never won then how could I stand a chance?"

He smiled mysteriously. "Because I have never known anyone that had such archer-eyes as you. It's like you were born for this and just have to unlock that potential Zhanshi within you." Destan motioned up at the sky where the warrior constellation twinkled down on us. Thgindim was entering the thick of winter, when Zhanshi's gleaming belt of three stars and shining shoulders ruled the heavens for the cold months to come.

I sighed, and couldn't help but smile. "Mmm, I don't know...my mom always said he had a club and shield, not an archer's bow."

"Bullshit. He's a hunter, and how're you going to get dinner with a shield and club?" Destan scoffed, shaking his head. "And just look at that in his hand, that gorgeous curve. That is a bow, I'd bet my wolf." To that, Siri even seemed to snort a little loudly, and we dissolved into hushed laughter.

"Maybe you're right, then," I said. "It's funny you mention him, though. I've always liked Zhanshi best, out of all the constellations."

"How come?"

"Because when it's coldest, hardest, when everything tends to suck the most, he's always up there. Even if I'm lost in the woods with frostbite or I've just fallen through ice, or I'm just in my hut looking out my tiny window, I'm under the same sky and not far from home at all, but in the same place," I mused, my head tilted all the way back to gaze at the stars again. I wrinkled my nose. "Does that make sense?"

"Mmhmm," Destan said, his eyes tenderly smiling at me. "You are an interesting person, Raine Ylevol. I want to know everything there is to know about you."

I glanced away, shrugging. "There isn't much you don't already know. All of my secrets at this point involve you, so there's not much to tell."

"True. But that can't be all." A few seconds ticked by and then he snapped his fingers, asking, "What is your favourite colour? This is one I've been waiting forever to know."

"Why does it matter what my favourite colour is?" I laughed, knocking his shoulder with mine. "I don't have one."

"*What?* I thought you were an artist!"

"I *am* an artist!" I protested, groaning and facing forward again. "If anything, that's why I can't just choose a favourite colour. I feel like I am only really in love with colours when they sit beside each other; when they form something bigger than they can do on their own."

Destan sighed, cursed under his breath. "Isn't there anything simple that you like?"

"I like you."

"Are you calling me a simpleton?"

"Well you aren't the sharpest knife in the drawer."

He launched into a tickle attack, making me squeal and jump as he got my sides and ribs, fiercely demanding, "You take that back! You know I am the future overlord of the Majesty Council! Under this hat is a brain as big as a pumpkin!"

I gasped for air, crying out, "Yeah, and like a pumpkin it's all hollow and squishy inside—"

This time he tickled my neck with the frayed end of his scarf, making me shriek and flinch away, and Siri stopped walking to keep us from tumbling off and over the edge of the cliff. I had turned completely around, Destan and I face to face now as we struggled to stay sitting up on the wolf's back. Destan chuckled quietly, holding up his hands in surrender. We sat there for a while just looking at each other and panting after all of that tickling, and I couldn't believe how easy it was now. It was comfortable, as easy as if I were looking at Chan or Gwen. And

Destan had such a kind face. Dirty skin smeared with mud and pale freckles, an angular, strong jaw, a slightly crooked nose that appeared to have been broken once or twice in his. A face still soft with kindness around his eyes and mouth.

He blinked, eyelashes glimmering gold in the light of the moon now hanging like a sliver of ice above us. "Is the guy you're courting as interesting as you are?" he whispered.

The lightness of the situation faded ever so slightly as Skye was mentioned. I nodded, curtly. "He's okay. He's nice, lives in upper Starshade. Works at Peak."

Destan eyebrows rose as I said that, and he nodded. "Not bad. Not bad at all. Seems like you're going to be in good hands." I must've frowned, or shown some sort of distress, because Destan's forehead crinkled in concern. "What is it, Raine?"

I was absently toying with my hair, loosening my bangs from my ribbon so that they fell more and more into my eyes. My voice sounded really raspy suddenly. "It's nothing. I just don't...I'm not sure if..."

"You don't love him," Destan whispered, shoulders sinking a little. Before I could answer, he patted my arm, giving me what looked awfully like a wooden smile. "You'll come 'round. That's how it is with a ton of parents down here. The whole falling in love and marriage thing has to be switched when you gotta put bread on the table before aiming to put a blush in your lover's cheeks."

He laughed, but I didn't feel in the mood anymore. Desperate to get off that topic, I tried to remember where our conversation had begun.

"So," I said, clearing my throat and forcing a tight smile, "I suppose I could try that shooting competition. But with all of the Fluxaria drama, and courting, not to mention my actual job, I'll have to get good fast."

"It's not for a couple of months, so we've got time. And you are improving at a remarkable pace, Bluehead, so I think you'll be shooting the flame off a candle in no time."

He guided Siri back onto the main road, picking up the pace as JPs started hollering us to get home and shut off the electricity as if our hut had any. I glanced back, smiling at him. "That would be a very cool thing to do. If I can do it by then, I'll compete."

Destan grinned. "So it's a deal?"

I nodded, once. "Deal."

chapter twenty-one

"First matter of business," Irene said, gnawing on some bread I brought her that Destan made magically tasty with his honey, "is we gotta get that tablet. It's that hologrammy thing all Majesty Councilmen and Peak workers carry around. It will have every file we need ranging from the threats sent to Fluxaria, to a map of the Tower, and any passcodes we need to get into where they might be hiding more weapons."

We were now actively plotting the route to saving Fluxaria, and yet while the theory of the plan made me equally excited as I was nervous, the actual going through with it continued to trouble me. It was mostly because of self doubt though, and Destan always managed to lift my self confidence with a goofy smile or comment about my mad skills.

"So, when are you thinking Raine and I would go up there? There needs to be a lot of planning if you expect us to actually make it to Peak," Destan told her, nudging me without a word and pointing at my bow leaning against the target. Sighing, I went to practice while he and Irene continued the discussion. My new targets were empty bottles I'd found sticking out of the trash. Not only were they smaller than the traditional target I'd been using before, but they were rounded and it was much harder to actually hit one and not just skim the edge, making it totter on the tree stump where it was perched.

"The next day *both* of you can take off. Can't be a weekend because I'm assuming that the dude we're stealing from spends his weekends out of the office. Just to be safe, at least, a weekday would be best. I have..." Irene reached into her satchel, her tongue stuck in between her teeth for concentration, and pulled out what looked like a scroll, "this! It's something an older spy stole from Thgindim a while back when I was still only an apprentice. If you call in to the Peak offices that you have something you believe to be an ancient mountain artifact, then they will provide transportation for you two to go up to the mountain and present it to a Councilman for examination. They will dismiss you after only a few questions so that they can run tests and check to see if they're missing anything like what you found, but instead of leaving, I want you to go to the floor where the Law Enforcement and Foreign Affairs guy is and find that tablet."

"And how do you suggest we make it inside this office without getting caught?" I asked, hands on my hips.

Irene pursed her lips, looking off to the forest as she seemed to be contemplating something. Then she spoke, slowly, "Well...it really only takes *one* of you to deliver the scroll. Then the other could have the job of getting the stuff we need."

"Which you still haven't explained," Destan pressed, agreeing with me about how unclear it was all beginning to seem.

Irene's eyes flashed. "The other person, which, in this case, let's say is Raine here, won't go with you into the Tower. My original plan of action was that I wouldn't go in at all or show myself unless it was a last resort and I'd have to use the scroll as an excuse," she began to explain, looking from me to him to get our complete attention. "I was set on climbing the Tower. I've got the equipment to do it. The tools can get through the metal and get you up to the floor, easy."

I gasped, "'*Easy?*' Maybe for you, but I'm not a trained and specialized spy, or even have much upper body strength!"

"That's why we're going to just have to practice," she insisted, punching her fists on the ground for emphasis. "Once you get the motion down and have a feel for the hand spikes and everything, it's not that bad. And you're lucky you've got this guy to help, because someone needs to be inside the office to let you in."

"And I could just walk right into the guy's office?" Destan asked, scratching his head as he struggled to grasp the full idea of it all.

"The person who you're bringing the scroll to is the same one who has that office with the files and tablet we need," Irene said, speech getting increasingly faster as she tried to make it seem less crazy than it really was. "Slipping inside will take a little stealth, but it locks from the inside and you'd at least have five minutes to scour through the place and get out with your girl before the guy returns. And if he does come back early, it's not like you two won't have your bows. Raine will carry up the weapons outside since I'm figuring you couldn't pass into the Tower with a bunch of arrows." She held her arms out, face bright with enthusiasm. "See! It all comes together just fine!"

It was seeming a tad more possible, but I still couldn't keep myself from frowning at her. "So…you're going to train us? To get in and climb and all of that?"

Her face split into a smile. "You bet your little blue ass. And we're starting today."

And thus began the weeks of utter *hell*.

"LIFT THOSE KNEES YOU SISSY GIRL, YOU WIGGLY-MUSCLED WEAKLING!" Irene roared at me from the base of the cliff, waggling her homemade crutch in the air as

I struggled up the cliff face, face redder than mountain berries, hair completely undone from my bun and hot and sticky on my face. "I could climb better than that *and I'm incapacitated!*"

I lost my grip on a branch jutting out from the rugged rock and whipped my head around screaming, "*SHUT UP, ASSHOLE!*"

I heard a whistle and then Destan's snicker, "Whew…you're making Raine cuss like…well, me."

"YOU SHUT THE HELL UP TOO, BEANIEHEAD!" I bellowed, wanting to cry, wanting to chuck a thousand bricks at the both of them, but only gnashing my teeth and struggling to get a new hold. I was only ten feet up, just about make it to the vacant meadowlark's nest three more feet up on a grassy cliff. That was our marker, and Destan had reached it an hour ago. This was regrettably my sixth attempt and I still found myself a hair away before plummeting down into the pile of pine needles we'd swept up into a big scratchy cushion. Even this sixth fall managed to steal the breath straight from my lungs.

From the squashy pine bed, my eyes burned in the onslaught of the high noon sun, my fingers ached from the stiff grip I'd been forcing them into with every reach, and my throat felt scorched from demanding it to send me so much air. Irene's face appeared above me, calm and placid, but then bursting into the wide, goddamn annoying smile only she could produce.

"Again!" she yelled, and before I could protest with a few expletives and maybe even some Fluxarian slurs I'd heard from JPs, Destan's hands went into my armpits and hoisted me to my feet.

I snatched my ribbon from the ground and began savagely tying up my hair again. "I do not know what you two expect of me. Why should the seventh, tenth, hundredth time be any different? I just can't climb!"

"No, you can climb," Destan said, crossing his arms against his chest firmly.

"Yeah, you were able to get down to me lickety split in

that avalanche, and those rocks were falling. That was much harder than this puny little cliff," Irene added, making my hands ball into fists defensively.

"Then, I'm definitely doing something wrong," I muttered, stretching out my hands and wincing as I heard a few knuckles crack.

Destan rubbed the stubble along his jaw and smiled, murmuring, "No...*we're* doing something wrong. Irene and I."

Irene raised an eyebrow. "Say what?"

"Raine doesn't want it," he said simply.

I blinked back at him, baffled. "Yes, I *do* want it. Why do you think I've gone up that thing six times now? Just for the hell of it?"

Irene giggled again, whispering into Destan's ear, "It's so funny hearing her curse. This is more fun than I'd thought."

"They say the quiet ones have the loudest minds," Destan agreed, chuckling behind his hand annoyingly and making me want to punch him.

I glared. *You haven't even gotten me started yet.*

"I think it's time we make you want it more, Bluehead," Destan said, smile vanishing completely as he clasped his hands behind his back and began to circle me like a wolf around a baby deer. "Sure, you want to show us you aren't a sissy-girl-weakling, but what are you climbing to? A meadowlark nest?"

I narrowed my eyes, feeling all colour drain from my face. Irene sucked in an excited breath and punched Destan's shoulder. "I like where this is going," she said.

Destan sighed, a sick grin on his stupid rotten face and his eyes went from the friendly, starry, grey to silver blades and he came toward me, making me backtrack into the nearest tree. He came so close to me that I could smell every grain of pine stuck in the fibres of his wool coat, and he caged me in by pressing his hands on either side of me onto the tree trunk. Unlike before when we had been talking so closely before on Siri, now I couldn't bear to look into his eyes, which were intent on my face.

"What are you doing?" I asked, in more of a squeak than what I'd hoped to be a bit more intimidating.

He cocked his head to the side and breathed through his nose, bringing his mouth to my ear and whispering, "I know what you want, Raine." His cheek grazed mine ever so lightly as he pulled away, setting my skin on fire.

My heart was drumming so fast and my face burning so hot, I could hardly think of anything but the fact that his face was no more than two inches away and his nose nearly touching mine. *I don't know what I want, you tell me. Why do you make my entire body feel like it's been hit by a lightning rod? This can't be good, this isn't what I'm supposed to feel, I don't know what to do if I feel this way, what to do with these feelings. I could either make them go away, or…*

My mouth opened to speak, but I couldn't produce a sound, my lips trembling. He was so close that I could count the freckles trailing below his eyes like indecipherable constellations. I could see the threads of milky white swimming in the silver of his irises. He was so close that if he were to take one more step—

"GET IT, NOW!" he suddenly shouted, slashing through my daze. I hadn't even noticed Irene limping over to where my precious bow sat upon a mossy rock. I was too wrapped up in having Destan so dangerously close that I couldn't make it away from him in time for Irene to take it and chuck it straight up into the meadowlark's empty nest.

I gasped, shoving at Destan's chest and charging to the base of the cliff. "You…*you*…" I fumed, struggling to find the cruelest word, but at the same time I could feel the anger begin to bubble through me like strength. I clenched and unclenched my fists and muttered, "Jerks." Lamest thing I could think of. At least Irene wouldn't have another naughty word from my mouth to laugh at.

I ignored Irene's still quite frail state and pushed by her, digging my boots into the first crevice and reaching up with my calloused fingers to find a good grab. My father's bow? *My father's bow* was the best thing they could think of? It's all I had left of him! If I didn't make it up, how could I enter that contest Destan talked about, how could I succeed to shoot the flame from a candle, how could I make Destan proud of me? No wonder it was the perfect thing to get me up the cliff all the way this time.

I made it to the nest and past it, slinging the bow across me and climbing and climbing higher. Ignoring their bewildered shouts to stop going any higher and come down before I broke my neck, I continued up until I reached a deep enough crack to use as a landing and rest. Flat on my back, I squeezed my eyes shut and felt laughter gurgle from my throat like a wild stream.

The world felt like it was spinning, the rock under my back the perfect resting place. I sat up and peered over the ledge, grinning and waving as Irene hollered up, "Okay, you did it, now come down, will you?! Your slowness has delayed lunchtime long enough!"

Feeling suddenly mischievous, I shook my head, taking from my pocket what I'd snuck from Destan's belt when he'd had me up against that tree. The plastic baggy of pork and egg rice balls shimmered in the sunlight as I held it up and grinned, "You're going to have to come here and get your lunch if you really want it, gimpy."

Destan exploded into laughter, hands over his mouth and eyes shining as Irene's jaw dropped in shock and I could see the bad words forming from her lips, aimed straight at me. I winked, wondering if Destan could see, and then he had the spy latch onto his back, monkey-style, and he scaled up the wall with the long, easy movements of his strong arms pulling them both up to me on the ledge.

I scooted back as he eased himself over the edge and onto the landing, carefully letting Irene climb off of him before he let himself settle on the cold stone. The spy brushed off her hands, looking at me with a fierce and loathsome and odd sort of appreciation. She snatched the baggy from my fingers, muttering, "You are one strange girl, you know that? You've got some guts,

I'll give you that much."

The maybe-compliment made me feel a wave of self confidence and I beamed, holding out my palm as Irene dished out the sticky rice balls to me and Destan, hers hanging out of her mouth, half-eaten and displaying the creamy pork filling inside of the chewy rice casing.

I tried to eat it slowly, savoring the only not-soup thing my mom had managed to make in the past month. She'd been given a rather large tip from Skye's mother the day after our date, with a large order of spinach dumpling stew. I was pretty sure the sudden generosity had more to do with her son finally on the fast track to getting hitched and she just wanted to keep the bribe going. I was glad for it, though, because it earned me and Gwen a trip to the market to pick up the not-so-cheap bean paste needed to turn rice and pork chunks into this tasty lunch.

As I chewed slowly, savouring each bite and letting it lay a little longer on my tongue before swallowing it down, Destan moved to sit beside me, our shoulders almost touching. Instead of giving in to the usual act of moving close enough that we were leaning comfortably against each other, I subtly slid a little farther, still shaken by the intensity of emotions I'd realized I'd had for him back in the meadow. He didn't seem to notice, taking a large bite of the rice ball and shooting me a grin, which I struggled to return just as whole-heartedly.

"Do you have a courting thing this weekend?" Destan asked, gulping down the entire ball suddenly and licking his lips in satisfaction. "I might have to work in the woodshop both free days…Ling is showcasing his work at Emergent and so this weekend I'm gonna be too busy with minding the shop to do this Peak expedition thing yet."

I twirled a wildflower in my fingers. "No official courting stuff. But the JPs are inspecting the house and installing the new radio and stuff so my mom'll need me home to keep Gwen from getting in the way of any of that," I said, shuddering at the memory of the time seven-year old Gwen had blown a friendly raspberry at the Captain of the Underbrush police fleet and had ended up with a hand-shaped bruise on her soft little cheek that lasted for two whole weeks. "Maybe next weekend though. I'm going to Skye's birthday party tonight, so I actually should start heading back so I can get ready."

I slung my bow across my body and had started getting myself back on the cliff to climb down, when Destan cut me off with his sudden bout of laughter, and I jumped, gripping the ledge more tightly.

"Wait— he's having a *birthday party?*" Destan gaped, "Like, with balloons and cakes and decorations? Well, fuck, he sounds real mature…"

"Not that kind of party! He's turning nineteen, not ten for crying out loud," I groaned, starting back down, Destan following with Irene clinging to his back again. Once we were a little lower than the meadowlark nest, we let go of the cliff one at a time and bounced on the fluffy pine needle cushion at the bottom.

Mom will go nuts seeing how much stuff she'll have to do to get me ready for this cotillion, I thought, picking some of the needles from my hair and observing my now blistered, and scratched hands. I prayed she wouldn't try to smooth out the calloused tips of my fingers and along the inside of my knuckles though, because they had come about from the regular shooting practice and they were helping it not hurt so much to draw the string back.

"Snag us some cakes and goodies?" Irene asked, her palms pressed together to beg. I nodded and saluted them both before trekking off.

On my way back home, I decided to first make a stop to see who I should've made an effort to visit at least once in the past few crazy busy weeks. I walked all the way to the Songs' house in southern Underbrush, and knocked on the door. Velle and Chantastic's grandmother came poking her raisin-like face out from behind the door and let me in, recognizing me by my hair in an instant. She was deaf and couldn't speak a word to me, but always smiled and seemed to know how to make me feel at home. I guess I didn't mind as much as Carmen seemed to since I had to deal with a near mute sister on a regular basis and was used to communicating wordlessly.

Chantastic was already home from work and came padding up the stairs from the cellar where she and her twin slept. When she saw me, she gasped, made a '*wahhh*' noise and opened her arms to embrace me. I rushed into her and held her close, overwhelmed by how many different flowers she could smell like all at once.

"Raine! I thought you'd dropped off the mountain," she whispered in her low musical murmur of a voice, burying her face in my shoulder and squeezing me.

I let her go, but then sighed and hugged her again. "I've missed you so much. I'm sorry I haven't come by, everything's been so crazy lately."

"I even went by your house a few times, but your mom said you were staying late working or out with Skye," Chan sighed. She pulled back, smiling, "How is the courting going?"

I caught her up on the lunch date and even vaguely mentioned that the Irene thing I'd been stressed about before was getting better. On the topic of the birthday boy, I then asked, "Would you come to Skye's birthday party with me tonight? I can't go alone and would rather it be you than my mom. I'm gonna ask Velle and Carmen too. We can all catch up with each other on our new life stuff."

She gasped, swaying back and forth excitedly as she said, "Yes, yes, that sounds awesome! Velle's going to get back home any minute too, so that's good." She smiled sweetly, and when Velle arrived and got the invite, we all journeyed back near my house to Carmen's to bring her along.

For Skye's birthday party, my Mom put me in my Career interview attire. It was ironic because despite me being a Laundress and washing thousands of clothes, I still hadn't gotten the mud out of the hem of my skirt, so I snipped about a foot off so that the skirt ended right at my knee. This way it wouldn't get in the way of my walking either. Mom screamed at me for cutting it, but I soothed her with a cup of tea and I let Gwen try to braid my hair. Mom nearly burst a vein at the terrible knotting Gwen had achieved and then told me to do whatever the heck I wanted with it. I grinned and reached for my red ribbon to make the bun I was so used to.

He was holding the party in Starshade's town meeting hall, and the simple hall was filled with candles and tables of food and people that I didn't know. Skye came over right away, beaming and bowing. "Raine! I'm so glad you could make it! Could you introduce me to your friends?"

"This is Velle, Chan Ai, and Carmen. We went to school together," I explained, motioning awkwardly at them as they curtsied. They all looked so beautiful.

Skye bowed to each of them. "Nice to meet you all. Help yourselves to any of the food and dancing." Then his eyes met mine, making me feel like he already wanted to pull me away from them but was too timid to say it out loud.

Though I wanted to spend some time with my girlfriends, I took the step for him, hoping maybe I could just get a dance over with and then return to them. "Skye, would you like to dance?"

His expression looked like it could cure any illness it was so happy.

"I'm an awful dancer," I warned him as we moved out onto the floor. I doubted he could pick me up and spin me like Destan had done back in his woodshop when we and Gwen had that spontaneous dance party, and also the music was slow and boring, emotionless without any singing. His hand was all soft and sweaty in my own, his cheeks pink with blush.

"Don't worry, they don't teach the lawyers how to ballroom dance up at Peak so we're on equal playing field, I'd say." He laughed but I couldn't really tell what was so funny.

I think it was moving with him that was the problem. He'd

213

move back and I'd move back too, but I was supposed to let him lead and go towards him or with him, and I always tried to dance in the opposite direction whether I was trying to or not. I stepped on his feet a few times too, and bumped into so many Starshaders that it wasn't even funny.

"I'm sorry if I may have pressured you into coming tonight," Skye said quietly, looking at the ground as he spun me and I went the wrong way and tripped over someone's foot. "I don't blame you if you want this to be the last time we see each other." I was so taken aback that I stopped dancing.

"Oh," I said, blankly, swerving out of the way of a couple who actually knew how to dance, "I mean…do you want this to be the last time?"

His face was beet red. "Of course not, I really do like spending time with you. But I also remember you said I'm the first person you've courted, so if you think you want to try with someone else, there's no contract binding you to me yet."

My stomach lurched, my mother's expression still fresh in my mind from when she'd scolded me about leaving him right after our first date at the cafe. "I would h-hope this isn't the l-last t-t-time." My words were as unstable as the lie was, and so I bat my lashes encouragingly, taking his clammy hand in my own again. "I really like you, Skye."

His entire face softened; his ears even seemed to perk up. "You do? You're not just saying that?"

No, I like you fine enough I just don't want to marry you and I think I might like someone else the way I'm supposed to like you, my mind was yelling over and over, and I struggled to collect different words to answer him, "Of course. If it seems like I don't…well…I'm just so new at this and still nervous."

"Oh, Raine you are talking to the shyest man in Starshade," he chuckled, taking my other hand too and planting a kiss on the top of my knuckles. Mom had worn down thecalluses, and now I felt his mouth touch my skin much more closely than I would have before. "It's all right. I just want to make sure you're still happy."

My throat felt tight and I couldn't reply. I just kept smiling with my lips tightly pressed together and my back against the wall to hide how badly I was shaking. Skye kept talking, still not convinced I was having the ball I claimed to be having at this humdrum cotillion.

"You're amazing, Raine," he said quickly as if he wanted to get it out, but had to do it fast or else he'd be too scared to say it slower. "And…you're beautiful and so different compared to all the other girls. I like the way you look at things…it's always a surprise, what you have to say."

Can't you think my disagreeing with you about jobs and meat and whatever is rude like my mother would? Can't you think I'm bizarre like all the other kids used to think when they saw this blue hair or saw me with my retarded sister and that was enough to drive anyone away? Why? Why, Skye? My thoughts were making me sick to my stomach. I forced a strained thank you out of my mouth, adding with complete honesty, "You're nicer than any boy I know." That was true. Destan wasn't as nice as this shy Starshader boy who had everything gentle about him.

After a few hours, I decided that I couldn't pretend to dance any longer. Velle and Carmen were dancing with some boys that were friends of Skye's. Velle was with a dark haired boy, they were awkwardly swaying back and forth while she looked at the ground and he laughed at her and tried to make her look at him. She glanced up at his eyes and he hugged her right on the dance floor. I was struck with a pang of loneliness and found Chantastic sitting behind the dessert table. She had a not-yet-eaten cookie in her hand, and when she saw me she smiled a little with her mouth still closed. I scooted down beside her and let out a long sigh.

"How you doing?" I whispered, leaning over to plant a swift kiss on her forehead.

She smiled at that, but then shrugged, and took a bite of the cookie, peering silently at the swirling mass of dancers. I put my arm around her and her head fell onto my shoulder. She sighed, "Not super great. Some boy asked me to dance, but I just sort of ended up here with a pile of cookies."

I trailed my fingertips gently through her hair. "I'm sick of this courting business, aren't you?"

Chantastic nodded. "I missed when we treated boys like Fluxarians."

She had meant it to be funny, but my laugh sounded hollow and fake. Without warning I started crying, overwhelmed by all of the secrets I was keeping from her and the lies I was telling and how much my whole body ached from the training we'd done today.

Chan touched my cheek, making me look at her, and we moved under the table completely for privacy. "Raine? Raine what is it, what's wrong?"

I struggled to swallow the sobs that were climbing like monsters up my throat, ready to howl, and just shook my head, tears skidding down my nose.

"I have to tell you something."

chapter twenty-two

We walked through the tunnel of willow trees, the branches hanging down and shielding us both from the forest and the Starshade town on the other side. Chantastic's small hand was in mine, and I pulled her along slowly, trying to find a place where we could be alone once the curfew gong rang and the entire mountain would go into a mad rush to get to their houses. We sat down at the base of the tree, my crying now calmed, but my breathing still coming in quick, panicked gasps that I couldn't seem to control. I should've known eventually all of this would hit me like a truck.

"Chantastic, please, I didn't want to keep anything from you," I begged, tucking my legs to my chest and laying my forehead on the scabbed tops of my knees, "I just c-couldn't risk…risk someone hearing, getting y-you in trouble, getting caught."

"Caught for what, Raine? What is it that you did?"

"It's not just what I did, it's a bunch of things," I said, digging my nails into the hard ground. "There's just so much and I know I should have told you…"

She hushed me, reaching for my hand and looking more worried than ever. "It's okay, I'm here now; just get it off your chest."

I closed my eyes, my head feeling light and dizzy from the panic attack. I didn't want to. I wanted to. Somehow both urges were equally strong, fighting inside me and knocking everything out of balance. Not letting myself be tortured over it any longer, I confessed it all to her, beginning with, "There was an avalanche. An avalanche right around the Starshade meadow where I work."

"Mmhmm."

"And me and Destan…remember, Destan Abrasha? The guy who left school kind of early?"

"Oh. Yeah, I think so."

"We…work together there," I paused, looking up at her, "and also sort of fool around. Nothing really bad before, just he wanted to teach me how to shoot and we just get to hang out and talk when we're done our work."

She nodded, so far understanding. But then her eyes grew serious, penetrating mine as she whispered, "Nothing really bad before what, Raine?"

"We found a girl caught in the rocks and got her to safety," I began to explain, choosing my words carefully as underbrush's first snow started flurrying down through the branches. I looked up, watching the flakes fall. "We've been taking care of her. I had to steal some medicine from my mom and she's been staying in the meadow where we work, which is trespassing, and we got caught once but we're pretty good at hiding."

218

"Caught by JPs?"

"I had to get probation paint." I lifted my thick drape of bangs and Chan gasped, her eyes reading the faded red outlines of *Thief* and *Trespasser*.

"Oh Raine…" Her face drooped sadly, and she took my other hand in hers. She moved closer so that we could lean on each other.

The next sentence coming out strangled and hardly a whisper from my lips.

"The girl's a Fluxarian, Chan."

"What?"

"A Fluxarian, a spy. I'm helping a spy, me and Destan, actually— we're helping a spy," I dissolved into crying, falling forward as she hugged her arms around me and rubbed my back. I felt like I was breaking into a bunch of little pieces and she was trying to hold me together in the process, and yet the relief of finally letting the crime escape my overloaded mind was so immense I was able to keep from completely crumbling into another panic.

"I know it's bad, Chan," I rasped, "It could get my whole family killed, it could get you killed now too…*fuck…*"

"Shh, shh, no, it won't. If you're honest when you report it, then the penalty won't be too horrible. Just tell the Council you didn't know," she said, trying to remain measured, but her touch beginning to tremble on my back.

I sat up, wiping my nose and gazing at her despairingly, "I'm not going to go to the Council, Chan. Not because I'm afraid, because I just…won't, not anymore. I can't."

She gazed back, taking a ragged breath. "I don't understand."

The curfew gong rang and I looked back through the trees keeping us from the town. I hadn't told Skye goodbye, not even any of the other girls. Chantastic had rushed me out the minute I'd started crying. And now I was scaring her, I could see how her almond-shaped black eyes were quivering as they tried to hold mine steadily.

"I promised her, the spy. I promised I'd help her," I said, watching Chan's eyes widen, her mouth form a shocked 'O.'

"Raine, you can't! It's too dangerous, please," she pleaded, seizing my shoulders in her cold, shaky hands, and blinking quickly in the now rapid onslaught of snowflakes. "You'll get killed, your family might…they could be….please—"

"That's why I'm preparing," I insisted, coming closer on my knees so that our faces were nearly touching. I spread my cloak around us both, pulling it tight. "There's only two ways out. And the risk is real for both. You know the Council doesn't care about accidents versus intentional; they'd arrest me for treason even if I'd smiled unknowingly at a spy, much less saved one! I gotta do this, at least this way Destan and I can maybe make a difference, keep Fluxaria from getting destroyed."

Chan didn't say anything. We'd always done so well in silence together. It was one of the reasons we got along so well. She was quiet because she's always been very fearful of other people, and shy. I was quiet because I was silenced early on by my mother and how much she'd scold me for saying anything she didn't like. And it didn't help when my dad, the only person I could really talk to, went away. But now, this quiet was different, it hurt the more it lasted, and then I saw some tears come streaking from each eye of hers, one at a time, and she looked away, wiping them away with her sleeve.

"Is he making you do this?" she asked, voice low and rough, stronger than I'd ever heard it before. "Is Destan threatening you? Has he hurt you, Raine?"

I gasped, shaking my head vigorously back and forth, "No! Of course not, Chantastic—"

"Please stop this, Raine," she begged, beginning to rock back and forth, her eyes darting from the trees to the sky to the road where we could see people retreating into their homes for curfew.

I took her face in my hands, holding her forehead to my

own and trying to calm her down. "Shh, shh, remember what you told me? What you told me not long ago about doing what I felt was right? That what mattered most was that it wouldn't make me feel guilty or regret anything? This is it, Chan." I swallowed, trying to believe my next words. "It's right. It's what I have to do or else I couldn't live with myself, she's just a girl and she's showing me things I never knew and she'll die if I don't, I just can't betray her."

Chantastic's breathing became less uneven, less sharp and panicked as we crouched there in the quiet of snow and swaying willow branches. Something had made her become very still. I closed my eyes, nuzzling my nose with hers, my thumb tracing under her eyes and wiping back a tear.

"What about you? What about you dying? What about me? I n-need you, too, Raine, I love you..." she rasped, voice catching on the last word.

I threw my arms around her, squeezing her tightly to me, burying my face in her back and stifling my crying into the hood of her cloak as she did the same. I ran my fingers through her long black hair, tucking my nose into her neck and breathing deeply, smelling roses and warmth radiating from her pale skin. "I love you, too," I whispered, shutting my eyes so tight so that I may never open them again.

I didn't wait for the sun to get up and I escaped to the meadow with the meager Underbrush load. The snow had crusted over the main gravel road with a crunchy sheet of ice dusted with the fine white powder. In Carmen's front yard, three snowballs had been stacked and decorated with chips of bark and small stones to serve as a tiny little snowman. A smile twitched on my lips as I imagined her brothers struggling to roll the balls with only the inch of snow to make do with, and I shoved my hands into my leather coat's pocket, pulling down the sleeves of my sweater to keep my fingers from freezing.

Once I was on my rickshaw, I replayed the conversation

with Chan over and over in my head until I could accept it had actually occurred. Someone knew now, someone other than me, Destan, and the fugitive herself. It made an odd, paranoid feeling spread from my shoulders down to my toes, making everything and everyone around me seem more threatening as I pedaled past with the Underbrushers' clothes not even filling up the entire bucket. *But it's Chan,* I thought, approaching the Starshade gate and trying to find my ID with one hand and keep the rickshaw upright with the other. *You can trust her no matter what. She won't do anything.*

But it didn't still the nausea coiling in my empty belly. She still knew. And she was upset with me about it, really upset. Was I supposed to tell Destan and Irene now? Was I supposed to take Chan and integrate her into our little group of rule-breaking misfits and make her help with breaking into Peak too? All of the new questions to answer made me feel even sicker, and I had to clench my stomach and breathe evenly to keep from getting too worked up about it.

I made it to the meadow after slipping (repeatedly) on the snow that had frozen into ice overnight in the forest, and when I trundled in with my gears squeaking and clunky bucket bouncing against its frame, I was surprised to see that Destan had already arrived to look over Irene. He was slumped against a tree snoring softly, his arms crossed, not even covered in a blanket. He looked so peaceful and vulnerable even though he was sleeping with a dagger in his hand. He was posed actually rather handsomely; his blonde head thrown back with the beanie hat falling off and lashes shimmery with snowflakes as his breath came out in a cloud every time he breathed.

Irene, on the other hand, was snuggled inside one of the big crates Destan had brought over to heighten some of my shooting targets, and she was tucked in like a baby bird in a cozy nest with knit blankets and a ratty pillow or two stuffed around her. Seeing that she was still contentedly snoozing, not to mention coated in a fine layer of snow, I tiptoed over   and brushed back some of the frost off the ground; making room for a campfire. I bent down and picked up some of the flat stones we'd gathered, and built them around in a circle, wondering if there was any dry wood to be found.

After fifteen minutes or so of hectically trying again and again to strike the flint Destan had loaned me to make sparks dance and catch onto the branches, I was finally successful and had a small kindling smoldering to defrost the frozen spy. Then I looked back at Destan, wondering if he'd need to warm up, too. Wielding a flaming stick, I quickly came towards him and set the burning piece of wood on a pile of pine needles, gathering up rocks from the river's shore and hastily putting a boundary between the fire and the grass where he lay, sleeping.

Wiping my brow, I sighed, unable to get myself over to my rickshaw and start washing when the stream had to be so cold it would make my hands numb in seconds. Rather, I slowly looked back at Destan, his sleeping face, the rising of his chest and the way his red hat hung askew over the wild, snow-whitened curls. Timidly, I laid beside him on my side, sketchbook out and open in front of me. *Just until they wake up,* I thought, reasonably. *I need to clear my head. Nothing does that better than drawing.*

My pencil short and nubby after prolonged use and shaving down to keep it sharp, I sketched his outline with thick, dark strokes, and started shading around all the shadows on his angular face. I darkened around his jaw where he had stubble beginning to peep through, and flicked my pencil quietly on the parchment where his long eyelashes fluttered in sleep. When I finished drawing him and had begun just adding some of the detail of the tree he was leaning against, suddenly his arm shot out and his hand latched onto my wrist, making me yelp.

"Who goes there?" he growled, face remaining as blank and asleep as before, save the movement of his lips.

I rolled my eyes. "Who do you think? It's Raine..." I cleared my throat, "It's Bluehead."

He hummed in disagreement, wrinkling his nose as he

muttered, "Can't be. Because I *know* my Bluehead would be practicing her archery most diligently and not fooling around while her instructor tried to get some shut-eye." His mouth made a tight, amused smile, and I playfully snatched the beanie from his head, making him wake right up.

"Oh, give me a break. The sun hasn't even gotten to work shining yet," I chuckled, turning on my heel and fingering the scarlet yarn as I heard Destan scramble to his feet.

He leapt in front of me, red-faced and a mix between embarrassed and angry. I clapped my hand over my mouth to keep from laughing as I finally saw just why he had to wear that hat all of the time. His hair was indeed wild, but I was blown away at how truly tangled and unruly it was. The pale gold curls shot out like springs being pulled and stretched, and they poked straight up from his head stubbornly in every direction. When he'd removed the hat inside the mountain, his hair had been so sweaty that it had appeared a little less crazy to me, but now that I saw Beaniehead in all of his glory, I couldn't help but gape.

Huffing and puffing, he grabbed the knit cap from my fist and shoved it down on his hair, pushing down the curls flat as he could. "Haha, very funny. I have to cut it, just haven't had time recently."

I shrugged, lowering my hand from my mouth and beaming at him. "Sorry. Good morning, though."

He reached forward and ruffled my bangs in revenge, sighing, "Good morning, Bluehead. Have a good time at your boyfriend's birthday party?"

Getting to that already?! I grit my teeth, rubbing my neck. "Not awful. But not that great."

"Why don't you just abandon the bore?"

Irene's voice came floating from behind me, and I turned to see her struggling to get out of the crate, face squished in concentration as each arm was freed. She shot me a broad grin, adding, "Good morning. But, to repeat, why don't you dump him?"

224

"I…" I knew that the longer I stalled, the more it would seem I was pulling the excuse out of my ass. So I put on a happy face. "I'll grow to love him. He's not so bad as he is now." I looked at Destan, continuing, "Like you said. Bread before blush, right?"

He snapped his fingers. "Yup. Gotta live to survive."

Irene snorted "'Live to survive.' As if that made any sense…"

"Well, I'm guessing you've never been poor," I muttered, in a much harsher tone of voice than I'd intended to use with her. I went back over to my sketchbook and stowed it away in my pocket before either of them could see I'd been drawing Destan while he'd been sleeping. "You can't do everything you want all of the time if you want to stay alive."

"I know, of course not," Irene said, shortly. She pursed her lips. "But isn't spending your life with someone a big deal? Would you really just marry him to get good money?"

"And he lives in a nicer part of town," I said, growing increasingly uncomfortable at how blunt Irene was making everything seem.

"Let's just leave it at that, yeah?" Destan broke in, stretching his arms over his head and yawning ferociously. He rolled his shoulders back and came up to me, pulling out an arrow and smiling. "Practice time now."

Destan worked me so hard that I punched him a few times and he screamed right back at me before we both broke off into laughter. I split my own arrows for the first time which was so amazing that he kissed my head and even Irene did a little dance with us. And for every mistake I made, Destan had an explanation for why it would fly the way it did.

My arrow went too far left? My grip is too tight on the bow and I'm throwing the bow arm to the right. My arrow went too far right? I'm plucking the string on release and I'm gripping the bowstring too high on the fingers. My arrow rode low? My anchor was too high. My arrow rode high? My pull on the string had increased slightly just before the release. And whenever he told me what I'd done wrong or the strategy to get the arrow to go a certain way, I could almost always fix it the moment after and I'd get it perfectly the next try. It was like magic. I could only wonder how he'd learned all of this.

One day later that week, I asked him. His answer wasn't incredibly surprising, "My brother. Griffin picked it up during the preliminary JP training he did while still in school. If you think I'm good, you should've seen some of his shots," Destan said, and a nostalgic shadow passed over his face, his mouth set in a droopy sort of smile. Then he met my eyes, smiling more genuinely and tapping his head. "Shot a curl or two off of this head whenever he needed to get my attention."

"Sounds like my kind of guy." Irene laughed. She scratched her nose, sighing, "My brother is a spazz with anything physical. All he does is read and stress out about everything."

"You have a brother?" I piped up, "How old?"

"Just three years between us," she said, shrugging. "Nineteen but might as well be forty with all of those frown lines and speeches about 'making adult decisions.'"

I went over to the shooting spot, attempting to nock in two arrows at once, saying, "I have a sister, Gwen." Arm quivering, I pulled it back, licking my lips as I considered my next words, "She's...technically ten."

"Technically?"

"She was born with some sort of condition in her brain," I said, slowly, trying to explain in the way doctors had told my mom without adding the bits about how useless she was to society. "She doesn't function the same way or understand the way other people do. But she's very perceptive. She once recognized my mom was getting the flu and alerted me before we'd even thought of getting her tested."

"Damn..." Irene nodded, a thoughtful expression on her face.

I released the arrows, hitting the target but still not close

226

enough. *Please stop this, Raine.* Chantastic's words hummed through my head, *You could get killed…your family…*

I quickly yanked out another two arrows, pressing my fingertips hard against the bowstring and drawing back my arm, muscles aching as I tried to sweep the thoughts away. It almost worked.

"When is the competition again?" I asked.

Destan came over and fixed my elbow, then moved the bangs out of my eyes so I could see the target more clearly. "Next weekend. Not this one, but the one after it. The day before we're stealing from the Majesty Council."

"Why must you say it that way?" I groaned, releasing and only having one of the two arrows I'd nocked in fly out to the rotten tree. The other flapped limply on my bowstring, and I frowned, wondering how both could fly off at once.

"You just gotta face it, Bluehead," he said shortly, retrieving the arrow and handing it back. "Again," he ordered. Then he backed up and continued as I loaded up the bow with two arrows again, "You're looking at it from a pretty angle of 'helping people not get blown up."

"That's the truth, isn't it?"

"That's not how the Majesty Council will look at it if they find out or catch us," he explained. "They're going to try and find the ugliest intention we could have so that they can screw us over. So we gotta learn how to take it and defend it."

"That is a good tactic," Irene pointed out from her perch on a rock by the stream.

"Fair enough," I said, this time making sure to surround both of the hooked ends of the arrows with my fingers spread. When I released this time, both arrows were launched, hitting the target's center at once. That gave me a big applause, but it was when I split my own arrow that Destan decided the next test of my very much improved skill.

"Raine," he said, "I think it's time to test and see if you can do the competition."

He dug around in the basket tied around Siri's back and took out a candle, grin spreading from ear to ear as the task registered in my brain. Irene didn't seem to know or remember, so I clarified, "I have to shoot the flame off that candle. If I can, then I'll do this competition thing he wants me to do."

"Oooh," Irene said, eyes bright and excited, "I'd love to see that." She rolled onto her stomach, propping her chin on her two fists and kicking her feet playfully in anticipation.

"Prepare to be amazed," Destan said, shooting a look from her to me, eyes glittering, making my heart race a little bit. Blushing, I avoided looking at him again, finding the two flint sparking stones and handing them over. He struck them together and dots of orange flew in the air. Destan had a piece of dry yellow grass in between his teeth, and he struck the stones together until some fire caught on to the fluffy end of the stalk of grass. Then he carefully took it out of his mouth and used it to light the candle.

I was so nervous I shot as soon as he'd backed up behind me and Irene had rolled herself out of the way. The arrow sang from my bow, curving off the arrow rest in almost slow motion, snatching the fire from the candle, finally piercing the tree as I dropped my bow in amazement.

Destan stared at the arrow with his mouth agape in disbelief, Irene hollering appreciatively and clapping, all of her broken fingers evidently healed. He looked from the arrow to me and then back at the arrow again. "Shit…you…you're going to win this thing."

I rushed to retrieve my arrow and before I got to it, he pulled me into a bone crunching hug. I patted his back, laughing. "You really think so?"

Irene struggled to her feet and hobbled over, her short arms not making it all the way around us as she joined the hug. She and I were close to the same height, but Destan towered over us both, and he seized the opportunity to pick us up and make us squeal before setting us back down.

"You've got this thing in the bag!" Irene exclaimed, leaning against me for support as we looked round at each other, grinning from ear to ear. She knocked my ribs, adding, "Not to mention your climbing skills have gone from awful to awesome."

"I think this calls for celebration," Destan said, jogging backwards to disassemble and hide the target we'd set up even though it was only morning and we'd hardly done any practice at all.

I came over, asking slowly, "Right now? What about work?"

"Get it done," he said simply, taking out his flute and licking his lips in preparation to play for Siri. "We'll help you."

chapter twenty-three

"Yep," Irene piped up, pulling on me to help her over to the river. Meanwhile I went to the rickshaw and took out the not so hefty load of Underbrusher clothes. "If it leads to a party, I'm all for it."

Giddy with excitement, I broke off the long bar of soap into three chunks so that we all could work on scrubbing at once, and it only took a few stern looks and quick comments to make sure they weren't adding dusty fingerprints or new wrinkles to any of the clothes. It only took ten minutes with all of us working together, and with our numb fingers tingling and aching, we got to work preparing the celebration Destan was so insistent about. He'd silence any concerned comment I'd offer up by plugging his ears and saying 'lalala' like a little kid.

I rode my rickshaw quickly back, shocking Jun at how soon I'd finished today's work, and then took the silver pieces Destan had forced into my hand and spent them at the moonshine hut. Well— technically it was supposed to be a produce store. But anyone in Underbrush could tell you that the creepy little fruit hut had a backdoor or secret basement where vats of simmering alcohol and other effective concoctions sat ready for bottling.

I'd never been here before, and timidly entered, looking around the sad little joint where a couple saggy apples hung from the ceiling in a basket and indistinguishable wrinkled fruits filled barrels only halfway. A mildly unpleasant girl I remembered from school was boredly plucking leaves from the tops of plums the size of cherries, sitting at the front counter with a smoking cigarette between her lips.

Attempting to look like I knew what I was doing, I went to her, my hands in my pockets. She didn't look up, just set down a plum and took a drag of the cigarette, blowing smoke over the pile of leaves. Some flew off onto the dirt floor, dancing around my feet. I gulped, and then cleared my throat to get her attention. She looked up. "What?"

"I'm here for…your special brews," I said, fingers nervously tapping on my thigh.

Her dark eyes remained on me, glazed and indifferent. "Could you be more obvious?"

I could feel the heat rising in my cheeks, but I kept my mouth pinched and unfazed as I replied, "Well, can I buy some?"

She sighed loudly, sliding off her stool and coming around to me. Her black hair was cut unevenly around her ears, and it looked like in the few months we both had been in work, age had already sucked colour from her skin. She coughed, handing me the cigarette to hold for her as she bent down to the floor, reaching under the little straw mat by the counter. Withdrawing a key, she shuffled over behind the counter again, crouching down. I followed awkwardly, my boots scuffing up clouds of dirt as I walked. There was what looked like a little trapdoor in the ground, and she unlocked it, groaning as she lifted it up. Before she stood back up, she spared a glance at me again, her raspy voice still cold, "How many quarts?"

"Three," I said, and she took three reasonably clean pewter ones from the shelf below the counter. We traded the cigarette and mugs and she stood back up, sighing heavily again as she cracked her back. Then she looked at me pointedly.

"Are you gonna go down?" she asked.

I nodded to avoid more conversation, hastily slipping through the hatch and landing on my feet. Destan had requested what he'd called the 'elixir of life,' but all five of the distilleries were unlabeled and the moonshine barrels bore names simple as 'wild strawberry' and 'ginger root.' The drinks still bubbling in the big metal tubs were all the same colour, as well, so to be safe I ladled up one quart with that stuff, another with a 'dandelion wine,' and the last with Irene's bizarre (or at least I think so) request: 'molasses whiskey.'

Moving fast to stay warm, I clutched the corked up quarts to my chest and hurried back to the meadow, awaiting what Destan and Irene had gathered. But rather than seeing the elaborate set up I'd expected, the meadow was cleaned up and same as before. Irene and Destan waited on Siri, each of them with something in their laps.

"Raine!" Irene chanted, seeing me. "Just in time!"

"Hop on, Bluehead," Destan called, patting the spot behind Irene.

I climbed onto Siri's back, excitement rising in my chest. "Where are we going?"

"His place, he said," Irene said, glancing over her shoulder at me.

"The woodshop?" I asked.

Destan shook his head, sliding his fur-lined mittens over top his ratty gloves and taking hold of the reins. "Not my 'place.' Just somewhere I know our party won't be crashed," he replied, shouting the command at Siri. We took off, Irene and I lurching forward as the wolf yearned to carry all three of us to wherever this place was.

We rode and rode for what felt like entire hours passing by us. It was obvious we weren't because there would have been no way. But with every blink, the woods around us were getting darker and darker, the thicker tree cover chipping away the sun one bit at a time so that it felt like night even though it could only have been noon. *Another secret place tucked away,* I thought, remembering how strange it had been getting to the woodshop. Not to mention the fact that Destan spent his days working in the secluded meadow I'd only found due to getting lost. *Why does he hide so much in the shadows?*

He slowed Siri's running, letting her rest a bit and trot along the invisible path we were taking. She took us under a low pine branch, and before I ducked, I noticed something strange. Something blue and silver glinting near the trunk. Looking back after we'd passed through, I realized it was a painted birdhouse, bells dangling down from the worn, wooden bottom.

"Are we there yet?" Irene whispered, eyes raking over the shadowed trees and the birdhouses and bells perched in each of them like colourful, singing nests.

"Almost," Destan answered, more loudly, as if allowing us to speak regularly even though it felt as though the hush of night had been wrapped around us.

And then I saw it— brown and grey stone softened with quilts of fine green moss that was so dark it looked almost blue. There were two buildings in total, but both were crumbling so haphazardly into each other that it seemed that they were one collapsing mess of stone and ivy and lichen. Around them were what looked lik glass statues of women or animals or some mixture in between. The glass was now so dusted with age and pine needles and dirt that they looked like they were filled with murky water.

"Where are we?" I gasped, easing my legs over Siri's flank to climb off, once we stopped.

Destan helped Irene down and opened up his arms to the sky, turning in a slow circle. "It's cool, right?"

"It's a temple," Irene said, limping over to one of the statues and brushing off some of the pine needles with her hand, "or *was* a temple."

I looked at Destan for clarification and he nodded, unfolding a cloth sack he'd packed up with food as he spoke. "She's right. I think those are statues of the spirits."

"For sure," she added again, stepping back to take in the crumbling arrangement of stone, the tangles of vines that throttled what was left of the temple so mercilessly. "I'm guessing Thgindim doesn't use it anymore?"

I shook my head. "I didn't even know we'd ever had any temples."

Destan shrugged, "Well, we'd always heard about spirits in old folktales and stuff, right? At some point we thought they were real."

"You don't believe in the spirits?" Irene's eyebrows rose, and she looked from him to me in surprise. Then she whistled. "You Thgindimmers really are a deprived culture."

"I guess we just don't need to believe in them anymore," I said, slowly, coming over to Destan and revealing the three hot quarts of drink. "Now we know why everything is the way it is with science and technology, so there isn't much more to make sense of and assign to a divine power. The stories are fun, but if there were magical goddesses in the sky then they would have helped us and blown up the Majesty Council by now."

"Is that what your parents taught you?" she asked, still thoroughly taken aback. It was strange to me that she seemed so invested in all of this spiritual stuff. I'd always taken her to be more invested in the logical than the magical due to the way she planned so critically and talked to us so bluntly all of the time.

I had just shrugged at that question, but, after passing around the drinks and taking a couple of gulps, Destan said, "My brother Griffin had been really into the spirit stuff. I'm sorta neutral about it, I guess, but he really, *really* was serious about it. Like, really serious. Praying every night and building those little treehouses for the forest spirits."

"Ohh..." I murmured, "so that's what those were. I thought they were birdhouses."

He smirked. "Most likely are. I don't see any elves or winged faeries around, do you?"

Irene and I opened up the warm packets he'd handed us, and the minute I tore through the wrinkled edge, steam came pouring out. Giving him an appreciative look, I ripped open the rest, my face breaking into a grin as inside I saw was a clump of still hot, candied lavender and pansy blooms. Irene fist pumped the air. "I knew it! I could smell that syrup even when we were still riding over."

"Where'd you get these?" I asked, snapping apart a pair of chopsticks and fitting them around a sticky pansy. I'd never tried these kinds of sweets before. I'd seen vendors on the side of the road in Emergent selling them, but I'd never had the time or courage to go up and get some.

"That's a secret." His eyes flashed, and he knocked his shoulder against mine. "Just know I didn't spend a cent."

"Good," I said, tentatively slipping the flower into my mouth and chewing. The petals had been caramelized in honey and maple sugar, and they stuck to my teeth and coated the roof of my mouth, "if you'd blown your money on sweets, I'd have to act like a mother and scold you for it."

Irene took a swig of her molasses whiskey and swayed on the log bench she was sitting on. The quart was half empty after getting passed around a few times, each of us taking a sip. I think this one was my favourite. The dandelion wine was sweet and had that slight tang that went up into your nose, and the moonshine I'd gotten straight from the boiler was dry and savory, making me want water. But the molasses whiskey seared my throat and warmed me all the way down to my boots. It lingered and lingered and even had a rich taste of cinnamon that came after your first gulp.

Drinking it made me happy. It seemed to make all of us

happier. Sometimes we'd just laugh and laugh without saying anything. Or Irene would burp and then Destan and I would join in without shame, clinking mugs and polishing off our flower candies all at once, making our tummies upset but tongues happy as could be.

"Is this what being drunk is?" I asked, eyes darting left to right as we lay on a bed of moss, watching fireflies twinkle in the thick canopy of pines. The ground rocked me like a baby.

"*I'm* not drunk," Destan slurred, jabbing my arm, "I would know, I've been drunk before and this isn't it, but you most definitely are because you, Bluehead, are a lightweight."

I scoffed, "I can handle some rotten batches of moonshine. I feel perfectly fine."

"Stop talking!" Irene whispered, arms behind her head, eyes closed, a pleased smile curling through her lips. "More relaxing. You two might be dead soon with the mission and all and I'm gonna be even dead-er with the police comin' after us, so let's just...let's just be quiet."

"No!" I suddenly yelled, feeling a strange bout of confidence claim me, as well as energy. I leapt to my feet, thrown off balance and grabbing onto the stone wall of the temple. "We can't just lay here! We gotta...we gotta..."

"We gotta run!" Destan finished, standing up and catching onto my arm for support. We giggled, locking eyes, as he announced, "We are going to live it up, you hear? Let's go running!"

"Let's be wolves!" I laughed, skipping over to Siri, tripping over my own feet as Irene tried to get up on her own, crashing down repeatedly as both her alcohol-fuzzy head and injured leg defeated her. Destan hoisted her up onto his shoulders, letting out the first ear-splitting howl of the celebration, and I joined in soon after, spinning round and round in between the trees.

We took off yowling, leaving the empty food wrappings and mugs behind, Siri gliding beside us in our shadow. Destan swung Irene over the rivers and I flew so fast over the rocks and roots I thought I'd grown wings. Even in the dark everything looked like it had a pearly halo, and even though I fell down more times than I could count, we kept dancing and dancing, Destan raising his hands, gripping an invisible glass as he said, "Cheers to us! And may the spirits grant us good luck with our most treasonous and valiant endeavour this weekend!"

Irene and I blew kisses at the colourful spirit houses peppering the trees all around us, snow spun down like little white dancers, and the ringing of our voices echoed off of the mountain into infinity.

chapter twenty-four

The excuse I gave my mother about the shooting competition was that I had a rare laundry order for the Base. This story was even fishier because the competition was during the middle of the night, but my mom didn't seem to care as she had been in the process of cleaning some dirt off of Gwen's cheeks and barely even glanced up. Chantastic had checked up on me too, apologizing for her heartbreaking response to my secret. I apologized as well, saying I was sorry I'd let it get so intense before telling her, but that I had to stick by my decision to help Irene; that I would show Chan why it was so important if she gave me time to prove it.

And she'd nodded glumly, staring at her hands as she whispered, "I don't understand and I don't know if I agree with your decision, but because I love you I'm going to be here for you, okay?" She looked up, her mouth set in a determined sort of frown. "If you need something, if it's what it takes for you to not be found out, I'll do anything. I don't think I could keep living if something happened to you. You're who I love most on this whole mountain, Raine."

I'd hugged her then, very tightly and for a long time, murmuring, "I knew I could count on you. I promise with all of my heart I will be careful, and I'll let you know what's going on."

She'd pulled back, giving me a small smile. "If you're not busy this weekend, Velle and I are going to stay up in Starshade for a night or two to bring back some stuff Granny wanted." Now her face glowed with a truer smile. "The snowberries are in season up there already! If we gather some on our way back, we could make some paint for you, and lip colour for Velle. She's got herself a crush on some Underbrusher waiter up at Peak and is starting to wear makeup."

My heart sank. That did sound like a good time. But as I'd promised, I had to tell her how extremely unavailable I was this coming weekend. "I'd love, love, love to...but this weekend Destan and I are sort of doing a big thing for Irene." I could sense the concern ready to fill up my best friend again, so I added, "This is really it. It's the only thing she super, super needs of us and after this she'll be ready to go home."

"And things will go back to normal? It'll all be over?"

"Yes. And maybe even better."

She'd nodded, pulling her white scarf over her mouth and rubbing her mittened hands together. "All right. I'll trust you."

"Thank you. And you can trust Destan too, okay? He's really...not so bad." I'd smiled, looking at the ground.

"Mmhmm."

Her eyes were saying more than her words. I stared into them, my suddenly rosy cheeks probably communicating what she was guessing. "I'm...trying to deal with it," I said, sighing.

"Think he feels the same?" she asked, slipping her fingers through mine as we walked up the Underbrush road. She was going to work; I was going to the meadow to meet Destan so that we could go down to the Base.

I shrugged, then shook my head, "I really, really don't know. He seems to care about me, though."

"And he makes you feel excited, like it's hard to breathe when you see him smile?" she asked.

"Yes…"

"And when he even brushes up against you, do you want to bring him closer?"

I felt like covering my face with my hands in embarrassment, and then I turned away from her, groaning, "Yes…yes, yes, yes."

"Does Skye?"

"There's nothing *wrong* with him."

Chantastic nodded slowly, nibbling thoughtfully on her lip. Then she gave me a curious look. "Does Destan have any money? Anything your Mom would consider?"

Now my face felt like it could burst into blue flames, and I pressed my palms over my hands, whining, "I don't know, I don't know! Thinking of marrying him is just weird, like…I haven't thought that far about it, I just think I might have feelings maybe, and I'm not sure what to do with them, if anything…"

"It's okay, Raine. Of course that's skipping ahead too much," she soothed, and I bent down and kissed her cheek, making her laugh as we hugged one more time. "See me when it's done," she'd whispered, stroking my hair. "I need to know you're okay. And I expect to hear about Destan, too, all right?"

I'd nodded, taking a moment just to hold her and memorize how she felt and how she smelled and the way her voice crackled when she whispered because I was suddenly struck with the fear that this could be the last time I saw her. I put my lips to her ear, replying, "I will. I love you. I'll make it back."

We parted ways, and even with the Peak mission tomorrow, going to the Base tonight for the shooting match was scarier and on the forefront of my mind. The competition had to have been secret and under-wraps because no one's allowed to go any lower than Underbrush unless they're getting trained for the Justice Police or are some important Majesty Council figure. But I decided I wasn't exactly concerned with rules these days, so I thought, *Why not break another and go down to the Base and try to enjoy the last night before committing treason?* This thought did nothing to make me feel better.

If this was going to be my archery debut, I didn't want the people I was up against to think I was as delicate and weak as my body suggested. There's not much a skinny, short girl like me could do to make myself look all that more powerful, but I put on a clean, form-fitting, jade-coloured sweater, some leather archery gloves and arm guards that were once my father's, long denim pants, thick socks, and my black combat boots. I tied my hair up in my red ribbon as always. It was the best I could do to look tougher than I felt. As I left my house, I saw Destan waiting on Siri already, his mouth smiling.

"Hey," he said, eyes looking over me slowly.

"Hey," I echoed, stomach swirling as I came up to Siri and pulled myself onto her back.

"You ready for this, Bluehead?"

I beamed at him, trying to appear confident. "You know it."

Instead of having Siri take off right away as usual, he spun around on the animal's back to face me, and he said, passing me a little wooden box, "Here. I wanted you to have this. For good luck and for keeps. You're the best archery student I've ever had."

I rolled my eyes, blushing. "I'm your *only* archery student, Destan."

He held my gaze and replied gruffly, "Then you're the best friend I've ever had. Actually…my only friend, just to make it more obvious how much of a loser I really am." He laughed it off easily, scratching his neck and looking away, but I couldn't help but feel sad at that comment. I was going to say something like, *Me too, you mean a lot to me too,* or, *You're not a loser, you're amazing.* But before I could, he sighed, poking my arm playfully,

241

"C'mon, c'mon, open the box."

I lifted the lid and took out the necklace from its little pad of pine needles. "It's nothing special," Destan muttered, showing that uncharacteristic sort of nervousness again. "It's just wood and some twine and I haven't seen you wear any jewelry before or anything, but—"

"Stop," I breathed, taking off a glove so that I could feel the smoothness of the pale birch wood under my skin.

He'd carved out and polished what at first I'd thought was a number eight; the two loops that connected in the center and swirled around and around eternally. The pendant was carefully strung on a long piece of braided red, green, and violet twine, and when it hung from its proper position, the eight was turned on its side. Destan whispered, "It's infinity. You know…the forever symbol?"

"You made this?" I asked, my voice sounding faint and higher than I intended. I wasn't especially familiar with the symbol, but in my hand I felt like I was holding a promise of some kind.

"Let me put it on you," he said feebly, and I handed it back to him. He tied it around my neck, trying to have it lay flat against the red scarf of his I'd kept.

Quick heartbeats and breaths were bubbling up inside me, and all I could think was, *What does this mean? Is your body acting so confusing? Do you actually have these same strange reactions when we're with each other?* But as I meant to open my mouth and finally try to clear some of these things up, Destan yanked on Siri's reins and we were flying.

We disappeared into tree cover and raced out of Underbrush to get to the Base. Destan had said he'd done this competition before, so he knew where to go and where there would be future JPs idling around, so I held onto him tightly and trusted his navigation skills. If I thought Underbrush had looked forlorn, it was nothing compared to the steely grey silence of the Base of Thgindim. We snuck past the electric fences separating us from the muddy barracks and training areas for the JPs, and even the woods we dove into were too quiet and a little less alive than the forests up the mountain. A strong decaying smell permeated everything.

The trees thinned. Suddenly the sounds of voices and maybe even faint music graced my ears, and Siri slowed and stepped into where a bonfire was burning and about one hundred people had gathered. The clearing was huge, a field of cleared out trees where stumps still remained like heads poking out from underground, and the area ran straight against the mountainside. Wooden bleachers were set up along the edge of the mountain, and real targets (not rotten wood slices) hung all over the mountain face, some up so high that my jaw dropped in reaction. There were tables sagging under countless quarts of ale and beer, an untouched roasted boar, a pile of apples, bowl after bowl of berries and dandelion greens. People crowded around it laughing and yelling at each other. Torches sprinkled the mountain face and were placed all over the field to give everything a golden glow, and as we came into view, a roaring of greeting erupted from all people, young and old.

"Destan Attila Abrasha! Here at last!" one meaty guy boomed, his long beard glittering with drops of ale. "*Now* we can begin!"

He crushed Destan in a hug and Destan looked at me with a pained and desperate smile. "Nice to see you, too, Guang! But I'm not competing this year," he wheezed, gasping for air as the big man let him go.

"Oh, but you must, boy!" a lady with two long red braids and two chins and rich-looking clothing moaned in her deep, drunken voice. She had to be from Emergent, and she came all the way down here for an illegal archery competition?

"This is my friend, Raine." Destan extended his hand and pulled me down off of Siri. I waved to them all a little bit shyly. They seemed so friendly it was almost intimidating. "I've been training her for the past few months, and I've got to say she might be better than I am."

"Naw, I refuse to believe that. A few *months?*" Guang guffawed, waving his hands in the air and gulping down some more ale. Wiping his mouth and swallowing a burp, he surprised me with a big bear hug. He was wearing a coat I could remember washing in a Canopia load because I had thought it was so impossibly huge and there were so many cigar stains that cleaning it was horrible.

"Well, Guang," a pretty, middle-aged woman with dark curly hair said, pointing at my face, "Look at those eyes! They shine like stars!"

"A true archer's eyes," Destan agreed, taking my hand and smiling at me proudly.

"And what magnificent hair!" The Emergent lady sighed loudly, clasping her hands together, "May I touch it? I've never seen such a colour!"

"Sure," I said with an anxious laugh, coming towards her as she touched the strands that had already fallen out of my bun.

"So lovely," she breathed, stroking my face with her big manicured hands.

"Would you like something to eat or drink before we begin the actual competition?" Guang asked, motioning at Destan and me. We looked at each other and silently agreed that before we could shoot anything, we'd need some of that boar and beer. The molasses whiskey from the previous night had felt like fire and had been so good; this beer was bitter and ice cold and much weaker. I didn't like the experience of that quite as much as I had with the whiskey, and decided that on top of not liking it, I didn't want to be intoxicated in the least when I had to shoot in a competition in so little time. But nothing I'd ever eaten before tasted like this boar. The meat was fatty and greasy and dark, but so juicy and I didn't feel like I had to be polite around these people. All hundred of us gathered around the long table passing along sauces and more drink, and Destan and I joined in on singing some of the few folk songs we knew, and feasted on the meat and apples like wild animals. This would be my last meal before stealing from Peak tomorrow, so I ate until I thought I might burst and took comfort that Destan was doing the same, polishing off plate after plate.

When we were all satisfied, those competing were called up to the area in front of the bleachers. About forty out of the hundred-some people gathered were competing, newcomers still showing up with their bows and quivers. It was mostly men and boys overdressed in armor with fancy crossbows and compound bows and metal things with all sorts of levers and steel bowstrings and titanium arrows that I knew had to have been made in Canopia and shipped to Emergent. There were also some girls, like the pretty dark-haired one who'd talked to me when Destan and I first arrived, and a tall, thin girl about my age who I thought I might recognize from Skye's party. She had dark eyes, a river of silver-blonde hair, and a long, impractical navy dress. Some of the buff guys were flirting with her, but she'd move away as if bored. I felt a vicious tug in my heart and realized that more than anyone, I wanted to trump this girl the most.

"Here are the names your sponsors registered you under. If it's wrong, suck it up because we wanna get this thing started," another man, even meatier than Guang, called to us, passing out signs that we'd stick to our backs so the audience could keep track of who was shooting. I took mine from him and turned to find Destan in the audience, so I could glare at him. I found his face instantly and as soon as he saw me his head fell back and he started laughing uncontrollably. I pinned the sign that said 'Bluehead' on my back and stuck my tongue out at him.

"First round— hit the target five times in a row. You miss, you're out!" the man boomed.

I picked up my slender bow, kissing its smooth ebony wood and whispering, fingers starting to shake, "Don't fail me now, please…"

"Begin!" the man shouted, dashing behind the line of

archers so as not to get shot. I nocked in the first arrow perfectly centered so that it rested on the bridge completely flat. The target was ground level, so much bigger than a piece of wood, and about 20ft away. Easy.

I released it and hit dead center while other archers fired all around me. I couldn't get distracted by how other people were doing though, and shot four more times, hitting very close to the center every time. Some kids I guessed to be the children of some of the competitors ran out and retrieved our arrows and brought them back to us. Then the targets were dragged away. Only six people had been eliminated, and heart pumping hard against my ribs, I exhaled. These really *were* the best archers of the whole mountain, and I probably wasn't close to being the best. The silver-haired girl had split two of her arrows in the first round and as she turned to wave for the crowd to cheer for her, I squinted my eyes to see what the name on her tag was: *Snake Eyes.*

Round Two involved shooting one of the targets stuck about 50ft up the mountainside. Shooters had to hit it at least three out of five attempts. I hadn't done much distance shooting with Destan, but could remember what he had taught me about manipulating where the arrow should go. Nocking arrows low will make the arrow ride high. But that's harder to have it come out straight, so my anchor angle would have to be much higher than I was comfortable. I shot five and got four to hit it. The third one had gone wonky and smashed against the mountain face.

"Come on, Bluehead! You're better than that!" I heard Destan scream from the stands.

I looked over my shoulder, yelling back, "I know! But shut it!"

The crowd laughed and eleven people were eliminated in that round. The third round would get rid of a ton of people. The kids came out with two poles that had a bunch of tiny bells strung on strings, and some assisting adults dug the pole-ends into the hard mountain ground.

"Ring five of the bells with only seven arrows."

I glanced at Snake Eyes, who was still in and having the best form. She nocked in arrows and fired faster than anyone here. Destan told me always to wait 2-3 seconds before releasing an arrow no matter how confident I was in the shot. I got into my stance and anchor, and took a chance. I loaded in two arrows at once, and they both hit the same bell.

Nineteen were disqualified in that round, leaving only four of us. It was Snake Eyes, Guang, the dark haired woman, and me. For the final round, it took some time and more than just children to set it up. They brought out about twenty poles of increasing height, and hammered them into the ground in front of not the highest target, but one that was maybe 40ft up the mountain. They were all perfectly lined up in front of one another, and an Underbrusher boy with a long flaming torch lit the top of each where I hadn't noticed a wick was standing on

each end. The crowd 'oohed' and 'ahhed' at the line of flame, and the announcer shouted out, "This part of the competition will be held one by one. Archers may choose their own order of when they will go, but the point of this is to put out every flame and hit the target behind the torches

without setting it aflame. Archers, line up."

We fell into our own order without any discussion. Guang stood at the head of us, the dark-haired lady second, me third, Snake Eyes last. Guang raised his bow confidently, his tongue flicking over his lips and eyes so slitted that I thought they could be closed. He took his time on the release and I heard Snake Eyes give a sigh behind me. I muttered, "Shh, let him concentrate."

She snorted dismissively, rolling an arrow in between her blistered fingers. How strange. I had blisters when I first began archery, but they went away after I practiced a lot and hardened up.

Guang released the arrow and I watched in awe as it flew perfectly through every torch and smacked into the target. I clapped and hooted for him in amazement and heard Destan yelling out, too. Guang fell to his knees, fists hammering his chest as he triumphantly roared into the sky. Then he got up and danced over to the back of the line where he boomed, "See if you can beat that, Moira!"

"I don't know if I can," the lady called back, sighing and getting a rather high anchor. The torches were relit and, without a moment of hesitation, she fired. Her arrow flew through the first eight torches perfectly before unfortunately decreasing in height and speed. The crowd moaned and Moira's shoulders sagged disappointedly, but she was led to the audience with big claps on the back and cheers following her for getting this far. The torches she had put out were re-lit in a blink of an eye.

My arms shook as I stepped up onto the shooting platform and nocked in my arrow. I smoothed my fingers over the cock feather and tried to breathe calmly. I couldn't remember being this nervous and under such scrutiny since my Career interview. I inhaled deeply, closed my left eye and envisioned where I wanted the arrow to fly. I brought the string to the tip of my nose, remembering how Destan had bopped it so many times to remind me to always make them touch, and when I felt like I had lined up my shot best I could, I let the string roll off my fingers.

I held my breath as it went through the first, fifth, tenth, twentieth torch, putting them all out and hitting the target, even closer to the center than Guang's by a good two inches.

I dropped my bow in shock as the crowd thundered with applause. Guang dragged me to the back of the line with him and screamed at me, "Archer eyes, indeed! I've won this thing seven years running and you just stole it from me unless this Snake Eyes gal can split your arrow."

Dizzy with anticipation, I turned back in suspense to watch her go. She didn't look half as haughty as she had in the beginning of the match. Now she couldn't seem to hook the end of the arrow well enough on the bowstring, and I could see her blistered fingers shaking. She had to have only been training for a few weeks, and she was already this good?

Snake Eyes put out every torch smoothly, but her arrow smacked against the mountain, missing the target completely. As soon as it came in contact with the mountain wall, the audience exploded into the field, all coming towards me in a mob.

Everything roared in glory. Flames of sound burning and erupting as a hundred bodies jumped towards me and rubbed my head and kissed my cheeks and embraced me. *I did this? I did this!* I thought, tears of joy flooding my eyes, everything so golden and shining and full of fire as I elbowed through the crowd to find Destan. Everyone was coming for me and the announcer was trying to put some kind of medal around my neck, but with Destan's red Beaniehead bobbing above the crowd, I just kept digging my way through until we came into each other's arms. He was hysterically beaming and crying, too. This was it, our last night before the mission. Our last night before risking it all. I could see the desperation and adrenaline and victory searing through his silver eyes, making them two shiny bullets.

When we met in the middle of the mob, he picked me up and spun me around in the air, and when he finally set me down I crushed my grin into his chest and tried to hold him as tightly as I could. "You did it! You did it, Raine!" he yelled, holding my face in his hands, eyes glistening.

"*We* did it!" I said. I threw my arms around his neck, feeling him lift me off the ground and spin me once more around. We were pressed together, screaming, crying, trying to make the moment last forever, and before we knew what was happening our lips came crashing into each other and we were kissing.

chapter twenty-five

I blinked up at my ceiling, unable to fall asleep. It was late. Probably 3am. Two hours and I'd be up and running to steal from Peak Tower. My fingertips ran over the dark circles under my eyes, traveling to my mouth, tracing the curve of my lips.

It was like he was still kissing me.

I could still feel him, all over me. His lips, eager and desperate yet careful and gentle, hot and tender, and his tongue had only moved inside my mouth and on my own like it was exploring me and telling me a secret all at once. He had tasted like beer and honey and…Destan. Like he was his own dessert that I was able to taste and experience.

How his thumb had caressed my cheek, his big hand on my waist pulling me closer and closer, his muscular arms supporting my back. How my chest had pressed against his, every molecule of me wanting him even closer, closer, in any way possible because I knew that if anything went wrong the next day,

I'd never have the chance to be close to him again.

I remembered the deafening roar of the crowd cheering as we kissed, and how it seemed to go silent in my ears the moment we pulled back to look at each other in shock and confusion and awe and then made the decision to keep kissing each other feverishly. We'd drifted from the field toward the empty stands; he picked me up and pressed me against the underside of the bleachers, burying kisses in my neck and running his fingers up and down my spine.

How his hair curled around my fingers and how he pulled my head back so he could kiss my neck and shoulder. The slight grittiness of his recently shaven cheek under my lips felt more perfect than velvet. How his hand snaked up the back of my shirt and held my lower back, his hand so warm and leaving shivers everywhere it touched, like magic. And then—

"Stop…Raine, stop."

That had been what he'd said. He had said it softly but seriously, his voice a little cracked and his lips coming back to mine for another fleeting moment before he drew back and cursed quietly. My lips still kissed his unmoving mouth passionately, but he wouldn't start again. Destan removed his hand from my back and tried to push down my arms so that my palms would leave his face, but I was stubborn and rested them on his shoulders, kissing his neck and jaw. Gently, but using his strength, Destan eased off my hands, stepping back and picking his red beanie off of the ground.

"Why?" I had asked, in a breathy voice that didn't sound anything like me. I was smiling. Destan, on the other hand, had looked hurt. Immensely hurt and about to cry not out of happiness anymore, but of pain. I stepped closer to him, confused, and tried to touch his face. Alarm spread on his features, he caught my hand and weakly threw it down. A few tears trickled from his beautiful eyes. "What's wrong?" I had asked, more forcefully. He looked me straight in the eye, almost shocked.

"*This* is wrong, Raine! We…we can't…you're courting someone else!" he yelled, and I had noticed that nearly everyone had left the competition grounds. It was just us and the trees and torches slowly burning out. Now, I cringed in bed. Destan hadn't been angry with me. He was in pain, which was so much worse for me to bear. I wondered what he was doing now. If he could sleep at all, if he was feeling the imprint of me still lingering on him as if I were there. His voice echoed again in my head, "You…you're going to *bond* with him in a matter of weeks if he proposes." His hand had covered his mouth as if to hold back a sob or scream or something and then he tore at his hair in anguish. He kicked over a table where the fruit had been set out for the archery match and beat his fist once against the mountain face.

"Destan, stop this please," I had begun to say, coming up to him, every inch of me shaking as I tried to calm him down, "I don't care about Skye. I care about you. I'll turn him down, Destan. I'll turn him down when he asks."

"No, I don't want you to do that, Raine. That's a fucking stupid thing for you to do."

"*Why?*"

My voiced died off because he laughed a loud, cruel laugh and for the first time in my life I was actually afraid of him. He spun on his heel, roaring, "Because I'm *nothing*, Raine! I'm the son of a whore! I live in an abandoned temple and can hardly feed my wolf a square meal everyday with the pay I get from the woodshop, and you think I could court you, could *marry* you?"

I stared at him, my body suddenly cold all over. "What? Destan…"

"I can't have you over for dinner, can't have you meet my parents or family," he rasped, arms dropped at his sides limply, eyes bright with pain. "I can't give you a dowry or pay off the taxes you need for your sister and mom and whoever. I can't be anything good for you." He shook his head, scoffing, "I…I can't even give you a good name! When I first told you who I was, I did it to scare you off! But you didn't understand."

"Understand?" I stammered, sick to my stomach, wishing we could just go back to holding each other.

"Abrasha. My mom. Tai Abrasha was the hottest whore in town way back when," he said softly, unable to look at me now. "I'm the son of some client of hers, just a whoops. My brother, too, but a different guy from years before when she was only sixteen or something. She got kicked off Underbrush and sent to work in Canopia because my dad pressed charges that she'd forced herself on him, a married man."

I gulped. "Is…is that true?"

"Why do you think the kids at school wouldn't talk to me?" he demanded, coming closer to me and making me walk backwards in fear. "Because I was weird? Because I picked my nose? All the adults around town know about the scandal, who would want their kids hanging around with the son of a prostitute and policeman?" We were face to face, only a little farther apart than we had been when we were kissing. Destan tentatively took my hand, whispering, "All I can do for you is bring you down, Bluehead."

I shook my head, placing a cold hand on his cheek, insisting, "No, no, you won't. Destan I've never felt this way for anyone before. It feels…right—"

"But it's *not*, Raine," Destan groaned, lowering my hand again."I'm the farthest thing from right for you. You can't have a normal life with me, you'll be living in the shadows."

"I'm already in the shadows with you," I whispered. "I don't care about any of that, I'll find a way to have this work out, I just know I need to be with you—"

"But I don't."

His words cut me like ice; I blinked quickly, unable to look into his now cold and frightening eyes. "W-what?"

Destan had his fists balled at his side, his jaw set so tightly I wondered if he'd even answer me. He did. "I don't…I don't want to be with you."

I shook my head, panic rising up in my chest, turning into anger as I grabbed the pendant he'd given me and snapped it off, straight through the messy knot he'd tied in the twine. Tears burned in my eyes. "Then why would you do this?" I asked, the words coming out forceful enough to have him take a step back. I continued forward. "Then why are you doing this to me? Why are you telling me secrets and trying to make me happy, why are you caring about me, why are you giving me necklaces and fighting off JPs for me if you don't want me? Why are you messing with my head like this, Destan?"

He shook his head, expression filled with sadness, "Bluehead, I don't mean—"

"Stop calling me that!" I screamed, throwing the necklace

down on the ground and roughly wiping away the onslaught of tears before they could fall. "Just stop, okay? Just go away if you don't care, just stop confusing me, please…"

"I do care," he sighed, running his fingers through his hair and pacing back and forth, "that's why I can't…why I won't…" He stopped, eyes glued to his boots. "I care about you more every moment I'm with you. I think of you so much it keeps me up at night and then you follow me into my sleep." Destan looked at me, his eyebrows drawn together in worry, and he whispered, "Raine I've wanted to kiss you since I first saw you trying to shoot me in the meadow. I do want you. I just…I don't want you with *me*. You deserve so much happiness and you have so many people to take care of and you have such a big future and other people who love you too and I can't tear you away from that, I just won't."

We came back slowly into each other's arms, my face burying into his shoulder as I felt the thrum of his heartbeat pressed to mine. My entire body was shaking, the trembling getting worse as he held me because of how desperately I felt I need to just kiss him or tell him everything was going to be all right. All I could manage to say, though, was quiet and hoarse and only made him let me go, "Please?"

His hand caressed my face, his lips just above my nose as he said, "We'll have tomorrow. We'll have until Irene can go back. And then you have to start your good life in Starshade, okay? You'll marry the rich lawyer who cares about you. You'll live in a house with a whole room just for drawing and doing your paintings…"

My heart was dissolving inside of me. "Destan, *no…*"

"And I'll go back to how it was before and we'll just have good memories," he continued, and I could feel him smile against my forehead, "really, really good memories." He took a last look at me, and traced his rough fingers down my cheek like they were tears before he closed his eyes and ran away from me, disappearing into the trees. I'd picked the infinity necklace back up then, but couldn't bear to put it back on.

I rolled over in bed, concentrating on Gwen's breathing from the other side of the curtain. I closed my eyes. I still felt him. All over me, I still felt his hands and mouth and heat and love and pain and yearning and longing, it all was branded on me. His body haunted mine like a ghost. My skin tingled thinking about the kiss and I my heart ached like a bruise someone kept touching.

Despite the awful exhaustion I had due to the insomnia, I arrived to the meadow the next morning right on time, trying to act as normal as possible for the sake of Irene who had no idea what had happened the night before. She asked about the competition, I told her I won, she congratulated me and then I tried to push the night away and asked where Destan was. She said Destan wasn't here yet; he was calling in to the Peak Offices from the public telephone box to report that we believed to have found an ancient Thgindim artifact. But after a few minutes of waiting, he bounded in, looking completely himself.

"Hey, the Peak lady said that transportation up there is gonna get here within the hour," he said, and I expected there to be some sort of tension but he sent me the same bright smile as any morning. "Morning, Bluehead. Sleep well?"

Taken aback, I stared at him for a moment, but he broke eye contact and started whistling and washing his hands in the stream. "Yeah," I lied, a little dazed. Irene then jumped in and we all sank into reviewing details of the mission.

We knew that weapons wouldn't be let into Peak Tower under any means, and we'd be searched if we were to be seeing one of the more important Majesty Councilmen, so Destan and I split up the duties. He goes in, fabricates the story about the artifact and keeps the guy temporarily busy before drifting off and making his way back into the office. I in the meantime would be waiting outside the window, weapons strapped to my back, completely successful in climbing the Tower.

Climbing the Tower.

I'd overcome my fear of climbing once I'd made it past the meadowlark nest, but picturing myself up on the mile high, completely smooth, titanium structure, still made my bones feel like jelly. I started to realize that my death was indeed *very* probable and that was harder to handle than I ever could have imagined. Irene had taught me some brilliant techniques though, and she'd passed on her climbing shoes and hand spikes that she had come to Thgindim wearing. She swore that the spikes were made of diamond and could penetrate or at least leave a dent in the titanium, so that all I could have to do is climb and hit the building really hard. Finding the window would be easy as long as I counted; the office I needed was on the 30th floor.

I'd hang out there for a bit waiting with weapons. Then Irene would distract the dude in charge by calling in with a fake emergency that involves a problem with the JP men not being at their posts and instead smoking in the woods. I know, it was a ridiculous scenario but it would surely get the Councilman out of his office, and he probably wouldn't need his tablet-thing with the information we needed for that kind of incident, so it was good enough. While he's gone, Destan would then sneak in and let me in the window and we'd dig around and find out as much as we could until the Councilman got back. Then we'd retreat to the meadow and share what we'd found out with Irene.

The only issue so far was transportation. Destan was getting a free ride to Peak, but I couldn't go with him with all this climbing gear and weapons. I begrudgingly had to take the route I'd taken for my Career interview. That stupid dark haunted lift. And this time I'd be alone and not have Chantastic to cling to, so it was going to be rough.

Destan took off his beanie and let Irene and me wash and comb through his hair to look more presentable, and he also dressed up in long grey corduroy pants, a nice crimson sweater, his boots (I'd polished them first). Irene laughed the entire time while I pushed his greasy blond head into the river and scrubbed at his scalp with my Laundress soap. He bid goodbye and goodluck, we nodded, unable to really meet each other's eyes, and then he departed in the weird shuttle thing that the Peak officials used.

For when I'd actually be climbing and inside of Peak, Irene had given me her black face mask. But so as not to appear ridiculously suspicious on my way up, I had a sweater and shorts over the hooded black jumpsuit, and the stealth clothes and climbing stuff in my knapsack. Irene called the Majesty Councilman Destan was seeing once the sun had completely risen (it was still near dark since it was so early), and then I began my walking; wondering if this would be the last time I stepped foot on the Underbrush road. I'd even left a goodbye note in my bedroom in case I didn't return and needed to explain to my mom.

It took a long while to get to the haunted lift in Canopia, but once I got to it I took down my hood and tried to appear innocent for the JP inside. He looked at me a little funnily. I was for once thankful that the lift-operating JPs had a code of silence so that he wouldn't ask me any questions about why a scrawny, blue-haired teenager like me would need to go to the mountain's capital. I couldn't help but feel a little bit scared of being in the dark with him for a half an hour as the lift shot up.

*I wish Destan was here…*I thought, crossing my arms against my chest and averting my eyes from the ones hiding beneath the tinted glass of his mask. I wondered if the lift-operating JPs were also known for taking advantage of girls who rode alone, but once the lift was in motion and before it went dark, the JP lifted his mask and grinned at me, I recognized him in an instant.

"Kris? What're you doing here?" I asked incredulously, remembering how he had ridden up this lift with me and my friends on my interview day.

"Ahh, you know how it goes. I didn't get the job I wanted, got drafted. But this isn't so bad." He shrugged, still looking like a cool kid. I smiled at him, but then we shot into the dark and he probably didn't see it.

"I know you're not really supposed to talk, so I'm sorry, but do you know if we could keep talking? I have an issue with dark as you might remember," I said, trying to steady my voice.

I heard him make a scoffing sound and chuckle. "Psssh, it's no problem, girl. The thing I HATE about this job is how I don't have anyone to joke with anymore. I haven't seen Aili or Pula in ages."

We talked about random things like school memories that he was more involved in than I was, and about our jobs now, and then he asked why I was heading up to Peak. I told him I had to pick up something from the Tower and felt my stomach get sick with nerves. He said good luck and that he hoped to see me again, and I said the same to him, wondering if this would be the last time I ever spoke to him, much less anyone.

Saluting him half as a joke because of the Justice Police code of conduct, I shot him a last smile before he tipped his helmet and slid the glass back over his eyes. Drumming my fingers on the dagger sheathed at my hip, I walked out into the suffocatingly crowded Peak square.

The mosaic-styled ground was thickly coated in snow, and I tried not to think about how even more impossibly thin the air would be once I was climbing I'd lost a lot of time taking that long lift, but the sun hadn't yet completely risen to its full height, so I had at least another half an hour until I would have to worry about the Councilman getting back from Irene's fake setup. It would send him to the lowest of Underbrush, giving us hours to search and scour through his office and tablet and then have to put it back together.

I moved casually, still looking out of place around all the professionally and richly dressed people. I strolled around the great Tower, eyeing the guards at the door, waiting for a moment to slip to the back. They looked away and I dashed to the back, gazing up in awe at the line of windows. I pulled my hood on and took off my grey sweater to reveal the black turtleneck of

Irene's, and hid the sweater and knapsack in a fern. I'd have to start climbing now. I tested the foot spikes and kicked the Tower.

It left an impression, all right. I smiled. *Well isn't that something,* I thought.

With great force, I dug my hand claw into the side of the Tower and pulled myself up, then kicked in my foot and continued the process as I moved up. *Wow, Fluxaria really does know how to weaken Thgindim's greatest achievement,* I thought, cautiously yanking free my foot spike and digging it again higher up.

I had gotten past the first five windows, and I stayed close to them, the cold of the metal seeping through the threads of my black turtleneck. I was freezing, but had to stick as close to the side as possible so that if a Councilman or Peak employee looked out, they wouldn't see me but I would see them. If I thought about falling, I would slip, and one slip of a spike and I would be a Bluehead-pancake at the bottom. *Just focus on what's in front of you and don't mess up, don't mess up and don't look down or up or you will die,* I told myself, every limb shaking, the diamond stake wedged deep into the titanium and even beginning to quiver. I closed my eyes and thought of Destan and found peace. I thought of the meadow and Chantastic and archery and Gwen and riding on Siri and Velle and Carmen and it quieted my nerves and I scaled up twenty more windows.

I had five left and the sun was making the once horribly cold metal hot as fire. My face was so sweaty that I could barely see as it dripped in my eyes. I was getting so close. I was almost a third up the tower, and by the time I made it to the 30th window, the bows and quivers on my back and swords and daggers on my belt were so heavy I struggled to keep from getting pulled down by the weight. I lifted out my right hand spike and clutched onto the windowsill with freezing fingers. Wind blew me a little bit back, I couldn't breathe and yet I was breathing so fast that my lungs would have to give up soon, I looked down and the mosaic ground looked more like fine rainbow grains of sand on a silver platter, I'd fall, I'd fall any moment. Panicking, I raised my hand to the glass and knocked, praying that the Councilman wouldn't be the one to peer out.

A pair of full moon eyes greeted me.

Destan pushed open the window. "Raine!"

"Pull…me…in," I rasped, "can't…breathe—"

His fists locked around my wrists and pulled me up. It was painful, but it released the tension and I let him support me, my muscles getting to relax. I kicked my feet to get the spikes out of the wall and then his arm went around my waist and pulled me completely inside.

"I got here five m-minutes ago, I-I thought you'd fallen." His voice was hardly above a whisper and shaking. Shutting the window softly, he gathered me in his arms, whispering, "Okay, o-okay, you're just fine, y-you're okay…"

I held onto him tightly, gulping in the fake but effective air that was pumped into the room, and I said, beginning to shake from the hysteria of where we were and what we were doing, "We're crazy, Destan. We're crazy. What are we doing?"

"We're already here and there's no going back," he said, pressing his mouth into my hair. For a moment, he seemed to want to kiss me again, twisting his face ever so slightly, but then as I began to move in as well, he looked away. Deflated, I let go of him and tried to focus on the more important problem at hand.

"Did he leave the tablet here?" I asked, taking off the spikes from my hands and feet before I accidentally impaled something.

"I'm not sure. I came in after he left, of course, so I'm guessing he could have. I've searched his desk and nothing yet," Destan said. The Majesty Councilman's office was neat as a pin; a huge bookshelf, incredible array of filing cabinets, an organized desk with locked drawers, a hi-tech glass telephone, organized stacks of mail. He had the same weird clock that had been in the interviewer's room hanging on the wall.

My heart sank. "Could you open the drawers? Are the keys anywhere near here?"

"No…but…could I see your hand spike?" he asked. I handed it to him and watched him jam it into the keyhole. He jiggled the diamond point in the lock with furious concentration burning in his eyes. If the spike could break through titanium, surely it could force the lock open. And it did! Destan tugged out the drawer, careful not to make too much noise, and stared at piles of typed up papers.

"I'll open all the other drawers, too. Look through these

and see if anything we need is there," he said, scooting over to the other side of the desk and working with the spike again. I pulled out a stack of paper and was surprised at how heavy they were. I skimmed over them and picked out the familiar words, getting lost in the lofty language. The next drawer was better. The documents were all schedules of JP stuff. It had numbers of the fleets, and where they should be and when, and even revealed the names of some of the officers. I took advantage of the moment and looked for my father's name, but quickly gave up seeing that I'd have to spend fifty pages-worth of reading for something not even related to the task at hand.

And yet, moving onto the next drawer Destan had managed to break into, there it was. *Ylevol, Solomon.* I yanked it out, resisting the urge to read it right then, pulling out mine, my mom's, Gwen's, and even finding Destan's. I didn't want this guy having anything on us. And there were so many Underbrushers' files he wouldn't notice a couple missing. I stuffed them down my shirt.

"Are they in there?" Destan asked. Without answering, I took the spike from him and hacked into the next drawer, then the next until I caught words I knew would have something to do with Irene's crisis. These were definitely on Foreign Affairs, and the only foreign territory Thgindim had to worry about was, well, Fluxaria.

"Destan, I may have hit the jackpot," I whispered.

His blond head bent down next to mine. "What do they say?"

"You can't read?" I asked, shocked.

He shrugged. "I don't use the skill very often is all. I can read if I really try, but since we're on a tight schedule…"

"Okay, okay, well these are all about Fluxaria. There's gotta be something Irene needs in here," I muttered, scanning through them. They were all conversations back and forth from Fluxaria and Thgindim and looked like they had been printed out copies of the virtual messages Irene had described.

"Listen to this," I began, and Destan sat back on his heels. "'Fluxaria nation, it is time you surrender to your sister mountain and return to us the mountain that was rightfully ours. If you do not oblige accordingly, then expect the land to be taken by force. It is either ours or no one's, and we will not let our other half of the mountain remain in the hands of savages any longer. This is no bluff. You have twenty weeks to respond or else we will take action on our own terms. We do not want that land lost or damaged, but can no longer let it remain under your dominion. Let us end this feud and become one mountain under the Majesty Council's rule. Let us together move into a future where we both can help the progress of a singular nation built upon loyalty and compliancy. No harm will come to your people by taking this generous offer. We will use our weaponry to clear out Mythland and connect our mountains, but if you refuse to cooperate, the weapons will be directed at you. You have twenty weeks.'" I glanced back up at him, passing the letter over. "This is the most recent document in here, only mailed a few weeks ago."

"Should we look through for other stuff? Like plans they haven't shared with Fluxaria?"

I nodded. "Yeah. But we've got to hurry—"

Destan immediately forced the top drawer open with an awful screech of diamond against metal. His eyes widened and I went up on my knees to peer inside. There it was. The tablet, enclosed in a case, a few pens attached. Destan reached in, carefully lifting it out and lowering it to the floor. We both took a moment just to stare at it. And then, as I'd meant to take it up and stow it safely in our knapsack, my finger brushed the small, triangle button on the front and in that instant a holographic screen burst from the projection lense and a voice blared from the speakers.

"WELCOME, COUNCILMAN LAO. ENTER PASSCODE."

"Turn it off, turn it off!" he hissed, shaking my arm as footsteps paused outside of the door. I jabbed at the button again and again trying to undo whatever it was I'd done.

"INVALID ENTRY. INVALID PRINTS DETECTED. ACCESS DENIED."

My whole body was trembling, "I-I don't know how—"

Someone began to knock and my voice cut off. We froze, not daring to breathe. The knocking became more insistent, voices calling for help to open the door. The Councilman might have been attending to Irene's diversion in Underbrush, but the tablet seemed to have alerted the secretaries and other Council members nearby.

Destan shoved the tablet and hand and foot spikes and the entire stack of threat papers into my knapsack so forcefully that the hologram switched off, and then he pulled my hood over my face and wrenched his bow and arrows off my back. It hurt and he looked at me pleadingly. "Get your weapon, it's going to be messy getting out of here, Bluehead."

I did as I was told and nocked in an arrow, just as the door was blasted open by Peak-designated JPs and they stormed into the office, their rods ablaze with lightning.

"Stay where you are!" one shouted, and in response I released an arrow pointed at his masked face. The arrow smashed into the helmet and knocked him off his feet, his cronies shoving past towards us. Destan yelled and plunged his dagger into one of their feet and without taking a moment to be afraid, I did the same to another, a frenzy of howling and desperation seizing every one of us in the room. Avoiding rods and crawling on our hands and knees, Destan and I made it through the crowd and into the hallway where more officers had shown up.

I made it to my feet and was about to take off running when I heard Destan cry out and saw him get yanked back by the collar of his sweater. A knife gleamed, and then plunged into Destan's shoulder. Another officer had his rod raised at the ready, and spinning back around I tripled the arrows nocked onto my bowstring and fired the three straight at it.

266

The power of the shot of three arrows tore the JP man's hand from his wrist.

I realized that Destan could be recognized without a mask on, so I did something so gross and crazy I couldn't believe it, but it felt necessary. As I got Destan to his feet and we started running I took his dagger and slashed my thigh. His eyes bugged out in horror, and he stole it back, screaming, "What *the fuck* are you doing?!"

"I need to hide your face!" I panted, turning a corner and racing with Destan down the steps, taking my blood and smearing it all over his face and hair. It made him trip a little and cuss even worse, but if we made it out of here, there would be JPsall over Underbrush looking for the fugitives who just stole from Peak Tower, so I had to hide his identity best I could. His hair was matted with dark red now, and his face unrecognizable and horrified at how I'd covered it with my own blood.

The JPs had been alerted all over the Tower and as we ran some thundered behind us. In the midst of this, more were coming up for us as well and we still needed to go down at least sixteen more flights from where we were now. "Dive straight into them!" Destan whispered into my ear as a huge mass of them appeared in front of us and the ones behind us got frighteningly close. Without another thought, I held my breath and jumped straight into them as he had said, and I elbowed through as best I could, but then I was hit with a paralyzing shock of electricity and crumpled.

"RAINE!" Destan screamed, lifting me up and taking the rest of the lightning. Though my vision was flashing red and black from the pain, I swung a punch and jabbed my dagger in front of me to get the JPs out of the way. I climbed over the bodies falling as they came in contact with my dagger and felt more bites of the electric rods as Destan and I escaped from the stairwell and came into the lobby.

The Peak employees screamed, seeing blood-faced Destan and the stampede of JPs behind us. More and more officers flew in, rifles blazing from all directions to stop us. Destan was sobbing and bleeding where I hadn't painted him, but through the panic I forced his bow into his hand and I loaded up mine with arrows too. We shot around the desks so that people ducked down and got out of our way, and by the time Destan was out of arrows, the innocent Peak people had scattered like jacks and only JPs were still blocking our exit.

We blasted out of the Tower into the unbreathable air, and as we headed to the lift, I heard a JP yell, "Close it off! Don't let them get away!"

Destan stole an arrow from my quiver and shot him and some JPs running to block the lift, but then cringed into himself, eyes rolling back in his head. He fell to the ground, shaking like there was still electricity inside of him. Light twinkled on his fingertips and his breathing became raspy and fast.

I used all my might to try and lift him, but with my slashed thigh and his just being too heavy, I couldn't, screaming, "Get up! Please, Destan, I know you're hurt, but get up, we're going to die if you don't get up!" I was in hysterics, shaking him furiously until he regained consciousness and could tortuously struggle to his knees. I pulled him all the way up, running and tripping and unable to use my bow anymore since I had to mostly support him, but when I got to the lift, I saw Kris and some nameless JPs standing guard with their rods hissing and spitting lightning into the air.

Kris's jaw dropped, his face white. He knew. He gaped at me in such shock that I thought he'd pass out like Destan.

"Stop running and surrender!" A JP at his side shouted fiercely. "We WILL attack if you come any closer!"

"*Please*," I mouthed. My eyes cut deep into Kris's, and he glanced around, breathing unevenly.

Kris didn't lose eye contact and then jabbed his wand into the sides of the guards on either side of him.

"33257, what the hell are you doing?" the JP hollered, bearing down on Kris. Immediately, I knocked him out with a single kick, and snatched the rod he'd dropped. Kris pulled me and Destan inside the lift and closed the iron netting. I forced the lever down without taking another look at the destruction we'd caused and shot to Canopia with such speed that if the lift was to finally give out, it would be now.

"Will you tell me what's going on and why I just risked my job for this?" Kris yelled as we sank into blackness. Destan's gasping for air was louder than the screech of metal. I laid him down and got to work on ripping at my layers of clothes to make bandages for his wounds.

"I can't tell you, Kris, but I can't thank you enough," I said hastily, touching Destan's face and wiping off my blood.

Kris cursed and begged, "Come on, Raine, I'm in big trouble! Give me more than that!"

"We just stole from Peak Tower," Destan coughed, and I fumbled with wiping off his face in the dark. "If you tell anyone it was us, I will kill you," he finished, letting out a cry and clutching his stomach. Destan vomited all over the lift's floor.

"No, he won't," I assured, seeing Kris' terror-stricken face. "Kris, swap the ID badge of one of the guys who you knocked out," I said, trying to comfort him as he began crying. "Take one of their identities, and no one will know it was you. If something happens to you, we'll step in, okay? Because you helped us, we're in your debt and won't let you get hurt, okay?" I said to him, feeling much braver than I knew I was, and Kris calmed down, agreeing that that would work.

When the lift came into the light and landed in Canopia, we all got out and Kris parted ways with us to return to Peak and trade his JP number for one that wouldn't get him banished or even executed. The shrieks of whistles ricocheted around the mountain, the ground shook from the number of tanks rolling down the street filled with armed JPs scouring everywhere for the Peak Tower Thieves. I heaved Destan along into the woods, my own injuries from the rods bleeding through the jumpsuit. Struggling to not keel over, I took his flute from his pocket. I knelt by him, soothingly squeezing his hand, whispering, "Play the song that will get Siri here." Destan opened his mouth to speak but then cried out again, what was left of the electric sparkling on his chest. *How much of it got into his body?* I thought, throat constricting in fear. *What if he dies?*

Eyes closed, he snatched the flute and blew hoarsely into it. He only managed a few puffs before falling unconscious again, and I tried to copy the song's pattern. After what felt like ages of tuneless playing, Siri appeared beside use, ducking her head so that I could slide Destan on, and then myself. I had the reins in my hands but didn't know how to guide her. Siri tried as much as she could to keep us moving, but when Destan nearly rolled halfway off, it took all of my might to keep control. My calves pressed against her sides, my fingers woven through her fur and body laying over Destan's in the desperate hopes of keeping him on, and by the time my strength gave out and we tumbled off, we'd smashed through the ferns and into the meadow. I hit the ground hard on my back, all air whooshing out from my lungs in a great burst as I turned to see Destan lying facedown. Still bleeding. He wasn't breathing.

"No," I whispered, terror seizing every nerve, shocking me into movement. I rolled him onto his back, feverishly trying to recall what to do. *Gwen had choked, Gwen had choked, Gwen had choked on a marble, Gwen had choked and—*

"Raine!" Irene limped over, falling to her knees and gripping my shoulders, shaking me as my own thoughts cycled endlessly on the wet softness of Gwen's throat on my fingers as I'd had to reach down, down...

"Dammit, Raine! Was he shot? Is he dead? What happened?" Her questions came like gunfire, and as she shook me more violently, I had to shove her off. He wasn't choking, he didn't swallow anything, how could I get his body working? I folded my hands over each other, pressing down on his chest in thrusts hard as I could. *Please-* thrust *-come-* thrust *-back-* thrust *-to-* thrust *-me.*

"I shouldn't have made you do this." The spy was weeping. I could hardly see Destan below me through my swimming vision. My hands were soaking and red as I realized I was pushing close to some of his injuries. "Raine, I'm so sorry—"

"Stop!" I panted. I brought my forehead to Destan's, my trembling palm resting on his cheek. "Please, please, please," I whispered. I opened his mouth and blew straight into it with the biggest breaths I could muster. Exhaling into him led to inhaling the air inside of him, and the uncomfortable mix made me cough. I breathed, I breathed, and before anything even happened my body was calming down. Irene had started the chest compressions again on her own, muttering to herself, her face blood-red in concentration.

I'd just sat back on my heels, gulping down air, ready to return and breathe into him again, when suddenly Irene proclaimed, "He's breathing! Raine, his stomach is rising again!"

My eyes found the movement, then my fingers felt the warm air steadily flowing from his nose and I cried out in relief, grabbing Irene and pulling her into a tight hug. We were both shaking, laughing and crying in response to Destan's revival, and after breaking away, we eased Destan over to the riverbank.

Each of us lay down side by side; Destan unconscious, but steadily breathing, wrapped up in what was left of the stolen bandages. I was out of the jumpsuit and swaddled in a blanket, Irene in the middle, clutching onto both of us. She looked at me worriedly, her owl eyes wide and shining. She licked her lips, and then whispered, "Did you get it?"

"Yeah, we got it."

"Are we gonna…y'know…be okay now?"

I stared up at the flat white sky patching through the trees. Destan's breath rattled through his lips. I laid my hand over his and shut my eyes, sighing. "I have no idea."

chapter twenty-six

"Stop this at once," she muttered, tipping my face up to look at her. "Since when does crying fix anything?"

She'd asked me this so many times after Dad was taken away. I swallowed, gasping for breath. "Never."

"That's right."

My mom let go of me, moving toward the doorway and looking out. She pulled her thin, grey shawl tighter around herself, watching as the snow came slowly down. I went back to picking up the glass. "You'll go to work today," she said, still just staring ahead of her as truck after truck of JPs barreled down the road in a seemingly endless flow of black metal and smoke.

I blinked slowly and in that split second, accidentally nicked my thumb on a shard of the broken window. Hearing my hiss of pain, my mother whirled around, eyeing me suspiciously as I sucked on the cut.

I removed my finger from my mouth, asking, "You don't

need me around here? I don't even think businesses are opening today, not with all that's happened."

She shook her head, absently looking out the doorway again. "I just don't know how such a thing could happen. If there's anything an Underbrusher learns in this life, it's that disobeying the power punishes all of us, not just the idiot who tried to act the hero. Why put the whole level in jeopardy for such pointless theft like that? I just can't bring myself to understand why."

I stared at the blood beading from my thumb. "I don't know."

"But you know how we'll get through this?"

"Same as we always have?"

She nodded. "Same as we always have. We're going to have to speed things up, though, if we want to get Gwen back before things completely go to hell."

My whole body went cold, remembering the morning. As soon as I'd gotten back to the village yesterday, I quickly realized all of Thgindim had been put on lockdown. No one was allowed to travel in between levels, and aside from me and Destan, no one knew why. And now today my sister and mother and I all woke up to the ringing of shots in Underbrush's square. It wasn't an unfamiliar sound, I'd seen public executions before— the bag over the head and gun at the person's hidden face. But I'd made Gwen stay inside despite her moans of protest, and my mother and I looked out to see what the commotion was about. JP 21996 stalked about the main road chewing on a cigarette, his gun twirling around his index finger. There were JPs everywhere. Barging inside houses, breaking windows, tossing aside whatever few valuables Underbrushers had, and even setting fire to trash cans. A trio of black-clad officers had shoved by me and Mom and tore apart the kitchen, opening every drawer, dumping out Mom's buckets of herbs and spices and digging the precious ingredients into the dirt with the heel of their boots. My mom had rushed at them, screaming, "You can't do that! What is this about? This is…this is all I have!"

They'd ignored her and headed toward Gwen and my room. Panicking, I struggled to get past and tell Gwen to calm down, to not be afraid, but one JP held me back as the others ripped through our bedroom and all of her toys. Gwen was humming madly and I elbowed the JP hard in the ribs to get to her.

"*Ray!*" she'd wailed, pummeling her fists against the JP's armour as he cut open her stuffed animals and glanced inside their stomachs. Then he turned around and hit Gwen hard across the cheek.

"Get away from her!" I yelled, grabbing my little sister's wrist and pulling her out of our bedroom. She'd cried so loudly that I'd had to strain my ears to hear what JP 21996 was saying outside. Another gunshot. I ran to the doorway where my mother had her hand clamped over her mouth.

"Hey!" JP 21996 hollered, a bitter edge to his usual drawling voice. "Stop the noise already you filthy— *BANG* — pieces—*BANG*—of shit!" He was only shooting the air for now, yelling at the Underbrushers who fought back against the violent destruction of their homes and workplaces. Shoving his pistol deep into the pocket of his pants, 21996 pivoted and let his yellow eyes run over each terrified face, landing on mine. "You've probably heard by now, but our Council has been bamboozled by thieves." Whispers sizzled through the crowd and he fired another silencing bullet to the wind. "And I don't know about you all, but if *I* were in your position, I'd offer up the two bastards before my neck is broken, yeah?" JP 21996 directed the gunpoint at seventy-year old Mrs. Tang, and as she cowered and began to cry he demanded, "Do *you* know who from this little rat nest might have spent their Sunday committing treason against their most loyal government?"

The woman was trembling all over, her silver curls bobbing as she shook her head insistently. "N-no, sir. I…I don't have any idea—"

"No idea? Well, that's useless," he sighed, clicking back the hammer of his gun and shooting the old lady right between the eyes.

I grabbed Gwen tightly and covered her face, turning away as the village burst into screams and JPs fired more silencing shots. Gwen sobbed loudly in my arms, scared of all of the noise, clinging onto the neck of my sweater. I backed us away into the house trying to keep her quiet so more JPs wouldn't think of coming over here. I saw Mom try to move the door over the entrance to our hut, but an officer saw her and yanked her by the hair, booming straight into her ear, "This level is in lockdown! All households must be inspected!"

He released her, shoving my mom back into the wall and standing in front of the doorway. But as soon as he'd stepped in front of it, he stepped aside, JPs rushing in straight toward me and Gwen.

"Why are you…don't you touch them!" my mother screeched, unable to fight her way through the flood of officers barging into our home. They hitched their arms under my armpits and dragged me outside, Gwen kicking and howling behind me. My boots scuffed up clouds of dirt as they pulled me out into the road where other adolescents were getting lined up, side by side. *Destan, where are you?* I thought, glancing around rapidly, unable to find his face anywhere. There wasn't a spot of red to be seen. He must've gone to the meadow already. Or maybe he had been telling the truth when he'd said he lived in the shadows.

"Very nice," JP 21996 sighed, rubbing his hands together and limping alongside the lot of us. Each of the kids brought out had two officers standing behind them; the insulated side of the lightning rod pressed against their necks in restraint. I struggled to breathe, reaching my fingers over to touch Gwen's hand beside me. She wasn't making a sound now, just shaking uncontrollably with the occasional whimper escaping her lips every now and then.

That's when I noticed the Majesty Councilman who was here with the police. It was the creepy guy I'd met in the elevator from what felt like forever ago; the guy I'd seen inside the mountain. I gulped, remembering his department. This was the man whose office Destan and I had barged into and looted just yesterday. He was going down the line with 21996, glancing down at print outs of fuzzy black and white photos and then up at the adolescent in question. Every now and then, he'd come to a certain someone, nod, snap his fingers, and the JP behind the girl or boy would zap him or her in the back, rendering them unconscious. Then the person was carried off to one of the trucks and piled into the covered back.

And now he was one boy away from me.

I shut my eyes, trying to make myself appear as calm as I could by taking deep breaths and envisioning myself somewhere else, anywhere else, even in the sled with Skye making awkward conversation, or by the stream washing clothes in the numbingly cold water. The Councilman cleared his throat and I was ripped from the daydream, face to face with the man who wielded the power to erase my entire existence.

"Hello, there," he said, a small, false grin on his thin lips. His flat black eyes squinted at me, and I suddenly felt very exposed, as if he could so easily invade my mind. "And you are...?"

I could see his mouth about to form my name, but then 21996 interrupted him. "Ylevol, your honor. Miss Raine Ylevol. I'd bet my money this little thief is a guilty one."

"Well, that'll be my judgment to make, won't it, officer?" the Councilman said curtly, a hint of annoyance playing on the edge of his voice as he looked from the paper to me. I peeped over the top of it, heat flooding my cheeks as I saw the hazy silhouettes of Destan and me in the middle of Peak Square, arrows poised in mid-flight. The figures were pretty incomprehensible. But then the Councilman paged to another sheet, and clicked his tongue.

276

JP 21996 craned his carelessly shaven neck down to inspect the photo, and flipping up his visor, he scoffed, "I'm tellin' you, sir. That is this girl right here, plain as day."

"Your service is not needed here this moment, officer," the Councilman snapped. "Go clean up the mess you made with that woman."

21996 looked down, stammering, "Y-yessir. Right away, sir." Crestfallen, he stalked over to Mrs. Tang's body, shooing away the crowd that gathered in mourning around her.

Sighing tiredly, the Councilman focused his charcoal-lined eyes back on mine. Even in this frigid, cold morning when I hadn't even slipped on my gloves or coat yet, I could feel the hot sweat trickling down my neck. My palms were moist and my hands balled into shaky fists as something scary seemed to flicker on his face.

He knows, I thought. *But how could he know, how could he; with only some blurry photos?*

He blinked. "I apologize for taking time away from your morning, Miss Ylevol." He took a bowler hat from inside of his big, black bear fur coat and set it on the bald top of his head. Tipping his hat, he gave me a last smile and then went on to scrutinizing Gwen.

"Your name?" he asked her, and I made a coughing sort of sound, making his gaze flicker back onto me.

"She...she can't speak," I said, shakily. "She's my little sister."

"Not so little, I would say," the Councilman muttered, eyes combing Gwen's figure. She was just as tall as I was, still horribly underweight, but she had a little more padding on her face and arms. She may have had the expression of a terrified three year old, but nevertheless she was also quite obviously in the stage of growing into a woman with her no longer perfectly flat chest and narrow hips.

A wrinkle appeared between his brows, and slowly, he looked from the photo to me again, then at Gwen, who whimpered, "Ray...Ray, no, no."

"Shh, Gwennie, shh," I breathed, straining against the JP's hold on me so that I could reach out and try to comfort her. But he didn't budge, and even pressed the rod tighter, hitting my windpipe, making me gasp for breath.

The Councilman licked his lips, then snapped his fingers, pointing at Gwen. "This one," he said, shortly, clasping his hands behind his back and moving down the line. As if the rod had actually shocked me, I jolted forward, straining against the JPs' hold as Gwen was zapped and slung over an officer's shoulder.

"No!" I shrieked, using all of my might to yank out of the tight trap of the JPs' arms, only to be hit right in the side with the prickly and horribly painful end of the rod. I crumpled, shocked, eyes watering as I watched the officer carry my baby sister away and drop her into the back of the truck with the countless others. *"Gwennie..."* I gasped, choking on my words as I was lifted up roughly by the collar and made to stand.

Once he had gone down and taken at least half of our village's kids and teenagers, the Councilman jerked his head at the trucks and the majority of the JPs piled into the front sections of each. As he strode by, his black fur coat billowed behind him like a storm cloud. His shoes left pointed footprints in the gravel. He whispered something into 21996's ear, and my least favourite JP declared, "These citizens will remain at Peak for careful inspection and proper detainment and questioning until the culprits come forward. If you cooperate, maybe all of them will come back as alive as they are now."

The crowd moaned in despair, Underbrushers turning and clutching one other as JP 21996 yelled for their attention to remain on him. He scowled at the lot of us, spinning his pistol around his index finger again, betraying a sick sort of pleasure in the excited red flush of his cheeks. "Oi!" he hollered, firing at the wind and then at Mrs. Tang's body; the impact of the bullet making it twitch. The Underbrushers shrieked in horror, and 21996 took up his pedestal for the last time. "Consider this your first warning. You want yer little kiddies at home with you? You don't want to wake up tomorrow with my gun at your cold nosey? Then it'd be best you stop covering for the two maggots who put your entire mountain in danger, all right? All right. *No one* is leaving this village until someone confesses!"

He slammed the truck door, waving at the driver to take off behind the growling line of vehicles returning back up the mountain. The JPs who stayed hollered at us to return to our homes. That was just a few hours ago. Now I was trying to get all of the glass off of the floor while my Mom thought up ways of how to fix this.

"As soon as they open up passage between levels again, you will go to Skye," she whispered, long black braid swaying as an icy breeze came into the house. "I'll call his mother, arrange the engagement. There will be no wedding. Not until Gwen is home."

"Of course."

"But you'll bond with him tonight. I believe Starshade has already prepared the arrangements for the ceremony, and if not, we'll make do with what we have."

"Y-yes, mom," I whispered.

"For now, I need some time alone." My mom padded into the kitchen, toying with the light on the stove. I could see the toes of her socks poking through the gaping holes in her beaver pelt slippers. When the stove's flame went out with another wind blowing in, she gave up. Leaning over her pot, fingers wrapped around the handles on either side, she spoke straight into the soup, "I need some time to think. To…figure all of this out. Leave me, now."

I hadn't even gotten up all of the glass yet, much less the shredded remains of Gwen's stuffed animals and our bedding. "But Mom, what about—"

"Please, Raine," she looked up at me, dark eyes as dry and emotionless as they'd always been. She was so good at concealing what she really felt. "Just go. Leave. Get Jun to give you work, go practice your archery with that boy if he hasn't been taken. I don't care where you go, just let me be here alone for a couple of hours." Her voice quavered and she buried her face in her hands, dissolving into sobs. This frightened me so much that I made to leave immediately, taking my gloves, Destan's scarf, and my wool cloak from the wall before dashing out.

As soon as I'd made it outside, I had to make a beeline for the side of my hut, stooping under the low-hanging pine branches and creeping along the edge of the woods. I'd never entered the forest this soon into my trek up to the meadow, so I tried to concentrate hard on my surroundings and black out all of the tumultuous feelings threatening to pour out of me. They threatened to take me straight to the JPs and tell them what I did so that Gwen wouldn't be tortured up there like I knew they'd done before last time she was brought up to Peak. *Therapy*, they'd called it. They thought a lot of thin, electrified needles going into her brain at once would stimulate normal activity and cure her of her *mental disruption*, or, *retardation*. All it did was make her burrow in bed refusing adequate food for two months with constant tremors racking her fragile body.

When I made it into the meadow, I couldn't help myself from running straight into Destan's arms, which had been piled up with lumber before dropping it all to embrace me. Irene stood, suddenly attentive as I remained holding onto Destan so tightly I was scared my bones would snap against his. He flinched at my touch, probably because his scorch wounds hadn't even begun to heal yet. There were still flecks of red on his cheeks from my blood, and I could hear him groaning as I continued hugging him.

"I was just going to go into town to look for you. Why are you so late?" he asked, pulling back and putting that dreaded distance he'd created after the archery match and our argument between us. It made my stomach heave, and I forced myself not to dissolve into crying. I squeezed every muscle I had to hold it together and not make him or Irene worry any more than they already were.

"Gwen," I said. Her name came out in more of a messy whisper than a clear statement. "They took Gwen. They took a bunch of us."

"Wait, who's Gwen again? Where?" Irene broke in, "Up to that tower?"

I nodded, shaking my long bangs into my face and looking off in a different direction so that they couldn't see how red and puffy my eyes were. Destan hesitated, lifting his hand to touch me, and then dropped it back down as he said, gruffly, "But why?"

"He's looking for us," I said, monotone. "The guy we took the tablet from. He's got the whole mountain under lockdown, he's got these really crappy photos of us, and there's no way you could tell it's us, but…" I ran my fingers through my hair, realizing I'd never even bothered to tie it up today. My fingers got caught in the tangles, ripping through them as I hissed, "he's just trying to scare us. He's trying to ruin everything so that we come forward and admit to what we've done."

"That's not going to happen," Irene snorted. When she noticed our solemn silence, her smirk lessened. "You two wouldn't, right?"

"Of course not," Destan said, stiffly. "But it does make everything else a hell of a lot trickier."

"Mrs. Tang was shot," I whispered, meeting his eyes, "that's our fault too, isn't it?"

He came forward and gripped my shoulders, keeping our eye contact firm as he insisted, "Not even a tiny bit. We didn't kill anyone."

"Incorrect passcode. Access denied," a cool voice spoke into the air.

"Fucking Thgindim…" Irene grumbled, blowing a wispy black hair out of her eyes, and jabbing at the floating image of a keyboard with the little pen we'd taken. After hearing her entry refused seven more times in the next couple of minutes, Destan had had it.

"If it wasn't so important, I would be smashing that thing to pieces," he growled, his arm over his face as he laid by the stream. His coat pulled up as he stretched, and I was sickened to see vicious purple blotches on his pale stomach, continuing up under his sweater and coat to stain the rest of his torso. I felt so ill, so angry, so guilty, and the feelings just kept building and building.

"How are you going to get into it if you don't know the password?"

"I know the passcode. Actually, I know all 182 of the possible passcodes. It's just figuring out which one…"

"You memorized 182 passcodes? How many digits each?" Destan asked, raising an eyebrow.

"Thirteen. All spies learn 'em," Irene replied quickly, staring off with an intensely thoughtful look on her face before typing in three more digits.

"Incorrect passcode. Access denied."

Now I was simmering over. I walked heatedly over to the spy, hardly able to keep myself under control any longer. "What's your plan?" I demanded. "Why haven't you packed up and left yet?"

"Raine, c'mon…" Destan warned.

"No, Destan," Irene said, getting up and glaring up into my eyes. "I wanna hear what blue girl has to say."

"It's supposed to be done with now!" I yelled. "You said get the tablet, get out, but you're still here, you're still making it so that me and Destan are one police raid away from getting executed—"

"So, you want me to go, huh?" she asked, eyes flashing. "Just take off, right now?"

"Maybe I do."

She licked her lips and smirked. "Get a grip, Raine. I *warned* you about what could happen, and you leapt right on the happy-treason-bandwagon, saying you'd accept the consequences, and now you're trying to say all this is my fault?"

Destan stood up. "Stop it!"

Something snapped inside of me and my hand came forward and hit hard against Irene's cheek. Her head whipped to the side, her mouth open in shock and skin red where my hand had slapped. I gasped, a tense silence settling on the meadow.

"Irene..." I whispered, eyes filling with tears, "I didn't mean...Irene, I'm so sorry—"

"Screw you, Raine," she said, pushing me out of the way as she stormed past, snatching up her comic book and water jug as she headed toward the trees.

"Irene, come on," Destan called, fingers raking anxiously through his hair, desperately following behind her. "Come back, let's work something out."

She kept walking, her free hand behind her back, middle finger jutting up. Destan stopped, sighing as she disappeared through the ferns. "Shit," he muttered, sparing me only a quick glance before continuing to stare at the trees she'd passed through. We stared after her for a couple minutes, not saying anything. Then he went to the riverbank, laying back down on the grass and covering his face with his hands. Hesitating, then deciding, I joined Destan on the frosted grass, lying down and placing my hands on my stomach. He subtly moved a couple inches away from me as soon as I laid my head back, but just as stubbornly, I scooted closer to him again. Nervously, I touched my hand to his, relieved when he didn't move it away that instant. Rather, he wrapped his fingers with mine, not breathing a word.

I forced myself to speak first. "Destan?"

"Hmm?"

"I'm going to have to bond with Skye tonight," I whispered.

Ten seconds passed between us. I opened my eyes to see his expression, but he had his hat pulled down over his eyes and nose. He cleared his throat, mouth hardly moving as he spoke. "So, he proposed?"

"Not exactly," I whispered, "but because of Gwen getting

taken and everything going on, our parents are arranging it all tonight."

"Ah," he said.

"Destan…I…" I trailed off, swallowing and pulling my knees to my chest, closing my eyes and wondering if Mom was still crying, if she'd already called Skye's mom and had everything organized like she always did. I wondered if Irene hated me, if Destan was hurting so much worse now that he knew I'd have sexual relations with Skye in just a number of hours, if I'd miss being called Bluehead once I was sealed as Mrs. Skye Zanying. Wondering if it was possible to simply melt into the ground and have the world go on without me for some time. Before my mind completely ran away with me, I heard the crackling of the cold grass, felt Destan's warm hand on my shoulder, and I peered over my knees. Destan had sat up, his head tilted to one side as he watched me in concern.

"What is it?" he asked, softly.

"I just don't understand it," I said, staring at the stream. "The whole 'bonding' thing. It's always seemed so alien to me."

"Well, I mean…I sort of get it," he murmured, shrugging. "It seals the deal for the wedding to come…forever bonding yourself to that person before making a grand public gesture of it all."

"I don't want to be forever-bonded," I whispered.

He gave a rough laugh. "Yes, you do, Bluehead."

"*No,* I don't."

He turned to me, eyes plunging into mine like silver bullets and hurting me all over. "Raine. Be real. You and me live in a world where everything is changing, all the time, forever, and we can't control any of it. The things that *can't* be changed are so rare and beautiful, and you don't want that? Infinite things are as rare as…well, as rare as having a hair mutation that turns it blue." For a split second, I saw a crooked smile rise up on his lips. Then it vanished just as quickly, and he looked away.

"But if change is so constant and inevitable," I reasoned,

284

frowning, "then isn't that a contradiction? Nothing is forever and true except that nothing is forever and true?"

"I guess, but all I'm saying is, once you bond with someone, you bond with someone and that's that. Even after you're both dead and in the ground, it doesn't undo the fact that you shared the most primal and sacred of moments together. Just as it is with who you saw first when you were born, or y'know who you first met at school, or who you first kissed…" He swallowed, scratching his head and standing up. He walked down the river a little bit, sticking his hands in his pockets as he breathed out a cloud of breath that smoked away in the wintry air. His voice came more quietly this time. "When you bond with someone, you're set forever. No matter how life changes, you'll always have that piece of them and they'll have that piece of you and that will never change. You'll never be the same again."

I came to his side, hair falling into my face as I looked down into the rushing water. "That almost sounds like an accusation," I said. "That I'll never be the same."

"You're already not the same," Destan whispered, meeting my eyes and making himself smile. "But I do believe that you've been changed for the better. You can shoot flames off twenty torches, climb a titanium mile-high tower, you can talk without hiding behind those big blue bangs of yours. I think it's safe to say you're doing just fine." His smile warmed, his eyes softly reaching mine. But soon I felt like I might dissolve again, and I leaned my head on his shoulder. He let me keep it there.

"I don't feel fine," I said. *I feel like I'm about to shatter.*

"You will. You're going on your right way, and…I'll still be here. If you need me. I'll be here," he whispered, gently taking my hand as the sun set gold before the trees.

"We can still try to be friends, right? I don't have to be up at Starshade forever, right?" I asked, and Destan rested his head on top of mine.

"This won't be the last time we see each other," he said, his jaw muscles clenching and tensing, as if he doubted his own words.

As it got dark, we remained there and I thought I heard Irene coming, but nothing came of it. I really didn't want to leave and go to Skye before making sure she knew how sorry I was, but it was getting dark so fast. Time was still moving so fast, so fast, and my eyes were burning in the effort of still keeping the crying at bay. My heart weighed so heavy in my chest, each thump felt like it left a bruise.

My fingers pinched on the stiff wool collar of Destan's coat, my forehead burying in his shoulder. "I don't love him," I whispered.

Destan's arms folded around me. "I know."

"And you're right, being bonded is something that I do want, Destan...I just...I don't want to let myself be forever bonded to him. If I ever do, I'd want it to be with..."

Destan grunted, taking his head off of mine and slowly moving out of the embrace. I swallowed what I had been planning on saying, and continued, even more softly, "someone that I actually care about. Someone that knows the real me even more than I do, and doesn't want to be trapped in this kind of life."

"Fate doesn't want to give you that person."

"Screw fate. Maybe I'm selfish and I want that anyway."

Destan laughed, "You really should get back. Your mom's fit is destined to be atomic because of how dark it already is." His jaw was set, his eyes shinier than usual. If he was going to cry, there would be no way I could hold it together.

"Are we ever going to talk about *it*?" I whispered, the words feeling urgent and unplanned.

He looked at me a long while, and in that exchange I felt us both recalling the kiss and the fire and the feel of each other and everything that he'd deemed a mistake. But even with the memories searing in his eyes, he could only glance away, go back to collect his lumber, sighing, "What do you mean, 'it?'"

I couldn't speak. I hated this ending. I hated myself for

getting so deep in all of these feelings I didn't understand, and above all I hated how now him, and his touch, and his presence was a distant land I'd never be able to travel to again. I was frozen stiff in my boots, holding my breath and trying to not say another word, and before he left, he gave me one last painful smile.

"This is 'it,' Bluehead. Nothing more."

chapter twenty-seven

I felt so sick I could barely stand. After getting back from the meadow, I'd fallen straight into bed, lying there with my eyes closed and blanket over my head for a couple of hours. If my mom had heard me come in, she'd have made me keep sweeping up the mess caused by the JP raid. It wasn't until I apparently started mumbling in my sleep that she realized I'd been in there for the past two hours or so. Usually she'd be pissed and complain that I should devote more of my time to helping her out, but this time she just hid her annoyance and told me to get up and get dressed. It took almost another hour just to get myself off of the sagging cot, and when my mom knocked on the wall asking if I was ready, I hastily brushed the dirt from my clothes and did up my hair. Now came suppertime, and my mom had spoken of nothing else but of the bonding I'd have tonight. The combination of having to swallow the lumpy eggs floating in the celery broth and remembering that I'd have my body invaded made everything entering my stomach sink like a rock. I set down my spoon, laying my forehead against the table as I whispered, "Mom, could you please stop talking about it? I feel kind of...I feel really ill..."

I felt her rough-tipped fingers rub the back of my neck gently, and I sat back up to see her smile at me. "Oh, I know you're nervous. It'll be fine. More than fine. My first time was something unforgettable, and Raine, it'll all be worth it, I promise, honey." Her lips touched my forehead and she handed me a box. "This is everything you'll need. I'll come for you in the morning."

I left and peeped into the box. I brushed my fingers over the garment. It was what my mother had worn, and grandmother had worn, and so forth. It was supposed to be symbolic, but thinking of all the girls who'd worn this and that now it was my turn just grossed me out. I pushed it aside and saw the other objects: a pill in a little blue bottle to take the morning after, a tiny vial of lavender oil, and a prayer book. I'd had to memorize the prayer anyway, but the book was there just in case. It says something about sealing our lives together and asking for the moon and sun spirits to create in us a bond that could never be broken, apparently. It was in the ancient language and no one really knew how to translate it anymore. I'd heard that up in Emergent and Canopia, couples didn't even complete the bonding a ritual. It made me wonder why the lower levels wanted to cling so much to these ancient traditions where the girls were picked like poppies from the ground, and left to dry out in the arms of a husband who might love you, but couldn't understand you. Or maybe that's just me.

No matter how life changes, you'll always have that piece of them and they'll have that piece of you, and that will never change. You'll never be the same again.

Trying hard to block out everything from thoughts of Destan to thoughts of even just showing myself so openly in front of someone, I walked up to Starshade and found Skye's house. It was so big. Two floors. And he had a television set. When I knocked, he came to the door immediately. He was wearing a robe and I could see the garment peeking from underneath. It was tradition for the betrothed to kiss in the foyer beforehand, and so without saying anything, he took my hand and pulled me onto the first step.

"Hello, Skye," I said.

"Hello, Raine. You look…magnificent, as always."

You're looking a bit fuzzy around the edges aren't you, Bluehead? Destan would have said.

I dug my nails into my palm, bowing my head. "Thank you."

"I have to get this just right…" Skye pondered, his dark hair perfectly combed, his brown eyes kind and worried as he stuck a piece of my hair behind my ear. His fingers tickled my skin. I closed my eyes, thinking he was coming in for that kiss, but he blushed, telling me, "Could you…um…get down on your knees, please?"

Taking a minute to understand what he meant, I suddenly remembered he technically hadn't proposed yet, so I clumsily crouched down on his front porch and bent my head down to the ground before him as was tradition. My arms were out in front of me, my eyes staring into the grains in the wood floor as I heard him clear his throat.

"Rise," he said, and I slowly looked up at him. My arms had started to shake. He held out his hand, and I took it, responding as I should.

"Am I to be chosen?" I asked, my voice so tremulous I wondered if he could even hear me.

Skye bowed to me, arms at his sides, "I have chosen you." I bowed in return, and then he reached into his robe pocket and withdrew three cloth bags that jingled as he held them out for me to take. "The dowry, or at least the first part of what I feel obliged to share with you. I am honoured to have found you,

290

Miss Ylevol...Raine," he added sheepishly.

I took the bags, and couldn't help but breathe a sigh of immense relief as they landed heavier in my hands then I'd expected. *I'll get you out of there, Gwen. You'll be okay, we'll pay the tax and get you out,* I thought, stowing the dowry in my belt pouch and smiling genuinely at the boy before me. "Thank you," I said, bowing again just to show how sincerely I meant it. He looked embarrassed at this, shuffling his feet as I came up.

And then, just like that— he kissed me. As soon as I looked up he came towards me, mouth open and I could tell he'd never kissed someone before. I barely had time to even slightly pucker my lips, when his touched against mine. They were cold and wet and soft, and felt like lips should. We held it like that for a few seconds, neither one of us daring to move them against each other. But I could feel his smile in the kiss. Destan had smiled when we had kissed, but still that had felt so different, so much warmer.

Skye pulled back quickly, and laughed a little. I looked at the ground trying to appear shy and flustered, but really just trying to hide the fact of how empty it had felt. Tears pricked like bee stings on my eyes.

"Wow. You taste like flowers," he whispered, cheeks blushing. He beckoned for me to come completely inside. "It's only us. For the ritual it said that there can't be anyone for a whole half a mile, or something strange like that. It's quite the event. My parents announced it to the whole village and they gave me oils and all sorts of gifts for preparation," he explained, meeting my eyes, to which I forced another slight smile. The tall brown walls of his house made me feel safe, and being with him, even safer. It was shocking how many less JPs were in Starshade than Underbrush. The division between our two levels was only seen as mild compared to the difference between Canopia and Starshade, but already the rumbling noise of police trucks shooting down the street had gone, and all was quiet. No shouting or shots being fired, no spontaneous officers barging in and looting. It was as quiet and sleepy as what would have been a fairly lucky Underbrush evening, and this was what Skye was saying was a not-so-peaceful Starshade evening. I couldn't imagine how it could be calmer.

You're going to live here, Raine, I thought, coming up the steps with him as the cold air drifted around us, *It'll be this nice every day. No more waking up to a nightmare. No more Gwen crying or Mom having to put up with JPs threatening her so much with higher taxes we couldn't pay.* We came down a short hallway, the sloped ceiling patched where some leaks had been. A long, nice, green rug was laid down on the wooden planks beneath our feet and I wished I'd left my boots near the porch rather than get dirt on it. Paper lanterns were attached to the wall, light tenderly tinting the hall golden. My long-legged shadow followed beside me, triggering another bout of sadness as I thought, *No more hiding in the shadows. Destan's alone in there again.*

He opened the door for me, and I slowly went inside. The bed could fit three people and his room was so big that I still couldn't believe he wasn't from Canopia. He had another nice rug on the floor and clean, soft, wool bed-covers and cotton sheets. A stack of feather roll pillows waited on the bed, thin candles clinging to the walls. The ritual candle was on his bedside table, which had been moved into the middle of the room.

Seeing my shocked expression, he laughed. "I assure you, that while I'm pretty well off, the sheets and pillows were given to me from the village for this occasion."

I nodded, a little reassured, but really just all the more nervous. *I think I'm going to throw up. How am I going to do this? How?* I thought, swaying on the spot and gripping the edge of the bedframe.

When Skye closed the door, he let out a deep breath, closing his eyes for a moment. He was realizing how big of a deal that action was. We stood face to face by the table; on either side with the candle in the middle still unlit. He removed his robe and I saw the thin, transparent silver garment. It shimmered over his pale skin and the threads were caught around some of his spiraling chest hairs. He was so skinny, and I couldn't let myself look below the waist where he wore the delicate shorts of the same fabric. The ritual said that the man would come dressed, the woman have to dress before him as a symbol of trust.

The ritual was in four parts: the initiation (that was the kiss in the foyer), the trust, the promise, and the bonding. He blinked his long lashes at me as if to say, *Your turn*. I tried to distance myself from what was happening; trick my mind into thinking I wasn't doing anything major at all. Just undressing. Taking fabric off of skin; just movements, simple movements. I slid off my cloak and my fingers started shaking so much that I could barely pull the cord. I was wearing what Destan had seen me in every day. Skye's eyes were subtly ecstatic, his teeth over his bottom lip in restrained anticipation.

I pulled the red ribbon from my hair and the bun fell out into midnight blue waves down to my waist. I lifted my favourite scarlet sweater over my head, then stepped out of my boots. I shakily slid off my fingerless gloves. They felt so naked, and now Skye definitely noticed how my hands shook. It looked like I was waving them.

We weren't supposed to talk yet, but he whispered, concerned, "Is everything okay?"

I nodded, too vigorously, my head feeling as if it were going up and down and up and down even after I'd stopped, "Yeah. I'm fine."

Why was this so hard? Couldn't I just turn myself off and get this over with? I clutched my hands for them to stop, but then a tear came streaking from one of my eyes. Every time I held a part of me together, somewhere else decided to start shaking, start panicking. I grasped the bottom hem of my undershirt and lifted it up over my head, only leaving a modest and worn out brassiere. I unhooked my belt, and had almost forgotten to unwind Destan's scarf from around my neck. I unzipped my denim shorts and let them fall from my narrow hips to the floor.

Skye let out a breath, gazing at me. Was he disappointed? What did he expect, that I'd have nice breasts or actual hips? That my ribs wouldn't come out farther than my stomach? I was scrawny and bruised and cut up, and every inch of my skin was getting dotted with goosebumps as the panic attack finally took hold of me.

What I'd hoped to just be a deep breath in became a moan, and exhaling I broke into sobs that came urgently up and out of my throat as if I were vomiting them. I unhooked my brassiere with wails rattling through my clenched teeth and my hair falling to hide my face. Mom said she had cried, but I doubted it had been like this. I couldn't breathe, I kept gasping for air and just heaving more gasps that made me more desperate for air. I held onto both sides of the brassiere, then let it fall to the floor. Skye was more focused on the crying than my half-naked body. I fumbled with the hem of my leggings, gripping them with my thumb and then sliding them down, my bare legs cold in the air. And to get it over with, I pulled off my underpants in a quick motion that made me trip, and I fell cold and naked to the floor. Skye gasped, and made a move, but had to stay standing as directed in the ritual, or else the entire thing could be rendered corrupted. I lay there trying to breathe, my fist tight around the infinity pendant Destan had made me.

Get up, I thought, *Get up, get up, please just get this over with.*

I grit my teeth, forcing myself to rise, wiping hastily at my runny nose and eyes as Skye once again broke silence, insistently asking again, "Raine, are you sure everything is all right? What's wrong?"

I didn't answer, just slipped into the ritual garment, the same transparent, shimmery-like-pearls fabric as his clothes. It was short, fell only past my thighs. I grabbed Skye's hand and pressed his palm to mine. My fingers were cold and vibrating against his.

He was so troubled by this that he kept looking up at me

as he went to light the candle. My eyes were dry now, and I stared at him calmly. My lips were glued tightly together so I wouldn't embarrass myself again.   Then, breathing loudly through his nose, Skye tipped over the candle and dribbled the red wax onto our intertwined fingers. I was so cold and numb that the hot wax didn't hurt as it scalded the same pattern on each of our hands.

"*Rednu Yin dna Yang, I esimorp ot evol dna hsirehc ruoy trah litnu ti on regnol staeb, dna enim ylno staeb rof ouy,*" he began, slowly and then more surely. I still wasn't sure what the ritual words meant, but I knew what to say back.

"*Rednu Yin dna Yang, I esimorp ot evol dna hsirehc ruoy trah litnu ti on regnol staeb, dna enim ylno staeb rof ouy,*" I repeated, but having to add, "*ouy era ym nus, I lliw eb ruoy noom, ew lliw erolpxe siht dlrow rehtegot.*"

We whispered in unison, "*I dnob flesym ot uoy. Ruo evol sreuqnoc egnahc.Ruo evol sreuqnoc lla.Ew era etinifni.*"All that was left now was the bonding. I felt dead, like the bed behind me was my urn and as soon as I'd lay down, I'd turn to ash.

We went to the bed in unison, and I was the one who would have to lay down.

I pretended I was laying on the grass by the river, Destan dangling a wildflower over my nose as I waved it away giggling. He'd say he'd found a great place for target practice, and then we'd run off into the woods with the sun chasing us and no one to hear how we'd laugh and scream as we lived the life we wanted.

But the bed creaked and I flew back to reality. I wouldn't let myself cry or think of Destan again. "Ready?" I asked him, my throat so dry. Skye was kneeling beside me, less frightened looking, but still visibly uneasy about how strange I was acting.

"Are *you*?" he asked.

With a jolt of sudden determination, I pulled him to me and made him kiss me hard. His mouth smashed against mine and he let out a quiet yelp, but then he slipped his body on top of mine silently. I felt his warm belly on my bony and ugly stomach and as he brushed back all the thick blue hair that was in my face, I felt myself crying again, nearly sobbing the kisses into him. He wasn't smiling and my tears were lost in his hair as he kissed my neck and along my collarbones. His hands traveled methodically, lightly down my chest and stomach and reaching to my hip.

Don't think of Destan, don't think of Destan. Raine, you're so terrible. That's so terrible of you. I kept thinking that to myself, but imagining it was Destan's big, ratty, calloused hands brought me comfort. Skye's hands were too soft and thin. He adjusted his body on mine so that we could bond and I felt him spread my legs gently, but as soon as I was about to lose myself to him, he drew away from me and sat back on his haunches.

He was sweating and breathing really shallowly, and as I opened my eyes, a single tear streaked down my cheek and left a dark spot on his sheets.

"I can't do it," he said dubiously, incredulously, looking at my naked body through the garment as if he couldn't comprehend it. "I can't."

He pierced my eyes and looked so distressed and handsome all at once that I felt something swell in my stomach. I sat up and hugged my knees to my chest, mumbling, "We have to, Skye…"

"You can't," he said sharply, getting off the bed and tearing at his hair while he paced. "You…you're so sad, Raine. This is supposed to be happy, joyous, reverent. You can't do this with me," he said, voice cracked and desperate.

"But you want me to—"

"*Fuck* what I want!" he cried, shocking me at how suddenly he'd changed from the timid Starshader I knew him to be, into someone so wracked with frustration that he threw down a pillow and pressed his forehead against the bedroom wall, his arms shaking as he clenched his hands in and out of fists. "Raine, tell me if you love me and don't lie," he said.

296

I pulled some covers around my body. "I…I love you, Skye."

"You can't love me, Raine, how could you love me if you can't even look into my eyes when I'm about to…when we're about to…" He sighed, stepping back from the wall and pacing away from me again. "I'm not stupid. I know why you're doing this."

My blood ran cold. "You d-do?"

He nodded, staring down at the floor. "I know your mother has been putting so much pressure on you to marry me, my mother's been doing the same thing. She wants me married off before her sickness gets worse and she…she dies. I appreciate you trying to help, and yes, Raine, I am very attracted to you, but I also really care about you and this…it's just too much for you—"

"It's not," I said, not even knowing his end of the story, but still set on just keeping my promise. "Skye, I need to marry you, too. I want to marry you."

His eyes flickered up from the floor and onto me at that, and in his gaze I could hear him pleading, *But why?*

I dug my fingernails into the mattress, struggling to keep my voice level. "You're right. I don't love you, not yet." Then I slid out from the covers and came up to him, hesitating between taking his hand or just leaving things as cold as they were now. I spoke again, more quietly, "Do you love me?"

Skye bit his lip, eyes staring somewhere far off. "I think I was beginning to. I'm fascinated with you. I like you, a lot. And I've always had a pleasant time with you, but it doesn't matter if you don't feel the same." He sighed, sounding exasperated, "You seem so smart and sure of yourself. You hadn't been afraid to disagree with me before, but now you're obviously in great pain over this and you won't even speak up or tell me how you really feel! Why?"

He was so right that even as he repeated the question, I couldn't answer right away. My throat was swollen with guilt. His face was fading steadily as I neglected to say anything, but before I could see that he'd truly given up, that I'd truly hurt him, I came forward with a burst of desperation, whispering, "Help me fall in love with you..." I took his hand and laid it on one of my breasts. Skye's head shot up to look at where I'd rested his palm, and looking in my eyes, both of his were tortured. But beneath the sadness, there was that spark of love. I could tell by how much resistance he was displaying for me, and I tried to look convincing, like his touch was affecting me. "Please, Skye," I breathed, touching my nose to his, "I *want* to fall in love with you, I need to, I do and I can, just..."

"You want to?" he asked, so softly, his hand nervously beginning to caress the side of my chest.

"Yes," I whispered, my finger tracing down his jaw as I felt his body press close against mine. Parts of him had seemed to melt, others grown rigid.

He moved his mouth onto mine, delicately at first, then giving in, moaning as I kissed him back. He moved his lips and then his tongue more earnestly. He tried pulling back every now and then to try and restrain himself, his fingers nervously traveling down the small of my back and then lifting off. He couldn't. Skye pressed me against the wall only with a moderate amount of force and kissed my cheeks. He kissed my eyes and nose; he kissed my neck and even sucked along my collarbones as shivers ran throughout my entire body.

It was then that I realized I wasn't moving. I hadn't been kissing him back or offering myself to him hardly at all, and until I did, he wouldn't make the bond. Skye was increasingly cleverer than I had imagined. And kind.

My hands were clammy on his face and I slid them slowly down his chest and soft stomach. He didn't believe me yet, wouldn't even begin to get the act over with. I grabbed his face and kissed it aggressively, filling him with so much of me that he moaned and touched my chest again, burying his face there and leaving one wet kiss after the other.

298

Then all of a sudden he swept me off my feet and we fell onto the bed, hiding under the covers. He climbed on top of me and we kissed for a long while, and without me even realizing it, he became Destan again. We were in the dewy grass at night, our meadow where we could see the stars. And his muscular body was heavy on mine and not like Skye's lithe form. His hand was on the small of my back, curving my body upward to his and a feeling shot through me like lightning at realizing we were about to bond.

"Your call," he gasped, words tickling my nose as my eyes fluttered open and closed madly. He was so close to changing everything.

"Fate doesn't want to give you that person."

"Screw fate. Maybe I'm selfish and I want that anyway."

I opened my eyes, Skye's own light brown irises an inch from mine. He was at the breaking point, our hips pressed together and our breathing the same frantic speed. My heartbeat slowed."I can't."

Skye touched his forehead to mine, laughing bitterly under his breath and lifting his hips off. I exhaled a big breath, tears springing in my eyes. Skye kissed both of them, and then planted a soft kiss on my lips."I'll close my eyes while you change," he said quietly, politely, as if he hadn't just been rejected by his fiancée. I slipped out of the bed trembling, and in shock, unsure if I should say anything more; hold him one more time to make it better. He was still recovering from the last moment though, and before I could approach him, he strode quickly over to the little table, picking up the candle burned down to a nub.

"Keep the dowry," he said. And with a last breath, he blew out the flame.

chapter twentyeight

A knock on the door. Looking up from my paper, I set my brush back onto my watercolour palette, and went cautiously to the door. The JPs had already come in three times so far today for inspection, and it was only noon now, so I doubted there was still a pillow unturned, a book not yet paged through for treasonous content. I pushed the door aside, making a mental note to try and figure out how to rehinge it eventually, and came face to face with no one other than Jun. My boss's grin felt out of place amidst all of the solemn quiet heavily weighing on the town right now.

"Is your mother in, dear?" she asked.

I shook my head. "She's taking a nap."

"Well then, I suppose the congratulations are for you alone, honey." Her eyes glittered, and she dug around in her cloth handbag before whipping out a folded piece of paper. "You've been doing so swell, Miss Ylevol," she bent forward, looking left to right conspiratorially, and then whispering quite loudly, "especially with these piss-pots running about, causing trouble. This curfew has been a damn mess with my schedule making." She handed me the paper, which I unfolded and recognized as my Laundress duties for the next month. She winked. "I gave ya mostly Underbrush and Starshade this month."

I bowed my head. "Thank you. I really appreciate it, Jun." She beamed and I had a sudden thought, skipping over to the kitchen, calling, "Just one moment!" I ladled some of the still-boiling split pea soup into one of my mom's containers, closed it, and then grabbed the crust of bread I'd been hoping to keep fresh until Gwen got back.

I gave my boss a quivering smile. "Here, as a thank you." Even when I definitely didn't do well or try my hardest, Jun pretended I was good at washing clothes, so the least I could do was give her something nice.

"Oh, my! And *I* appreciate this, dear," she cackled. "And congratulations on winning that match last weekend, by the way."

She winked at me again and I stiffened, feeling my face grow hot and panic creep its way into me. "You...you saw me?" *Did she also see the kiss afterwards? Is that why she winked? Could she know I broke off the bonding, too?* The thoughts came quickly and uncontrollably.

"No, I wish I could've made it; just been too busy this year, y'know? But my older sister went and said a little girl with blue hair shot the straightest. And well I just said, 'I'll be darned if that's my Miss Raine!'" Jun laughed heartily, trying a nibble of the bread I'd given her.

Relief filled me, and before my loud but lovely boss could wake my mother from her nap in her room only a few feet away, I bid farewell and closed the door again, slumping down the wall and rubbing my temples. *I have to stop being so goddamn paranoid*, I thought, my eyes traveling to the table where my mom had dumped out Skye's dowry money and had been carefully dividing it all into different expenses. I couldn't remember the last time

I'd seen her so happy. I also couldn't remember the last time I'd felt this conflicted.

I'd decided this morning to wait until I could regain my sanity and for us to send in the money to reclaim Gwen before I told my mom what had gone down with Skye. All but only a little of the dowry would be what was required to get Gwen freed from the Tower's ward for the 'mentally-inhibited.' Skye's mother must not have been told either, because I would have awoken to the infuriated screams of my mother and ended up deaf from her boxing my ears. Instead, I'd woken up to fairly okay split-pea soup and a tired *good morning*.

JPs filled every and any crack in Underbrush that I used to be able to slip through, so seeing Irene and apologizing was not an option, and neither was going to Destan and telling him about Skye. At home, I tried to scavenge what I could of my used up watercolour paints to keep myself distracted. But all I found myself painting were smeary red and grey blobs again and again, and thoughts of Destan just wouldn't leave me be. I wasn't sure how to go about all this, and before I'd had crazy feelings like these I would have thought it was beyond idiotic to be preoccupied with love while people were getting shot and an execution was probably in my near future! But despite how rational and focused my head tried to be right now, my realization that I loved Destan and couldn't be with anyone else consumed me and felt so earth-shattering that I knew I couldn't contain it for long. And still, Destan meant too much to me to receive a random outburst of feelings again. The night of the archery match hadn't gone well, but when we had approached our situation more calmly the last night before I went to bond with Skye, things had gone more smoothly. I had to talk to him today, I had to. If I didn't get this out of the way, there was no way I could sneak out a spy and help to divert an all-out war between mountains on top of that.

Then there was another knock, gentle enough on the wood that at first I didn't notice it. But then the second came hard against the door, and I scrambled to my feet, now beyond annoyed with the frequent visitors to what used to be a nearly invisible household. But the moment I'd shoved aside the door and was hit with a gust of cool morning air, it was quite obvious that no one was waiting to be greeted. I stuck my head out, looking around the corners, but no one was to be found. *Am I going crazy?* I thought, shaking my head and rolling up my sweater sleeves to heave the door back into its place. But just as I'd gripped the splintery wood with both hands, I noticed a fancily wrapped package sitting on our beaten-up doormat.

I eyed it suspiciously, taking another glance around to see if someone was sticking around to see me open up the thing. The streets remained abuzz with the shiny black suits of police officers and the red-eyed wolves that walked beside them. After only a couple moments of standing out there, I'd drawn the attention of a certain officer burning a pile of books across the street. He whistled through his mask, making some rude hand gesture. And so, using all of my resistance to not return the favor, I slipped inside with the parcel, slamming the door back in place and most regrettably waking my mother.

"What's that?" she snapped, finding the tissue-wrapped parcel right away, even though her eyes still looked half-open and bleary with sleep.

"I...don't know. It's addressed to me," I murmured, undoing the navy blue ribbon and tearing through the wrappings. Something silver glittered under the paper, and I pulled out a long garment covered in beads that shimmered like fish scales and glistened like a pool of rainbow motor oil in sunlight.

"Oh, now that's not the dress I ordered for the wedding," my mother sighed, annoyed and coming over in her ratty slippers and robe. "We have to send it back. This isn't for a stick like you. It's probably for some Emergent girl who has the little white wedding dress I paid for."

She went padding into the bathroom, leaving me with the beautiful and peculiar gown draped across my lap. I peered inside the box again and withdrew a card written in fancy calligraphy:

Miss Ylevol,

It has come to my attention that you will be attending the celebratory feast for your companion, Master Atrasha. I wanted to make sure you came dressed fit for the occasion. Receive this as a gift in thanks for whatever contribution you made to Master Atrasha's finding of a valuable Thgindim artifact, and for being one of our favourite Laundresses. Hoping you are well, and I cannot wait to get to know you at the celebration tonight.

Sincerely,

Sebastian Lae

```
Head of Law Enforcement
    Foreign Affairs
          and
      Archaeology
```

I yelped, dropping the card and rushing straight to the coat rack. I coiled Destan's red scarf around my neck fervently, frustration pulsating through me. *Accompany Destan? To a feast? Come to this Councilman's attention? What's that Beaniehead gotten up to since I last saw him?!* I thought, and I bundled up in my coat, hastily searching the floor for the gloves that'd slipped out of my pocket.

Then I paused, sitting back on my heels and gritting my teeth together. What was I going to do now? Leave my mom here to go back to the meadow? I'd wanted to stick around until Gwen was returned. I had to be here for when she came back or else I'd never forgive myself. The streets were swarming, if I got caught trying to move between levels nothing would keep them from shooting me on the spot. *But Irene needs to leave, now, before not even the meadow is safe. And getting a gift from the guy you stole from seems like a big deal, I have to see Destan and know what all of this is about,* I thought, drumming my fingers on the floor and chewing on the dry skin of my bottom lip. A gunshot went off outside and I jumped, pulling my knees closer to my chest and closing my eyes. *And I need to just get out of here, just even for an hour. I'll be back in time for Gwen.*

So, getting to my feet and snatching up my bow and quiver, I left out the back and crept along the edge of the forest as I'd done to sneak between levels now that border security was so much tighter. It took painfully long, and I had to duck behind trashcans and into the thickets of bamboo repeatedly as JPs patrolled the forest perimeter. Not to mention I was exhausted from the sleepless night I'd had post-Skye, and I'd been too distracted by everything else to bring myself to eat much of anything this morning, so I was already tripping over my feet and struggling to stay alert. Buzzing in my head were the same thoughts over and over, each with their own sharp hit to my heart, *Destan, Gwen, Skye, Mom, Chantastic, Irene, Destan, Gwen, Irene, Destan, Destan, Destan...*

And then, right before I crossed into the meadow where I could already hear Irene and Destan laughing about something together, another thought pierced me. *When should I tell him about what happened with Skye?* But I wasn't able to ponder any longer, because Irene seemed to have spotted me before I'd even pushed aside the branches of pine and fern that covered the opening.

"Hey! Raine, come on in here, you gotta see this," Irene hollered, on tiptoe so that I could see her high black ponytail and broad white grin through the veil of crisscrossing pine needles. Seeing her filled me with such immense relief that I couldn't help but run straight at her, lifting her up off the ground in a bone-crunching hug.

"I'm sorry, I'm sorry, I'm sorry," I said rapidly, squeezing her and then feeling her wriggle out of my hold, moaning and groaning about personal space.

"Okay, okay, you apologize, I get it!" she grumbled, a side of her mouth twitching up into a smirk. She stood so straight and tall, no longer hunched or using a staff to support her. Irene's torso was still wrapped in a bandage, but less to contain bleeding and moreso to keep the ribs in a good place for healing back together. She eyed me quizzically, a thick eyebrow arched. "Now you're freaking me out. What's your deal?"

I followed her into the meadow, carefully avoiding the slippery mud patches and ducking under the ferns. "I just felt awful about what I did. And I missed you."

"It's hardly been a day, dude," she sighed, rolling her eyes and squatting down near a campfire she must have put together the night before. She rubbed her palms together, chuckling, "Don't fall apart once I'm actually gone."

"I'll try," I smiled, joining her by the fire. "Where's Destan?"

"Taking a piss. He'll be back," she said, poking the fire and then reaching behind her for her spy knapsack. She fished out the tablet, and with an impish sort of grin tweaking her lips, she scooted closer to me. "I got it," she said, "Totally cracked the code."

I gasped. "That was...fast. How'd you figure it out?"

"Tried all the ones I'd memorized, and then when those didn't work I just scrambled them up until there was a click, a whoosh, and a screen that very wonderfully read 'access granted,'" Irene said, quite pleased with her work as she tapped in that series of numbers, symbols, and letters all on that hovering sort of keyboard. "You never doubted I'd get it, right?"

"Of course not," I shrugged, smiling a little at her as she logged in and out again and again just to prove that she'd been able to hack it, "you *did* say you're Fluxaria's most notorious, most feared spy, didn't you?"

"I'm the shit, honestly," she laughed, bumping her fist against mine and smoothing back the little black hairs that'd fallen in front of her eyes. There was a sudden, sharp crunching sound, and we both glanced behind us. Without announcing himself, Destan had reappeared; splitting logs with a composed yet brutal amount of force, splinters flying out in all directions as his axe came plunging through the soft, white wood. Irene called for him, "Hey, Destan, tell Raine about that thing you got."

He set his axe down, exhaling a great breath through his nose and coming slowly over, appearing just the same as any other day; with his tall black boots and high collared wool coat with the brass buttons, his beanie slightly askew and his cheeks a little chapped with cold, his face as unreadable as ever. The only thing out of place was how both of us seemed to be making it our priority to *not* make eye contact.

"Big news," Destan said, his gaze focusing somewhere right above my forehead. "A fancy messenger man came by the woodshop with this letter." He waved it and then tossed it to me. It fluttered in the air the way paper does when it is tried to be thrown, and I saved it from falling in the river as he further explained, "I don't even know how whoever it is knew to find me there, I've been going about my life as much off the grid as possible for as long as I can remember." He crouched down closer to me and Irene, and beckoned for me to start reading.

I nodded, assuming it had to do with the weird package and note I'd received this morning as well. I skimmed through the short invitation. I was right.

"Destan…" I said, glancing up at him and then back down, "that 'artifact' you returned as a distraction so we could steal the tablet is some really important scroll from when Thgindim and Fluxaria were one mountain…because of this, you've been invited to a feast held by…" My heartbeat stuttered. "The head of Law Enforcement and Foreign Affairs and Archaeology."

"All right, he knows we stole it, I'm outta here," Irene scoffed, leaping up and putting her hands on her hips. "Isn't it fishy that the *one* guy we steal from is the one who wants to hold us a feast for something that doesn't even apply to his Career?"

My throat went dry. "Well actually it does apply…it says he recently also took over department of Archaeology due to a death of that Council member."

"That's convenient," Destan snorted, shaking his head.

"More like strategic," Irene said. "Just don't reply, 'kay? It's gotta be a trap, you guys, you know that, right?"

"Shit." Destan's brows were dug hard over his lids, his jaw clenched and stiff as he spoke, "Doesn't sound like I've got much of a choice."

My eyes wandered back to the invitation, which was now slightly fluttering at the edges as the winter breeze drifted over it. Then, I noticed that beneath the signature of Council Sebastian Lao was one more line of thin and slanted handwriting. I snatched it back up, eyes skimming over the words:

Seeing as the feast is quite the traditional affair, we humbly ask you to consider inviting a guest to accompany you to this engagement; a relative, a friend, a close colleague from work. Just something to consider. Simply notify the Peak representative of your level and we will make sure to accommodate you and your guest as sees fit.

"What is it, Bluehead?" Destan whispered, nudging my foot with the toe of his boot.

I opened my mouth hesitantly, and then closed it, considering my words. My own invitation seemed to vibrate impatiently in my shorts pocket. "Um…nothing, it's nothing…"

"*Raine*, what is it now?" Irene said, voice rising in volume as she came storming back up to me, stealing the letter from my hands and reading it quickly before I could stop her. She rolled her eyes, tore the invitation in half, and walked away, growling, "Well this is even more super duper…"

"C'mon, Raine just tell me what it says."

"You…you are being asked to bring a guest to the feast."

We held each others eyes for a moment. Siri snored softly under the tree we used to lean the archery target against. "But apparently, you already invited someone," I sighed, sticking my hand into my pocket.

"How could I?" he asked, furrowing his brow. "I didn't know what the letter was even about until now."

I withdrew my own token from Councilman Lao, the card that had been wrapped in with the dress. "This came this morning," I said, about to pass it to him, but then reading it aloud when I remembered he couldn't by himself.

Destan gaped at me, licking his lips and scratching his head thoughtfully, "But…I swear it, Raine, I didn't know about any of this until now."

I nodded. "I believe you."

"It's a set-up," Irene said, shortly. "It's a set-up and if you two go, you're not going to come back." She crossed over to her knapsack, packing up the various items she had laying around it.

"Regardless," I began, choosing my words carefully, "we still have to go. This is less of an invitation and more of a heads up that they know it was us."

"*I* have to go," Destan whispered, looking at me seriously, "*you* have to stay here."

I gave him a stern look, saying, slowly, "I can't. You need someone to back you up if something goes wrong."

Just as I'd known he would, he shook his head, again, "No, Raine, you're not. And there's nothing you could really do anyway if it's a trap."

"The Councilman *knows* I'm a part of this too, it won't save me if that's what you think you going alone will accomplish—"

"It's not about that!"

"Then what?" I begged, holding my hands out in front of me, "We…we're a team," I whispered, more to myself. More just because I still believed it.

He sighed. Irene was silent as a tree. Destan looked at me again and his eyes searched mine for that something that was different, that change that he still thought had occurred overnight because of bonding. I looked at him and I tried to have my eyes say, *No, I'm the same and I love you. I love you Destan and I can't love anyone else.* And I looked at him, and I felt my entire being filling with yearning because the longer I did, the more my heart jumped and jumped inside me; the more restraint it took from kissing him right then and there with Irene still just a few feet away and a thousand miles of responsibility and conflict between us.

"Destan," I whispered, so quietly it came from my lips as thin and fragile as a breath, "I have to tell you—"

Gunshots blasted the sky wide open. And with a roar, the trees glowed red, then orange, then burst into pieces, all of us flying back with them.

chapter twentynine

Trees tipped like pitchers of fire, spilling the flaming needles in a bright and lethal shower over us. Destan and I darted left and right, crouching down to avoid the onslaught of rubber bullets being shot straight through into the meadow. Irene had climbed a tree to get to safety, only to crash down with it as that tree too was blasted apart by a JP bomb. Destan leapt toward it, doing a roll on the ground and catching Irene in his outstretched arms. She scrambled out, backing away, screaming something at us but we couldn't hear anything except for the shrieking sirens and thunderous gunfire.

Thinking fast, I snatched Destan's hand, pulling him toward the opening of the meadow to get us back to town. Irene disappeared into the brush, and I was only able to catch a quick glimpse of her big, round, black eyes before another tree fell and she had already escaped.

Siri howled at the top of her lungs, nudging at both of

Destan's and my legs until she stuck her muzzle between our legs and had us slide onto her neck, then secure us on her back. I clutched tightly to her fur, twisting my fingers into it and pressing my face into her soft neck, Destan's arms folding protectively around me as Siri dodged in and out of the burning trees. As we ran and ran, more and more black silhouettes of JPs dotted the woods, and the screams of the town just grew in volume and pitch.

Two JPs threw out a long chain, tripping up Siri and making Destan and I have to cling to her try not to fall off as she pitched to the side. Siri shook it off, not letting her hind legs get caught as she bounded over it; and then behind us came more JPs, all riding on the backs of shiny black bikes that didn't even touch the ground but zoomed right over the lumpy roots and piles of rubble.

"Faster, girl, faster!" Destan commanded, smacking Siri's flank and then rubbing it encouragingly. She pumped her limbs faster and faster with more force packed behind each movement, and her pink tongue was pressed to the side of her face as we flew into Underbrush square— straight into a swarm of police officers.

They threw out an electrified net over us, sending Siri down spread-eagle where she stood, Destan shielding me from the sting of the wire as he laid across me, his back taking most of the attack. Siri squealed, each of her paws strapped down to the ground in a flash, Destan's body convulsed above mine, and just as I was sure we'd be shot and it would all be over, the net was removed and we were dragged out into the road where hundred of Underbrushers lay on their stomachs, hands behind their necks as JPs trooped in between the rows of them.

My face scraped against the gravel as they dragged me along, pulling me by my ankles, and through the pain I frantically tried to look around to see where Destan had been taken, to see if my Mom or friends were anywhere in sight, if Gwen had been brought back home yet.

"On your back, scum!" the JP yelled at me, and I obediently rolled over, my face dirty and stinging as he shined a red light into my eyes. I flinched, meaning to cover my eyes, but had my arms forced back down and cuffed together at the wrists. Then he rolled me back onto my stomach and pulled me into line with other people my age.

Destan was thrown beside me, a thick slug of blood coming down from his nose, and since his wrists too were cuffed behind his back, he couldn't wipe it away; only snuff it back up as dirt was scuffed into our faces with every stride the JPs took. We looked at each other helplessly, not daring to speak as more kids were added to the lines, getting thrown or dragged screaming beside us as JPs forced parents back into their houses and made a fence of black uniforms around us in the road.

"Repeat after me," one officer with a megaphone ordered, "I am loyal to the Majesty Council."

I am loyal to the Majesty Council, the crowd shouted.

"I hide no truths from the Majesty Council."

I hide no truths from the Majesty Council.

"Bluehead?" Destan whispered, just as everyone was calling back their responses. There was a loud, shattering sound, and then a crunching of wood and blade, and even from the ground I could see police tanks driving straight into the makeshift Underbrush huts and cabins. Glass sparkled in the air like rain, and landed with the music of demented wind chimes.

Every inch of my body was quaking in fear. "What?" I asked him, then making myself yell back with the crowd, "I am loyal to the Majesty Council."

"It's going to be all right," he insisted, his face somehow measured even as blood continued pouring from his left nostril and screams of Underbrushers getting herded with electric nets filled the air. "Raine we have to look as calm as we can or we're totally busted."

"Destan, this is too much, we can't just keep hiding anymore or it's going to leave the whole level in ruins!" I pleaded,

314

hoping the JPs trooping around didn't notice that my lips were forming very different words than what they were supposed to be. I looked at him, fiercely whispering, "Just because you don't have anyone left here to worry about doesn't mean that other people don't, that other people couldn't lose everything because of us." I felt like the biggest jerk in the world the moment those words left my mouth.

"Raine, I *know* that," he groaned, zipping his lips instantly as the officer standing at the head of the fleet hollered out another order.

"I will surrender all knowledge of malicious intent to the Majesty Council, or else suffer the full extent of the Justice Police's power. Say you will!" the JP screamed at us.

"I will," I replied, only because a general wielding two extra long and lethal looking lightning rods came stalking by. But I also realized my answer was what I was leaning towards. There was a continuous crashing, and an entire row of pine trees around the town's border came plunging down on top of houses. I found myself breathing more sharply, more in a state of panic that was getting harder to control.

"No you won't," Destan whispered, his voice rough but eyes softer. "Raine, just for now, we have to still keep it to ourselves."

"But all I can think about is how many people are dying right now, Destan, how many houses are getting wrecked, how many trees are falling, how much time until they find Irene and kill her too," I said, words blurring together, throat constricting in fear.

"Then..." Destan's eyes looked left then right, and he paused waiting for another reply to be issued. Then he whispered, gently as he could, "Once a long, long time ago there was a hunter guy named Zhanshi. And...and he went down in history as being the strongest, most best-looking and friendliest dude you could meet."

I shook my head. "Destan, stop. Why are you telling me

this?"

"Because he wasn't this cool guy at first," he continued, edging ever so slightly closer to me so that I could feel his warm breath brush against my cheeks with every word he spoke, "He was lonely, he grew up hidden away and chose to stay there because he was scared of all he didn't know. Zhanshi was about to just wipe himself from existence and save the world the trouble of ever knowing a shadow like him, and he'd have never become that strong warrior, if it hadn't been for this um…this nature spirit. Yingsu, the spirit of the poppy flowers that sprung up out of nowhere one winter. Charged right into his territory, all red petals, just sprouting everywhere and brightening up the dark woods he'd always hid away in. When he first saw them, he took his sword and went to cut them all down, only to see the spirit living inside come rushing out, with a fierce, and frightening, and beautiful, and kind, and strange pair of eyes and voice that made him drop the sword right then.

"And it wasn't until she showed up that he felt like life was worth living. Because she…she was his light," he said, now unable to meet my eyes for even a second. His voice was shaking, my eyes couldn't contain the tears anymore and a few skidded out down my cheeks. "And, fuck, as magnificent and otherworldly as she was, she claimed to be alone too. She gave him her friendship; they were friends, the best of friends, running all around in the forest, him teaching her the lay of the woods, and her telling stories of the spirit world. She started hanging around the mortal world so much that she was losing her divine form, and the heavens weren't too happy about that. But…" he trailed off, biting his lip and taking a breath before continuing, "…she loved him. And he loved her. And there wasn't really much more to it.

"In some versions of this story, um, you know…" He smiled slightly, wincing as another series of gunshots were fired, more shrieks, "The big bunch of other spirits and goddesses got mad and took Yingsu back, sent a white tiger to kill Zhanshi and it was all pretty damn sad. But…did you ever hear the *real* version, Bluehead?"

I swallowed, voice quivering, "No."

Destan now smiled fully, a smile so out of place and warm that it was all the more comforting, "They ran away together. When that tiger came down, Zhanshi and Yingsu teamed up and lassoed it, climbing on its back and running away. Yingsu eventually was unable to revive the spirit energy she once had because she was now banned from the heavens, and she and Zhanshi became just a pair of humans wandering and wandering, never safe. The two of them were always running and having to change where they slept and how long they could stay where they ended up, but they always made it out together no matter what punches were thrown, and they found and fought in battles they had not much of a place in and ended up making the world a prettier place—"

"Attention, citizens of the Underbrush level."

Destan cut off, giving me a last pleading look before we both had to focus our attention to the front. Standing there was that same Councilman from the day before, with his bald head and black robes and eyes like two black beetles encircled in charcoal. Sebastian Lao, head of the department of Foreign Affairs and Law Enforcement and Archaeology and who knew what next.

"While I hate to see a mess made in any area of this beautiful mountain," he began, a smirk evident in his voice, "I cannot say that this destruction is not without purpose." He stepped down from the podium the JPs had set up in the center of the road, walking through the police to us.

"Do unto others what shall be done unto you. You took Majesty Council property, we took your children. You damaged what is the pinnacle of democracy, our very own Peak Tower, and so is it not only just that we show you the same common courtesy?"

He snapped his fingers, and brought everyone's attention

to the podium where he'd just been. Now there were four Underbrushers standing there, burlap sacks over their heads as they shifted from foot to foot. They also had their hands cuffed behind their backs, JPs in a row behind them. I tried to figure out who they could be from the state of their clothing or the dark hair that spilled out from under the bag of one woman, but it was useless. They looked as dirty and plain and average as any Underbrusher. The only thing that worried me was the height difference between at least one of them and the rest. The way that figure teetered wobbily on his own two feet and seemed more frightened than the others made me realize with a lurch that it had to be a child.

"Now, of course, dear citizens, it is not the direct fault of your level that these acts of treason were committed. No, no, I am well aware that only two of you are actually to blame. Two adolescents it seems from the evidence we have gathered," he said, striding closer and closer to where Destan and I lay.

"However...I must stress that it is the fault of *each* and *every* one of you that your efforts have not been focused toward unveiling and turning in the criminals. Rather, that you have attempted to carry on your merry ways and keep secret who of the lot of you were radical enough to disobey the very Council that mothers you. The Council that led you from the tyrannical rule of the so-called Fluxarian nation, the Council that does its utmost to secure your safety and wellbeing on this mountain."

Just as he came nearly a step away from where he'd get sight of Destan and me lying guilty among the innocent, Sebastian turned on his heel and went down another line of Underbrushers. "And so it is with the heaviest of hearts that we are being forced to take such drastic measures." Sebastian flicked his fingers. With a quick rattle and then an ear-splitting blast, a bullet was fired straight into the back of one of the four, bag-covered Underbrushers' heads, the bag not being able to hide the spew of dark red streaming down the corpse's front.

I buried my face into the gravel to keep myself from seeing

any more of it, inhaling a noseful of dirt and coughing violently in response, earning a kick to the ears from the officer trooping by. I looked up, gasping, eyes watering and stinging with grime, and found myself staring straight into the beetle black eyes of the Councilman himself.

He was crouched down, silk robes fluttering ever so delicately around him, the rabbit fur of his scarf rippling in the chilled breeze. His eyes were narrowed, his nostrils flared. "Good evening, Miss Ylevol." Sebastian turned back, smiling at Destan, "Mr. Abrasha. I can assume both of you received your invitations?"

I didn't answer, every inch of my body petrified. Destan nodded at him. "Yes. We...we'll be there tonight." His voice was still strong, gruff. But every word that left his lips quivered on the last note.

"Splendid," Sebastian grinned, thin lips spreading up and then dropping back into a grimace. "I will see you at the Peak shuttle pickup, then. Heroes such as yourselves should not have to witness the coming demonstration. You're excused." He snapped his fingers, ordering the JPs to undo our handcuffs and help us to our feet. As Destan and I stretched out our wrists, avoiding eye contact with the Underbrushers watching us, Sebastian bowed, walking back towards the podium, announcing, "Officers, show our people what will happen if they continue to be dishonest with the Majesty Council."

"Raine, let's go. Now," Destan muttered, hurriedly, grabbing my hand and pulling me toward the trees. I stumbled behind him, letting him lead, but unable to escape before watching a blade slice through the neck of one of the Underbrushers on the podium, seeing another have their head forced under water, held down by three officers, the final one, the child, getting shoved to the ground and kicked repeatedly.

I scrunched my eyes closed, trying to keep up with Destan as he ran to Siri and untied her from the restraints the JPs had put on her. As she whimpered and howled in pain at the spiked chains that had been wrapped around her paws, I thought I heard someone calling my name. I glanced behind me, scanning the crowd who was now being ushered back into their homes systematically. And then I saw her, waving her arms, mouth open wide as it could go and screaming.

"*Raaaaaaaaaayyyy!*" Gwen yelled at me, on the opposite side of the road. My mother had her arm around Gwen's shoulders. Even from here I could see the bruises on my sister's face, the hospital's uniform still hanging loosely on her tiny figure. My first instinct was to run straight through the mass of people still lying on their bellies and crying about the execution, I felt a sudden wave of peace come over me. She was here. Skye's dowry had gotten her back, and now she was home. And looking at Destan, who was gently leading Siri along, I realized that had to be enough for now. Just a few lines down Chantastic and Velle clutched onto their Granny. They didn't see me.

"Bluehead?" Destan said softly, touching my arm. "We have to go."

I nodded silently. Unable to tear my eyes from Chan's tear-streaked face, her arms pinned behind her back as a JP ran a gloved finger across her cheek. *I'll be back, Chantastic,* I thought, rubbing Siri's flank affectionately and disappearing into the trees. *Tonight won't be the end. I promise.* But I realized I couldn't have told her that out loud, to her face. Because not even in the back of my mind, did I believe it.

chapter thirty

"Are you keeping your eyes closed?"

"Jeez, Bluehead, yes, they are closed."
"And you're facing the other way?"
Destan sighed, "Can't you see that I am?"

I flushed, tucking a strand of hair behind my ear and coming out from behind the tree, or...what used to be a tree. The attack earlier had ravaged the forest, shredded the meadow to nothing but a clogged up stream with fallen trees and scorched rubble everywhere. I had to step carefully over what remained of our archery target, my feet crunching on the blackened grass. It was unrecognizable. It hurt my heart so much to think of how it used to be. I tried convincing myself this was somewhere else, that this hadn't been a place filled with so much history and life. The only reminder was Irene, who had taken cover up in a tree while the destruction had raged. She was sleeping there now, tucked up with her knapsack and blanket like a baby bird.

"Okay," I said, about to touch his shoulder, but then thinking better of it. "You can look now."

When he finally saw me, I thought something was wrong at first because his face went so red and his mouth fell open.

"What?" I asked, stopping, suddenly terrified I'd forgotten to zip it up or that I really looked as stupid as I felt. I had put on the pendant he'd made me, but I didn't think that would cause for such alarm.

He cleared his throat and stared ahead nonchalantly. "You. Um. You look beautiful."

"It's the dress. Councilman Lao sent it to me this morning. Isn't that weird?"

"The dress wouldn't be half as cool if you weren't in it," he laughed quietly, rubbing the back of his head. He had fixed his hair again, but a few blonde bangs still stuck out over his forehead. He was in a midnight blue tuxedo a little darker than the colour of my hair, and it was made of some shiny fabric that looked expensive, so I knew it must have been a gift from Sebastian Lao as well. We both looked so different from ourselves that maybe we wouldn't look like the criminals who robbed Peak Tower.

After we'd gotten back to Underbrush, waiting at the shuttle station like we'd been told, I murmured, looking at the gravel, "You look pretty cool, too."

He shrugged, trying to stuff his big, rough hands into the narrow pockets of the suit jacket. "Uh…thanks, I guess."

Should I tell him now? Destan must be looking at me and trying to find that something different, that change that had occurred. He'll probably make something up to notice since Skye and I called off the bonding. My thoughts were racing in circles, my belly unsettled and anxious.

"So...last night went well?" he asked, speaking to the ground. I knew what he was really asking. Nope, I wouldn't give it away just yet.

"I'm feeling better. I made the right choice last night."

I wanted those words back instantly. Because even though I *had* made the right choice, Destan didn't know that choice meant choosing him and those words had to have stung.

I saw his fist clench inside his pocket, but he smiled. "I'm glad. I knew you would."

The shuttle pulled up and it was fancier than I had expected. Destan had ridden in one of these before when he had gone up to Peak to deliver the scroll. As the metal thing pulled up floating on air and not even using wheels, I moved closer to him, a little scared because I couldn't understand how it worked.

It was shaped like an egg or pod, smooth silver metal, and the door slid open and Councilman Sebastian Lao stepped out. It hurt my face to smile at him, and it took great control to curtsy politely after all of the awful things I now knew he was up to. He came over to Destan and shook his hand. "Ah, Mr. Abrasha, so glad to officially meet you when you are *not* witnessing an execution." He laughed heartily, Destan obviously uncomfortable and hardly able to force out a chuckle. Then Sebastian turned his glittering black eyes onto me. "And you as well, Miss Ylevol. You wear that dress like any lady from Emergent."

I bowed. "Thank you, your Majesty," I said, so quietly I was shocked he could hear me.

"There is no need to thank me. It's a pleasure to get to honor your friend and to meet his companion tonight. Shall we go inside now?" he motioned towards the pod and I looked at Destan worriedly.

Sebastian had already climbed inside and Destan breathed into my ear, "Don't worry. It flies faster than Siri and the lights are on the whole time."

My hand locked on his arm as we got inside. The shuttle was lined with dark lilac silk and had plush seats going all the way around the interior. In the center was a glass table with a bucket of ice where a bottle of some kind of drink I didn't recognize sat comfortably. Sebastian sipped the rosy-coloured liquid from his glass and offered us both one. I politely declined and said I was only fifteen.

"It's a celebration!" he laughed, sliding a glass towards me. "I won't report you to the Head of Underrage Misdemeanors. It'll be our little secret." He winked slyly, cocking his head to the side and watching me intently as I still wouldn't take the cup. I couldn't get past the feeling that it was a goblet of rose-coloured poison.

But more concerned that I'd create suspicion, I pretended to sip it, gulping down air and wiping nonexistent moisture from my mouth. Destan's arm curled around my waist and I instantly felt more at ease. I let myself lean ever so slightly against him.

"So, could you tell me the story of how you found this scroll? The old bat who was in charge of archaeology before me died right after he talked to you. I never got to hear the wild tale of how this amazing thing came into your hands," Sebastian said, and Destan shifted in his seat. I saw him blink slowly and knew from the way his mouth twitched at the corners that some magnificent lie was about to peel from his lips.

"Raine and I were in the woods because I had thought I'd left one of my carving knives near the grove of elms. I'm apprentice to the woodcarver, you see," he began, voice up to perfect speed with his brain as the story unraveled, "and I went back to where I had been working, and saw that there had been a rockalanche."

"Oh, now here comes the climax, I'm guessing?" Sebastian droned, almost sarcastically, eyebrows raised. I hated him.

Destan laughed and drank from his own glass. I smiled seeing that he subtly spat out the wine, but made it look like he had just simply choked. "Funny enough, sir," he grinned, his silver eyes shining, "it was Raine who found the scroll. We dug through the rocks looking for my knife, you see, and she dug a little too deep and asked if it was mine and I said no.We unrolled it and knew it had to be something important."

"We didn't find the knife though," I added with a coy smile.

"Oh, darn! Well," Sebastian chuckled, Destan and I joining in nervously, "you found something better! And now you get to have a nice, private night at Emergent, which I know must be so glorious for you. Life at Underbrush is so hard, isn't it?" His voice was caustic again and so Destan and I just nodded hesitantly.

"And I really did mean it, Miss Ylevol, when I said you two did not deserve to witness that horrible display today," the Councilman continued, tutting and leaning his chin on his fist. "But, alas! Justice must be served. I hope you two understand. This mountain is balancing on the edge of a razor blade when it comes to the enemy across the valley, and having internal affairs interfering with such delicate matters has set us on the fast track to war."

There was a beeping noise around us suddenly, and I jumped. Sebastian raised an eyebrow, instantly taken out of the lecture he'd been giving us. "Calm yourself, Miss Ylevol. We've just arrived." There was a break in the smooth lilac silk wall on my side and it pulled away as a door.

"Ladies first," Destan whispered, beckoning for me to go out. I picked up the hem of my dress and stooped down to fit through the door opening. I stepped out onto glassy smooth ground in the shoes that had come with the dress, little silver heels that pinched at my skinny ankles. The Emergent Hot Springs were more beautiful than anything I could have imagined.

There were about ten of them, all steaming and filled with flower petals and foam. There were big stone dividers to separate them from each other, some that even completely enclosed the baths, and racks of fluffy white towels were ready in each area. A little while away from the springs was a long table filled with decadent foods including a series of five different meats and bowls of fluorescent-coloured punch speckled with yellow lemon zest and fruits I'd never seen before. I breathed and found it surprisingly easy and not chemically tasting either.

"The steam is therapeutic and vaporizing. Good for the lungs," Sebastian sighed, my hair standing on end seeing as I hadn't noticed him coming so close to me. "You may eat first and then bathe, or bathe first and then eat. The night is yours and Master Abrasha's. I'll be floating around inside the building nearby if you need me. Try and relax, Miss Ylevol. I didn't bring you here to kill you." He touched my shoulder and smiled in a way that was so horrible I couldn't even feign that I was okay with him being around me anymore. I backed away from him fearfully, but he spun on his heel and walked into the building by the hot springs that I guessed held even more wonders inside.

As I approached the spring, I stared at my reflection and was taken aback. It didn't look anything like me…I looked…pretty. Almost normal, if not for the hair. My skin was still dirty and bruised and cut in weird places, but paired with the silver of the dress, my skin shone like porcelain. My eyes were like two almond-shaped blue moons, my lashes thick and dark from the makeup I'd taken from my mother. My lips were the colour of dark blood. The dress hung on me loosely, the thick straps silky and with excess fabric hanging off, creating a wavy look. The dress fell to a little past my knees, ruffles like river-foam at the bottom, and the rippling water of the springs made my long, scrawny legs look shiny.

I knew Destan was behind me before he made any kind of sound. "Could we talk?" I asked, heart rate starting to quicken nervously. I turned to him and tried to convince him with my eyes. "Join me in the water?"

He nodded and walked to another spring, sliding out of his jacket and starting to unbutton his shirt. But before he could undress anymore, I jerked my head toward the right, hoping to put across that I wanted us to go in one of the more private springs; the ones completely enclosed. Destan clenched and unclenched his jaw uncertainly, but nodding again and following me around the big, curved slab of stone that surrounded one of the smaller baths.

Inside was a big rock wall dividing the spring in half, and Destan and I each picked a side. I slipped out of the princess gown, the humidity dewing on my bare skin, and then I eased myself into the hot water, feeling almost like I was boiling in a pot of my mother's flower petal soup. If there hadn't been a divider, I wouldn't have completely undressed with Destan being right there. But now that he was bathing in the spring behind me, I leaned against the rock wall that separated us, wondering if he was pressed against the other side and thinking of me too.

"What do you need to talk about?" he asked, voice echoing dully off the walls of the rock-dome. I closed my eyes and went completely under the scalding water for a moment to calm myself. When I came back up, I had rose petals plastered on my hair.

"I didn't bond with him," I said, loudly enough so that I wouldn't have to repeat myself.

There was a splashing from the other side. "What? Why? I thought you—"

"I never specified what was the 'right choice' I made, did I, Destan Abrasha?"

"Well, I assumed…"

"Do you think you'd win that easily?" I spun towards the rock wall and pretended I was looking into his grey eyes and not the grey stone. "Destan, I can't be with him.Not at all.It was killing me. I got so close and just couldn't…I kept thinking of you and I just couldn't— "

He groaned,"Raine, we can't go through this again…"

"Destan, please listen," I begged. "Tell me what you *want*. Not what you think is the right thing, not what you think you need or I need, but what you want."

"You're expecting my answer to be 'you,' aren't you?" he said, and it stung a little bit, but I knew he was just trying to push me away again.

I moved away from the wall, floating on my back and closing my eyes. "I don't know what you want anymore."

After a moment of swimming around, Destan asked, gently, "Could you come over to my side of the hot spring? I *want* that."

I covered my chest self-consciously with my arms.

But then I saw how thick and frothy the bubbles were all around the surface of the water, and I just crouched down a little lower so that he'd only be able to see my neck and what was above that. My heart was still racing madly. "I'm coming," I said, wading over to the other side and seeing him leaning against the wall as I had imagined.

He reached out his hand, and it was strange to see them without his ratty gloves. I took it and his other hand touched my cheek delicately, making my whole body feel suddenly cold with nerves even in the hot water. "Raine...I...I want selfish things that won't do you any good. Do you want to hear them anyway?"

I nodded, my thumb tracing over the calluses on his fingers. Destan looked up at the ceiling of the dome for a moment as if he was trying to remember a speech he had prepared, and then he looked back down at me again with a sigh. "I want to run away with you. Into the woods with just our bows and your sketchbook and some lanterns, and I want us to build a house in the middle of nowhere where the JPs won't get us and I want to kiss you again like I did that night, but kiss you like that every night and I want to hold you when you sleep and make your face go red when I call you Bluehead and I want to go exploring with you all the way to the ends of the earth and save the world with you and take you to Fluxaria to see all the pretty things Irene told us about," Destan rambled out in one breath. He wasn't finished and looked at me expectantly but I could barely focus anymore on anything except for him and the beautiful things he wanted.

"I want...to be better for you, and by better I mean that it kills me when I think about all the danger I put you in all the time, even if it's consensual, even if you say you'd risk your life. I hate the thought of anything bad happening to you, because you have so much more to lose than I do. I could walk right off the edge of this mountain and maybe one person would blink an eye. And it kills me thinking about how your family would react to you marrying the son of a whore who doesn't have a home, who's got nothing but a bow and a lot, a lot, of love for you. I scare myself at how much I love you. I've never felt drawn to anyone before. I wouldn't have dared step foot in the village again if it hadn't been for you being there, being a reason for me to stop hiding for one goddamn day. Just because I can shoot well and chop logs doesn't make me a hero or a good, strong guy, Raine; just because I love you, doesn't mean I'm what you need, and at the end of the day you're the one who should be drawing for the Majesty Council and I belong at my woodshop post, or with a bunch of logs that need splitting," he sighed, anguish streaking his face with worry lines. I rubbed his arm with my clumsy fingers, and tried to speak without making him more upset.

"I'm afraid, too," I said softly, and his eyes landed on my face, holding me in a gentle gaze. "I understand the risks. I understand the stigma against you and what it feels like never being good enough," I whispered, "but I want...I think I need to be with you, anyway. Because if it were possible for me to move on and go onto someone else, I could've bonded with Skye and saved myself the humiliation of running away from the ceremony. But I kept seeing your face and wishing it was you, and I can't sleep or focus anymore ever since you kissed me, Destan— "

"Raine, wait," Destan said suddenly, holding up a hand and edging close to the rock wall behind us.

"What?" I hissed, glancing around as his ears pricked up like a cat listening intently to something. We were still completely alone in here, but suddenly this cold sort of dread sank through me that we were being watched, all of the tension that had been dissolving before coming back into the air with full speed.

"Do...do you hear that?" he asked, and I strained my ears. There was a faint ticking. Like a clock, but louder and gaining speed. Had the sound been there all along and we were now just noticing it, or was there something wrong?

Then there was a knock, and the door to the enclosed

spring opened. Destan had grabbed my arm, shoving me behind him protectively, but then we realized it was just a couple of servants rolling in with carts of towels and robes. His shoulders relaxed, his hand loosening on my arm. The servants were all men, all rather strong-looking men dressed in white with blank expressions. They stood, arms behind their backs, against the curved stone walls of the spring, and then continued to unload the stacks of towels onto the shelves. Destan whispered out of the corner of his mouth, "Don't speak anymore. Not until those guys leave."

"Okay," I replied, softly, taking a tentative step farther from him since the whole nakedness thing was still making me anxious. The water continued swirling around, milky and bubbly with hot fumes rising up. And now that we'd stopped speaking and the servants had stopped making all that noise, I noticed that the ticking hadn't stopped at all. If anything, it was getting louder. Faster. I could feel a tremor in the water. The rose petals floating on the surface trembled from some force that felt like it was coming from under us, and Destan and I exchanged puzzled looks before diving under.

I opened my eyes, struggling to keep them open in all of the heat, and puffed up my cheeks with a supply of oxygen. Destan and I swam close to the bottom, hand in hand, and the water became hotter and bubblier as we got lower. Squinting my eyes and feeling the air begin to throb in my lungs, I saw that an object that looked like a clock was at the bottom of the pool. I would say it was a normal clock, except it had seven numbers and four hands and the numbers weren't sequential either and some were upside down. There was a light blinking in the center of it.

It was the same kind of clock from the interviewer's room, and Lao's office, that weird, nonsensical clock. *What's this doing down here?* I thought, turning to Destan who was slowly reaching his fingers towards it. But as it ticked and the water got hotter and bubblier, something inside my brain clicked, making me seize his arm and wrench it away in the slowed down way of underwater movement.

I sucked in a gulp of water in panic, Destan and I kicking our legs as fast as we could and swimming up. But before we could break the surface, flickering above I could see what looked like silver circles falling towards us, and as we came up and gasped for air, I saw for a split second that at least twenty men in white had appeared surrounding the pool, all of them dropping their twenty lightning rods right into the water.

I was filled with a pain so intense that I couldn't hear my own screams, I couldn't see anything but red, I couldn't tell if my eyes were open or closed if I was even alive or if this was dying. And as we fried in the water, the clock bomb went off, blowing us out of the pool and slamming me into a slab of rock. I heard Destan shout my name and then the sound cut off with a thud, sending dread hot and horrible through me.

Rocks and towels and boiling water were strewn and flying and burning all around, white uniforms now mixed with the glossy black of JP armor all swarming in haste to pull what they probably hoped would be our dead bodies out of the rubble. I was getting blown in and out of consciousness, a blackness that came in bursts as I remained trapped beneath a piece of the wall that had been sliced from the force of the explosion. My eyelids fluttered weakly, body still feeling like it was on fire, and I saw red draining from every pore of me onto the stone. There was a lot of shouting, a lot of loud blasts of lightning in the air, and then Destan's face appeared, hazy and bloody and dirty as he crawled over to me. He wrapped me up in his button down shirt and towel and he had his pants that were ripped to shreds, and everything spun around me as he ran with me in his arms.

There was so much still exploding around us as he stumbled over all that what was left of the spring. Bullets darted to and fro like wasps around Destan's face, which was all I could see. I kept fading in and out, one moment hearing him scream as something evidently hit him, the next moment in the dark and

332

lively Emergent woods, overgrown and filled with annoying chatter that made my head throb. He was carrying me, breathing laboured, tears falling from his face onto my cheeks. Time moved in illusionary, staccato bursts: one moment I was swallowed in green ferns and the next I could hear water or see Destan's face close to mine.

He ran into some strange place that felt and smelled damp like a cave, and gently laid me down on the ground. He fell on his back beside me. We winced and flinched from the electrocution at the same time, and he held my hand saying in a garbled voice, "Raine, Raine, don't let go of my h-hand, okay? Okay, j-just don't let go."

"Okay, I won't...I won't," I gasped, feeling as if the cold ground beneath my back was spinning. Every inch of me hurt so badly that I couldn't even breathe without falling into that blackness. "I can't keep my eyes open," I whispered, coughing and feeling drops of something wet splatter my cheeks.

"Try, Bluehead...please," he moaned, moving my head to look at him. Blood dripped from his temple in a thick, scarlet, slug.

"Destan, I think we're dying," I said, coughing and rolling onto my stomach as blood and dirt came pouring out of my throat. My eyelids fluttered, my burned arms giving out and making me collapse. Destan caught me, reaching out his arms and pulling me to lay on his chest. It was bare and streaked with fierce red burns.

"No, not yet," he begged, voice dry as rice paper and filled with agony as his whole body shook, trying to keep mine close to his. "Don't go to sleep. Please, stay awake. We have to..."

"I promise," I said, but my eyelids closed without my permission and everything went black and silent.

chapter thirty-one

I woke up. I didn't think I was going to, and as I sat up, my entire body prickled and ached and my arms were speckled with blood. There was a deep gash in my shoulder, and every time I moved and tugged at the skin, I had to bite my tongue to keep from crying out. Destan was still beside me, passed out and just as beaten up and dirty. I was no longer naked, but pulled his shirt around me, and a shiver ran down my entire body. It was so cold, we were barely wearing anything, and Destan hadn't been able to grab our weapons. Panic seized my every nerve, and I struggled to get to my feet. I couldn't feel them, or my hands, and my memory felt frozen too as I groped around in my mind and the cave to get a grasp of what the heck had happened last night and what was happening now.

It had been a trap. Sebastian had found out it was us who stole the tablet and broke into Peak. Sebastian had tried to kill us a safe distance away from the public eye that would actually care, and when the bomb had gone off—

The bomb.

I pressed my forehead to the cave wall, feeling the cold seep through my skin. The clock bomb. From what I had seen, every room in Peak had them, or at least I could assume that, if even Sebastian had one and he was one of the most prominent Councilmen. But why would the Majesty Council have themselves constantly two feet away from death machines? Why hadn't they enforced the clocks in Underbrush, in the citizens' homes? Why hadn't the clocks been inside the mountain with the other weapons when Destan and Irene and I had broken in?

They must have some other purpose, I thought, peeling my skin from the wall to keep it from growing numb like the rest of me. *Maybe the bomb feature is just one aspect. What if they are cameras, or surveillance where they can push some button and see what video cameras down in the levels are picking up, to spy on us? What if they're so dangerous that by some twisted logic, that's why hidden in plain sight, under the noses of the only ones who know about their true power, who can protect them? What if they're the final blow to Fluxaria?*

I tried to stop thinking, then. It all seemed too farfetched now, too much like I was grasping at straws, stretching my brain to its maximum capacity to the point where it could barely keep me standing without my vision fuzzing black at the edges and making me teeter. Even speaking inside of my mind exhausted me, hurt my throat. Or maybe I was just so thirsty.

Destan and I hadn't drank that wine, hadn't enjoyed the feast laid out for us, and I was a little glad because it probably had been stocked with poison. But I couldn't help but ache with hunger and thirst. If we had eaten, maybe we would have died peacefully talking about feelings in the foamy waters, and not starving and freezing in a cave in the middle of nowhere. The cold was getting to me even worse now that I was conscious, and with it being this unbearable I couldn't fall back to sleep. *Would it be safer to stay here and hide away from the JPs and the Majesty Council who are still on the hunt, or try to find Irene? Maybe I should tell her about the not-clocks.*

I gave up trying to stand, and fell beside Destan, curling into him, my whole body racked with tremors. This was the first time he wasn't warm and it hurt my heart. I pressed my hand to his chest to make sure he still had a heartbeat. I could feel its steady thrum and calmed, but he was still so cold. His arm tightened around me, chapped lips moving in the dry air of the cave, trying to speak. His voice sounded like feathers.

"Raine…Bluehead?" he asked, touching my shoulder, reaching for my cheek.

"I'm here, I'm here," I rasped, a drought in my throat.

He coughed, choking on his breath, his body spasming from cold. "Get….hand me my flute. I'll get…Siri."

I nodded, bringing my hand to his pants pocket. I made an involuntary strangled sound of disappointment, realizing that it was torn as well as completely empty. "Destan, you don't have it—"

"It…I put it in my shirt pocket. On you, my shirt…is on you," he said, exhaling and opening his silver eyes.

I patted the shirt, and in the breast pocket I could feel what had been making me so uncomfortable: his little flute. It had been cracked during our escape, and one of the holes drilled into it had been completely split. I slid it into his fist. He didn't move, but looked at his unmoving hand and cursed. He couldn't move it, the cold had made him too numb. I knelt and blew on his hands, trying to warm them up. "Just hang on a bit…I'll make it better okay?"

After some blowing and rubbing of them, he wiggled his fingers, and sighed, "Good enough." Destan raised the flute to his lips, and it was shaking so much and his breath was so thin that no sound came out. He licked his lips with a paper dry tongue and tried again, making a low hoot. Slowly, he got better, and played the series of notes he used to call Siri. The flute rolled out of his hand, and he launched his gaze on me, eyes bloodshot.

His thumb traced my cheek, breath jumping. I held his

hand there and whispered, "Help's coming, right?"

He coughed, took a shuddering breath, "Right."

"Good," I said, quietly, and tucked my head into the crook of his neck. It wasn't long until he fell unconscious again, arm going limp. Even though it was hard, I stayed awake to make sure he didn't disappear. But seconds passed, minutes, and then I was sure it had been hours and there was no Siri. *Maybe we're too far away for her to hear it…but it's at wolf's frequency, isn't it? Why isn't she coming?* I sat up and hugged my knees to my chest, starting to rock back and forth. *Irene's with Siri. Maybe something had happened to her, maybe the JPs found her, maybe they killed Siri and Irene and*—

"Bluehead? Don't cry…Raine, no, don't cry, it's okay," Destan's voice broke through my panic of thoughts and I felt his arms wrap around me from behind. Tears flowed steadily from my eyes, and as Destan pulled me into his arms I only cried harder.

"She's not coming. Neither of them are coming…" I whispered, and Destan made us both stand to keep our muscles from becoming too stiff. I tugged down on the hem of his shirt self-consciously. It fell past my thighs, but I felt worse being so exposed compared to being cold. It was like being with Skye all over again. I couldn't handle being vulnerable like this, even if it was with Destan. Allowing someone to see this much of me was like telling a secret I'd kept since birth.

He held my hands, leaning down to touch his forehead to mine. It instantly brought me comfort. "Where do we go from here?" he asked in a gruff whisper. Having his face so close to mine made my heart pound in my ears. And I knew that he wasn't just referring to escaping the cold, and fleets of JPs ready to shoot us, he meant what had been said while we were still pleasantly floating in the bubbles of the hot springs.

"I have no idea," I confessed, closing my eyes and tilting my head up to kiss him. I waited for him to meet my lips so that I knew if it was okay, and he dropped my hands, his arms starting to fold around me. Our lips met and feeling his kiss felt as it does to recall a good, distant part of a dream. I hadn't forgotten the physical feeling of it, but I had forgotten the way my body, my brain, everything melted with only the caress of his lips.

He lifted his mouth away reluctantly, whispering, "We can't leave yet."

"And we can't stay much longer either," I added with a shiver. Destan's palm slid up and down my arm, warming it ever so slightly. He was looking at me in wonder.

"Raine, you have to make a promise to me, alright?" he stammered, full moon eyes landing on mine. I had to fight the urge to kiss him again. I nodded as his free hand started playing with my hair and then the infinity necklace. His voice was shaking and a tremor rolled down his body from the cold. "I don't know what we're going to do next. I'm guessing we should sleep on it and I'll have a brilliant plan by tomorrow," he began to say, and I listened closely, "but no matter what happens next, or where we go, or who finds us here and what they do with us, I want you to promise...to promise..."

He shuddered again, and his odd bout of nerves was frightening. "To stay with me. I can't lose you, Raine, I just can't. And I want...will you marry me if we get away from all this?"

"I'd marry you even if we don't," I said instantly, pulling his face to mine and kissing him, another overflow of tears pouring hotly down my cheeks, our faces coming together again and again.

"Even though I have crazy lumberjack hair?" he asked, breaking away to make sure.

"Even though you have crazy hair."

"Even though my fingers feel like sandpaper, and I can't cook or sing or read to save my life?"

I nodded, taking his hands and laughing shakily, "And you want to marry me even though you'll have to deal with this Bluehead forever?"

"That's exactly why I want you in the first place..." he said

338

in a low rush, gathering me up in his arms again and knitting his fingers into my hair securely as he kissed me so fiercely that I became unsteady. Both of our mouths were dry and gross, but I didn't care, and I let his rough tongue slide over mine and his teeth tug at my bottom lip though it was cracked and trembling. I was the first to pull away, my knees gave out a little, Destan's hands catching my arms and holding me upright. He swayed on the spot too. We sighed, looking at each other longingly.

I silently traced my fingertips down the planes of his chest, touching the thin gold hair that curled from his skin, avoiding the spots still scarlet from the lightning rod burns. My palms slid down the sides of his stomach, ran up his spine and down again. He, meanwhile, pushed my bangs out of my face, resting his chin on my shoulder and hesitantly letting his hands rest on my bare back under the big, ripped shirt he'd given me to wear.

"I love you," I whispered, realizing how much warmer I was now that we were closer, our bodies moving, off of the icy floor where we'd been so still.

"I love you," he said, lifting his head from my shoulder, coming back to my face and kissing me deeply, his tongue soft and passionate in my mouth. His fingers were lightly brushing the buttons of the shirt I was wearing, the sensation making my hair stand on end. Ever so subtly, I nodded, smiling into the kiss, and taking a shaky breath, he fumbled with the buttons, undoing them and hastily sliding the blouse from my shoulders and onto the ground. The first instance of cold hurt, but soon was soothed as he pressed his chest to mine, our bellies warming each other as we kissed and began slowly lowering ourselves back to the ground, his body hovering above mine the whole way down.

It was different with him. Feeling him touch me didn't send me anywhere else but here, in this ugly place in the ugly cold, but where a beautiful boy was bonding with a girl he thought was beautiful too. I didn't want to be anywhere else, didn't have to think of anything else, I was here and with every kiss he gave me, I felt myself sinking into a thrilling sort of comfort, no longer afraid or nervous or uncertain.

We continued dizzily, fervently, kissing and touching, and I felt his lips graze my heart and I couldn't see anything but him. Even when my eyelids were closed and his mouth trailed down my body, across the trembling slope of my thin stomach and across my hip bones to where I felt fire race throughout my entire body. And that night he filled me with light and I filled him with everything I could offer from my body and spirit, and I wish I could have remembered the proper ritual words that were to be said when you bond with someone, but in the heat of the moment, I could only recall the final promise and I knew it was the most important part but I couldn't place what it was supposed to mean.

"*I dnob flesym ot uoy. Ruo evol sreuqnoc egnahc. Ruo evol sreuqnoc lla. Ew era etinifni,*" I whispered, brushing my fingers along his jaw and pressing every nerve of myself against him. Destan's arms formed a cage around me and he pulled the red ribbon from my hair.

And I'm not sure how it could be possible he knew this, but in the dark I could make out his response as well, "*I dnob flesym ot uoy. Ruo evol sreuqnoc egnahc. Ruo evol sreuqnoc lla. Ew era etinifni.*" And we silently faded into the night.

Tangled together, we lay pressed into the pile of clothes we'd shed, keeping ourselves from sleep. Every time I closed my eyes and tried to drift away from the cold and hunger for awhile, nightmares began drilling into my head, and I'd have to leave my slumber immediately. I could sense the same thing happening with Destan, noticing how he whimpered quietly and how his muscles tensed up as he tried to dream.

He'd just woken me up again, kissing away the remnants of the bad dream I'd had until I couldn't remember hardly anything at all. The only thing that remained was the vision of Sebastian's black eyes locked with mine, digging deeper and deeper. I opened my eyes, looking into Destan's to try and remind myself of who was actually watching me.

"Destan?" I whispered, fingertip gently tracing Destan's frozen lips. His were dusted with dry blood and seeming to turn bluer every time I blinked.

He closed his eyes, nuzzling his nose with mine. "Hmm?"

I swallowed, saying softly, "We…we can't stay here much longer. I think we should leave as soon as possible."

"Where do you think we'd go?" he scoffed, "The meadow? I think it's been a little burned to a crisp."

"No," I said, "I think…I think we should go home. To Underbrush."

Shards of sunlight came streaking like spears into the cave, a few landing on Destan's eyelashes, making them glint with gold as he blinked, deep in thought. He spoke gruffly, "Your friends and everyone are in danger too, aren't they? Because of us."

"You saw that execution. I think Sebastian will do whatever it takes to get us to him. Our families will be next," I said, then pursing my lips, looking at him inquisitively. "Your family…you said you just have your mom and sisters, right?"

He nodded. "Half-sisters."

"Are they on Underbrush?"

"No. Everyone's up in Canopia. Don't know where 'cause I haven't exactly been in touch for nearly a decade. And who knows where dear old dad is."

My stomach clenched up as I thought of my own father. *Daddy…oh, Dad, what do you think of me? Do you know? Have they punished you?* I rolled to the other side so that Destan couldn't see the red panic I knew was blooming in my cheeks. His body followed mine, curling around it so that we were still together and warm.

"I'll follow you anywhere, Bluehead," he said softly. "You're the only thing keeping me here."

"Don't say that," I murmured, squeezing my eyes shut. "We still have Irene, too."

Destan's hands tightened around my arms for a moment,

and then relaxed as he sighed, "I hope to the *spirits* that they don't have her. Oh, Raine, if they've got her, then we're so fucked."

"She's got to be safe. She was almost all better," I said, trying to believe my own words. "And with all of the craziness going on back in town, I bet she could slip out and start heading into Mythland without anybody noticing."

Destan was quiet for a beat. Then he said, "Yeah." Silence wrapped around both of us in an icy blanket.

We lay there, struggling to stay awake, struggling to keep our blood flowing to our toes and fingers as we found ourselves nearly immobile with exhaustion. I wanted to return to that happy place we'd achieved just hours ago, when just touching each other could freeze time and make everything seem like it would wait for us. But that was gone. And now every breath I took filled me with guilt because I wondered if Chantastic or Gwen or Mom were breathing their last.

Destan delicately combed through my hair with his fingers, the rhythmic brushing making me doze again. He broke the quiet, "Bluehead...you want us to turn ourselves in, don't you?"

My throat constricted into a ball of pain, keeping me from swallowing as I fought back the tears springing madly in my eyes. "Yeah," I said, and I tried to concentrate on how my fingernails scraped at the fine grey rock-dust on the cave floor. "If we run...if we hide...we're no better than killers. All of those innocent people dying."

"We're not guilty, Raine."

"I'm pretty sure theft and harboring an enemy spy is a universal no-no, Destan."

He sighed, burying his nose in my hair. "They'll kill us, Bluehead. Who's to say they won't get everyone else after they're through with us?"

I shrugged. "They don't wanna look like bad guys. They wanna be the good guys killing the bad guys, so I don't think they'll get all of our friends and families involved if they don't have to."

"Is it just us involved?" he asked, under his breath.

I bit my lip, uncertain of how to explain about Chantastic. They didn't really know each other, so I knew that if I mentioned her, he'd jump to the conclusion that she'd have something to do with them finding out it was us who did the stealing. I'd only told her about Irene and our plan against the Council because I couldn't hold it in anymore. We hadn't hardly spoken since then. And if there was anyone other than Destan I could trust with a secret, it was first and foremost Chantastic.

"What do you think?" I said, coughing and wiping at my eyes. "You, me, Irene. We're the only ones who did the crime."

"But did you tell anyone?" he pressed, fingers impatiently drumming on my calf.

I groaned, covering my eyes with my hands. "No, well...I...I confided in Chan. You know, Chan Ai Song. But that was before we actually took anything—"

He gasped, "Then what did you tell her? Did you tell her about Irene?"

"Yes, I did, but Destan she hardly says much to even her friends, so I doubt she'd go to the JPs about us," I explained, and the slight trembling of his body worsened a little with the added anxiety. I rolled back to face him, resting my palm on his cheek, gazing straight into his eyes. "Destan, I trust her with my life. She'd never dare do anything to hurt me, and you have to trust me that I knew what I was doing, who I was telling. She's been my best friend all of my life. She's like my sister."

He still looked obviously shaken, but after a couple of seconds, he silently moved closer and kissed me again, arms enveloping me. I kissed him back, hesitantly, and then passionately, wanting to engrave the feel of him on my lips and every cold limb of my body. Destan pushed my hair aside and kissed along my throat, up my jaw and then across my collar bones, whispering all the while, "I trust you. I trust you, I trust you. And I love you so much, you have no idea..."

I twisted my fingers into his hair, breathing shakily as our chests touched and his hand moved down my back. "I love you too…but after the sun sets, we have to go back. Destan, we can't keep hiding."

He drew back from me, smiling sadly. He had dark, ashen circles under his eyes, his thick blonde hair in tangles. Destan blinked, and two tears skidded down his cheeks, leaving shiny trails behind them. "Let's make the most of it, then," he whispered, trying to keep his smile as the edges of his mouth quivered. I held back my own tears, squeezing my eyes shut, sitting up and pulling his face back to mine, kissing him and kissing him and wishing the night would never come.

chapter thirty-two

We stole some clothes from the Laundress pavilion, quickly dashing back to the woods and slipping on sweater upon sweater, and trousers over trousers (and an unholy amount of socks) to chase away the chills we feared we'd have forever. And once we were properly bundled up in what I was pretty sure were garments belonging to some Starshaders, we kissed quickly and I headed to my hut and he to the meadow to see if Irene was safe and sound.

It had started to rain really hard, everything around me grey and dripping like a watercolour painting with too much water. My mom hadn't lit the lanterns, and I shivered in the doorway, leaving little muddy puddles where I walked. The radio was turned up to a more audible volume level than we usually had it, and I took that as a bad sign. The 24/7 Peak reports had everything to do with crime, Fluxaria news, all of that. I could only wonder a moment if Destan's and my name had been released yet, before I heard a creak of the floorboards and the radio's buzz was switched off. My mom came out into the hall, her eyes round and bright as orbs. Her hands shook at her sides, and I had been prepared for an explosion, for a, *Where have you been? Do you have any idea how awful it is for you to leave at a time like this?* Rather, she just kept staring. And I stared right back.

"You're here," she whispered, immobile. She nearly made it over to me, before planting herself once again at the end of the hallway.

I gulped. "Mom…mom, I need to talk to you."

Her lips twitched almost into a smirk, but she cleared her throat, coming forward and pulling a stool out from the table, seating herself in the one across from it. "Sit down, Raine," she said, voice measured.

Cautiously, I came forward, sitting down and folding my hands under the table. Even though my hands had suffered frostbite in the past night, they now felt burning hot and slick with sweat. I laced my fingers apart and together as I tried to bring myself to speak again. I looked back up at her face, her gaunt face with shadows so black and deeply etched that I wondered if she'd completely starved in the little time we'd been apart.

"Gwen's back, right?" I asked, and she nodded slowly.

"Was brought back a morning or two ago," she said, eyes narrowing ever so slightly. "Won't speak. Won't eat. Can't even sleep. I think they made her into a vegetable while she was up there."

My stomach heaved, my nails digging into my palm so hard I felt wetness dew on my skin. I opened my mouth, then closed it. Took deep, shuddering breaths, and had to focus my gaze on the grey grain of the wooden table. "Has Skye's mother called you?"

"Course she has."

"I'm s-sorry, mom. I…I fell in love with someone else." It didn't even sound like my own voice, and as the words rolled off my tongue, I felt like snatching them from the air and swallowing them back down with the cold cup of tea set in front of me.

Her eyes flashed. "That's not all you want to tell me about, is it?"

I shook my head.

"They announced who the thieves were this morning," she said, quietly. "Tell me it isn't true. Tell me you haven't been doing these things they say you've been doing."

Every bit of me shriveled in shame. "Mama…I didn't have a choice. She fell into our laps and all of the things she showed me, that we found out, just—"

"Our laps?" she breathed. "You and that boy? That archery boy from the blackout that you *fell in love* with?"

I nodded, and before I could even open my mouth to speak, her hand met my cheek with a sharp smack, and I toppled back on the stool in pain. I touched my stinging face, eyes watering, looking up at her pleadingly as I got clumsily to my feet. "Mama, just let me explain—"

"'*Explain?*'" she mimicked, in a high whimper of a voice. I'd never seen her this mad. She'd been maddest the first time the police showed up here with me for stealing some perfume from an Emergent woman's purse. She'd been maddest the night Dad said he was getting drafted even though he'd already served a term years before. But still, I'd never witnessed her this mad before. "How dare you think you have a right to come into this house to 'explain' when your sister is screwed up as ever after getting taken back up there and getting who knows what done to her? When your neighbours have been shot and their houses burned and their savings emptied because you couldn't resist the devil inside that son of a whore?"

I stormed towards her, frustration boiling inside of me as I demanded, "This has nothing to do with him! I *chose* not to turn the spy in. I chose to steal from the Council for her. I chose to do something about the shitty state this mountain is in, the shitty state this whole world is in because of the Council destroying everything!"

"How dare you speak like that!" she yelled, looking behind her to make sure Gwen wasn't coming out to see what all of the commotion was about. "I didn't raise you this way, your father didn't raise you this way. What makes you think an Underbrusher girl like you could do *anything* for the state of the world? All you had to do was worry about the state of our family, and you've pretty much ripped us to shreds, just gone and ruined it all." She hit me again, the other cheek, and I let her do it just twice more before I ducked under the next hit and held up my hands.

"I'm sorry. I'm sorry, Mom," I pleaded, unable to keep from sobbing now, "I didn't mean for any of this to happen. I just couldn't keep living like this! I couldn't marry Skye, I couldn't just let the spy be killed, I couldn't just leave Destan. I couldn't let myself because it all felt so *wrong*, Mom. I love you, I wanted to do what you wanted, but I just couldn't anymore!"

"That's enough," she said, no louder than a whisper. Fat tears rolled down her cheeks, "That's all you had to say. That's all you had to confess to them."

I stopped breathing, gasping, "What?"

She closed her eyes, staring beyond me. "Take her. Just get her out of here."

An arm reached across my throat and yanked me back as JPs came slithering out of the shadows of the hall, lightning rods raised and ready. I choked on my words, reaching out with my fingers at my mother as the betrayal sank in, "Mom, please! Why are you doing this?"

My arm was shoved down by an officer, who also cuffed my wrists together. "I'm your daughter," I whispered, voice breaking as I was pinned to the wall, my view of my mom blurry and distorted from tears building up on my eyelids. "I'm your daughter, Mom, why did you do this?"

"You are no daughter of mine. I don't even know who you are anymore," she hissed, shaking her head back and forth, backing away. "I'm done with you. I told him I'd take care of you but I'm done. You're not even mine, I won't have you anymore." The door was knocked aside, cold rain blowing in.

"Mama!" I screamed, digging my boots' heels into the doormat. I caught sight of Gwen peering out from our bedroom, her face white and stricken with terror and confusion.

"Get her out of here!" my mom cried, slumping down at the table, burying her face in her hands as she fell into weeping. "Just get her *gone*, please…"

"Ray?" Gwen squealed, her brown eyes meeting mine. She reached out with the stuffed wolf in her fist, her curls springing as she shook with fear. I lunged for her, terror seizing me in realizing that I might never see her again.

"Gwen—!"

"Don't touch her! Get out!" my mom shrieked, shoving everything off the table and coming towards us. I pressed my hands against the doorframe, trying desperately to stay inside, but she slammed the door, forcing my fingers off, and I felt myself float backwards for a moment before hitting roughly into the steps and rolling down into the road. I tried to get to my knees, but the rain made my vision so blurred that I only dizzily staggered back down into the puddles.

The JPs soon heaved me up, lightning rods at my back as they ordered me to walk. I raised my head, gasping for air, as I saw Destan in the same position in front of me, but with his mouth bleeding steadily as if he'd been punched. He turned back and saw me, his face an awful mask of sadness and longing as rain drenched down it. I looked right back, feeling like we were somehow speaking with each other in the silence.

I'm sorry, Destan, I thought.

Should've known it'd end this way, right? His face seemed to say, his eyes darkening as we were loaded into the back of a JP truck and separated by metal bars. His fingers curled around one of the bars, his sad smile trembling. *Not all endings are happy, I guess.*

I rested my hand around his fingers, touching my forehead to his through the bars. *It's enough if we end it together.*

He nodded slightly, *Together.*

chapter thirty-three

"Level 15, Correction Units," the elevator voice spoke, and the silver doors of the Peak elevator slid apart.

Destan and I were rushed through the elevator's jaws and onto the level, bare feet hitting the cold shock of metal floor and blindfolds and gags being removed. As soon as I saw the horribly familiar, long grey hallway, I couldn't help but start hyperventilating. Memories of my Career day and how I'd seen the torture going on inside one of the rooms still fresh and bleeding in my mind. In between my rapid gasps of protest and straining against the JP's firm hold, apparently I was making an unacceptable amount of noise, and Councilman Sebastian Lao struck the side of my face with the back of his hand, silencing me instantly.

Destan jolted forward at him furiously, but Sebastian managed to slither out of his reach and type in a code at the door to the first room. I was so repelled at the sight of it that it might as well had been dripping in my own blood.

"23876, take your men back to the perimeter. I have them from here," Sebastian whispered, eyes trailing over my face curiously as he shoved at the door. The JPs bowed to him and vanished, leaving Sebastian to hold both my arm and Destan's. And before I could even use what was left of my strength to fight back, we were forced into the room and the door slammed shut behind us.

Complete blackness gobbled us up. Sebastian's hand left my arm and reached to the wall where I figured he'd be searching for a light switch maybe, but as soon as his fingers brushed whatever it was on the wall, spikes sprang up in all directions from the door frame. Destan grabbed my waist and held me to him as so many spikes filled up the doorframe that any light from outside disappeared fragment by fragment. *No,* I thought, desperately, *not the dark, please not the dark I can't bear for Destan to see how I act when it comes to the dark.* Already I felt like my lungs had decided not to work, already the confusion of if my eyes were opened or closed had sent me plummeting into a panic that shook my entire body, and I ached all over for Chantastic to be here to hold me and make it all better because even Destan didn't understand how he made it worse by trying to talk to me and touch me. I couldn't answer; I couldn't tell if my mouth was moving I felt so numbed by it all.

The floor was nonexistent, not like the cold metal of the hallway, but soft and sinking. I stumbled and couldn't tell if I was falling or if I'd even hit the ground, it felt like we were suspended, the only thing I knew was real was his hand secure in my own, and the knowledge that Sebastian was lurking in here somewhere made it all the worse.

Then, as sudden and abrupt as we'd been plunged into dark numbness, I felt something, and noticing how Destan squeezed my hand I guessed he had to have felt it now too.

It felt bad, it felt hard and rough against my bare back, but it was feeling and it made me real again. It was a chair, and ropes were coiling all about me and pinning my arms to the sides of it and even though they pulled so tightly that I thought my arms would go limp, I forced my hand to stay around Destan's. I heard the faintest sound of motion from across wherever we were, and all of a sudden, we were brought back into light.

The room was small and square, entirely free of furniture aside from the two chairs Destan and I had been forced into. We sat back to back under a harsh fluorescent ceiling that was one big light that stung our eyes every time we looked up. The walls were sliding into each corner, they looked black and soft and now they were being replaced with dark silver metal. They were gross and in some places there was evidence of dried blood and our reflections in the metal looked warped and twisted and dark. Sebastian stood near the door, hands behind his back as he began striding around us. The ropes seemed to be moving, but no one else was in here but us, and so I didn't understand how they could be possibly getting tighter, but then I heard a hiss and understood perfectly.

The pythons spat and flicked their forked tongues, their black scales shiny as volcanic rock as they flashed in the light. Mine wound around my neck in a smooth coil, and trying to keep it away I tipped my head back, teeth ground together as the snake opened its jaws and then closed them over and over.

"Creative, isn't it? My idea, the snakes. Better for persuasion than chains, I think." Sebastian smiled, and I felt my python's heavy body weigh down on my windpipe.

"Pretty sick, actually," I rasped, struggling to keep from appearing too fazed as the Councilman prowled around us.

"Yeah, no one would guess the little makeup-wearing-Council-member-of-everything would be this twisted. Wow," Destan added caustically, and as if the snake could sense his insolence, it flashed its fangs right in front of his eyes, nearly giving me a heart attack. Destan forced out a strained laugh and I joined in nervously, feeling ourselves teeter on the edge of hysterics.

"You should consider your mortality, you two," Sebastian chuckled, cocking his head to the side and bending down to me. I shut up instantly, gasping as he tilted my chin up and brought his face closer and closer, our noses nearly touching. I held my breath as his almost licorice-scented whisper blew hot against my skin, "After all, Miss Ylevol, it's up to you if you want to leave this room…" He traced a finger down my thigh, "…untouched."

"Get your hands off her, asshole," Destan growled, making his chair rock back and forth as he pushed against his serpent binds. I turned my face away from Sebastian's, breathing slowly through my nose and closing my eyes, wishing with all of my being for the Councilman to move away from me. He laughed under his breath, and then drew back.

"You seem much smarter than your boyfriend, Miss Ylevol," Sebastian said, raising an arched eyebrow at Destan. "I have a proposition to make, one that will take your necks off the chopping block. Will you lend an ear? I promise it satisfies each of our needs."

I stared at the ground, heart beating faster and faster. "I'd rather you just get it over with and punish us," I said, unable to conceal the malice from my tone of voice. "You got us. We lose, you win."

"My dear girl, *nothing* is that simple," he sighed, a frown finding its way onto his smug face. "If it were as easy as taking out the problem like a piece of garbage, don't you think we would have handled it already?" His eyes flickered onto mine, black and brutal. "It didn't take any longer than a week or so to decode surveillance that showed your defacing of Majesty Council property with foreign tools of destruction, breaking and entering into a private Majesty Councilman's office; not to mention the footage of you with that Fluxarian spy handling weaponry inside of the mountain."

I felt all heat leave my face. "But…that was months ago. We went into the mountain at least a month before we went up to Peak…"

"Correct. So, as you can see, things have played out just according to a plan formulated long, long, ago by yours truly. Started with catching that spy in an avalanche, our tactic being to try and take her out as we've done time and time again with the others in the past, only to be interrupted by a pair of fresh new adults and witness a heartwarming story of sacrifice and going against all odds to understand and help each other. Does that sound about right?" he asked.

Destan and I sat in shocked silence, no longer frightened by the snakes or the ability Sebastian had to send us into numbing darkness, now only preoccupied with the absolutely terrifying knowledge that we had been watched all along. Every arrow shot, every plan formulated, every stolen bandage, every garment of clothing I'd washed in the river, ever since my new life had begun, I'd been living it under the supervision of the Council themselves.

"You let us rob your office," I whispered, entire body still cold with shock. "You knew the artifact had been a diversion. You took our bait, you even let us bring it back to Irene?"

"Irene is the spy, correct? Why, yes, of course I did. As nerve-wracking as the whole process was, it was my own little social experiment. My own little glimpse at getting to know the lowest of the mountain better and the lengths at which they would go just to deceive the mouth that so willingly feeds them."

"Bullshit," Destan hissed, and I could feel his whole body shaking even from my chair. "There's no way you would let us go this far into stopping you, altogether. You'd never let something precious as your tablet and power get into the hands of your enemy."

Sebastian was across the room now, running his fingers over the stained wall thoughtfully. "You'd be surprised the lengths the Majesty Council is willing to go to achieve the desired purpose, Master Abrasha. And if we'd ever thought that you *would* get away with it all, then of course we'd interfere." He turned and smiled at him. "What do you suppose this ordeal is?

You two have run your course."

"And what about Irene?" I asked. "She still had your tablet...unless you caught her too?"

"Sadly, no. Even after burning through your hideout in the forest, the Fluxarian managed to slip between our fingers," Sebastian sighed, looking obviously a little put out at this. He soon recovered, face returning to the smooth mask of superiority. "But, alas! There are armed forces driving into Mythland as we speak, and the situation will be, once more, controlled. I wouldn't worry about the girl and your wolf or the tablet reaching Fluxaria at this point."

"Wolf?" Destan interjected, "My wolf?"

"Yes, your wolf. The spy was spotted fleeing the scene on the back of a large, grey wolf, yesterday evening," Sebastian said, patting Destan's shoulder.

Siri, I thought, a lump in my throat. I looked up at him, swallowing. "What's...what's the deal you mentioned earlier?"

"You know of information only the Majesty Council was supposed to be aware of, and I am willing to overlook the housing of a Fluxarian, and even perhaps the stealing of my tablet if you keep silent about everything you know. No proclaiming about the war against Fluxaria, or our plans on clearing out Mythland, and especially nothing about what Fluxaria is like because I'm sure that spy filled your odd little head with fantasies all about her kingdom. I can assure you—*they are lies*," he said earnestly, pushing away from the wall and leaning in close to us again.

"Fluxaria isn't supposed to exist. We were one mountain, one tribe, and as soon as order tried to come about, they formed their own being and revolted, shattering our peace and making the spirits so angry that they had to separate us like school children quarreling. And while they have advanced greatly as a country, it is evident that they still pose a great danger to us, Miss Ylevol. We've killed a number of their spies and why would they be sending over so many if they weren't up to something?

Thgindim is your country, not Fluxaria, I assure you. And it is unknown to me why you would let yourself be swayed by the obvious enemy rather than stand by your country during this critical time.

"I urge you to listen. As frustrated as I am with the blatant disobedience you two have demonstrated, I must be impartial and realize that my dislike of you and Master Abrasha in general has to stay out of this. The fact is, the citizens of Thgindim cannot handle anymore than we are already telling them, and if you so much as speak one word, there could be people flocking to Fluxaria and dying in Mythland on the journey there. Is that really what you want? For us all to escape to the 'better mountain' where they still have a near monarchy, and as much dislike for us as we have for them? Even the ones that make it there will be executed, and even more friction will arise. I'm a politician, and have been for over thirty years. I know quite well how these matters play out. Answer me, now, Miss Ylevol. What do you want to happen?"

I twisted my fingers around Destan's as I tried to find words that could express all of the emotion pulsing through me. What could I say? Nothing I felt would even make much of a difference. I watched him, calmly saying, "I want us to stop teaching everyone to hate Fluxaria, to fear them, to want to hurt them. I want the Council to stop blaming their twisted agenda on the nation across the valley who has no intentions of starting another full-out war." I paused, trying to keep myself composed as the stare-down between me and the Councilman intensified. My voice came out more quietly now, "With all due respect, sir…I think this mountain is worse off than before we were separated from Fluxaria."

His mouth tightened. "How so?

"You said you've been watching us this whole time, right?" I asked, voice shaking. "Then you should know that the bottom of the mountain is just about in shambles. And you've said it's because of us, that because we showed disobedience we had to be punished by watching our village suffer, but if you were keeping an eye on us all along…it is your own fault for not stepping in before we were able to get away with it."

The silence that followed was satisfyingly heavy, pressing down on even the snakes and causing the Councilman to pause in his pacing. His tan, lined face suddenly stricken with paleness. Destan rubbed my hand, calming me a little as he himself spoke as well.

"If you see all, then you've seen your officers beating, shooting, raping our people day after day," Destan began, voice rising angrily. "You say that it's all under your control, so how can you expect us to trust you and be obedient when you allow people to starve and die and get taxed into oblivion every single fucking day?"

Sebastian's robes swirled as he faced us, face livid with rage. As he stormed over, Destan kept at it, "Give us a reason to listen and we will! But all the Council gives are reasons to disobey and stay alive, to reach out to the other nation you're constantly trying to kill off! The nation who could help us—"

"You know nothing of this world!" Sebastian roared, gripping the back of Destan's chair and shaking it. "Fluxaria is not going to help us. They will destroy us, and I've given you my reasons and I've given you the choice to stay silent. This is the deal. You can have your opinions, your whining, but promising me your silence is what will keep you alive."

"How can you expect us to?" I asked, exasperated, and Sebastian placed another snake on both of our laps. Where did he get these things? I wouldn't be surprised if he'd kept his little serpent buddies in his silky pockets.

"The Majesty Council's advanced surgeons can remove certain memories from your brains. That is how," he said, clearing his throat. "We'd remove everything from the past seven months. We do not know yet how to sort through the memories to find the information or read the thoughts for what specifically you cannot know, but we destroy the memory tissue only so far as to relieve you of whatever has happened during that time. It is a drastic measure, but if you accept this procedure, I will even reward you."

"It'll have to be a pretty hefty reward," Destan grumbled.

"I understand, Mr. Abrasha, that you've been an undocumented resident of Underbrush for quite some time. Such a misdemeanor would usually result in up to twenty years imprisonment in this Tower. However, I will waive the charges and make it so that you can be reunited with your mother and your three half-sisters in Canopia and together you can live in the lap of luxury on Emergent."

"I don't care much for that—"

"I'm not finished," Sebastian snapped, his smile vanishing. "If you let me take away those seven months, I will make it the Justice Police's utmost mission to locate your father and make sure he is punished for the harm he has caused your family's reputation. Your mother will receive such a bounty of wealth that she will no longer have to take part in the sex industry any longer. And if you still wish to remain distanced from your family, we shall provide you a house of your own right on Emergent in fact, or we can make it so that a bigger one is built on Underbrush if you, for whatever reason, desire to stay down there."

Destan didn't speak out. He breathed evenly through his nose, and I wished so badly that I could see what expression was on his face. Then Sebastian addressed me.

"Miss Ylevol, you will be rewarded differently. I have come to learn, over these past days of trying to get to know you and Master Abrasha more closely, that you are a talented artist…"

No. Please no, don't Raine, don't listen to him, the voice in my head pleaded.

"And that the position of Sketcher was not awarded this year to anyone. The only promising talent was yours, in fact, but Career Agents are always wary of choosing Underbrushers because of lack of available artistic education on your level."

I couldn't help myself. My ears pricked up in interest and I realized I was sitting up stiff and straight as a board. *Stop it, stop it, stop it!*

"But I am willing to give you this job. You can be our Sketcher. You can even count on your mother receiving some financial aid for her hard work, and I think that after all these years, it would be best for your father to come home. He's been most valuable in our service, but with you making such a sacrifice to better Thgindim, it is only right that you should reunite with him."

I sank low in my chair, staring into my lap as the snakes continued to hiss and a headache continued to throb and my mind continued to spin and spin until I thought I could throw up. Sketcher was one thing, a tantalizing thing. But I didn't care so much for my dream job if it came between remembering my past seven months with Destan and Irene. When it came down to my mother, my father...everything felt muddy. I couldn't think in a straight line. Every time I thought I was coming to a conclusion, I'd veer off to another side and try to make a decision from over there. All I kept envisioning again and again was my mother's face, all of the horrible things she'd said to me before turning me in, and that without me there, now she and Gwen would be worse off than ever. The dowry wasn't enough because the bills and taxes just kept coming. I didn't know if I'd be executed, imprisoned, banished, who knows what, yet. But all I knew was that if I didn't accept Sebastian's offer, I wouldn't be going home. I wouldn't be able to try and rebuild the family I'd torn apart, as my mother had said. And my father...just the acknowledgement that he still existed, that it was a possibility he could come home, made everything the more complicated.

"Can you...can you give us a moment alone to consider your...offer?" I asked, voice hardly reaching above a whisper, and Sebastian nodded, going towards the door.

"I'll be back in no more than three minutes. I hope you make the right choice," he said, clearing his throat and he, for once, didn't sound full of malice. He pushed an invisible switch on the wall and as the lights went out again, the snakes slithered away somewhere, I heard the soft walls come sliding back, and as soon as the binds disappeared, Destan and I stood and held each other so tightly that our bones creaked.

chapter thirty-four

"You're not considering, oh, you're not considering it, right? Please tell me you aren't," Destan moaned, hand rubbing over and over on my back as I pressed my face to his chest. The dark now was the worst it had ever been for me. I couldn't breathe even a gasp and I felt like I was falling through the floor with Destan as my only anchor.

"Raine, Raine, talk to me…" he whined softly, thumb caressing my cheek, the bridge of his nose pressed flat against mine.

"I don't want to lose those seven months, Destan. If we agree, we'll probably never meet each other again, and I'm never going to find anyone like you, and I'll suck at archery again, and Irene will blow up, and it will all because I'm selfish. And if you think about it…Sebastian will have to brainwash more than just us because we've met so many people, like the other Laundresses, and my mom, and just…I can hardly breathe…" I coughed and forced my lungs to keep working at their proper pace. I closed my eyes and tried to imagine being in the light, not a tiny dark room, it wasn't dark, it wasn't dark…

"Then we…won't? Raine, why is it so hard for you?" he asked. I drew back from him incredulously.

"Why is it so hard?" I echoed. "For one thing, we'll be allowed to live through the night! Destan…I could have my father back. After all these years, I could see him again, and I could be Sketcher and both of us would be getting just what we want and need, and no one else would have to die at all. My whole family is on the edge of *bankruptcy* because of me, and Sebastian could change all of that with a snap of his fingers if we agreed—"

"You believe him!" Destan took my hand off his arm and nearly shouted at me, "You completely believe he can do all this stuff? Raine, why are you letting him get to you?"

"Because maybe we should just make the sacrifice to prevent any more of this…this bloodshed on our own mountain," I said, yearning for him to understand. "Destan, even though we did all this for the right reasons, Underbrushers are dying. The woods, our meadow, it's all burning. Sebastian is sending people after Irene as we speak…"

He cursed under his breath. "Sacrifice each other? Sacrifice Irene and her entire country so that you can draw pretty pictures and have a pretty daddy and I can live in a pretty house with a pretty normal wife who isn't you?"

"Destan, that's not what I mean—"

"No, thanks. I know what I need, Raine Ylevol, and I need you, and I need Fluxaria to stay, and you need to listen to me." His voice was fierce and urgent, his hands gripping my shoulders tightly. "Please, Bluehead, even if I did sacrifice meeting you, so much more would go, too. This is bigger than us. And if he takes our memories, we won't remember the deal in the first place so who's to say how we'll actually end up? Let him get inside our heads and he could screw up so much more." Destan waited for my retort again, breathing quickly, but I couldn't make one. I leaned forward, forehead resting on his chest. He wrapped his arms around me.

"Either way I just feel like things are going to get worse," I murmured. "All this began when we just didn't want to have a girl's blood on our hands. Now look where that's gotten us."

"I don't want to be anywhere, but here," he whispered, finding me in the dark, his palm sliding up my arm and hip, warming me, easing me into a kiss. "If we're going to lose either way, please don't make me lose you, Bluehead…" His lips gently kissed my eyes, his cheek resting against mine as we held each other.

"I'm still so scared, Destan," I breathed. "I'm so scared of everything that's happened and what's going to happen…"

"Just let it all go," he whispered earnestly, brushing away a stray tear on my cheek and touching his nose to mine. "What's done is done, yeah? Just chin up and let's make these Majesty Council sons-of-bitches eat their hearts out, how's that?"

My smile trembled. "Yeah," I said, taking a couple deep breaths, trying to calm the anxiety making me shake all over. "So, we're not going to fight it? We'll turn down the deal?"

"Turn down the deal."

"And if we're put on trial? Then what?"

"Then we get away with as much preaching as we can," he said, moving back, still holding my hands. "Major stuff like this is broadcast all over the mountain. Raine, we probably won't be here much longer after the trial, and I'm pretty sure we can't break out of Peak Tower twice. Especially without our bows or daggers or anything. This is it. We get to speak, or at least one of us, and I'll nominate you. Speak as long as you can about Fluxaria and the bombs and everything, and I promise that even Sebastian won't have the authority to stop you if you keep it tied in to the testimony."

"This will get us killed," I said shakily, the dark wrapping its tight black hands around my neck. I already felt like we were starting to die.

"But it might save everyone else, hopefully," he sighed, kissing me softly, and then passionately, his fingers twisting into my hair. I shuddered and pulled him closer. He was shaking. I wanted to say more, I wanted to thank him for everything and get out my goodbyes, but we didn't have much time before Sebastian silently came in and switched on the lights and the room felt real again.

"I hope you two have done more than that since I've been gone," he snorted, watching as we hastily broke away from the kiss.

"Yes," I said, facing him, "in fact we have come to a decision."

Sebastian's eyes glittered. "Really? And…?"

Destan stood, brushing off his pants and getting so close to Sebastian that I thought I saw the Councilman wrinkle his nose in discomfort. "Fuck you and your deal to Mythland. We want those seven months, and a trial."

Sebastian chuckled, a dry and disturbing sound, and he took a step back, shoes clicking on the floor. He blew some air through his lips, rubbed his chin. "Well, I don't wish to be a killjoy of any sort," he said, fixing his cruel eyes on the both of us, "but I'm afraid you've attended your trial."

I couldn't breathe. "Excuse me?" I gasped.

"Your crimes have to do with no one in the Council but me. Remember? I deal with Foreign Affairs, Law Enforcement, and Archaeology. It would be a waste of the Councilmen's time to have them come in for a crime they have hardly any interest in, don't you think?"

He crossed over to the door and slid his finger down it, the spikes that had shot up in the doorway lowering back into the floor. "Not to mention, you've confessed, both of you. All evidence is against you. It's clear you know the consequences and willingly…how did you put it, 'fuck my deal to Mythland'?"

Destan's hands balled into fists at his side, shaking as the knuckles went white. "So, that's it then?" he snarled. "You'll execute us tomorrow in front of our village, and have it all be done with?"

Just Destan's mention of such a thing sent me rollicking into nightmarish imaginings, and I felt my palms grow sweaty the longer Sebastian stared at us. He tutted quietly, shaking his head in disapproval. "Unfortunately, no. To lower the risk of explicit information regarding your misdemeanors getting inflicted upon the public, you will not be executed."

"You...you're not going to kill us?"

One side of Sebastian's mouth tweaked. "I wouldn't go as far as that, Miss Ylevol. I guess you'll just have to wait and see." And with a jerk of his head, and a small rush of JPs coming into the room, Destan and I were separated, dragged away to opposite ends of the Tower.

I stared at the tiny window, watching the snow fall. It was really coming down. Underbrush didn't see many blizzards; most of them hit the higher levels, but now from my cell in the Tower a second wouldn't go by when the entirety of my limited vision outside was blindingly white. *Who knows what's going on out there,* I thought, *who knows what's going on in here?*

The double-layered door was opened one layer, so that now I could see through the thick crystal bars keeping me from the hallway. "You have three minutes," the JP standing guard said to someone outside of it. I scooted around to look out, my fingers curling excitedly around the smooth bars, eyes trying to see between them.

"Three minutes?" a familiar voice gasped. "We just went through four *hours* of inspections, can't we have a little more time?"

"Shh, shh, Carmen, it's fine..." another whispered.

"I'm already counting down," the officer grumbled, making the person sigh as she and her two companions came over to the door. I was filled with a swell of emotion seeing that it was my old friends, Carmen, Velle, and especially Chantastic. They were all dressed in starchy white clothes, had their hair tied back and masks hiding their mouths.

As they knelt down and reached through for me, I struggled to find my voice. "You...you're here? How did you make it up here?" I rasped, seizing Carmen's hand and pressing it to my lips, bending forward and kissing Velle's cheek, my eyes falling longingly onto Chantastic's. Compared to the others, hers were unbelievably sad.

"Just did about everything," Carmen explained, trying to smile her feisty smile and only managing more of a scowl. She rubbed my hand, averting her eyes. "Raine, you know how damn furious I am that you never once came to me or us about this. But let's pretend otherwise, 'kay?"

"You forgive me?"

"You're going away," Velle said, in a quiversome voice. Her forehead was wrinkled with wavy lines, her fingers laced together as she paced back and forth. "Forever.I don't know if I'm forgiving you, but I'm not gonna let you go out there thinking I'm on the same side as the guys who put you in here..."

"Two minutes."

Carmen cursed, gritting her teeth together. Her brown curls danced as she brought her face so close to mine that our noses nearly touched between the bars. "Raine, look there's not much we can tell you that you don't already know, but Underbrush has been alerted about you and the Abrasha boy's banishment tomorrow. I've been briefed again and again by the security of this place that if I ask you just what happened and what you found out, I'd get in a cell myself, so I'm not gonna ask that."

"Banishment," I echoed, sitting back on my knees and shoving my bangs out of my eyes. Swallowing, I looked up at her, then at Velle, still pacing, and Chan, still nearly cloaked in shadow away from the other two. "So, that's what's happening,"

I said, dumbly, suddenly empty of all of the words I needed to get out in these stinking two minutes.

"Just…um…stick to…you know, your stuff," Velle said, voice trembling up an octave. "Don't eat the poison berries, don't go into swamps, keep far, far *away* from anything that look's like it could be a nest for a snake or flesh-eating bug or—"

"One minute. Wrap it up," the JP coughed. Velle burst into tears, and I reached through, taking her hand and squeezing it.

"Shh, shh, I will, I will," I whispered, watching as Carmen got up off her knees and stood by Velle's side. I let myself cry at last because I needed them to know just how much it hurt to have to talk to them like this. "I love you. I won't let anything eat me, I promise."

Chantastic finally looked up, light glinting off her black eyes. Velle and Carmen edged away as she came quickly over now, with a fervent manner unlike anything I'd ever witnessed her showing before. And bringing her hands inside my cell, placing both warm and shaking palms onto my cheeks, she suddenly pulled my face to hers and kissed me. Chantastic kissed me, her lips hot and tears hotter as they mingled with mine, or maybe it was just the shock boiling everything to a new heat inside of me.

"Reach me," she whispered hoarsely, drawing back with her mouth, but her hands still firmly planted on my face. Then one hand slid to the back of my head, fingers reaching into my bun. "Just keep it warm and it'll reach me…"

"Chan?" I didn't understand, the kiss, her words, anything.

"Time's up!"

It only took a fierce look to get Velle to scurry down and away from me, and a shove to get Carmen running after her. But for Chantastic, the JP had to bend down, seize her by the shoulders and wrench her off of the ground.

"Keep it warm—" she gasped, her expression so determined and then so full of pain,and before I could tell her goodbye, that I loved her, she was stolen from my sight.

I crumbled into weeping, scared of how much just kept pouring out of me, as if everything I'd held back until now was finally flooding the fortress I'd built around myself. It went on like this for who knows how long, but when I was just too tired and even the thoughts of Destan didn't draw moisture from my eyes, I laid flat on my back and waited for my breathing to get back to normal. The metallic ceiling was still swimming above me.

"Keep it warm," I whispered, unable to make sense of Chan's last words to me. No 'I love you' no 'I'll miss you,' or 'be careful.' *Keep it warm*, she'd said, and as I tried to mull it over and keep myself from getting into that awful crying again, I felt a discomfort lying there on the floor. It felt like I was lying on top of something, but that was impossible because there was absolutely nothing in here, not even a place to go to the bathroom. I'd already had to ask for the toilet and was guided to the floor's restroom, one with multiple stalls. My stall had been kept open, armed female attendants' prying eyes keeping watch. It only reinforced my dread that my cell had been made so useless and bare because it was specifically for the criminals about to get the boot.

But now, reaching back and lifting my head up, I felt around my hair for the lump I'd sensed beneath me. And sure as anything, after taking out my bun and sitting up to shake it all out, something light and round fell from my hair, like it had been nestled behind my ear. I caught it before it fell and broke, safely nestling it in my hands and cautiously glancing back to make sure the guard hadn't come to take a peek after hearing the slight ruckus I'd made. He had returned, but made no move. His back was to me, and I turned my back to him, gazing at the delicate thing before me.

It was an egg of some kind, definitely a bird's egg, only a couple inches long and very white, with spots of lavender and rusty red all along its outer shell. The JP sneezed, and I gasped,

369

nearly dropping the egg and having to scoot myself into a corner to look at it more closely. *A bird's egg?* I thought, perplexed to the highest degree. *Why would Chantastic give me an egg? How come she waited until the end to talk to me, and why was she so cryptic about everything?*

I fixed my hair back up, tucking the egg back into the thick nest of ratty tangles. Then I laid down, carefully, on my side, very conscious of every movement, so that I wouldn't break it. And hardly able to keep my eyes open any longer, I let myself slip into a quick, shallow sleep.

chapter thirty-five

"It's just woods. We'll make it," Destan said.

"Woods.Right.Good." I rasped, the trembling reaching it's peak.

As we marched through Underbrush, we passed ghostly faces of our friends and family that just stared back in what felt like betrayal. Jun eyed me in pure shock, the other Laundress girls whispering into each other's ears and averting their eyes from mine. My mother and Gwen stood in front of our house, forced to watch as citizens were when it came to banishment. I'd never witnessed one in my lifetime, and evidently neither would my mother because her eyes glued themselves to the gravel. I felt desperate for her to just look at me, just one glance and I would be okay because the last time I'd seen her eyes, they were full of fire and malice and I didn't want to remember them like that. Gwen had a thin arm extended out to me, her own eyes glassy and imploring as I was forced to walk by, rifles at my back.

"You'll see them again," Destan whispered, so quietly that only we could hear. "Eventually, at least."

I sighed, "When I'm dead, you mean."

"Eventually," he repeated, flushing and getting urged to keep up to speed with the procession of police.

Ling the woodcarver was crying, holding his hat in his hands as we passed, and Destan gave him a stiff nod, hardly able to look at him. We were nearly out of Underbrush when I saw my friends again. Chantastic, Velle, and Carmen weren't crying, but they looked proudly at us, their faces unreadable. And as we walked past them, they tossed handfuls of flower petals at us, letting us walk through a fragrant shower of mountain poppies and white roses. Councilman Lao eyed them in disbelief, and he opened his mouth to shout something, but then closed it without a word. There was no law he could use against them.

Even though Destan and I had been to the Base before for the archery competition, we hadn't seen the true nature of the lowest level of Thgindim. We'd taken a detour into the woods, but by continuing on the main road, we trooped through the Justice Police camps and training grounds. Officers walked in single file along the edge of us, wielding their rods and disappearing into the hard black buildings or into fenced-in yards to practice fighting. The eeriest thing was how silent it had become. The JPs didn't make a sound: I could hear my boots crunching on the road, and Destan's breathing, and the clicking of Sebastian's tongue against his teeth. "He must be loving this," I hissed to Destan, "He must be so excited to see us go."

"I still think he'd rather see our heads on pikes," he snorted, giving me a sideways look.

We approached the gate: huge, shimmering, titanium bars, surrounded by the meanest looking JPs I'd ever seen. And Sebastian saluted them, yelling, "Open the gate!"

Every one of them grabbed a handle, and pulled at once, making the pieces slide apart with a screechy creak. Beyond the gate, were endless trees taller than any on Thgindim, and Destan wound his arm around my waist to try and keep us both calm.

"Good luck out there, Miss Ylevol," Sebastian hissed, an evil smile on his thin lips. He moved us so that I stood side by side with Destan, and the JPs rolled out a big cannon looking thing with a long thick tube and darkness inside. "To show just how generous the Majesty Council can be towards its citizens, even the disobedient ones," he began, turning and ushering over three officers to stand before us. "We will allow you two to pick a single token to take along. Choose wisely."

A bow, arrows separately. A heavy bag of packaged food. A gas lantern. I flinched as my handcuffs were unlatched, eyeing the three. I didn't dare just reach and take one, though, and I nodded at the bow, not allowing myself to rethink my decision. The JP holding it instantly strapped ii onto me, Destan choosing the arrows, and having the same done to him.

"I think a *thank you, sir* will suffice," Sebastian chuckled, nearly giddy. I wouldn't speak. Just stared at my boots and watched my blue strands of hair flutter in the breeze. The Councilman draped an arm across my shoulders, giving me a gentle squeeze as he whispered silkily into my ear, "Oh, Miss Ylevol, I really will enjoy thinking about what sort of beast will feast on you two tonight. If only I could see."

I whipped my head around and spat straight onto his cheek, making him stumble back in surprise as my saliva gleamed on his skin. His eyes flashed madly, and he snapped his fingers, giving me a last livid look before ordering, "Shoot her out first! I want the girl gone—*now!*"

Destan and I clung to each other frantically, eyes locked and terrified, my hand on his neck, accidentally pulling off his red beanie and making his blooming head of curls spring out. JPs cut through us, backed me against a sheet of black metal. As soon as I touched it, it sent off a mechanism that made a thick clear dome surround me, enclosing me in an orb that sat snugly in the mouth of a cannon. I came at the glass, hammering my fists against it, screaming straight into the tiny air holes punched into it.

"No! No, not without Destan, Sebastian, no!" I yelled, entire body flaming in panic as I realized Destan was still restrained and struggling, JPs pinning him to the ground as he yearned to get up and over to me. His face was smeared into the gravel, his bloodshot eyes piercing mine in horror as Sebastian made an order that resulted in Destan's entire body getting kicked by the police officers circling him. There was nothing I could do but scream my throat raw in those last seconds. There was a whir, air shot out of the cannon at full speed, and I soared through the gates, completely airborne and powerless as a leaf being knocked about in the wind.

Thgindim was left behind me in the dust, the gates closing as the air lost its power and my pod slammed hard into the ground, bursting open on impact and sending me somersaulting through the dirt.

I stood up, taking out my bow, spinning in a circle as dread sizzled through my veins and his red hat pulsed in my fist. *Just wait*, I thought, *He's coming next, he's got to be coming next*. I waited a couple more seconds. Minutes. I was alone. There was no movement but in the horrible, mountain-high trees towering above me, the beasts waiting in the shadows, and I fell to my knees in a daze.

"Destan?"

In hardly a particular order...thank you to...

Nick and Faith for being the first to read and making me feel like a real writer. Also thanks for letting me know to NOT mention a character peeing in the woods EVER again.

Mrs. Supplee for being my writer mommy and always supporting my writing to the max. I really really cannot believe I have been able to be taught by someone who inspires me so much as a person and writer, as well as someone who always knows how to soothe creative constipation and give really nice hugs. I really love you so much and don't think I could have asked for a better teacher to guide me through my fiction writing.

Michelle! Holy cow this would not be the book it is if it hadn't been for your most wise and honest critique. It's like you took my little shrub of a plant and watered it so that it grew into a majestic unicorn flower. Thank you to the moon and beyond!

Mommy and Writer-Mommy and Rosie for all of the copy-editing and hard work you spent helping me polish this up for the presses.

Iryna, my Sargasm and badass Ukrainian wonderwoman. You've always encouraged this Polypen's writing escapades and made her feel so appreciated as well as respected. When you get a motorcycle, I'll get a sidecar so we can wreak havoc together.

Anita, my first writer buddy. You are such a blossom of beautiful writing and elegant imagination. Thank you for all of the movie nights where we raved about fictional heartthrobs and drank all of your marble soda. You're who I think of first when it comes to who should take a peek at a project.

My litkids, all 18 (whoa how'd we get so many?!) for being the grooviest bunch of people I could have asked for to have as editors and peers these past four years. It was fun standing on desks like in Dead Poets Society and running through rivers and eating blondies and knocking and picking up knocks and through all of this I think we all became the writers we were hoping we could be by the time we graduated.

Fleet Foxes, First Aid Kit, Sigur Ros, Of Monsters and Men, The Staves, Daughter, and a whole bunch of other bands and artists who sent my creative juices flowing and helped churn out this novel.

Irene and Chantastic for letting me put you two into here and for being my best, best, best friends in this whole milky universe. Glub Friend, Water Lily, I love you beyond anything and everything. Also this shout out is for Irene for specifically helping me with those beautiful, beautiful character portraits.

Ronen. For such a beautiful cover, and all of the good times we've had. I'm still rooting for you, Yabukov! Keep your head off your desk, hands off your phone, and you're bound to do amazing things!

Taffy, for existing.

Nat, for being cool and playing Barbies and thinking I'm crazy in the good way and not the bad way and letting me sit behind the passenger side and for dealing with me shaking my leg and for pretty much everything. I would be so lonely without you and just as Quinn sang to Finn, you keep me hangin' on. For real. I really wouldn't be here writing this if it hadn't been for all of the times you just held me and reminded me of all the good stuff.

Mom and Dad for making sure I stayed alive to write this. I love you, I love you, I love you, I love you.

about the author

R.R.S. hails from Baltimore, Maryland. When not writing books, the author is usually at home watching *Buffy the Vampire Slayer* with a soft and petulant cat called Taffy, at a dance party with a bunch of three-year-olds, or looking for faeries and wild Totoros in the woods. R.R.S. really likes China and hopes to visit there and perhaps live there to climb mountains and find inner peace (and pandas).

Wanna say hi? Send your messages to:
tolcdin_forever@yahoo.com

or just follow R.R.S.'s personal tumblr:
totoroses.tumblr.com.

WANT MORE OF THE INFINITY CHRONICLES?

CHECK OUT THE BLOG!

WWW.THE-INFINITY-CHRONICLES.COM

AND COMING SOON...

PART TWO:

LOST CONSTELLATIONS